south ᵒᶠcentre

a novel
by Andrea Carter

Cover illustration and book design: Andrea Carter

ISBN 1453789502
EAN 9781453789506

Andrea Carter
Santiago de CHILE
www.andreacarter-stories.com

Printed in the United States of America

south of centre

This book is dedicated to the people of Tocopilla,
especially to my mother-in-law, Edith Ayala-Araya.

*Este libro esta dedicado a la gente de Tocopilla,
especialmente a mi suegra, Edith Ayala-Araya.*

Many thanks to
my husband Alex Hernandez for his amusing
anecdotes, insights, and constant encouragement;
my Mom Dolores Carter, my sister Marcia Harris,
my daughters Sandra and Cathleen Schmitke,
for the boost only families can provide;
Luca Tripaldi, Sharon Lamontagne-MacDonald
and Katja Preston, and for their kindness,
early reviews and gentle suggestions.

CHAPTER 1

Clorinda

Tocopilla, 2001

Clorinda exhaled heavily and watched as the taut strands cut her breath into thin slices. The wooden hand loom was braced in primitive blocks so it leaned slightly away from her. She tied a knot around the last nail and sat back to scan the result of her efforts.

The warp stared back at her, its vertical lines submitting themselves to the crazy idea that she would make something of them. Knotted together across her ambitious three square metre wooden frame, the threads were strangers to one another. They were disenfranchised scarves and sweaters that had been reduced to random lengths of yarn of various colours and textures. They cringed at their forced intimacy. Imagine the atrocity of genteel red English wool united against its will with loutish brown llama yarn and in turn, the loud protests of these coarse yarns raging against the weakness of such refined threads. Clorinda's indiscriminate fingers had tied them tightly together and then drawn them up and down around the metal posts that restrained them. These silent stringed prisoners quivered with tension, if not with a certain bizarre and perverted excitement. They were the foundation of her 'life's work.'

Clorinda dared to lightly caress the woollen strings. Her hands were rough and gnarled for a young woman who wasn't yet 28 years old, and her nails were ragged and broken but when she touched her precious yarns, her fingers became graceful ballerinas that danced across the bows of so many violins. Clorinda's olive complexion was somewhat lighter than the other locals who were a heavy mixture of *altiplano Quechua* native with Spanish blood. But her eyes were black diamonds that glinted from within the shadows between her brows and high cheekbones. They darted crazily as one thing or another caught her interest and then like a cat, she focused single-mindedly on the object that was her prey before pouncing and playing with it in her mind.

Clorinda had thin, unremarkable lips and when they parted to form one of her infrequent smiles, a full set of teeth, somewhat yellow but still all there, was displayed in straight rows, top and bottom. Her sleek black hair was cropped just above her shoulders with bangs that ended in a straight line barely covering her eyebrows, a rare style for a Latina woman. She was influenced by photos she had seen of Joan of Arc and didn't care what anyone thought about it because somewhere in her own mind she too was a heroine directed by an inner voice. Clorinda's trademark characteristic was her 'calendar' wardrobe – an eclectic collection of clothes she designed and sewed herself, outlandish outfits that fell into one of seven themes according to the days of the week.

She sat up straight, which for Clorinda was still decidedly hunched, a habit her spine had developed from bending over her fabric treasures and, as a young girl, skulking around school yards spying on the groups from which she had been excluded. Today was Saturday so she dressed in one of her semi-full skirts – a patchwork of yellow floral print and green jungle motif, and she complemented it with a green and orange striped cotton pullover. Since she had stricken Wednesdays from her calendar, she re-assigned her traditional Wednesday flower and scarf accessories to Saturdays, meaning she was permitted this yellow and orange polyester bandana around her head. Her ears protruded from under the bandana, parting her hair around them and assigning her an attribute akin to a perky feminine monkey.

She leaned forward, closed her eyes, and touched a line of fine grey alpaca wool with her tongue several times. She was careful not to lick it as she did with cotton or silk garments because that would leave little beads of saliva on the wool, something she didn't want to do. Rather she simply wanted to identify it for certain. It tasted like the sweater of the old man across the street who had died last week. The flavour stabbed to her heart and she sat silently praying for the wind to come and carry away the pain.

She thought about him at the cemetery. Three weeks ago the old man's coffin had been pushed deep into the hollow concrete niche, scratching roughly along the bottom until the end with his head brusquely collided with the back wall. The cemetery worker unceremoniously heaved a concrete block across the opening and with a fresh cement mixture he sealed the old man and his coffin into darkness with only Clorinda as witness.

Clorinda had stroked his name, Orlando del Transito Ortega de Riveras, with red house paint onto a board that she ripped from his patio and she leaned it against the cement seal of his tomb. His name revealed nothing about him and his date of birth was unknown, or at least no one took the trouble to research it. And it didn't make much sense to note the date of his ending if his beginning was a mystery. Clorinda had placed a single yellow daisy and Señor Ortega's stylish black fountain pen on the ledge beside it. She blessed herself and asked God to please ensure that no one would steal the pen. To help God in his vigilance, she reached up and carefully wedged the pen into the wet cement just behind the name board and repositioned the daisy in front. Only she would know about the pen, she and God and Señor Ortega, just as it had been when he was alive.

Inside his coffin, Señor Ortega wore his British wool sweater and Italian-made trousers. Only a week earlier, he had stopped wearing his finest alpaca wool vest because he had donated it to Clorinda. –What do I need this vest for?– he said to her. – I won't be invited anywhere these days.– Obviously his burial, which he knew was imminent, was not going to be very elegant. He knew he would not attract a crowd of townspeople to say goodbye to him. He would not feel one hand after another, planting a kiss on the top of his coffin as he was carried past a steady stream of inconsolable onlookers. He wouldn't hear anyone say, "Go with God" or "I'll miss you, my old friend."

The day of his funeral, Clorinda wore her special frock, the one made with deep turquoise, blue and purple satin patches joined so the light reflected the various deliberate angles of the nap. It was Señor Ortega's favourite dress. She started sewing it the day after she first saw him and finished it only six months ago. It took a long time to come across just the right garment swatches and she considered herself blessed to have found them at all.

Now Clorinda studied the soft grey threads of the vest that were stretched up and down on the frame in front of her. It, like the old man's life, had unravelled in the most unexpected of circumstances. The vest gave her far more yarn than she needed to finish the warp. She would use the rest to weave across itself. She imagined a large grey, nonuniform area. It would be the base for Señor Ortega's patch on the world.

She stared at a grey and red knot near the bottom right corner of the frame. This is where she tied the yarn from her favourite red sweater to Señor Ortega's grey. – This, Señor Ortega, is where you end – she thought. She followed the grey yarn upwards and let her eyes scan the rest of the threads to find where his life might begin. Her eyes stopped and focused on the knot that joined him to a string of rough ochre llama wool.

She stretched her legs out in front of herself, dropped her arms, fell back into her wooden chair and squinted her eyes until the coloured threads blurred into one solid canvas. She had hopes that images would magically emerge from the warp, especially at the point where her red joined Señor Ortega's grey. But they didn't. It is Señor Ortega who should be red – she thought – his life was much more vibrant than mine.

She reached into the plastic bag on the floor beside her and drew out a short piece of the grey wool from Señor Ortega's vest. She would allow herself this luxury. And as she pulled the strand of wool across her tongue she tasted a bit of his life. It was a foreign flavour that both saddened and excited her, arousing great curiosity.

She stood up, short piece of wool still in hand, and walked out of her patio and across the street where she planted herself in front of Señor Ortega's abandoned house.

She remained there frozen, just two metres from his front door, staring at the dark windows, dragging the short piece of grey wool back and forth across her tongue like a bow over a violin. The sound that she heard was the emptiness from Señor Ortega himself.

CHAPTER 2

Clorinda

Tocopilla, 2001

Clorinda had spied on Señor Ortega from the day he moved in across the street a year ago. She remembered his arrival on that first day. It was a Wednesday. She remembered because she was wearing a heavy patchwork linen jewel-neckline shift with a pair of dangly earrings that chimed in the wind.

It was mid-winter and she was sitting on a wooden kitchen chair outside her door watching the vultures circle above the black and rusted-out mine ruins down at the shore. A few small fishing boats bobbed a short distance out in the water and a Japanese freighter was being loaded at the dock. From the distance, noise from the town centre was muffled but she could see the activity on the main street from where she sat. Intercity buses arrived and left as usual, cargo trucks headed back up the main road towards the desert high plains to the copper mines.

Tocopilla was no longer the commercial hub it had once been but ships continued to dock and car loads of saltpetre from the world's only remaining saltpetre mine still made their way down from the *altiplano* to be loaded before setting sail for somewhere. Clorinda never asked where. The town's location on the coast about eight hours south of the Peruvian border and two hours from the world's largest open pit copper mine in the high desert interior used to be strategic. But the port city of Iquique to the north and Antofagasta to the south had become more important in recent decades and the powers-that-be relegated Tocopilla to become the centre for two highly-contaminating electric plants. The electricity was pushed along a set of huge transmitter lines that crossed the south end of town and climbed up over the mountain barriers until they were free to hum eerily over hundreds of kilometres of otherwise empty desert plain to the mines.

Some people accused Tocopilla of being an ugly little place because of its monotonous blend of grey metal roofs, grey cement walls, grey and rusted corrugated metal fences, its lack of greenery, and its otherwise broken and disorderly makeshift buildings. But Clorinda didn't know because she had never been far beyond its borders and couldn't make a comparison. She heard that the Andes were covered in trees in some parts of the country, and that streams ran through them, but she couldn't imagine such a thing. The mountains that punctured the blue sky on Tocopilla's eastern edge were rocky and barren. Nothing grew out of such hostile soil. Nothing grew anywhere in Tocopilla unless someone had money to water it. The place saw rain only once every 25 years, and even then the drops would evaporate before they hit the ground. Townspeople were proud of the palm trees in the plaza and those that had been planted around the main traffic circle by the gas station, no matter if they were covered in dust and assaulted by diesel fumes.

Tocopilla was trapped in a slightly concave strip of land between the Pacific Ocean and the high Andean *cordillera*. The town had limited options both in terms of space and opportunity. Men eked out a living either at the electric plants (if they were lucky to have a cousin on the inside), by labouring in their own small mining stakes or for a corporate mine outside of town, or as a fishermen. Sometimes they just laid around on the beach or sat on a bench at the central plaza and waited. It was never clear what they waited for.

Occasionally Clorinda wandered down to the beach at the shore two blocks from the main street, where the sand was black and the water was always cold. She watched boys play *fútbol* and sometimes hovered above couples who were oblivious to her presence as they locked in passionate embraces. She passed the ancient Bolivian mine ruins that they said were being kept as an historical reminder of Chile's victory in The War of the Pacific in 1876. But even she had to admit that it looked like nothing more than piles of gnarled, rusty metal and was a playground for rats. Even so, it held a mysterious attraction for her.

Today she was spending the afternoon at home. She turned to watch the ore train snake its way down the scar that scratched a spiral path around the steep back of the Andes. It had just wound its way to the base of the closest mountain when her attention was captured by a red convertible Bel Air that pulled up and lurched to a halt in front of the house across the street.

The driver, a man in his early 60s, sat for several minutes studying the house, melancholy *tango* drifting into the air from his car radio. Clorinda watched as the man slowly ran his fingers through his hair, massaging memories that had lain undisturbed for years. He had a handsome, boldly defined face, dark-skinned (or tanned at least) with black eyes and thick greying hair. He reminded her of Clark Gable, whose face was on the faded remnants of the old poster still hanging at the entrance of the long-since-closed movie theatre on Esmeralda Street. Gable, the gringo who made all the *Latinas'* hearts throb. She had always admired the poster and once even tried to steal it by scraping it from the wall but the glue was too strong and it began to tear into small pieces. Better to leave it intact where she could at least admire it once in awhile. 'Gone with the Wind' the poster said. She imagined herself being caught up in a gust and carried high into the clear blue over the town where she could oversee everything, like she was a goddess or at least an angel. She would glide through the air, arms open wide, and Clark Gable would suddenly appear and float along beside her, take her hand, smile into her eyes and together they'd fly over the Andes. After that her imagination got stuck because she didn't know for certain what lay beyond and she would sigh as the dream faded into blue.

The man turned off the radio and in a single smooth motion

he opened the car door, planted one foot after the other firmly on the ground, stood up and closed the door so it latched gently as he stepped away. He proceeded in long strides to the front door of the little house. She had never before seen a man walk in that manner, with such confidence and dignity and grace. Yes, she decided he was graceful. He looked taller than most men. Clark Gable came to mind again; yes, he was Clark Gable, slightly older than when he was gone with the wind, and without the moustache, but Clark Gable just the same. She leaned forward fascinated, elbows on her knees and chin on her hands, dark eyes squinting as she studied him.

He pulled a key out of his pocket and inserted it into the lock, hunching his shoulders and leaning into it as he wrestled for a few minutes trying to get past the rust. Finally he straightened and pushed on the door. It creaked open, he took a step inside and stood for several seconds at the threshold, his eyes adjusting to the dim interior light. Then he disappeared, leaving the door hang open behind him.

Clorinda instinctively jumped up and sidled quickly across the street in her customary crab-like mode, arms bent weirdly away from her sides for balance, until she reached the exterior wall of his house. She flattened herself against its concrete surface, sniffing a little and shrugging her shoulders nervously. She was no James Bond but she'd been successfully sneaking around her whole life. Her sideways shuffle did not help make her less visible as she had believed when she was a child; she just never outgrew the habit. It was something she had developed when she started school. She was too shy to join the other girls but too curious to be left out, so she circled around them believing that if she was crouched they wouldn't notice her. In fact, this manner of moving from place to place had become somewhat of a trademark and instead of providing her with a cover, she was actually more easily identified, even from a distance. But she didn't know that and was now too old to care. Her heart raced with great anticipation as she listened to Clark Gable's movements.

The house had been empty for several years. An old lady named

Doña Miranda had lived there and Clorinda assumed she had died quietly, abandoning it to no one in particular. She didn't remember a wake or a funeral at the house but maybe it happened during one of her rapturous periods when she locked herself in her bedroom (sometimes lasting days at a time) to unravel, taste, and manipulate the woollen sweaters she had found at the back of the second-hand shop. The mystery of the empty house had never mattered before, but now it was suddenly extremely important and she berated herself for not having investigated at some point over the years.

She slapped herself lightly on the cheek, both in punishment for her past lack of attentiveness as well as a sharp reminder to capture everything from this point on. She craned her neck around the open door and peered inside. The man was nowhere to be seen. She slithered around the door frame and entered the hallway, poised crookedly with weight on one leg, leaning away from the door, careful not to make any noise.

Clark Gable re-entered the house from the back patio and strode into the sitting room, did an about-turn towards the small room at the back of the house, and walked directly to an old desk in the corner. He reached for a key from his pocket and opened the desk drawer. He emptied its contents, two thick stacks of yellowed papers and envelopes, onto the dusty surface and slid the piles of paper into an old basket beside the desk. Having obviously found what he was looking for, he tucked it under his arm and prepared to leave.

Clorinda gasped and slipped silently back behind the door, willing her feet to shrink. Clark Gable's musky men's cologne floated past her nose as he passed her. She swooned a little and promised herself to always and forever remember the scent. He locked the door and Clorinda stood alone in the silence. She listened as the car motor started, music resumed on his radio and Clark drove off to a *tango* rhythm. "Clark!" She breathed.

Initially she was so excited to be on this side of Clark Gable's personal history that looking for a way out of the locked house did not even enter her mind.

The house was typical of all the places in the neighbourhood. The entrance hall led past a sitting room, three small bedrooms and a kitchen that opened into the back patio. She noticed the tile and wooden floors were still in decent condition and the walls had not been damaged by the various earth tremors that had hit the region over the past several years. Doña Miranda was not a remarkable woman in terms of what she kept in her house so Clorinda considered that if there was anything special at all, it was already in Clark Gable's basket. However, she was compelled and could not pass up the opportunity to look around.

After about four hours, which included sitting down for a cup of tea in the kitchen and then at the desk in a back room near the patio (she found tea leaves in a can on the kitchen shelf and was surprised there was still gas in the cylinder beside the stove), she decided the best way out was via the back patio and over the roof. Her skinny legs scratched their way up the patio wall and carried her in a crouched sideways motion across the roof to the front of the house where she scraped her way down the corner using protruding uneven pieces of rebar as a ladder.

CHAPTER 3

Orlando Ortega

Tocopilla, 1952

For Orlando del Transito Ortega de Riveras cosmic justice did not exist. As a young man he realised that justice was nothing more than a random consequence of man-made rules or perhaps a lucky coincidence. Some people were luckier than others. He didn't ask if it was because of the star sign under which they were born, or if God was on their side or if they were simply good people and got what they deserved, because in his opinion it was none of these.

Growing up, he was unlucky no matter what. His life was plagued by mishaps and complications of mishaps that never seemed to completely unravel, one thing constantly becoming knotted up in a remnant of something else until it became a way of life. Just when he considered a subject closed and wrapped in a neat little ball, he discovered it had a loose end that was tied to something totally unexpected. Therefore, in his early life he found himself falling into one pothole (or man shaft, as it were) after another, often around the edges of a smouldering, man-eating crater that he imagined must be something like hell.

Being born into a poor family in the town of Tocopilla at the edge of the Atacama Desert was the first sign that justice was a mythical concept. The perverse poverty of the place and the fact that a population struggled for survival in the harsh desert climate was enough in itself. But add to that an enormous wealth of ore and saltpetre just asking to be exploited by greedy foreign companies and the inevitable result was a tendency to-wards unbridled corruption and repression.

Orlando del Transito Ortega de Riveras was the last in a long line of increasingly less impressive and more downtrodden Spanish immi-grants who had produced offspring by *Quechua* women. By the time what was left of the fighting and adventuresome spirit of Don Julio Ortega Villegas de Pamplona reached Orlando del Transito Ortega de Riveras' father, it had been watered down to complacency within an at-titude of compliant servitude.

For an unexplained reason a flame from Don Julio Ortega Villegas had buried itself within generations of offspring until it found oxygen in the spirit of Orlando del Transito Ortega de Riveras. He discovered it when he was 15 years old working in a lower shaft of a British-owned gold mine several hours inland from Tocopilla.

As with all the small, light-weight young workers at the *El Camino* mine, he was tied to the end of a rope and lowered head first to pass through the narrow crevices into low shafts. Using a small pick and the lamp on his helmet, he worked alone hacking at the rock, with the boss occasionally barking instructions. Several times per shift he was raised back up with a heavy bag of test samples. Sometimes, and especially if he had a stub-born boss who was sure the location was the site of a rich ore grain, he was lowered into the same crevice for weeks on end in order to do a thorough test. The gases were intoxicating and by the end of each day, his head was pounding and his young mind as pliable as that of a newborn baby.

By 15, he had learned to add beer and home-made *pisco* or *chicha* to the mix at the end of his shift. Most days being too tired to finish even one drink, he fell onto his bunk in the workers' shack where he lay still as death until the whistle blew him out of bed the next morning.

He was underground each morning by the time the sun heated the earth and mirages undulated across the sand. He was underground each afternoon during the relentless sand storms. And he was asleep each night when the moon hung over the sandy domain's peaceful star-filled sky.

Orlando Ortega was a bright young man who was following in the footsteps of his father. He was small for his age but that was what made him a perfect candidate to explore promising crevices. He was quick to catch on to new techniques, although there weren't too many tricks to hanging upside down on a rope. But by the time he was 15, his body filled out and he proved that he could handle a pick as well as any of the grown men. He sprouted quickly to become taller than many of them and he carried himself with confidence. Other than that, it would be difficult to pick him out of a crowd of shift workers, everyone with the same black hair, dark eyes, and solemn, sooty faces. To this point all he could remember of his life was being in the mine.

All he knew of the *altiplano* was its eternal underground and all he could see for the future were dark rock caves – that is, until he knocked free a piece of quartz about seven centimetres in diametre that was more gold than crystal. Standing at the end of his rope, his helmet lantern focused on what was sitting on the palm of his oversized glove, Orlando del Transito Ortega de Riveras made a decision to run with it.

The only way to get past the fastidious British shift boss and the routine body search was to be injured, but it had to be something serious. Minor cuts wouldn't get him anywhere. Workers with major injuries were immediately hoisted up to the shack near the office. If they stopped bleeding, they'd be bandaged and sent back down. If not, they'd be bandaged and dismissed, replaced immediately by one of the hopefuls peering in from their perch on the big rock just outside the gates.

That's how Orlando del Transito Ortega de Riveras came to have two less toes on his left foot. It was the most major minor injury that he could think of as he stood in the semi-darkness of the underground inferno staring at the chunk of gold in his hand. He ripped his handkerchief with his teeth, wrapped half of it around the gold and tucked the small package down into the front of his underwear. He adjusted his balls to make room for his golden extra and then closed his eyes and swung his pick into his boot. His prolonged scream of pain and freedom echoed through the shafts.

They pulled him up, the boss cursing him for losing valuable time and occupying man power that was better spent hacking rock and not hauling the body of a useless boy up to the surface.

That afternoon Orlando found himself on an ore train headed towards Tocopilla. With his duffle bag and the gold quartz still stuffed in his crotch, he jumped onto a car loaded with saltpetre and rumbled across the *altiplano*, swirling white tornados picking up around every ore car on the train. Descending the mountains towards the coast, his dark eyes blinked through the thick white powder on his face. Except for a persistent, growing red stain on his left foot, his hair, his arms, his legs, his entire body was covered with the acrid dust of saltpetre.

When the train slowed to round the curve near the first group of houses at the outskirts of Tocopilla, Orlando grabbed his duffle bag, heaved himself over the edge of the car and rolled down the hill.

Still white from head to foot except for his dark brown eyes and the red stain on his foot, he walked into his mother's house and slumped onto the nearest chair. She shrieked and hugged him tightly to her ample bosom. Once she realised that his unexpected presence at home meant that he wasn't at the mine earning money, she swiftly swatted him across the ears and berated him for his carelessness. How long would it be before the mine would take back a boy with two missing toes? Now he'd have to stand at the end of the line, and God knows how long it would take for him to get close enough to have a seat on the rock nearest the gate once more.

He limped to the patio where he stripped and washed and rewrapped his foot, careful not to look too closely at the half-cauterised wound where his toes used to be.

That night he climbed onto the roof of a bus heading south and held on for dear life as it zigzagged along the coastal road. Half way to Antofagasta the bus stopped for fuel at Michilla, a *pueblo* consisting of a gas station, a restaurant, 3 bare-bulbed street lights, and about 20 concrete houses with plywood-covered windows, lining either side of the highway. He slithered down the back and joined the four solemn hopeful workers who sat on the ground waiting for a ride to the Michilla mine. Before dawn, what was a dot in the distance turned out to be an approaching pickup truck with one good headlight. It rattled to a stop and men who had already hooked themselves onto the broken wooden sides of the pickup watched, uninterested, as the others climbed in. The truck turned and rambled up into the mountains, reaching the mine gate just as the sun peered over the tallest peaks.

Michilla was a small mine as mines went, but it was well-protected against unauthorised visitors. A barbed wire fence was strung across the mine entrance, which was blasted out of a cliff. A heavily-whiskered man with a shot gun stood vigil at the gate. The guard's hut was inside on the right, his family subsisting in a cramped one-room adobe house at the back. The ore-buying office was on the other side, in front of the chief engineer's hut. The on-site buildings, all unpainted plywood caked in black grease and dust were slightly larger than outhouses, boasting one door and no windows.

The armed guard refused to allow him to pass until Orlando was finally able to convince him with three home-rolled cigarettes that he had stolen from his mother's cabinet on the way out the door, that he was there to sell gold and not to look for work.

Inside the buying office, a stout, unshaven man with dirty, thick-framed glasses, wearing a heavy jacket buttoned up to his chin, beckoned him to step forward. He rubbed his hands trying to warm his stubby fingers, the valuable instruments with which he weighed gold and counted money.

"What have you got?" He asked without looking up.

Orlando reached into the front of his trousers and rummaged for a few seconds before pulling out the half-handkerchief. He laid it on the counter and unwrapped the gold quartz. The man said nothing as he scrutinised the ore with a magnifying glass. After a minute, he glanced up at Orlando.

"How much do you think it's worth?"

"That's your job. You tell me, and then we'll talk." Orlando tried to sound confident, as though he had some idea of its value.

The man picked up the ore in his grubby fingers and tossed it up and down a few times, feeling its weight in the bloated palm of his hand.

"Not as much as you think," was his estimate. Then he reached under the counter for a small cobbing hammer and his thick fingers expertly chipped away at one corner until three small chunks of pure gold lay beside the large crystal. Most of the gold remained embedded in the quartz. Orlando shifted nervously from one foot to the other.

Corruption, like lust, sometimes erupts in a powerful unexpected explosion. Maybe it smoulders undetected beneath the surface but once you taste it, the flavour becomes a powerful addiction and the sickly-sweet smell of its smoke hovers and clings to you until it becomes part of your person and you don't even notice. Some people can sniff it on you, some can't.

That day in the buying office of the mine located halfway between Tocopilla and Antofagasta, Orlando lost his innocence to a foul-smelling, grubby, fat-fingered man with dirty glasses. It was his first taste of the real world of business, Chilean style. "We help each other, *compadre*."

Lust at first sight.

There was a lot of gold in that chunk of rock. "But," said the dirty man, "I have to offer you the going rate, which unfortunately isn't as high as it was just last week." And to emphasise the point, "Not even as high as yesterday's price."

He leaned forward and Orlando noticed the bread from this morning's breakfast stuck like glue in the wide space between his front teeth. The two centre bottom teeth were missing. He had long hairs hanging out of both nostrils and his breath smelled like fish. Orlando thought he saw a flea jump from the man's left forearm to his shoulder.

The man winked at Orlando, "I know something about the world gold market, my boy, and the price will be higher tomorrow. So I can offer you in pesos the equivalent of $350 US for this piece of rock."

"I want the American dollars, Señor."

"Hmm, yes," the man rubbed a stubby finger under his nose and sniffed several times. "But in that case, I will be able to pay you only $300 American dollars because there is an unreasonable exchange rate these days and it is a lot of trouble for us to get American dollars in this place. You see..." He gestured with open arms, "We are hundreds of kilometres from civilisation."

Orlando's two missing toes suddenly began to ache and the desire to rub them became unbearable. He shuffled. He was overcome with pain but didn't want to give the fat man an advantage. He grimaced and fixed his gaze on the crystal and three gold chunks that were still on the counter, reasoning that if he concentrated on it hard enough he would forget about his toes.

The fat man interpreted Orlando's hesitation to mean that he might snatch the rock and run, and he didn't want to let this opportunity slip away. "Listen. Listen. We can make a deal, just between the two of us."

A glint in his eyes, he leaned forward and beckoned Orlando to do the same. "I can do us both a favour." He winked, as their faces met, nose to nose for just an instant. The smell of the man was too much and pains were shooting up from his foot, so Orlando drew back, driving his left foot into the floor in an attempt to mitigate the torture of his two missing toes.

The fat man glanced over both shoulders and then half-whispered, "I can do you a favour because you look like a nice kid. I can pay you $400 American dollars even though it will be more than this rock is worth."

"I will accept $450." His two missing toes were really putting on the pressure.

"Okay, but there is something else – because of the exchange problem," he feigned an expression of sympathy, "You know – the one I just explained to you – you must give me $75 for my trouble."

"Yes, okay, I understand. Something for you... I will agree to accept $450 and pay you $50, not $75. If that's not enough, I'll take my gold elsewhere."

No point in arguing, he would make more from this than the kid would know anyway. "Okay. It's a deal, but I'm doing you a favour because you are just a kid." The dirty man smiled, exposing the breakfast in his teeth once more and rubbed a chubby hand through his hair. Orlando thought he saw at least two more fleas escape.

He kept his distance while the man filled out several forms and then turned his back to search through a box of official stamps on a shelf behind the counter.

With the speed of a lightning bolt, Orlando reached forward and snatched two of the three small chunks of pure gold the man had chipped off the rock and slid them into his pocket, backing silently away from the counter so as not to arouse suspicion.

The man at last found the three necessary stamps and held them up with a broad smile. The importance of a man with stamps in his hand cannot be underestimated. Then he needed to locate the ink pad. This took another several minutes. Finally he stamped the forms with a pageantry common only to isolated mining offices in northern Chile.

With one hand he reached under the counter and brought out a tin box with a big padlock. He set it down with a thud, and with the other, he pulled out a shiny Colt .45 that he slowly and deliberately positioned beside the box, nuzzle pointing in Orlando's direction. He smiled directly at Orlando. "Insurance." He said. Orlando stared back at him.

After his stubby fingers had been licked repeatedly and he had counted the American bills several times, the fat man set them in a pile beside the official document and moved the Colt .45 to rest on top of them. "Sign where the X is."

Orlando signed. The fat man counted out $400 and slid it across the counter to Orlando, then flashed the $50 for himself and stashed it into his pocket.

"Everyone is happy." He said.

"Yes, everyone is happy." Repeated Orlando. "*Adiós*". He turned on his heel, bills scrunched tightly in his sweaty fist, and walked as swiftly as his two missing toes would allow, saluted the guard at the gate, crossed the road and headed down a path that he knew would lead him back to the town of Michilla.

The man in the buying office quickly slipped the third small chunk of gold into his pocket and went crazy looking for the other two. Orlando was long gone before he could stop him.

The next day the English boss at Michilla valued the gold in the quartz rock at 700 US dollars. The company was not stupid enough to inform their employees about the real value of gold from day to day. Their healthy margin to cover 'employee error' at the buying office increased profits dramatically.

When Orlando arrived in Antofagasta two days later and sold the small chunks of gold at the regional survey office, he received an additional sum of $70.00.

He calculated that each of his toes had a value of $235 and that, given the fact that their absence did not inhibit him to a great extent, especially now that the bleeding had subsided and the pain diminished, it had been a brilliant decision to end his work at the mine as he did. However, there was a niggling measure of anxiety over the suspicion that if he had sold the entire rock at the Antofagasta survey office rather than in the Michilla mine office, the value of each of his toes would have been even greater.

CHAPTER 4

Clorinda

Tocopilla, 2001

Clorinda invented her 'calendar wardrobe' long before Señor Ortega arrived in Tocopilla. Her neighbours judged it to be an incredibly original idea that sprung from her eccentricity, which itself was the result of a deep well of creative genius. The truth is that it was simply the result of total lack of self-control. She lusted after fabric and threads of all kinds, and needed to be surrounded by it, to work with it, feel it and manipulate it. She wanted to weave herself into it, knitting the threads across the surface of her skin, penetrating, and shaping them around her organs. Tasting and even consuming yarns was her first and strongest impulse, but it was uncivilised and impractical, so she could see no better solution than to envelope herself in it, to turn the idea inside out and herself become a meal for her fabric. She submitted herself to its appetite.

While the calendar concept provided some structure, it also allowed a great deal of freedom to mix and match textures and colours. She wore the skirts that were constructed from old bleached jeans patches and blouses with sleeves of at least two different colours on Mondays. Tuesdays were her heavy cotton, full-length patchwork circle skirt days with soft, fuzzy sweaters (cashmere if she could find it). Wednesdays she donned one of her simple but elegant jewel-neckline shifts accented with a feather or flower in her hair to brighten up the middle of the week. Thursday was broadcloth caftan day, especially nice when the wind ducked underneath and the fabric rippled against her legs. Friday was 'casual Friday' (something she overheard her neighbour Norma say was a North American custom) so she slipped into heavy cotton trousers that zipped up the side, the back of the jeans always a different fabric than the front, and she imagined her life as a casual North American. She was known to swagger like a cowboy on Fridays. Saturday was 'retro day' and she liked to dress up in calf-length semi-full skirts made of a combination of floral prints that she complemented with striped cotton or linen pullovers. Sunday was reserved for slightly more formal a-line dresses with cap sleeves. She patched together several of these from crepes and taffetas, mixing different weights and patterns into one finished garment.

Clorinda was pleased with her calendar wardrobe creations partly because they spoke for themselves, but mostly because they fulfilled their obligation to provide a medley of constant fabric delight. Angélica, and her mother Norma who lived down the street, caught onto the calendar concept only weeks after its inception and were quick to point out to the rest of the town that if anyone was in doubt as to what day of the week it was, they need only see what Clorinda was wearing. Perhaps their astute powers of observation were due to their experience with garments. Norma worked as a clothing sorter at the dock, which put her on the front lines of the second-hand clothing business.

She saw the items before anyone else, including her boss. In fact, he rarely saw anything. He offered the dock workers a flat rate per container of clothing, which they slid into their pockets, and he paid a low wage to Norma and a handful of others to sort garments according to his instructions for 12 hours per day, six days a week. As soon as the container of donations from well-meaning foreigners hit the South American shores it was fair game for profit. Norma saw no reason why she shouldn't share in some of it, and she stole select items when the surveillance camera was not working (which was the majority of the time) and threw them, one by one, over the wall to where Angélica waited on the other side. Mostly Norma and Angélica treated themselves to the new clothes, but if the garments didn't fit as expected (very often a problem because they saw themselves as slender beauty queens rather than the short, stout figures with extra belly rolls that they really were) and if they couldn't find a buyer, they gave them to Clorinda to disassemble and recreate.

Nothing could explain Clorinda's deep desire to taste and sometimes consume the very fibres that she needed to touch. When she was a young girl she assumed it was a human instinct and that the whole world managed to politely resist. But for an unknown reason it overpowered her. She thought it must have been due to a faulty gene and she left it at that. Her unnatural talent had its benefits. If ever in doubt about the origin of a thread, she identified it by its taste.

Some threads were so savoury that she bit off a short length and chewed, closing her eyes, the ecstasy of its flavour penetrating her senses until she achieved a taste orgasm that was even better than chocolate. She was able to distinguish fabric dyes by their plant origin and sometimes she even knew in which part of the world the plant had grown. All of this was self evident, and obviously a God-given intuition, a blessing.

She could distinguish the purity of material, the characteristics of Egyptian cotton versus Indian cotton, the rare pleasure of Italian silk, the weave of a double-faced satin, yarn-dyed versus piece-dyed, the luxury of a fabric with high thread count. All of these things were second nature to her. Fabric was her passion. Ever since she could remember she had dreamed of flying across the desert sky on wispy flowered chiffon or washing herself in a sea of deep blue silk and then lying under the sun on a flowered-appliqué velvet field.

Clorinda's new project – her weaving – which she proclaimed as her 'life's work' was much more ambitious than her calendar wardrobe and would of course mean that she would sacrifice plans for further calendar wardrobe items. All of the fabric would have to be categorised and all knits unravelled for use on her new tapestry. She perused her wardrobe and stood tall, chest expanding with pride as she proclaimed aloud that she had enough clothes to last 100 years after she died. Her closet was an patchwork mosaic of textiles and colours, each with its own inspiration and schedule for use.

Clorinda had become aware of her special talent with yarns and threads at a young age. No one had to tell her. In fact, she never discussed it. But she felt that her intrinsic knowledge could be augmented with specific information. She discovered the local public library when she was ten years old and her eyes were opened to stories and photos related to (but not restricted to) fabric. Even though the library collection was very small it provided a narrow glimpse of Asia and Europe and the Americas. Her heart quickened and blood rushed to her face whenever she happened upon an image associated with textiles. The library rarely acquired new books but when a new donation was made, the librarian always informed Clorinda because, although the librarian never admitted it to the rest of the community, this odd, rag-tag little girl was her most loyal client.

Her first visit to the library happened quite by accident when Clorinda ran, practically tripping on her own feet, from a gaggle of school girls whose accusing fingers pointed in her direction. She had just managed to slip a small cotton handkerchief with pink lace edges into her pocket after one of the girls dropped it at Clorinda's feet. How could she resist? She ran with it. Desperate to escape, she threw herself through the first entrance she came across, ducking through the old, infrequently-used glazed glass doors of the local library. Her eyes adjusted to the soft golden light, dust sparkling in the quiet air over stacks of books. A small woman with the thickest eye glasses she'd ever seen looked up from her desk and smiled. Clorinda's world stopped for a minute as she realised she had just entered an other-worldly chapel for books. She froze, nostrils expanding, eyes alternately growing round and then squinting, ignoring the smiling lady as she gazed around the room. It was a new sensory experience. She loved the musty odour of the shelves that were home to a small collection of mostly hard cover books in various states of disrepair, some of which had not been moved in 20 years. The earthy smell of old paper provoked a nostalgia for something but she didn't know what. External sounds were muffled by the thick walls and a single, square, double-paned window (unheard of in Tocopilla and no one could explain the reason for such an installation in the library). There was a magazine rack with a label at the top announcing the news of the day in playful art deco letters. It was partially filled with 30-year-old publications. There was even a low shelf at one end with a dozen children's picture books. Someone had pasted small white paper shapes with neatly printed Spanish translations over the original text.

"How can I help you?" The lady with coke-bottle lenses sidled up to her.

"Well... I don't know. I mean... I just came in...."

The glasses lady was obviously thrilled with Clorinda's presence. It was as though she hadn't spoken to anyone in years. She anxiously emerged from her cobwebs to be of service. "Well, what are you interested in?"

"Well, I like textiles and yarn and fabric of all type." Clorinda wondered if she answered the question correctly.

Before she knew it, the lady had her seated at the rectangular wooden table that was blemished with carved hearts and initials, and she was piling books in front of her. "We have something about the history of cotton production. We have this wonderful book with an amazing photo of a silk worm. We also have something about weaving, but the illustrations are not very good." The lady bustled back to the shelf and returned, her face beaming, coke bottle lenses magnifying the light in her eyes, with something about Andean art. She said it had a few black and white photos of ancient belts and hats amongst some facts related to pottery.

Not only did Clorinda find astonishing new information, she warmed to the librarian, who was especially kind. Her flight from the schoolgirls as a response to the accidentally dropped, and subsequently stolen handkerchief was a stroke of pure luck. Clorinda was safe here, even welcome. The girls' chides disappeared once inside this haven.

Now, rather than slinking from one corner of the school ground to another in her sideways crab walk in an effort to make herself invisible, she actually could disappear into the safety of the library. The girls teased her because she was friendless, and they openly mimicked her habit of avoiding eye contact. The unexpected result of their cruelty had not been pain, but comfort and joy – in a wooden chair at the quiet table beside the main library stacks where she was served by a be-spectacled librarian who, she knew instinctively, could remember similar schoolgirl taunts.

Clorinda dedicated many afternoons to sitting at one of the two tables in the open library space. The librarian's magnified eyes watched as Clorinda's scrubbed but stained fingers turned pages and lightly caressed the photographs. When she turned her attention to written content, she ran her index finger under each line of text, sucking the words in and exhaling them without pause. Then she would pass over the text again and again, finally smiling to herself. One of her favourite books was the one with an illustration of a black slave picking cotton in southern USA and, as predicted, the other was the one with the amazing full-page macro photo of a silk worm. Without fail, she requested these books upon each visit. The librarian made a habit of pulling them and placing them on the counter and eventually they were never re-shelved. Clorinda would walk through the door, collect the books with a silent nod and sit at her table to pour over them.

In the library, she also occasionally browsed through books with photos of chocolate. One such book had colour photographs of chocolate-sculpted animals (not just rabbits) and balls covered in chocolate flakes and slices of deep chocolate layer cakes adorned with glistening cherries. Next to fabric, chocolate was the next favourite thing to put into her mouth. The first time she stole chocolate was when she was barely tall enough to see the top of a sweets counter. Her 6-year-old nose led her into the shop just as a clerk was preparing to wrap some beautifully formed chocolate drops for a customer. The customer distracted the clerk with another item of interest, and when they both moved away leaving the drops unattended, Clorinda swiped them with both hands and ran like the wind. By the time she hunched down behind the deserted shack at the beach, the drops were nothing more than brown, greasy liquid squished between her fingers and smeared over the dusty palms of her hands. She had never dreamed appendages could be so delicious. She sat, skinny legs outstretched on the sand, for an exquisite hour of licking and re-licking the chubby valleys between her fingers, her tongue repeatedly revisiting every crease of her palms.

She missed the chocolate evenings with Señor Ortega.

She missed the world he introduced her to – chocolate being part of it – chocolate and other things that required money. She tried to imagine having enough pesos to buy tea and still afford chocolate. If she allowed herself to question much beyond that, her head began to spin and she had to abandon any attempts to connect her reality with Señor Ortega's world of riches and the kinds of things she saw in library books. She was an adult woman but before meeting Señor Ortega, she had never travelled beyond Tocopilla, and had never dreamed to come close to a vehicle as beautiful as his red convertible. Even the cost of a ticket on an old micro-bús to María Elena was out of the question.

Clorinda didn't resent people with money. But it was a mystery how they came upon it, how they gathered more than they could spend on tea and bread and electricity and water. All the people she knew carefully juggled their pesos day by day while individuals like Señor Ortega thought-fully and even playfully invested their dollars. She was wise enough to understand that probing this gap between herself and Señor Ortega was futile, so the questions were either discarded altogether or they took their rightful place in the back of her head as he described fine sculptures and paintings in beautiful buildings, gold-plated altars in churches and exotic clothing on the backs of gentlemen and ladies.

Her personal environment was a barren one, but it was something she had become accustomed to at a young age. Things had seemed to slowly decay after her mother disappeared – dishes broke and were never replaced, the radio stopped working and was never repaired, one of the gas burn-ers on the stove gave out, so they cooked on three, the walls of the house cracked and needed paint, so she lived with the shady crevices and small black holes. Years later, after her father died, because of the cost of doing so, it was difficult to replace items that other people took for granted such as an electric kettle or an iron. When the cost of electricity increased, Clorinda counted the broken appliances as a blessing in disguise.

In fact, Clorinda had two true blessings in her life. The first was her friendship with Señor Ortega and the second was her life's work. Señor Ortega was key to both, not only because he bought her the loom and made the project physically possible, but also because he was the inspiration for the work itself. And she was free to move it forward on a whim – if only she could find her muse.

At this point her tapestry was still just a blank warp created with her found threads and recycled yarns. She looked around at the plastic bags of fabric she had accumulated in the last few months. She had years' worth of yarn in the closet in her room and bags inside bags in the far corner of her father's old bedroom. She had to be attentive to them, opening them, shaking them out, ensuring no insects feasted or nested. Apart from tending to them, every spare moment was spent picking apart the seams of second-hand lives and unravelling fabric stories of strangers that she collected from behind the second-hand clothing store. Fortunately, with the recent boom of North American and European second-hand clothing shops, she no longer frequented the garbage dump. And with Norma's and Angélica's generosity (largely because of their erroneously selected 'slim line' items) she had years' more worth of raw material. Surely, despite its humble beginnings, her tapestry – her life's work – would be a beautiful piece of art. If only she knew where to commence.

Of the one dozen plastic bags of textile and yarn that Clorinda had selected for immediate use on her life's work, three of them were filled with the most exotic, refined fibres and swatches. These bags were branded with shop names that didn't exist in Tocopilla, which gave them an elite status. One was a green Falabella branded bag, the other a blue Almacenes Paris version (both, she knew were from Santiago) and the third and most impressive was a heavy off-white plastic bag with a stiff cardboard bottom quietly but powerfully labelled 'Marks & Spencer.' She had no idea where this bag originated but there was no doubt it advertised a quality company, so she designated it as the temporary new home for Señor Ortega's vest. The grey balls looked rather lonely in their rows at the bottom of such a spacious bag so she covered them with her favourite fabric swatch, a luscious emerald green square of crushed velvet that she cut from one of Norma's too-small dresses. She regretted not having the foresight to have draped it like a small flag across Señor Ortega's chest, tucking it under his chin, before closing his coffin. He would have appreciated its lush sensuality. She imagined him smiling up at her, a corner of the emerald crushed velvet brushing against his cheek.

Clorinda also had a lovely supply of small silk remnants, some as big as table runners, others as small as handkerchiefs. The other nine bags were used to store polyester blends from China and sheep and llama wool from locally produced sweaters. If it was an appealing colour she also kept some of what she referred to as 'plastic wool,' mass produced synthetic fibres from unknown sources. Since she wasn't sure yet what fibres and colours she would need to include in her tapestry, it was best to save everything.

Clorinda's special bags of wool consisted of strands she had unravelled from fine cotton or woollen European and North American-made garments. If she had known about the donors, she would have predicted how delighted they would be to have their old things transformed into an exotic tapestry – someone's life's work – rather than remaining intact and warming the body of a less fortunate South American.

CHAPTER 5

Orlando Ortega

Northern Chile, 1961

A nickname like *Pelota Dorada* – Golden Ball– or *Dedos de Plata* – Money Toes – can take a young man a long way in the wrong direction.

At the age of 24, Orlando del Transito Ortega de Riveras was the youngest president of a first division *fútbol* club in Chilean history and he was thinking about retiring. He managed it (in a small town in the interior of the third region) with a trademark nonchalance, making dispassionate decisions. His style was either harshly criticised to the point where the mere mention of his name triggered whistling and booing among *fútbol* fans, be it at the stadium or the local pub, or he was duly praised with compliments by businessmen who raised their glasses to his good health.

Orlando was so hated by his fans that midway into each season, he had to increase his personal security at the stadium to four policemen, who escorted him in, sat with him during the game and escorted him back out. Other than to watch games – the essential public duty of any team president – he endeavoured to keep an extremely low profile.

Nonetheless Orlando became accustomed to his VIP status and developed a certain personal style that earned him either greater disdain or deep admiration, depending on where you sat in the stadium. He was taller than normal for a northerner and had a naturally thin, well-proportioned frame over which he liked to drape clothes of only the latest style from the most exclusive men's shop in town. Fine wools and linens were his preference along with a few favourite felt fedoras. His fingernails were impeccable, something that set him apart from other working men, and his thick black hair was always neatly trimmed and combed. He preferred to be clean-shaven rather than wear a moustache. The thought of catching crumbs or bits of vegetables from his soup in a brush of hair on his upper lip made him shudder. Orlando had deep, dark eyes that revealed only the fact that he kept a thousand secrets. He was one of a select few men that, at his age, had been able to maintain a full set of white teeth, which was so distracting in its completeness that when he talked, people often focused on his mouth rather than looking him in the eyes. Whether he intended it or not, he had a magnetic charisma that few men or women could resist. Even if they hated him, they secretly loved him.

While the fans saw him as cold-blooded and disloyal, the businessman applauded his astute decisions and timing. He was able to maintain the team in first division by calculating exactly when to sell star players for a sizeable profit. As soon as, and only when it could be safely determined that the team would remain in first division where it would benefit from higher corporate sponsorships, radio royalties and gate revenues, he sold his best players for all he could get. At the same time, he sent scouts out to small desert towns to pick up young talent at no cost and he exposed them the next season, so the wolves of the wealthier teams in the Capital could prepare acceptable offers.

By the time Orlando del Transito Ortega de Riveras sold his second player, he had learned that if he negotiated to lower the official asking price by 10% and then asked for 5% under the table, everyone would be happy. The other board members were none the wiser.

In addition, he made friends among the referee community to ensure no-risk, highly profitable wagers for himself and his associates. He also greased the palms of mid-level municipal bureaucrats to ensure that stadium rental remained a minor, if not a nonexistent expense. He knew which players he could illegally sign on under false names for low one-time fees in order to ensure a strong team in an important game. He also knew which bookkeeper would do a good job of balancing gate revenues in his favour against actual attendance. If Orlando del Transito Ortega de Riveras did anything honest at all, it was to pay his players. *Azul Unido* was the only team in Chile to keep their promise to the talent, albeit with traditionally low salaries, reminding them that their greatest reward was the mere privilege of participating in this most glorious of games.

Although, at this point, he had never been to the Capital, his reputation preceded him in some of the Santiago coffee bars and private business clubs. The story around town was that this youthful club president was nicknamed 'Golden Ball' because as a young player he was able to score from midfield with an incredibly powerful, well-placed kick. And others referred to him as 'Money Toes' because of his magnificent dribble, the ball clinging like a magnet to his shoes, from one end of the field to the other, never disappointing a betting man. He had been the all-round superstar player of his barrio whose potential career ended in tragedy when he tripped into an old sink hole on a dark night. Apparently he was lucky to escape with his life, the broken ankle was never properly attended to, and it ended his career before he ever really got started. That, they said, was the reason for his slight limp. "Raise your glasses to Money Toes."

These fairy tales that had been concocted to account for the nicknames, are what originally qualified Orlando to become president of *Azul Unido*. But it was his excellent performance as a businessman – benefiting not only himself, but associates – that kept him there. He was elected unanimously by the contributing investors, a group of *pirquineros* (small, independent miners) who contributed a minimal percentage of their weekly salary to the club. The general expectation was that they would see a return equal to what they had invested, and most importantly they would have free passes to each game. Once the club investors realised that Orlando was also skilled at making money, greed overtook pride as the reason for loyalty to him. Before the 'Ortega era,' participating miners sauntered the downtown streets proudly sporting team shirts on their backs. But now they strutted around the main plaza with rat tail combs waving stiffly to the world from their back pockets. They all wore thick-framed, reflective sunglasses and greased back their hair. Their gold chain-adorned chests were so inflated by their own importance they looked like mating pigeons. They frequently waved to one another just so their smug, square-faced club rings that signalled exclusive membership, could be exhibited.

Orlando never corrected any of the stories that led him to this point. Once a rumour started burning through the minds of men, it gained a momentum and life of its own and didn't, at least in this instance, cause any harm. If it served a good purpose, then let it be.

In truth, the events leading up to Orlando's nickname were sometimes a little blurry even for himself. The afternoon he escaped the Michilla mine, American dollars stashed in his underwear, he headed south by bus to Valle del Elqui where he found lodging in the adobe house of a *campesino* who was renting rooms by the night. He felt safe there and stayed for several weeks, heading into the bigger centre of Coquimbo to change some of the American bills to peso notes. In order not to be an easy target he exchanged small amounts of money in various different places over a period of weeks. Meanwhile his underwear was a vault. Unfortunately, his mouth was not.

On one of his visits to town, he entered into a conversation with a typical, hard-working miner at a local bar. Weeks had passed since his escape from El Camino mine. It was hundreds of kilometres behind him now. After more *pisco* than he could handle at his young age, he couldn't resist leaning across the bar and whispering his story to his drinking companion. The miner was outwardly impressed not only with Orlando's audacity but also with his apparent success – stuffing the gold into his crotch and then cutting off his own toes! Brilliant! He immediately turned around and with pisco sloshing out of his raised glass, invited everyone and no one in particular, "Hey, let's drink a toast to *Pelota Dorada* – 'Golden Ball.' This," his index finger pointing at Orlando from above his head, "is *Pelota Dorada*." A communal '*Salud*' rang through the bar as everyone turned to raise their glass in obliging good humour. After more low conversation during which Orlando earned more of his companion's appreciation – who was shaking his head in disbelief and repeatedly pounding the bar – the companion turned again to the crowd, and raised his glass, *pisco* sloshing onto the floor, and said, "Hey, I have another one. Let's drink to *Dedos de Plata* – 'Money Toes' here!"

"Cheers to Money Toes." The bar crowd, undoubtedly all *fútbol* experts, focused their attention on Orlando and murmured about his physique – perfect frame, good height, strong arms, just the right build for a *fútbol* player – and the speculation about his level of *fútbol* skills began. Within days the murmurs that were sparked by the nicknames the young miner had given him, grew to a steady stream of gossip about *Pelota Dorada*. It was only a matter of days before *Pelota Dorada* was a *fútbol* legend. Out of nowhere, there were even incredible eyewitness accounts attesting to his rare skill and everyone lamented its loss on the tragic night he tripped into the sink hole. These tales were repeated so quickly and from so many different sources that no one knew exactly who the eyewitnesses were, but their authenticity was never doubted.

The night that his *fútbol* legend status was born, Orlando and his companion left the bar together. Having consumed several glasses of *pisco*, they decided to return to the valley on foot. Neither of them had a grasp of the distance they needed to cover as they stumbled drunkenly, leaning on each other for support, beyond the lights of town and into the quiet moonlit hills. Once they had meandered a few kilometres from the outskirts, the companion suddenly planted himself solidly in front of Orlando and surprised him by drawing a switchblade from his pocket. Wavering unsteadily like a dead tree in a strong wind, he held the knife to Orlando's chest, and spit out his demand, "Give me all of your money, *Pelota Dorada*." Shocked and too drunk to respond, Orlando could only stare down at the knife, the tip of which was about to pierce his sternum. When he raised his bleary eyes to look up into the smirking face of his drooling companion, he lost his balance. He wobbled and shuffled in the sand attempting to regain his equilibrium and trying to locate his wit. However, any creativity and all instincts were swimming in his *pisco*-pickled brain and he was not successful. He just stood there numbly, in no position to argue, with his ankles about to give way.

Agitated, the companion shook the knife, poking Orlando in the chest. "Cough it up, Golden Ball."

As Orlando nervously reached into his pocket to pull out some bills, he shuffled, slipped on the loose gravel and fell to the ground, landing on his back with a heavy thud, one hand still in his trouser pocket. He noticed for the first time in his life how the multitude of twinkling stars hung so close he could almost touch them. But he was too drunk to extend an arm.

The companion was short on patience and he threw himself into a crazed, childish tantrum. Threatening the moon with his knife and punching into the night with his other fist, he jumped up and down several times on the spot. Suddenly exhausted, he leaned forward, hands on his knees and he leered down at Orlando. "You useless, toeless little runt. You thought you didn't need your toes, but now you can't stand up. Well, you'll need more than your missing digits to save you tonight, you smart-ass."

The companion lunged forward in an attempt to grab Orlando's foot. Orlando kicked at him and succeeded in throwing him off balance. The knife slipped out of his hand and flipped through the air. The companion fell back several steps, arms flailing in wide circles as he to tried to regain his footing. After skidding and tripping across the sand, he performed a couple of clumsy half-cartwheels and disappeared over a mound. There was a high-pitched, drawn-out yell that fell away into the distance. Then silence.

Orlando lay frozen for several minutes, leaning forward on one elbow, eyes squinting into the starry sky. He turned onto his belly and slithered over to the embankment where the companion had dropped from sight.

In the moonlight, he couldn't see the true depths of the shaft, the edges of which had surrendered under the companion's weight. He doubted whether even the light of day would reveal the body that lay broken numerous hundreds of metres in the shadows below.

Old ghost shafts were occasionally discovered by chance, normally by fatal accidents such as this. Earthquakes frequently rearranged the land, slyly folding sand over lightweight tin shaft lids, fooling even the miners who had left them there. One of Mother Earth's cruel tricks, it was the most underestimated danger of walking across desert mine areas, day or night.

The unexpected disappearance of his unfortunate companion immediately sobered Orlando. He pushed back from the edge, brushed himself off and began the long walk towards his lodging, gazing at all the lucky stars in the naked desert sky. He reached up and felt their light bless his fingertips and smiled. If the companion had not stopped to rob him they would have both staggered into the shaft and disappeared forever. His luck, if he dared to believe in it, had turned.

CHAPTER 6

Orlando Ortega

Northern Chile, 1961

If the world spinning on its axis is explained through the laws of physics, then it involves neither luck nor love. But very few people comprehend or are concerned about astronomical equations, particularly those born into extreme poverty. Questions about the world as a whole are not only irrelevant and useless but are ridiculous in the face of constant urgent quests for food and shelter. These have to be obtained through the acquisition of an arbitrary amount of money that is determined each day by someone else, who for all intents and purposes, is living on another planet. But it is what it is and there seems to be no changing it.

Even if the world turning lazily on its axis, is explained through the miracle of God's love and creation, the resulting situation is basically the same as if it is explained through physics: poverty and inequality, accidental deaths and natural disasters.

Very few mothers send their teenaged sons to hang on the end of ropes in narrow, toxic mine shafts out of love or because they are hoping for a miracle. Very little love is needed to explain how sacrifice will eventually lead to a blissful afterlife somewhere in the heavens where money is not essential for survival. Here, however, where it is a prerequisite, mothers sometimes sell their bodies to feed their children, and still others sell their body parts for cash. Therefore, in the grand scheme of things, Orlando believed his sacrifice of two small appendages was a sound decision.

His life had changed dramatically from the days when he was low-ered head-first into mine shafts, but the memory and niggling fear of one day having to return, occasionally gave him nightmares. The fear of being penniless was, for Orlando, synonymous with hanging upside down in a bottomless, rocky cavern.

At the end of his fourth season as president of *Azul Unido*, when it often took him more than a full day to count his money, he noticed a shift in his sentiments. Perhaps it was the physical sensation of handling paper bills – bundling them, folding them, smelling them, arranging them into piles for one purpose and then dividing them into different stacks for something else. Towers of coins were lined up alongside each other, like walls of a fortress or like pawns, ready to move out onto the front lines.

He ignored the fact that bills were nothing more than paper, and coins nothing more than metal discs, each their own perfect set of mol-ecules designed by Mother Nature and shaped by man. Paper and metal, like pieces on a game board, had since ancient times, been assigned a val-ue, and a duty. These molecular combinations had the power to define the fates of families, and in fact, entire nations. With the capacity to purchase tangibles the metal discs decided whether or not someone could afford to live, and if so, under what conditions. Most often the cost of living in even the most reasonable of states required more than the amount most peo-ple were allowed to possess. And for Orlando, although paper and metal could not buy intangibles, it certainly bought him peace of mind. And of equal importance, it permitted him to play the game with which he had become enamoured.

By the end of his final term as president of *Azul Unido*, Orlando had become an adept player in the money game. Encouraged by the creed of 'Go forth and multiply,' far from being a tool for survival, money was a tool for accumulation of the same. The game was without rules and per-petuated itself on the premise that, one: you needed to have some to play and, two: that you could never have enough to be declared the winner.

Each minor decision of his everyday life was driven by whether or not the cost of something would result in a financial benefit and if he could justify spending an extra peso here or there. His only nonprofit extravagance, driven by an aspiring social status and growing ego, was in creating his personal façade. He splurged on fine suits, silk ties and socks, imported woollen sweaters, soft leather shoes and felt hats.

He was not unaware of the poverty that surrounded him but he was unable to rationalise donating money to charity because doing so did not result in a monetary reward. He did not drop a peso into the hand of a poor woman on the street, nor did he agree to donate to established charities unless they reciprocated with public fanfare from which he could draw indirect financial benefit. He ignored the poverty in the shadows of his self-imposed blindness when he surveyed the everyday landscape. This blindness led to an unnamed insidious infirmity that was a veil across his memory, preventing him from relating current local conditions to his own miserable childhood, and therefore relieving himself of any responsibility to help. It also gave him a reason to blame poverty on the poor themselves.

In the same way the world rotates on its axis for no other purpose than to rotate, counting as it does, each day and every night, the perpetual money game counts its gains and losses for no other purpose than to continue counting.

The vast majority of fans of *Azul Unido* were ecstatic over the news of Orlando del Transito Ortega de Riveras' resignation, although some predicted a certain nostalgia for the days when they had witnessed the president fleeing enraged fans, his assistants in tow, policemen unable to protect them from sharp insults and hurled objects. They were going to miss hating him as he sat in his private box, seemingly uninvolved, silent amidst the raucous exchange between his assistants and those of the opposing president yelling at him from the other side of the stadium. Many fans had perfected their imitations of the man, especially his limp. It took nothing more than one man to walk across a bar, favouring his left foot, for others to pipe up with imitations of Orlando's phrases of how the team will overcome adversaries with his own special vision and planning.

Orlando del Transito Ortega de Riveras decided that he would return to Tocopilla to invest in mining interests about which there was a lot of buzz recently. In the midst of a national tendency towards reform for small miners and land-owners, he saw an opportunity to profit by entering in the back door, so to speak.

CHAPTER 7

Orlando Ortega

Tocopilla, 1961

Orlando's mother was in the patio, a dirty striped apron thrown loosely on top of her oversized blouse and faded cotton skirt. A few long strands of grey hair had fallen loose from the bun at the top of her head and she puffed them away out of the corner of her mouth. She didn't see him as he watched her from the doorway. She was cleaning fish. The skin peeled off, she drew out the guts with her fingers and threw them into the bucket on the ground beside her. She was expert with the knife, but the blade had long ago lost its edge so she grunted her way through the job. Cats peered down at his mother's fish from the edges of the patio roof, incessant meows, demanding their share. A couple of them were bold enough to jump down onto the plywood sheet, the makeshift table that had been there as long as he could remember. She rapped them across their hind end with the back of the knife and sent them screeching back up to their lookout.

Orlando smiled remembering the day his younger brother Jorge was cleaning fish in this very spot. He had tossed some guts up onto the roof for the cats, but misjudged the distance. The neighbour, who was bent over washing his face in the basin in his patio on the other side of the wall, felt the fish guts slop onto his back and slide coldly down towards his waist. Before he knew what was happening, two cats lunged after the guts, claws scraping across the poor man's shoulders and scratching down his back. Insult following injury. The enraged neighbour grabbed the cats and tossed them, along with the fish innards back over the wall, cursing and screaming for no less than an hour. It took several months before he acknowledged anyone in Orlando's family with anything resembling a civil phrase.

Orlando noticed that his Mom still saved her fish guts, probably to donate them to Señor Casali, the local pig farmer. He probably still came by every two days with his burro-drawn cart to collect food scraps for his porkers. In exchange, he rewarded his faithful clients with a generous cut of meat for New Year's dinner. Orlando realised nothing had changed. The four local pig farmers probably still threw clumsy punches at each other if they met on the street corner, their burros waiting patiently in front of the carts until the frenzy of old fists finished without a decisive winner. It was well-known that housewives were loyal to only one of them at a time, but there was always a fight as to which one.

Orlando picked up a smooth stone from the pile of rocks in the patio and threw it at the loudest cat. After all these years it was still an automatic reaction, something he had learned as a boy. His mother used to send him to the beach to collect smooth stones for the anti-cat arsenal they kept in the patio. He wondered who did it for her now.

He considered stone-throwing more humane than hiring the *mata-gatos*, the cat killer. The *matagatos* was a crooked old lady with a notorious burlap bag. She responded to requests to get rid of nuisance roof cats and she pocketed more than a few pesos doing so. She could be seen walking down the streets, alternately holding the bag with its wriggling contents well out in front of herself or dragging it behind her on the ground. When it was full she made a trip to the cliff on the north shore, where she swung the bag lasso-style above one shoulder before sending the clawing, meowing contents flying over the edge and into the surf. The *matagatos* was always in high demand, her service considered an essential one. Orlando guessed that she, or perhaps her daughter who would have inherited her job, was still around and wondered whether or not she could sleep at night.

"*Buenos Días, Mamá.*" He was aware that he was just a tall, well-dressed stranger in the shadow of her doorway. His voice reached her ears at the same time as his stone clipped the cat on its rear end.

She jumped back startled, dropping the knife, "Son of a bitch!" Escaping from her mouth. She shielded her eyes with her hands and squinted over at him.

"How have you been, Mamá?" He guessed not well, by the state of things around here. The lone tree in the patio was nothing more than a fusion of dry sticks, gnarled fingers reaching out for help from a thick stem that leaned into the wall. Two plastic bird figurines were wired to two separate branches in a no-doubt once-inspired but pathetic attempt to add colour. Now the birds were just dirty shapes on brittle branches that blended into the homogenous grey dust of the patio. Dog droppings sat in small, fresh yellow puddles that hadn't yet been absorbed by the rock-hard soil in what used to be a garden. Flies buzzed in and around them.

Attracted by the dead fish, three vultures circled down towards the target. They would fight it out with the cats if they had the opportunity. Orlando's mother was oblivious to it.

She fumbled roughly with the bottom of her apron and rubbed her hands on it. "Orlando?" Her eyes widened. "Orlando!" She made a self-conscious attempt to arrange her hair, pulling the strands away from her face with her fish-bloodied fingers and she rushed past him, going directly across the patio in her floppy shoes to the bathroom, washed her hands, splashed water onto her face, inserted her false teeth, ran her fingers through her hair, removed her apron and tucked her blouse into her skirt.

Now ready, she approached him slowly and deliberately, slippers flapping against her heels as she crossed the dirt floor. She looked up into his eyes and slapped him firmly across his clean-shaven cheeks, first one side, then the other, both hands put to use. "What have you got to say for yourself?" She didn't wait for an answer before guiding him back into the kitchen. "Come, I'll make us some tea."

He didn't say much and she didn't ask. He looked good and she looked terrible. It was only after they had drained the last drop of tea and he stood up to help her remove the cups from the table that she turned to offer him a hug. She grasped him by his shoulders and leaned in towards him, brushing her cheek against his chest but remaining close for less than three seconds . She went through the motions but the feeling was hollow. He guessed he had been away for too long.

Orlando was relieved to learn that Jorge had moved to Santiago more than a year ago, attracted to the national workers' union which had made great strides in the past few years. His mother bragged that Jorge had become inspired by the book, 'Unions: History, Theory and Practice' by Father Hurtado a priest (recently deceased and no doubt headed towards sainthood) at the head of social justice causes in Chile. Orlando and Jorge had always fought as children, perhaps natural sibling rivalry, and as adults they were still sure to disagree on everything from shoe style to politics.

Their father, his mother said, had died a typical miner's death two years ago – his lungs holding out for as long as they could. He worked up until the day before he died. She said he collapsed at home walking through the front door at the end of his 10-day shift. He didn't want to die up at the mines, she supposed. He must have used all of his strength to hold on so he could see her once more. And that's all he did. He raised a hand without having the strength to utter a hello or a goodbye and collapsed in front of her. His mother recounted the story without emotion as she stared at the ground. "He's there now," she motioned weakly in the direction of the cemetery. "They gave him a niche in the miner's union wall. Your brother saw to it." She didn't mention Orlando's absence or lack of responsibility in the matter. He felt a twinge of guilt and swallowed hard.

CHAPTER 8

Clorinda

Tocopilla, 2001

Clorinda's tapestry was going to be her life's work. She wasn't sure what 'life's work' meant to anyone else, but for her it was an interpretation of the activities, both physical and spiritual of the universe itself. This consisted of the town of Tocopilla and its population, both human and animal, that dotted a patch of desert ground about eight hours south of the Peruvian border, trapped between the Pacific Ocean and the steep, barren Andes, but mostly it consisted of Señor Ortega. It was an ambitious project.

The blue sky, the sun and moon knew all the places in the universe but that they smiled down on Tocopilla which was all that mattered to Clorinda. They didn't smile down on it in a way that made it a fortunate or a wealthy town, perhaps quite the opposite. Maybe the smile was twisted into a sneer born of an unjust universe with an outward disdain for the town's poverty. But she had learned from her father that life was what it was, no matter what the universe thought.

Her father, along with half the population of Tocopilla, was a mine labourer. He worked for one of the big corporations in the *altiplano*, ten days in and three days out. On the ninth day of one of his shifts, just after Clorinda's eighteenth birthday, two men in a company truck knocked on Clorinda's door and delivered her father to her in a box. "It was miner's lung, Señorita. No doubt about it," was all they told her.

The company had been kind enough to supply the coffin, and the miners' union efficiently arranged a cheap burial plot in the ground at the edge of the syndicate wall in the municipal cemetery. Because of the alarming rate at which empty syndicate niches had become occupied by relatively young miners, they had to expand into the ground beyond. She and Norma and Angélica attended the burial along with an evangelical preacher who was doing some promotion to increase the size of his flock and as such, volunteered to say a few kind words about a man he'd never met. He was pleased to do it, though, because he said he was a 'fisher of men,' and 'kindness was the best bait.'

There was no wake because the men who delivered her father in the box said that their truck broke down on the road from the mine and her father, God rest his soul, had to wait in the middle of the desert, sun beating down on his coffin in the back of the old panel truck for nearly a full day while they repaired the motor. That, coupled with the fact that he had been found dead on his bunk the morning before meant that his body (sorry to mention this, Señorita) had begun to decompose perhaps as many as seven or eight hours previous to when they had kicked at his cot to rouse him for work. Therefore, there would be no time (hygieni- cally-speaking) for him to lay idly by as people who were dressed in their Sunday black sat respectfully on chairs beside the coffin to silently wish him farewell, stuffed their mouths with sandwiches and requested wine to wash them down. No, there would be no leisurely send-off for Clorinda's father. He would have to be rushed to his final resting place.

From that day forward Clorinda visited her father every Sunday without fail. She swept away the bits of garbage that had blown onto the hard dirt surface of his grave and she washed the simple wrought iron cross to which a flimsy piece of wood on which his name was neatly print- ed, was attached with a wire. She picked up the miniature model air plane, dusted it, and replaced it at the base of the cross.

Most families decorated their loved-one's grave with little ornaments and photos and trinkets that had sentimental value to the deceased. The glass display cases of children's niches, for instance, were filled with small stuffed animals, plastic rattles, miniature vehicles and wooden blocks. Family members occasionally changed the collection of toys to provide fresh entertainment for the child, always careful to include at least one favourite type of toy. Sometimes there were heated disagreements about the child's best-loved toy, with aunts and cousins insisting that their gift from Christmases past was the child's true choice. Hands were slapped, little toys roughly tossed to the ground to be replaced by another, then quickly grabbed and replaced by yet another. On occasion, punches were thrown and toys broken. In that case the old toys had to be re-inserted into the display and apologies offered to the child for sentencing him to boredom beyond the grave. Curse words were thrown over the shoulders of each family member as they stomped away in single file down the path towards the gate. Everyone knew that the true power of choice was with the keeper of the niche's key. Usually this was the mother and she could count on being lobbied during the week by the most insistent of aunts.

In Clorinda's case, because the only thing she knew about her father besides his job as a miner was that he had an interest in travel, she settled on a miniature grey painted model of an air plane that she found one day on the road not far from home. She could have used a bus or maybe a ship, but the toy airplane was the first thing she came across once she had decided on the travel theme. It looked good at the foot of the cross, but the overall decoration lacked colour. So she inserted a bright red plastic rose into the neck of a dirt-smeared glass coca-cola bottle, and placed it beside the air plane. May he rest in peace.

Although her father had spent more time in the mines than at home, and even though he had always been a solemn man of very few words, and she should have been reconciled to the quiet, after he died, the silence of the house became immense. Without his silence it was just hers. She never would have imagined that her own silence would be greater than the two of them combined. To fill it, she began to sing. She sang when she washed clothes and hung them to dry in her patio, she sang as she hunched over her sewing machine. She sang unselfconsciously when she sat outside by her front door at night to watch the sun set over the ocean and she sang herself to sleep in the same wooden-frame single bed where she had fallen asleep every night of her life.

Her songs were not sad ones, nor were they songs of joy. To say she was surprised to find herself singing into the hushed air of her hollow house would been untrue because it seemed such a natural solution to an uncommonly quiet and therefore disconcerting environment. What was surprising, however, was that she had never before been inclined to do so. Clorinda had never had the urge to sing along to the radio or hum snippets of songs she remembered hearing. Now she generated her own spontaneous melodies, rarely singing the same thing twice. They arrived at her creative centre from the blue sky as though transmitted through a pure golden thread from ethereal stringed instruments somewhere in the heavens. She had the voice of an angel. When she first started singing she was unaware of the beauty of her voice, its purity, the innocent timbre, its force and striking clarity, and of the effect it had on neighbours and passersby.

Once, as they sat in the evening air outside of Señor Ortega's house, he had commented on her lovely singing voice and requested a song. He asked if she could sing *tango*. Of course she couldn't sing *tango* and the request made her very uncomfortable. But only yesterday when she went to visit Señor Ortega at his niche, she tried to sing him a *tango* called 'She's never had a boyfriend' made famous by Julio Sosa. She heard it on the radio and paid special attention because of its significance. She was only a few bars into the song when she stopped, embarrassed, feeling that although the lyrics were appropriate, her version was dishonest. She was not a *tango* singer. She apologised to Señor Ortega's niche and vowed to never again attempt to sing someone else's song, even for Señor Ortega who was prostrate in his tomb, his ears disabled by the natural processes of decay.

She sang for herself now, gazing at the vertical threads of her tapestry, watching them vibrate in the sunlight as they anticipated her touch.

And she theirs. They were like lovers, she and the threads. Still singing, she leaned forward and licked the centre of the strung loom, savouring the foreign flavours. The strings parted for her tongue. Perhaps if she sang for them alone, they would paint images across themselves and she would see what it was that Señor Ortega knew, what this tapestry was finally meant to express, realising the testimony to her universe. And finally her life's work would blossom, poignant and brilliant in its truth.

Unfortunately, in spite of the erotic pleasure she shared with her threads, this fecund ecstasy was insufficient and her muse continued to elude her.

CHAPTER 9

Orlando Ortega

Tocopilla and María Elena, 1961 – 1973

Orlando spent more than the next decade in Tocopilla with his mother. Jorge was much too busy to return from Santiago; the socialists were gaining ground all over the country and things were volatile. Orlando could see it happening in Tocopilla, which had a reputation nationally as a communist haven. That's why he did his work out of town, often travelling into Peru and Bolivia to meet business associates. Although he called Tocopilla home once more, he was almost never there because he had set up an office in María Elena, a mining town about 45 minutes east of Tocopilla and 1,000 metres closer to heaven.

He relied on the local miners' rumour mill to glean information on where to buy good stakes and from whom. The small-time miners had big ideas. Their downfall was that they had never been outside of the region and their ideas were only big in proportion to their narrow scope and limited business environment. Their other big problem was that they had no capital and out of necessity, they were forced to sell at low prices for immediate gain. Truth be told, they were no match for Orlando who was in an entirely different league and he knew it. His business flourished as the miners scrambled and argued amongst themselves about petty concerns, ultimately of no consequence. Each small man wanted his small share of power but lacked perspective. Understanding the force of the rumour mills in small towns, Orlando planted ideas that started the wheels turning, using the miners themselves to generate his growing business which was built upon them selling him their mining stakes for shamefully low prices.

The current political climate and mounting confidence of the socialists helped to propel his success. All he had to do was whisper into the ear of one miner after another that the government was poised to immediately nationalise all the mines in the country. Convinced that they had to get out while they could, they lined up at his office in the plaza of María Elena to sign away their livelihoods for practically nothing. Because political progress in Chile was slow, he was able to profit for years by this ruse before the government finally took steps to realise his prediction. When miners accused him of deception, he would say "Wait and see. Can't you see the writing on the wall? It's just around the corner and when it comes, it'll be too late. Take the risk, if you want, but think first about your children."

At the same time, he counted on big foreign companies (at once too naïve and too arrogant) to believe they would ever be pushed out. He sold the rights he had purchased for a pittance from the poor miners to the international mining corporations for a profit. The companies were confident. They had faith that their mere presence was enough to bring Chilean government ministers to their knees. The added safeguard of 'promotional and public relations' expenses in their corporate budgets – generous sums for dinners and vacations for ministers and staff of various ministries, not to mention the presidential executive staff and several senators – was their insurance. Both the foreign companies and Chilean officials rationalised that Chile's rich mineral wealth should benefit all citizens, not just those who actually hauled the ore out of the ground. As always, they ignored the fact that the men who hauled it out of the ground were the ones who gained the least.

Perhaps even more gratifying for government officials than the corporate promotional expenditures were the direct gifts of neatly bundled small denomination bills delivered in quiet paper bags through the back doors of offices in the Capital, as one might deliver sandwiches. Foreign mining companies became widely and affectionately known as 'the delicatessens.'

For added insurance, Orlando always kept himself abreast of the foreign mining company rumours. He discovered that he had a remarkable gift for languages; was almost fluent in English, and he knew some French and enough German to impress when it counted. He was invited to play golf in the sand courses designed by the Americans, pretended to enjoy their game of baseball, and accepted dinner invitations at the homes of foreign executives. When asked, he always said he was born into the mining business and avoided further discussion on the topic. Because of his language skills, it was assumed that he had lived and worked abroad, something he never bothered to correct.

Orlando del Transito Ortega de Riveras was a Latin charmer. Although he never took in business partners, he nourished close ties with corporate executives, rogue players and the wives of both. A young man of medium height (tall by Chilean standards) and build, he considered himself neither ugly nor beautiful, but he dressed according to his own inclinations which were cosmically synchronised with some of the finest international designers. He was aware that this gave him good leverage. He was grateful to have a nice, thick head of hair, no signs of early baldness, good teeth, and a natural slim physique – although not muscular, he was blessed with a semi-sculpted masculine trim. He had developed a unique quiet style, and could be a man's man or a woman's man, depending on the circumstances, but always first and foremost, his own man. He was aware that foreign women gossiped about his enchanting aloofness, and although he was not necessarily impressed, he took advantage of it where possible.

Orlando's office in the dusty, central plaza of María Elena was in a 2-storey wooden building, which also housed the offices of, among others, four sleazy lawyers, the government land registry, a notary public who was known to be crooked, a shoe store, and a button and zipper shop.

There was no sign hanging outside of his office. The narrow 2-metre high exterior wooden doors opened to a small enclosed porch and a set of interior security doors with two opaque glass panels. Each set of doors had one long deadbolt and, as if that wouldn't be enough, and to quash any expectation whatsoever of elegance, an industrial padlock hung on a heavy chain. A small glass door knob opened only one of the interior doors. The other door was permanently closed, requiring stout men to pause and then wriggle sideways through the door that was allowed to open. The common understanding was that fat thieves would not escape without a struggle.

The porch opened into a single office which was a spacious, dark, square room. Tall wooden shutters were nailed closed across two narrow windows. A bare light bulb hung halfway down from the 2.5 metre-high ceiling over a wooden table that served as Orlando's desk, behind which was a wooden rung arm chair with armrests. Its faded green upholstered cushion was the only attempt at luxury in the place. An upright iron safe was shoved into the corner and beside it a heavy marble-top armoire with individual padlocks on every single door and drawer. A wardrobe with a broken full-length mirror reflecting what little light there was in the room stood in the other corner. Everything was covered in dust. There was a small, peculiar wooden chest with a lid, also locked with a padlock, on the corner of the table. A wire ran across the floor and into the box. Inside was a black telephone with a rotary dial. No one had seen Orlando use the phone so rumour was that it was there for appearance only. Beside his phone chest was an ink bottle, a fountain pen and several blank sheets of writing paper, everything set perfectly perpendicular to everything else.

A dirty horse-hair sofa upholstered in deep red chenille, with stubby, claw feet and large round arms worn down here and there to grey threads was pushed against the wall opposite the table. Small clouds of dust arose whenever anyone made contact with it. If Orlando ever invited a visitor to relax in his office, he directed him towards the sofa while he sat up straight behind the desk and puffed on a fine black tobacco cigarette.

They conversed across the long, hollow distance, their words echoing off the walls. Sometimes he interrupted the conversation to unlock a cupboard of the armoire and pull out one of many small wooden boxes in which he filed documents. They say he kept precise notes on everything.

His in-office business was done mostly with the miners themselves. However he occasionally entertained rogue businessmen. Even less frequently a mining executive was seen to walk through the doors. If, for whatever unusual reason, he invited a foreign executive to his office, he explained that the décor was deliberately designed to gain the confidence of local miners, who would be uncomfortable and mistrustful of anyone with a more elegant place of business. And he was right. The executives congratulated him on his astute psychology and were entertained by the somewhat tranquil circus atmosphere of his odd professional establishment.

He paid a municipal guard who worked at the plaza to watch his office during his frequent absences from María Elena. In turn, he paid a young boy who hung around the plaza taking bets on *fútbol* games and train arrival times, to watch the guard. In nine years, his office had never been burgled but to err on the side of caution, he always carried his most valuable documents with him in a locked briefcase, and as long as he was in the country, he never went anywhere without his two armed *secretarios*, a couple of stout, moustached men in dark suits with greased-back hair and dark glasses. He had picked up the *secretarios* as body guards when he was president of *Azul Unido*. He paid them well and they were blindly loyal.

When the *secretarios* weren't each occupying one of the two shoe shine stations at the plaza, they spent a fair bit of time spitting on and shining their patten leather shoes or cleaning their glasses with handkerchiefs as they idly observed the comings and goings from the corner.

Pigeon droppings frequently soiled their shoes or the shoulders of their dark suits, so they avoided whenever possible, passing under the main set of electrical wires that were strung around the plaza perimeter. Over time, the weight of the pigeons and their droppings had caused the wires to slacken and bow down so far into the centre that if a tall man extended his arm, he could touch them. The boys that hung out in the plaza used the pigeons for slingshot target practise. Orlando's men preferred multifunctional long sticks, using them on more than just pigeons.

Although the initial reason for Orlando's trips to Potosi, Bolivia and Iquique was to buy and sell silver, an impelling factor for return trips were the wives of a foreign mine engineer and diplomat, one in each city. He would never allow them to be the sole reason for his journeys, but whenever he could work either of these cities into his business agenda, he did so, his black fountain pen smiling their initials across his calendar page.

They both offered him foreign delights, teasing his senses with exotic perfume, words with exquisite new sounds and porcelain skin, soft as the satin sheets they climbed into. Once in Imogen's husband's bedroom in Potosi, he realised that he enjoyed the feel of satin slinking between his legs and gliding across his back as much as, and possibly even more, than running his hands along the curves of Imogen's refined English body. Nevertheless, sex at high altitudes was an exhilarating experience, and enhanced by fine wine, perfume and luxurious fabrics he saw no reason not to return for more. Besides Imogen would not be long in Bolivia and he could take advantage of an affair without demands or complications.

She had agreed to spend two years there with her husband, and complained that she spent the first few months testing, without positive results, various recommended methods to alleviate headaches and nausea caused by lack of oxygen at this altitude. How people ever considered populating such a place was something she would never understand. She refused to chew coca leaves, but made tea of them and sucked on raw sugarcane. Neither of these methods, as it turned out, was foolproof and she was still occasionally overcome with the negative effects. Orlando was quite possibly her only cure, making her forget all about the altitude maladies for up to a week after one of his visits.

He always stayed at a quiet hotel on a narrow passageway behind the main plaza, with a window opening out onto a view of El Cerro Rico (the

Rich Hill, or, 'the mountain that eats people,' as some locals referred to it because of the number of natives who had lost their lives in the mines since the arrival of the Spanish 500 years ago). Orlando contacted Imogen's husband after he settled in, and accepted the inevitable dinner invitation.

Imogen's husband sold him refined silver which he stole from company sample rooms and Orlando sold it to his contacts at the port of Iquique upon his return to Chile. While in Potosi, Orlando also contacted a Bolivian shift boss who sold him his stash of silver at an even better price.

In addition, he stopped at the central cathedral to buy selected items from the local priest's bags of solid silver coins and collectibles – gifts from poor peasants willing to trade found antique artefacts for a hope and a prayer. He never queried the destiny of the cash he paid the priest, any more than he would have asked what the peasants hoped to gain in exchange for their donations. Their destiny was sealed before they were born no matter how many times they kneeled in front of Jesus or the Virgin at the cathedral to watch their prayers rise in smoke and disappear. The difference, he thought, as he stuffed the peasants' gold and silver treasures into his leather suitcases, was that the rich engineer and well-off shift boss at least realised something in return for their valuables.

He visited Imogen at her house in between these brief business dealings, always satisfied that he was able to take advantage of everything on offer during his business trips.

The arduous train journey back over the salt flats from Bolivia and into Chile's interior was a long, cold one, even in the first class car, and it was never on schedule. But Orlando's relationship with all the border guards at this entry point made it worthwhile. There was no need to haggle over how many pesos to press into their hands for passing his suitcases across the checkpoint without opening them.

Because Orlando's policy was to never return to María Elena with anything but cash or bank transfer slips in his suitcase, he disembarked from the *altiplano* train, legs stiff and bones shaken, and stepped immediately onto a bus heading for the coastal city of Iquique.

He stayed in a one of the new high-rise beach-side hotels at the south end of town, treating himself to the view across the expanse of white sands that gently disappeared into the cool Pacific waters. He allowed the swishing of the surf to lull him to sleep and for a couple of days he lounged between his bed and the terrace, building up a reserve of energy to spend on Tookie, the wife of the American diplomat he had met some time ago at a formal dinner hosted by the Chilean governor.

Tookie was bolder than Imogen and liked to tease her husband by flirting openly with Orlando or whoever else she chose as the flavour of the week. Her husband was seemingly unaffected. There was always a party. He learned that Tookie and her husband hosted at least two parties per week. Men and women exchanged flirtatious glances and made bold advances in all corners of the room as the satin voice of Elvis Presley crooned over their heads and small Chilean women dressed in black and white uniforms wove in and out, offering cocktails and seafood delights. Orlando mingled, making witty comments in English, and listening intently for openings to business opportunities until he saw Tookie crook her index finger and pull him over to her with just three slow indications. They usually went to the walk-in closet of the guest room where it was not necessary to remove his socks. In fact, most of the time, he managed to participate with his shoes still on. Unlike Imogen, Tookie never asked why he always kept his socks on. She didn't even notice.

He sold his Bolivian goods at the port in Iquique and stopped in to visit his mother in Tocopilla.

The mining rights business was successful up until a few years before the socialist president, Salvador Allende was elected in 1970. At that point even the most influential of mining companies could see the writing on the wall and decided to be more cautious. It had been a lucrative run for Orlando. He quietly closed his María Elena office but continued with his buying and selling trips because the black market was thriving.

When he made his final trip to Potosi, Imogen had already returned to England. He felt a certain nostalgia as he sat alone on the upstairs cafe of the downtown hotel. The city's undulating terracotta rooftops settled over the depressing reality of a shrinking population, the wealth of the region being sucked out by foreigners not unlike himself. A slow reluctant migration was underway, like animals who had circled round the edges of a dry watering hole, many dying of hope because they refused to believe it would not fill up again. Even donations to the church had dwindled to the point where the priest stood unabashedly, open bag in hand, asking in vain, for Orlando to drop something into it rather than to buy from its contents. The Bolivian population was increasingly impatient with weak political leadership and, as usual, government infighting was a signal for violence on the horizon. Although the foreign mining companies would no doubt be spared serious losses because of their own government backing of the political change most convenient for them, Orlando decided to remove himself from the scene in search of something more tranquil.

Unfortunately he was not to find it in Chile, because, as he had predicted, socialist plans to nationalise mines were starting to take shape, and resistance to it would soon follow.

He retreated to Tocopilla, where he lay low with his mother during the drastic changes brought about by the Allende government. Brutal struggles for special interests – both national and international – obscured the original determination to move towards a more egalitarian society. The result was unwanted food shortages, constant changes of currency and power sharing that did nothing more than weaken the governing coalition.

CHAPTER 10

Orlando Ortega

Tocopilla, 1973 – 1974

The *Coup d'Etat* (some would say it was inevitable) took place on September 11, 1973. It was probably the most organised operation in post-Inca South America.

In spite of his initial shock, Orlando found himself secretly impressed with the precision and coordination on that terrible day. As the reality of it took hold, he was surprised by his own detachment, his ability to be in the midst of this massive turning point in Chilean history and remain remote from it. He realised that although he was a son of his mother, a son of this desert and this country, he felt he was nothing more than a visitor, that the wind could pick him up at any moment and whisk him elsewhere, anywhere, and his life would continue without a pause.

This sensation made him the owner of a kind of perfect power that assured command over himself (if not others) no matter what the situation. It also filled him with a great sense of isolation and loneliness. Thus, rather than sympathising with any one of the players on either side of this new game that had come raging from just beyond the horizon, he turned inwards.

He was at his mother's side around the clock during the first few weeks of the general curfew that was immediately imposed by the military. She sat shaking with fear at the sudden and overwhelming presence of military vehicles, by the seemingly random but apparently systematic shots that cracked through the air, day and night but especially during the night. Helicopter search lights routinely penetrated their windows as they hovered overhead transporting commando voyeurs. Glaring pairs of head lamps illuminated their street as one military jeep after another shifted gears, grinding past them up the hill and around corners, like high school bullies, hurling loose gravel into confused, innocent walls on sharp turns. Suddenly there would be the sound of tires screeching to a halt followed by slamming and crashing, then several sharp commands yelled into the faces of people being dragged out of houses, their high pitched screams filling the darkness. Cracks and skidding tires, engines roaring off in the distance and then silence. People sat in their houses, senses heightened, ready to run – but to where?

No one, unless they were intimate friends (and even then there was room for doubt) knew what happened to some individuals. Stories were told and retold with both subtle and gross discrepancies. It was better not to ask. The heap of stories grew very high and no one was ever able to burrow to the bottom of it and return with enough of the real truth, and nothing but the truth to tell the tale.

People peered out from behind the bars on their windows, the safety of their little homes now turned inside out. Houses that were once secure fortresses against petty thieves were now converted to individual prisons with armed guards on street corners, their neighbourhoods one large cell block after another.

The dock was overtaken by naval vessels. Military personnel poured in from land, sea and sky and the town realised that it was locked-down and helpless. Orlando sat in the patio and marvelled at it all, one arm around his trembling mother.

A heavy cloud of fear and disaster imposed itself over the town. It stole in from all directions, billowing up from the sea and rolling down the steep mountainsides. It converged on the main street and stealthily dispersed to every corner of town, as though itself under military command. It rose up along the roads and crept under doors, seeped in through windows, forced its way through cracks, filled closets, lay across beds, hid in bathrooms and lounged in back patios.

Everyone felt its eerie presence. In spite of it, or perhaps because of it, people eventually escaped from behind the bars of their insecure prison homes. They began to cautiously step out to the bakery and sit with some trepidation in the plaza, careful not to form a group of three or more people, which constituted an illegal meeting and was grounds for arrest.

They could not escape the repressive atmosphere which, they were told, was called 'order' (as opposed to happy chaos, they thought, but no one dared speak such thoughts).

Students were ordered to attend school once more, this time under the supervision of their new military head teachers, the original teachers having retreated to their back patios or disappeared altogether. To where, no one knew. Workers resumed their jobs, following orders of their new military shift bosses. Everyone was suspect. Everyone was under surveillance. Neighbours watched their own neighbours without knowing why.

Sometimes questions were yelled out from civilian queues on the street in front of the local military holding cell. Mothers demanded to know where their sons had been taken and wives begged to be informed about the whereabouts of their husbands, but they were silenced with threats or even shots. So the questions had to be whispered amongst each other. Questions that received no answers just the same. Questions about the fate of a cousin or a friend were rebuffed with unsatisfactory responses that added to the mystery.

"I last saw him only two nights ago." Said a low voice.

"Yes, but he hasn't been around since. They say he went to work in the mines." The whispered response.

"So suddenly? Without telling anyone?"

"I guess so. That's what we are told."

Eyes were lowered and heads hung down to hide the disbelief. Mass impotence raged on but had to be buried inside the bodies of the living.

Later, or perhaps not at all, bones were found in old mine shafts or bodies washed up on the beach. The invasive cloud of new order that had rolled into town demanded obedience and silent acquiescence. Memories became blurred in its fog. But loved ones were not forgotten, only missing.

Although he retired to Tocopilla before the dictatorship began, and doing business was no longer a necessity, Orlando del Transito Ortega de Riveras had, in spite of himself, become king of the local black market. The wealth he had accumulated since he ran out of the mine at the age of 15 with a golden rock in his crotch had multiplied so many times that he couldn't keep track. Not that he didn't delight in trying. He smiled to himself as he lounged in the back patio at night, arms folded behind his head as he gazed up at the stars. He could no more count the number of times he had turned a profit from one of his deals than he could count the stars in the sky.

He got involved in the black market trade because he couldn't help himself. Simply being removed from the business of buying and selling mining rights and ore, did not mean that he had kicked the habit of sizing something up, anything at all, and automatically calculating the money to be made. He was still in love with the money game. The local market was small-time but it didn't deter him because it was, nonetheless, recreational negotiation. It was impossible to see anything in life from an angle that didn't involve making money. He didn't particularly care if what he did was clever or challenging (although that provided an added buzz), as long as it jingled in his pockets at the end of the day.

A large gypsy caravan had become stranded in the municipally-allotted camp area since the *Coup*. General Pinochet had ordered all gypsies to abandon their nomadic lifestyle until further notice. They were beginning to get restless and had dispersed into the community in search of opportunities and entertainment.

Orlando had never done business with gypsies before but he understood they, like himself, considered everything negotiable. He especially admired the obvious mechanical skill and attention to detail where their

66

automobiles were concerned and he had his eye on a prize red 1957 Chevrolet Bel Air convertible that he noticed in their camp. It had white leather bench seats with what appeared to be an original polished red dashboard, and an impeccable convertible top. It was parked in the centre of the camp, always under someone's watchful eye and covered with a protective tarp except for once each day when a couple of the younger men tended to it. They would rub it down, stroking and talking to it like it was a valuable stallion. Only once had Orlando seen the head of the caravan, a large man of happy-go-lucky outward demeanour named Boldo, drive the car, and even then he just circled the edges of their camp a few times as though he was training a champion for a show.

Orlando was not the sort of man to splurge on anything other than clothing, but this car became like a magnet for him. For the first time in his life he became obsessed with something other than money. He was obsessed to the point where when he woke up each morning it was the first thing he thought of and it was the vision of this perfect red machine that he saw as he closed his eyes at night. Perhaps he had simply become bored with life. But no matter, he reasoned that such an obsession would not cause him any harm and he decided to pursue it, knowing in the back of his mind that he was helpless in the face of it in any case.

He struck up an acquaintance with Boldo. Intrigued by Orlando's reputation and enticed by rumours of his large quantities of silver ore, Boldo eventually invited Orlando to sit and drink coffee with him outside of his tent. "We can do business." He said. "What do you want? We can offer you many different things."

Orlando did not commit to anything in particular. "Well, what have you got? I, too, am a businessman so it has to have some value for me and it has to pay off – and sooner rather than later." Orlando was aware that the gypsies' prolonged stay in town had exhausted their business prospects and that time was on his side. Boldo was getting anxious to feel the weight of silver in his pockets.

CHAPTER 11

Orlando Ortega

Tocopilla, March, 1974

María Jacobé appeared in Orlando del Transito Ortega de Rivera's life one early autumn day. But she was like a spring sea breeze with the beauty and freshness of a thousand delicate flowers, as though the wind had detoured through Chile's southern valleys before deciding to swing north, out over the sea and return to grace the barren northern landscape with her mere existence. Her presence lingered momentarily like dew in cool air as she stepped slowly into view in the centre of the arid gypsy camp and caused the entire desert to shiver awake in unspoken whispers. "Enchanted..." Orlando thought he heard himself say.

The unexpectedly powerful effect of her presence threw Orlando off balance and he lost track of what he was saying to Boldo. He felt like a schoolboy and babbled a bit of idiotic nonsense about profit and loss in order to conceal his sudden disconcerted state.

For a man who was accustomed to sophisticated but transparent coquetry of married women looking for a fling, María Jacobé was a manifestation from heaven. He had never in his entire life been so captivated by even the most beautiful of women. 'Smitten' and 'bewitched' were two words that he least expected to include in his vocabulary.

María Jacobé was a typical gypsy girl with long black hair that hung down over her full skirts, her complexion somewhat more pale and her facial features somewhat sharper than Chilean women. You could perhaps even say her beauty was more refined. She was slim and slightly taller than northern Chilean girls of the same age and she carried herself with the unusual grace and confidence of a young queen. Her dark eyes shone with a love of life and her full smile expressed genuine joy rather than simple courtesy. Orlando noticed her thin tapered fingers with carefully shaped nails and imagined how sensitive they were to everything they touched. She had an overall air of elegant precision, like she was a carefully designed and crafted work of art.

Although Orlando could have had a daughter her age, youth was not the reason he was drawn to her. When Boldo barked at her to bring them coffee, two puppies and several kittens jumped playfully at her heels and she laughed (the sound of soft chimes) and waved them off. Out of nowhere, feathery images of a European children's fairy tale washed in front of his eyes. He wasn't certain which tale it would have been because one blurred into the next, but his impression was of someone's innocent, young darling skipping carefree through a meadow. He also remembered something about wolves but wasn't sure what. She lifted her eyes to boldly meet Orlando's, and quipped something in *Romané* to Boldo. He laughed. She turned to finish serving the coffee with no sign of self-consciousness and disappeared again into a tent opposite the Chevy Bel Air.

"My daughter." Boldo said as he jerked his head in her direction. "She, my friend, is the only thing that is not for sale here." When he laughed, three gold fillings glinted past his yellowed front teeth but his eyes were serious as he trained them on Orlando.

Orlando nodded and wisely chose not to answer. One does not comment to a gypsy about his daughter. But in spite of the warning, he was intrigued. He decided to delay expressing any real interest in the car for a few more days, which was longer than he had originally planned. It was an excuse to return to the camp again the next day... and the next and the next so that he could observe María Jacobé. Therefore, he suddenly excused himself to Boldo with a lie about remembering some urgent business in the centre of town, and he promised to pick up where they had left off tomorrow. Boldo's expression turned to one of undisguised disappointment.

Although he had rehearsed a few possible scenarios, it was not necessary for Orlando to invent a reason to meet María Jacobé because the next morning he encountered her away from, but still within view of the camp. She was standing alone, one hand on her hip and the other shielding her eyes as she looked out to sea, like the woman on the cover of a romance novel waiting for her lover's ship to come in. The wind played gently with her hair, and her full skirts rippled around her legs. She reminded him of the heroine in 'Gone with the Wind.' She could have also been one of the carved mermaids at the bow of a ship, still and perfect as she leaned out over the water. What had he heard someone once say? 'A monument to womankind.' Yes, that's what she was. A very young monument, but no matter.

She saw him approaching and turned around to walk back slowly towards camp. He caught up with her within a couple of strides. Two gypsy women had stopped to watch as they approached, so both María Jacobé and Orlando maintained a polite distance between each other as they strolled across the loose dirt path.

María Jacobé opened the conversation. "You have business with my father."

"Yes."

"It's a lovely morning, don't you think?" An abrupt change of subject. She smiled a generous smile but did not turn her face fully to his.

"Yes, yes it is." He was almost tongue-tied and his mouth was dry.

"Well, I will prepare some coffee then." She quickened her pace, leaving him in the dust.

It was not much of a conversation but she had given her words freely and Orlando would repeatedly replay them over the next few days, allowing the memory of her voice to titillate him.

As Orlando settled onto the wooden crate opposite Boldo, María Jacobé served coffee and smiled at each of them in turn. Boldo appeared not to mind the attention she paid Orlando. Either that, or he hadn't noticed. He was obviously about to put his cards on the table. Lately the days here were adding up to nothing, his resources had dwindled and rumours of the General announcing a lift on their travel ban made his feet very itchy.

"Mirko!" He yelled to a younger man who was pounding out a copper pot several metres away. The young man set down his tools and stood up.

Boldo barked an order in *Romané* and Mirko sauntered over to the Chevy to remove the tarp from the car.

Boldo waved his arm, a broad gesture towards the vehicle. "Look, *Chileno*, I know this car interests you. It's for sale."

Orlando was impressed with Boldo's astuteness because he had not insinuated for one second his interest in the car. He glanced sharply at Boldo wondering if he had also instinctively felt Orlando's interest in his daughter. There was no indication. Probably Boldo's choice of the car was nothing more than gypsy luck. Or perhaps desperation. He relaxed and decided there was no reason to credit the gypsy with extraordinary intuition.

"Yes, it's a very nice car."

"What do you mean, 'a very nice car'? It's the nicest one we have and the best you'll ever see in northern Chile... probably all of Chile. It's a gem, well-preserved and maintained, has a great deal of sentimental value..." His voice trailed off but there was no reason to listen to him. If Orlando was going to splurge, he definitely wouldn't pay extra for the man's sentimental attachments, neither was he going to spend the energy pretending to care.

"I don't think so. I'm not in the market for a car." As though the thought of purchasing it had never entered his mind. "As you know, I'm looking for something to generate a profit. These days no one can afford a luxury item like this."

"Don't underestimate how such a car will add value to your image, the impression others will have when they see you in it. They'll know you are a man of means and substance, not someone to trifle with. This car will bring you more money than you can earn transporting yourself around on foot." He looked down deliberately at Orlando's impeccably polished boots where fresh dust had settled. "And especially if you have any problems at all with your feet." He referred indiscreetly to Orlando's limp. "This vehicle," he indicated the car with a broad sweep through the air like a magician about to perform an incredible act of magic, "is a powerful business tool."

Yeah, thought Orlando, – he's just feeding me a load of sentimental nonsense and he steeled himself to resist and make his exit. But Boldo reached over and gripped Orlando's shoulder with his magic fingertips. "You must at least look at the interior, Chileno, check the motor. You can't say you are not interested in such a beautiful machine. She purrs like a kitten too." His voice was so sweet Orlando could almost taste the honey. But Boldo would not trap him in it today.

"No, thank you, Boldo. Not now." He almost barked the response, suddenly feeling cold towards the gypsy. It was the remark in reference to his feet. The only man who knew the truth about his two missing toes was long forgotten at the bottom of a ghost mine shaft. He hadn't thought about him for years and he didn't like to be reminded. He had made a childish mistake when he confided in the companion at the bar that night. But the dark memory had nothing to do with his companion's demise; rather it was about the death of his own innocence, or what was left of it up to that point. The memory took him down to the black pits of the mine and it made him feel ill, like someone was swinging a pick into his brain, digging for golden thoughts. He was compelled by a sudden splitting headache to immediately depart from the camp.

For three days he almost succeeded in losing interest in the car and he avoided the camp, observing it from afar while harbouring hopes of glimpsing María Jacobé. He saw her once again standing on a ledge looking towards the sea but she returned to camp before he could even plan his approach. He wondered if perhaps she really was waiting for the return of a lover. Probably not. She was not the picture of despair. And it wouldn't deter him in any case.

On the fourth morning the relentless pounding in his head had subsided and he felt more like himself. So he sauntered over to the camp and María Jacobé and two young women waved handkerchiefs as he neared the perimeter. They followed him to where Boldo had just emerged from his tent, grunting and tightening his belt like an old, starving bear.

Orlando was aware of, but wasn't sure why there was a growing audience. People continued to exit their tents, all on the same bizarre psychic signal. He and Boldo simply picked up as though a time warp had transported them back to the very same place they stood three days ago. Boldo waved Mirko over to remove the car's protective tarp as he led Orlando towards the Chevy. Orlando deliberately furrowed his brows, as though the whole exercise was a nuisance, a waste of time, and that he had returned out of nothing more than curiosity. He had to admit, however, to a twinge of guilt because of his rude flight three days ago.

The car was truly a gem. Boldo hadn't lied about that. The interior was impeccable. It was an automobile for a movie star, from its white leather upholstered bench seat with red trim, polished red dashboard, with chrome-rimmed gauges, to its spotless red floor mats. Boldo had even added a soft red leather cover on the steering wheel. The exterior had been waxed and there wasn't a scratch anywhere. White-wall tires and original hubcaps over red rims, gold Chevy logo and carved details on the hood, its characteristic wing-tipped, low back end with chrome streamlining along the entire length of the vehicle, to say nothing of the fine leather white convertible top. He could see his reflection in the side of the car. Or was it perhaps really Clark Gable? He licked the saliva that materialised in tiny bubbles at the corners of his lips.

"Come on. Get it. I'll take you for a ride." Boldo opened the passenger door and practically pushed Orlando onto the seat and then advised him against such brusque entry. "Careful! Careful, *Chileno*. You must enter with caution when you are invited into such a work of art!" He motioned to his two daughters. "Mariá Jacobé, Jackza, you two get in the back." He clicked the door shut with the grace and poise of a rotund royal footman.

The ride consisted of a short tour around the fringes of the camp because, as Boldo explained, he kept very little gas in the tank. – Just a precaution – he winked – in case anyone gets any ideas. He drove at the speed, and with the skill, of a stubborn mule, slowing to a snail's pace as he navigated the corner at the end of the dirt field. "See how the engine purrs. Just like a kitten." He made a low growl in his throat then laughed, spittle on his lips, glints of gold in his front teeth. His eyes shone with the excitement of his slow ride and the anticipation of more silver than he'd ever held in his hands at one time.

"I'll come back tomorrow." Orlando teased him. He knew there was no chance of any other buyers in Tocopilla. He could drag this out as long as he chose. And today he was in a playfully antagonistic mood. His main objective of seeing María Jacobé had been met, although he still hadn't decided on how to extract her from the clutches of her family for even a few minutes.

"Listen, Chileno," Boldo put his big hand on Orlando's shoulder and dug his fingers in hard. His expression was serious, a hint of something sour around his lips. There were small beads of sweat hanging on the ends of his hair and his forehead was so shiny that Orlando could almost see his own reflection. "I'll give you a better price than you deserve. I'll give you a gypsy-to-gypsy price. You'll still be able to make a profit on resale if that's what you want to do. Either way, you can't lose."

"I'll come back tomorrow and we'll talk about it." Orlando shrugged free of Boldo's grip and made his exit. María Jacobé and her sister both watched the exchange in silence. Orlando imagined that María Jacobé was studying his stride as he walked off, and he was very self-conscious about his limp.

The night before Orlando made the purchase, he found it impossible to sleep. For the first time in years, his two missing toes caused him a great deal of pain. It could have been the result of one of three things: the thought of finally possessing the car, or the fact that he was haunted by María Jacobé's smile and a fantasy about also possessing her, or the urgent call his mother had just received from his brother in Santiago begging for Orlando to help him escape the country.

The next day he made Boldo the happiest gypsy in the world. They were both satisfied with the deal which was why, as Orlando settled into the white leather seat of in his new Chevy Bel Air convertible and started the motor, he wondered if, after his hard bargaining, he had still paid the gypsy too much.

For no reason other than to listen to the purr of his new acquisition and perhaps because the memory of last night's pain from his missing toes played games with his head, he found himself cruising along the road leading to the Virgin shrine in the mountains east of town. Boldo was right. The car was a treasure and Orlando was now certain that no matter how much he had paid, it was a good buy. He turned off the road, the shocks performing beautifully over the rough gravel. When he reached the path leading to the shrine, he parked the car where it would still be in sight and proceeded on foot towards the makeshift grotto.

He hadn't visited the grotto for years but things never changed and the Virgin would no doubt be in the same condition as always – hands gracefully folded in prayer as she watched over Tocopilla in her role as holy chaperone. His mother used to hold her in high esteem, but since the *Coup*, she stopped visiting the grotto. The Virgin mutely observed any and all types of crimes without a single attempt to report them. Had she done so, her son or his father might have seen fit to intervene in the cause of justice. Perhaps a sudden rough sea or a maybe a harmless earth tremor here or there could have been employed to bring a temporary halt to the military atrocities and even small insults and petty sins committed against and amongst *Tocopillanos* themselves.

Orlando was not a religious man, and did not even consider himself a spiritual one, yet here he was padding his way along the path towards the Virgin. It was just a whim, he told himself. Or then again maybe he was driven by a sudden intuition that told him about María Jacobé's occasional visits to this place.

Whatever the reason, that's when he encountered Mariá Jacobé alone for the first time, away from the camp. She was leisurely choosing her steps up the sloped path and she allowed him to fall in step beside her as though expecting him. They exchanged polite greetings and strolled along without conversation, aware of some kind of magic and mutual satisfaction that came from simply sharing the same close air space, like two dizzy birds. Orlando felt the distant, piercing gaze of a condor, unusual at this low altitude. He shivered and carried on. The condor's huge wings cast a shadow over the rocks until it found them. The shadow was like a missile honing in on its target. It locked in place, hovering over the two of them as they walked the distance up to the Virgin. They ignored the omen.

Even though he was well aware that she was much younger, he felt he had known her all his life. He wondered what it meant to fall in love at first sight and realised the question didn't scare him. He looked down at her sandalled feet stepping carefully over the rocky surface and was aware that nothing about her made him uneasy, surprised him or caused him any doubts. This was something novel because if he wasn't born with a suspicious nature, he had definitely developed one, to the point where outside of his own mother – who even occasionally instigated twinges of anxiety – he was on guard with absolutely every living creature. He felt an immense warmth and compassion towards María Jaobé and he was certain, against all of his customary logic, that he would protect her with his own life. It struck him that she was the first and only person in his life with whom he felt true affinity.

Without analysing his feelings, he could distinguish between the simple lust for a woman (of which he was more than familiar) and the deep physical attraction he felt towards María Jacobé. This attraction was different. It was rooted in his soul. He could feel it germinate. It sprouted uninhibited, tantalising his senses, taking over his flesh. The desire to hold her was, he rationalised, a manifestation of the only earthly means bestowed upon less-than godly creatures with which to unite two distinct beings.

Orlando did not possess a natural instinct towards sharing anything at all – his money, secrets, ambitions, or ideas – and he didn't immediately recognise the desire to do so. At first he felt a fleeting stab of sorrow, akin to nostalgia for something he didn't even know he missed, followed by the sensation of relief that a gaping hole was about to be filled. He wanted to share something with María Jacobé. The first and most practical thing that came to mind, in hindsight, appeared somewhat juvenile. But his decision to chauffeur her in his new car would not only take them away together, it would provide an unprecedented opportunity to share his joy in something with another living soul, in this case, the pleasure and luxury of the vehicle. So he invited her to ride with him past María Elena, towards the salt flats, just, he said, to feel the desert wind on their faces and allow themselves to be overtaken by the wide open spaces and eternal blue sky. It would be, he said, an attempt to catch up with their wandering spirits.

A young gypsy girl who roams away alone, out of sight of the camp is at risk of being punished for a grave lack of prudence. Orlando guessed as much and knew there was a good chance she would be obliged to say no, but he let his invitation stand.

María Jacobé told him that her mother allowed her, without her father's knowledge of course, to visit the Virgin grotto alone. She had convinced her mother to grant her these solitary pilgrimages because her sister was nothing more than a nuisance and distraction and she prevented María Jacobé from having a serious conversation with the Virgin. At least her mother was wise enough to understand that.

Orlando was delighted (a word to describe a feeling he previously attributed only to gay men, not for someone as worldly and manly as himself) that María Jacobé agreed so readily to do something that they both knew was prohibited. The strict cultural rules as well as (he imagined) Boldo's stringent enforcement of them, didn't allow much space for her to make her own decisions. He was, therefore, extremely impressed by her wilfulness, and charmed by her somewhat rebellious spirit, which thankfully lacked the tendency towards belligerence that less mature individuals might display. Perhaps that's why, in his estimation, she was much older than her years. He would, he told himself, proceed with some caution to see where it led, although the truth was that caution had already been thrown to the wind and the wind had carried it across the eastern horizon, letting it slip through its lanky fingers, sprinkling it liberally over the salt flats and flavouring them with a sweet vulnerability.

María Jacobé agreed to meet him three days later on this same path. From here they would drive together up to the desert *altiplano*.

Everything Orlando did between the moment of his invitation and the planned trip was coloured with the anticipation of her company. While he was not a man to spend a great deal of time asking why, he was aware that he spent a lot of time suspended in an ethereal reality in which she seemed to accompany him.

An as yet unidentified but profound feeling associated with María Jacobé had travelled a long distance from somewhere in his soul to awaken a spongy forgotten sector of his consciousness. He was himself, he mused, a character in a European fairy tale. Was it the prince who had slept for a hundred years or the princess? He couldn't remember. After contemplating it as coolly as possible, he allowed himself to admit without fear, that he was in love. The feeling left him no choice and he was wise enough to understand that denial would end only in misery. Besides, he had no reason to negate such a feeling and suddenly at his 37 years he felt he had come of age.

Words are trite in the face of emotions that defy mere verbal communication. In any case, obvious mutual sentiments eliminate such a need. Orlando and María Jacobé travelled together under the broad desert sky in the comfort of the lush white leather bench seat, attentive to one another and to the sound of tango as the wind swallowed it from the dashboard speakers. María Jacobé let her head fall back and she sang, wrapping her own voice around the melancholy music, her notes mingling with it into the air and beyond.

They were a single red and white arrow shooting across a sandy golden landscape towards a blue heaven. Orlando and María Jacobé inched closer to one another until their shoulders touched and he could feel the tension in her thigh. Every now and then he looked down at her and she met his eyes with an undisguised expression of devotion.

So it was that on their return trip when they pulled off the road to avoid a military patrol before the initial descent through the mountains that would lead them back to Tocopilla, they held each other in silent confidence on the white leather seat of the car that used to belong to María Jacobé's father.

Orlando pulled a blanket out of the trunk and laid it over a sandy shelf not far from the car and they made love. He was conscious of María Jacobé's light perfume, one he didn't recognise, and he wasn't sure if it was the mystery of it or the scent itself that added to his excitement.

Although she was trembling she didn't pretend to be coy and she helped him undress her, all the while looking squarely into his eyes, perhaps daring him, perhaps afraid to look elsewhere, before he slipped out of his own clothes. Her eyes were moist and wide as they sought his out, trusting that he would bring her no harm. She was small and he was conscious of his weight on her. He moved gently and she gave herself to him without hesitation. He felt his heart beating against hers and his spirit soured. The sensation that she was absolutely joined with him was a new experience. It was the first time he ever felt an absolute and complete union with another human being.

CHAPTER 12

Clorinda

Tocopilla, 2001

Clorinda was encumbered with the dead weight of Señor Ortega, heavy and static in the absolute obscurity of his niche. It struck her that he should be driving his Bel Air convertible across the vast *altiplano*, wind blowing through his hair, music blaring from the radio, laughing at her for gripping the dashboard with one hand and her hair with the other. She had no idea it was possible for anything to move that fast. And now she didn't know anything could remain so still.

Perhaps she could weave the bright red Egyptian cotton threads that she had painstakingly released from their past life as a woman's vest. She could begin at the far left of her loom and send them shooting across the variegated warp like a bullet over the desert. And no one would be able to catch them. They would disappear just as Señor Ortega had dropped off the planet, as an early explorer sailing past the edges of the earth or like the wind running away with his life beyond the horizon.

Clorinda nearly fainted with the dizziness as she recalled how she and Señor Ortega ascended together through the mountain pass in his 1957 red Bel Air convertible. It was the magic realisation of the recurring dream in which she flew across the sky with Clark Gable. She merged her memory of their ride in the car with her fantasy flight through the sky. Señor Ortega's leather bench seat became exotic fabric, rippling around their legs as they leaned back into the soft cotton cloud seat and the wind roared past them, like translucent chiffon angel wings in open heavens. Nothing could stop them.

But now, here she sat across from his niche, looking up at the concrete slab situated in the third row of the wall, asking if he would be comfortable like that for the rest of eternity. It was Sunday and she wanted to feel special in her Sunday wardrobe selection. She had chosen a soft pink taffeta dress with a slightly lower hemline than normal so that she could enjoy the swish of the extra fabric around her calves. In an effort to lift her spirits and to emphasise what she hoped was a happy face looking up at Señor Ortega, she tied a floppy bow in the long purple crocheted sash that she wrapped around her neck, and she slipped on a pair of oversized hoop earrings. She probably looked stunning/ But she was worried. She still hadn't touched the warp of her tapestry, having done nothing more than consider it all these weeks since Señor Ortega died. She came to him now, asking for advice.

"Señor Ortega, I'm still waiting for the bright ray of inspiration to carry me forward." She was aware that she mumbled in a monotone voice. "But I can't get used to you being here, I mean, in one spot like this. I wait every night for you to come out and sit on the chair at the front door of your house. But you don't come out to sit there anymore."

He was nodding, understanding.

She continued, "Have you seen me looking for you at your house? I don't mean at the front door. I mean inside?"

No, he wasn't aware of that.

"Well, I've often gone over very early in the morning, at the hour that the bakers remove the first batch of bread from their ovens. Most people are asleep and no one notices me. I still go to spy on you, you know – just as I did before you became resident in this new neighbour-hood." She swiped her hand through the air in front of herself, indicating the cemetery in general.

She heard him twitch uncomfortably in his coffin. He didn't know that she used to spy on him, both before and after they were friends, did he? Would he not have been pleasantly surprised by her interest?

"Yes, Señor Ortega, I was very attentive, from day one. Of course, I have spied on other neighbours over the years, but no one has meant as much to me as you do. When you moved to Tocopilla, it was easy to forget about everyone else because you were obviously so much more exciting. And of course, as it happens, you are the only one of my subjects I have ever become friends with. All the more reason to watch and ensure you were safe and well."

She could feel Señor Ortega's face flush in the dark. He must understand how she cherished him. She bowed slightly and rubbed her sweaty palms on her lap. She had never admitted this to any of her subjects before, but because he was the only one that she ever loved, she dared to confess. That he was dead also made it easier.

"I must admit Señor Ortega, that I almost fell in love once, but it was well before we met. I doubt if you remember him. It was Jimmy Zurieta, the once beautiful young man who still lives at the end of the block with his mother and two sisters. It's amazing how quickly someone can change. He wanted to borrow your phone once or twice, remember? No? Well, anyway, now he's older and toothless and not at all attractive. But one morning several years ago he caught my eye when I was creeping across the roofs like a cat. Did I tell you I used to do that, Señor Ortega? But only before you moved to town. After you arrived, I only spied on you, I promise." She winked up at him and felt him blush.

She leaned back to settle onto the wooden bench in front of the wall and recounted the day that she decided she wasn't in love with Jimmy Zurieta. But first it was necessary to explain that he came to her attention early one morning, within the first week of her discovering 'the route of the cats' over her neighbours' roofs. Following the route of the cats began quite innocently one morning when her own cat (a grey tabby kitten that she had never bothered to name) made a playful getaway with one of her new balls of yarn. The night before, because it was a chilly night, she had tucked herself into her bed to unravel a purple 50/50 polyester-wool sweater. She had harvested six medium sized balls of yarn from it and feeling satisfied, leaned back into her pillow as she rolled the last ball. She fell asleep like that, purple balls scattered on her bed, the small one having rolled away just out of reach.

At sunrise, she felt the kitten jumping and jabbing into her legs, a small ball of purple yarn bouncing and unravelling, sharp claws flying through the air in playful pursuit. The cat batted the little ball onto the floor and out the door. Clorinda quickly slipped into her sandals and chased after it out into the back patio. When the cat jumped up from the pile of empty crates to the roof, Clorinda followed it, scratching her way over the wooden boxes with surprising ease. She found herself standing on the roof at sunrise in her nightgown, surrounded by no less than eight roof cats, all of whom had a sudden interest in her purple ball of wool. One of the big cats grabbed it with his teeth and ran off, followed by Clorinda and the other felines. She trod carefully, always only along the walled edges, never in the centre of the metal panels, which gave the cats the advantage. Finally, out of breath and tired from the energy required to maintain her balance and concentration, not to mention sprinting like a fairy in a flannel nightgown down and around the corner, she admitted defeat and decided to turn back. She would have to make up for the lost purple yarn somehow.

On her return she took her time, peering down one by one, into neighbours' patios and on occasion, through gaps in the metal-panelled roofs into sitting rooms, kitchens and bedrooms. Most of the households were still asleep. It was at one corner when she skidded, and was forced to lean down, hands on dirty metal to maintain her balance and save herself from falling down into his house, that she spied Jimmy Zurieta. Her weight on her fingertips, toes curled with tension around the ends of her slippers, she froze, her eyes round, her mouth forming a big 'O' above Jimmy's bedroom. He was pulling on his trousers, probably preparing to go to the bakery. His mother must have been adamant about getting the pick of the fresh bread for breakfast. Clorinda had heard about such families, fighting over buns at six in the morning. Sometimes bakeries had had to call the police. It probably didn't help that many people simply were not morning people and couldn't hold their tongues while others refused to say a word.

Holding her breath, she snuck around the edge of Jimmy Zurieta's roof, watching him as he entered the bathroom through the patio and stood over the toilet, where he lingered for several seconds. Then, still half asleep, he bent over the sink to splash water on his face and run it through his hair with his fingers. None of this was earth shattering. She'd seen her father go through the exact motions since she was a little girl. But Jimmy Zurieta, well... he added something sexy to his morning performance.

The cold water zapped extra life into him. He closed the toilet lid and jumped up on top of it so that his torso was directly across from the mirror above the sink. He was so close to her that she could smell his morning breath. And he started to gyrate, converting to a sultry singer, tossing the comb from one hand to the other. One second it was a microphone and the next it was a slick tool to flick wet hair back from his forehead. His smooth motions made her swoon.

After a few minutes the music in his head stopped, he jumped onto the floor, gave the mirror one long, seductive look and sauntered out the door and onto the street, with an occasional rock star swing of the hips. Clorinda's eyes followed him from her crouched position on the roof. A female gargoyle in nightie and sandals, suddenly smitten with an Elvis Presley not-so-look-alike.

Her one-sided love affair with Jimmy was relatively short-lived. She watched him perform his routine each morning. Sometimes during the day she caught a glimpse of him when he passed by her sitting room window, sauntering along with a group of friends who kicked a ball back and forth between each other. The infatuation came to an abrupt end when Jimmy's father gave him a haircut. Not just any haircut – it was a buzz cut that made him look like an army recruit. Clorinda yelped the morning she saw the new Jimmy. Not only could he no longer flick his hair back off his forehead, which made it an even bigger stretch for his Elvis look-alike routine, but without his long hair, the odd, block shape of his head was obvious. It was like a cardboard box that had been partially flattened by someone's boot. Her sexy Elvis had been converted to a monster with a three-dimensional trapezoid on his shoulders. Clorinda felt she had drowned in ice-cold water. What had she been thinking?

That was the beginning of her career as a roof spy and the end of her infatuation with Jimmy Zurieta. Just as well because in addition to his trapezoid head, he grew up to be a bald, toothless man with an un-attractive paunch. Anyway, after that, she rose early to walk around the neighbourhood from one roof to the next, stopping whenever something interesting caught her eye. She became familiar with the layout of every house in her block and she knew who slept in which bed and with whom. Admittedly, much of her voyeurism was boring because it was too early for activity and after awhile she lost interest in watching people sleep but she never lost the skill of a rooftop spy.

The first few times she spied on Señor Ortega, it was late at night rather than early in the morning. She waited until the activity in the street died down and she sidled across the road, up the rough exterior wall of his neighbour's house, and over the roofs towards the room at the back where he always sat at his desk.

She watched the top of his head and wondered how it would feel to run her fingers through his thick hair. He sipped from a glass of whiskey, thought for a few seconds, sipped again and picked up his pen, writing at a leisurely pace. He filled one line after another, page after page between sips and thoughts, before he finally closed the notebook, set the pen at a 90 degree angle, turned off the light, and went to bed.

She trod softly along the walls, following him, trying to see through the cracks in the roof. Every night she willed herself into his dreams as he turned off the light. She remained crouched on the metal roof above him for up to an hour, imagining his face in the dark. When she was sure he was sound asleep, she ventured along the roof again, scaled down the neighbour's wall, walked, as if on air to her house, opened the door and re-entered her own silent, fabric-filled life.

CHAPTER 13

María Jacobé

Tocopilla, May, 1974

María Jacobé watched her own fingers reaching up into the night sky, nearly touching the stars that hung so low she imagined everyone on the beach could snatch one from its orbit and take it home to wish upon. The gypsies clapped and swayed to their complicated staccato rhythm and María Jacobé and her sister Jackza danced as the bonfires crackled, sparks like miniature golden fireworks shooting into the dark.

If one of the stars would make her wish come true, she could allow herself to become lost in the dance, she could be exhilarated once more by the lament and joy of the transient strings. She would fling her skirts round into the air and fly free as the bird she was born to be. She would allow herself to become entranced and she would laugh and cry with the violins. Her life would be her own again. She would perform in the circle of bonfires for the people who clapped in and out of the shadows, her toes sinking into the black sand, light flickering off the faces of dazzled onlookers.

Tonight though, it was with great effort that she feigned this spirit, and she had to call on memories from years past to perform. She was in a pit of profound loneliness. Her voice rained over the black sand, merging with its dark crystals as they were dragged out to the melancholy sea and washed up again in its unrelenting surf.

At last the dancing ended. It was time for the climax of Santa Sara's annual pilgrimage. Santa Sara, the black Virgin icon of the gypsies was solemnly placed onto her makeshift wooden raft and gently sent out from the shore. The crowd watched her bobbing lightly over the rippling surface. This ritual was symbolic of her arrival after a long journey across the sea. Everyone watched in anxious anticipation until the salty water licked up to the hem of her holy skirts, the signal for them to follow the Virgin into the cold water and guide her back to dry land. The crowd lunged into the sea towards the raft, laughing and screeching as the dark waters reached their chests. Finally a few of them were able to lay their hands on the raft and pull Santa Sara to safety.

She was welcomed back to dry land, dozens of trembling hands excitedly reaching out to touch her robes with the tips of their fingers in gestures of love and respect.

The gypsy couple who had been selected this year to carry the icon back to the chapel, cradled her carefully between them, faces beaming with the pride and responsibility that comes with leading the procession. The colourful crowd wound its way up from the beach to the camp, a serpent with multiple yellow candle eyes in gypsy camouflage floating and murmuring its way along the streets. Local residents stood smiling from their doorways, moved to tears by the spectacle.

"Please Santa Sara..." María Jacobé begged the little statue from where she had dropped back to the end of the procession. She fixed her eyes on the tip of the Virgin's golden crown as it jogged up and down between the shoulders of the special couple and pleaded silently for the saint to save her from this most sinful and shameful predicament "If you can't help me, I have no escape other than death itself."

Only hours earlier, before the commencement of the trek to the sea, María Jacobé had lit a dozen candles and placed them in front of the Virgin. She stood to one side of the altar at the small chapel near camp, praying for guidance, pleading for intercession, begging for something, anything but to live this new reality, which she could no longer deny.

At the beach, she danced and sang for the Virgin as she had each year since she was 10 years old but tonight Santa Sara showed no sign of compassion. Mariá Jacobé stopped and allowed the procession to continue without her. Careful not to be noticed, she turned and drifted back towards the beach, where the fires had burned down, now nothing more than smouldering signs of their earlier life. Like herself, she thought.

She wandered along to where the sand was black as coal. The tide was rising, the waves tumbling over the rocks at the north end of the beach. She continued until she reached a shallow sand-filled gorge just before the mound of rocks that blocked the view of the beach from the road above. This spot had always been a sort of refuge even though she knew it was not a secret place. She found comfort in its seclusion, and ignoring her sister who always accompanied her, often sat for ages in a semi-trance induced by the steady rhythm of the waves and intermittent 'caw' of the seagulls.

Tonight she would lie down on the black sand in this tide pool and let the waves wash over her. The moon would pull the watery blanket over her feet, up her legs then across her belly and beyond her chest, and she would lie still, eyes closed, tasting the salt on her tongue, feeling her ears and nose fill with water.

It would be a peaceful communion of her own spirit with the earth and the sea. She would rather deliver herself to the universe than to the wrath of her father and the disdain of the rest of the gypsies.

She lay on her back, arranged her skirts around her thighs and she combed two long strands of hair straight down over her chest, a final preparation for when they would find her. She rested her hands on her belly and tried to feel the baby inside, this baby that was to be the reason for her own death. She imagined it curled up inside of her, smaller than her fist, a tiny body of flesh and soft bone, inside of which was a heart of its own.

She opened her hands and spread her fingers around to measure the size of her slightly bloated belly. No one had noticed it yet. The moon had just completed its second cycle and still there had been no bleeding. The nausea in the morning, extreme fatigue in the late afternoons and the tender, enlarged breasts were symptoms she remembered from when her aunt was pregnant with her youngest cousin. She had heard similar complaints from other women, shortly before their bellies gradually protruded to the point where they finally waddled around camp supporting it under their hands.

There was no doubt that she would bring shame on all of them because of her one and only secret rendezvous with the Chileno. It would have been serious enough if she had become pregnant by another gypsy, but for the father to be *Chileno* was an even worse curse upon her and her family. Better she sacrifice herself than risk this malediction on the entire caravan.

As María Jacobé lay waiting for the water to cover her, she thought about Señor Orlando del Transito Ortega de Riveras. She pictured his deep dark eyes and chiselled, masculine features, and remembered how a dimple appeared on his right cheek when his face broke into a smile, how straight and white his teeth were, not missing a single one. His thick hair, curled slightly over his ears and she pictured the small patch of grey on either temple. He had beautiful hands, like he had never worked a day in his life, long fingers with immaculately manicured nails. He smelled clean with a touch of musk and his breath carried a minty scent over a hint of something like whisky. He was tall and walked with broad strides and a very slight limp, which added a mystery to his character.

Señor Orlando del Transito Ortega de Riveras had chosen to cast his magic spell on her, María Jacobé Jankolevich, the 17-year-old daughter of a gypsy who was already promised in marriage to a gypsy youth in the same caravan. She was helplessly attracted to Señor Ortega, largely by the certainty that she had known him since before she was born. Whenever her father invited Señor Ortega to sit down outside their tent to discuss business, his presence overwhelmed her.

He had not exactly invited her the day they met along the path leading to the Virgin shrine but she sensed he would not object to her falling back in step with him. Since everyone she knew made frequent trips to the Virgin, it didn't occur to her that he had no plans himself to pray to the icon. She had stepped aside, making room for him to walk next to her, conscious of maintaining a polite distance as she glanced up every now and then at his face.

They walked much of the way in silence but she offered, "I come here every month to light a candle. I prefer our Santa Sara, but when we are here, it's a good idea to pray to the Virgin María too." She was confident in her knowledge of Virgins.

Señor Ortega was smiling when he looked down at her. He said nothing. They continued along the dirt road, keeping the same safe distance but she felt attached to him with an invisible thread. The road wound round to the back of the hill and the path narrowed and continued up along the side in between huge boulders that had settled there after tumbling down during an earth tremor perhaps centuries ago, perhaps only last year.

"Sit here." Señor Ortega motioned to a wide slab of rock, from which they could see the Bel Air he had just purchased from her father. "I have to keep an eye on my car."

They sat in silence, both looking straight ahead. He inched his fingers along the rock surface until he touched her hand and gently covered her fingers with his own. He smiled down at her, a warmth in his eyes. His expression lit a fire and she had to look away. Either that or burn up. She quickly turned her face, focusing on a small lizard that clung just outside a narrow crevice on the rock opposite them. His simple touch, quiet fingers lightly over hers, was so intimate that she shivered and felt blood rush to her face. She didn't remove her hand. She was aware of his musky smell, of his slow, even breathing, of his eyes scanning her face, then her shoulders and her chest, then back up to her face again.

"I like you." He said so softly that she thought maybe she had imagined it.

She turned her face up to look at him, her eyebrows furrowed slightly as she mused over such a simple statement. No poetic phrases, no obvious attempt to seduce her with clichés, just an unusual candour. She smiled, aware that a response was not necessary.

They both sat looking silently at the lizard until it disappeared into the rocky shadows. The sun began its descent towards the sea.

"Meet me here again and we'll ride up to the *altiplano*." It was not an invitation as much as a plan for which he seemed to take her assent for granted. She knew she should have rejected the idea but instead had agreed in an instant. That was her mistake.

Now María Jacobé lay on the black sand staring up at the stars. The water was lapping in around her. She recognised *Las Tres Marías* constellation twinkling amongst the other celestial fires and asked them to deliver her safely into the arms of the Virgin, and prayed that her baby would become a star itself, hanging in the sky, interceding on its mother's behalf, praying for forgiveness for her terrible sin against God and her family.

She could still feel Señor Ortega's arms wind around her waist when they laid on the rock ledge the day they returned from the *altiplano*. He pulled her to him and she felt his muscles down the length of his body. The excitement of being so close to him was mixed with the odd sensation that making love to him was familiar, that although she had never touched him before, she already knew the curve of his back and the pressure of his thighs. She simply allowed herself to give into this feeling of ecstasy, which she could describe only as a union of spirits manifested in flesh. They moved slowly into one another without urgency. They were fluid, like the water that washed over her now. They were rhythmic, like the waves that came in and retreated. Their lovemaking was new, but it felt mature and wise and as natural as the earth upon which they lay.

María Jacobé opened her arms straight out from her body, dragging them up and down over the wet sand, creating black angel wings that grew out from her shoulders. With each swipe of her arms the waves washed the wings away and she remained mortal, succumbing to the waters of the incoming tide.

CHAPTER 14

Orlando Ortega

Tocopilla, May, 1974

For more than six weeks after their unforgettable desert journey Orlando tried in vain to find an excuse to visit the gypsy camp, but since the day he bought the car he had been unable to make contact with Boldo. By now Boldo would be doing discreet deals with the silver. He assumed that María Jacobé had been equally unable to arrange more visits to the Virgin without arousing her mother's suspicion. Each day he wandered nonchalantly past the camp and drove along the road to the Virgin grotto but there was no sign of her. He wondered if her mother had somehow discovered their indiscretion. There was no way of knowing.

Lately the nights were filled with music and there was dancing in the camp. He was told the gypsies were rehearsing for a celebration. Finally, and with a mixture of relief and jealousy, he heard talk about how Boldo's daughter, María Jacobé was their most accomplished dancer and singer and that if you stood on the high ground at the edge of the camp, you could see her practising every night. This meant life for her at camp continued as normal, but he was bitter because of his exclusion and he stubbornly refused to watch rehearsals from the fringes along with other curious onlookers.

For the time being, the two of them were forced to remain on either side of the invisible social barrier. Orlando was frustrated at each unsuccessful attempt to encounter María Jacobé but was determined to be patient.

His hopes for an excuse to visit the camp were raised when he successfully opened negotiations with a scrawny middle-aged gypsy named
Jerko who said he could arrange to provide Orlando with pure, refined
copper at a substantially lower-than market-price. But Orlando was disappointed when Jerko insisted that their deal had to be done in private,
away from the camp. For the time being he could only go along with him,
and trust it would soon lead to a path inside.

Jerko was to deliver the copper a week after they agreed on the terms
at a prearranged location at a side road off the northern coastal highway.

Jerko skidded to a halt in an old Ford truck that was laden with several industrial bags cinched tightly with wire. He hauled the smallest bag
out of the back and opened it. It was full of miniature corrugated sheets of
refined copper, a form with which Orlando was not familiar.

"What is this?"

"It's pure. I told you. I melted it down myself. I set up a small plant
that no one knows about, which by the way, I would appreciate you never
mentioning to Boldo. We've been stranded here for so long I decided to
set up shop. I work it myself." Jerko pushed his prickly chin forward, in-
flating his chest like a preening pigeon with too many gold chains. Jerko
was a slimy creature whose individual ambitions were far too strong for
the gypsy community lifestyle. Orlando knew that such a man was not to
be trusted.

He hesitated. They were standing alone on a deserted road, surrounded by nothing but rocks, under the fixed gaze of two vultures that
were perched at a distance, feathers slightly ruffled, reflecting the tension. He should have invited his *secretarios*. He felt uneasy but could see
no logical reason for such disconcertedness since, although Jerko was a
distasteful character, he was probably weak and harmless. So Orlando
yanked each bag off the truck to feel its weight. Satisfied, he piled them
into the trunk of his car and observed the springs adjust to the load. Jerko
beamed a dirty-toothed smile as Orlando counted the cash into his grubby, quivering, ring-adorned fingers. He indicated his appreciation with a

nod of his head and a limp-wristed half-salute, jumped into his truck and sped off, leaving Orlando standing in the dust.

It wasn't until the next day, when he went to unload his copper at the local ore trading office that Orlando discovered all but the one small bag Jerko had opened for display, contained stolen copper cable, some still inside its rubber casing. That would explain the power outage in the southern sector of town that had been mentioned on the radio the other night. The next day, still without lights, hundreds of local housewives had marched on the central military commission to demand their service be restored. Repression was one thing, basic services another. Orlando had had to do some fast-talking and pay off the clerk in order to avoid being fingered for questioning by the authorities. He was fuming for having fallen for such a scam and enraged at Jerko for assuming he could get away with it.

It had been several months since he had had to call his *secretarios* into action. Orlando found them at a cafe-bar on main street, faces swimming above bowls of beef and corn soup. They smiled up at him, broth dripping from the ends of their moustaches, grease glistening on their clean-shaven chins. Orlando gestured for them to wipe their faces. It was distracting to talk to someone like that. They looked around and grabbed the waitress' damp rag that she used for cleaning the table tops, took turns swiping it across their chins and threw it back. She picked it up and proceeded to clean the tables. Orlando made a mental note not to eat here.

The *secretarios* assured him that they were more than pleased to be of service and would not let him down. In fact, they had their own score to settle with that weasel of a gypsy. So that night, careful to avoid the military patrol, the pair of them interrupted Jerko's clandestine poker soirée that he had arranged under the light of a kerosene lamp in a deserted rail car at the edge of town. They could see him through the dirt-streaked window, very animated, waving his arms, throwing back his head and laughing, brazenly puffing on a Cuban cigar. He was focused, confident and fully enjoying his role as illustrious rail car host. The *secretarios* looked at each other and grinned. They had, themselves, sat in on a few of Jerko's poker games in this very car. Jerko always won and they suspected him of cheating but couldn't prove how. To say this would be satisfying was an understatement.

Jerko stopped being the life of the party when the *secretarios* burst in, each with a gun that they nudged against Jerko's temples. Jerko's stale, smoke-filled poker heaven was converted into the siege from hell and he knew his lucky streak had dried up forever. No one would ever agree to sit at his table again after an incident such as what he predicted was about to occur. The other players, two of whom wet themselves, yellow poker puddles on the kerosene soaked floor, were easily convinced to empty their pockets, leave all their money on the table and abandon the rail car. "Let's just call it your unlucky night, girls." The *secretarios* grabbed the bills, pistols still touching Jerko's head and slid the money into their pockets before getting down to business. Jerko panicked when he noticed what could only be blood and guts stains on the lapels of both *secretarios* and he cowered onto the floor, his skinny, ring-adorned fingers covering his face. He had no way of knowing that the *secretarios* never soiled themselves with other men's body fluids. They had simply been sloppy when they wolfed down a mayonnaise and salsa-laden hot dog, an evening power snack before the job at hand.

The next day Jerko's Ford pickup truck, driven by one of the *secretarios*, pulled up behind the rocks on the familiar deserted side road off the coastal highway where Orlando stood waiting. The other *secretario* sat on the passenger side and Jerko was wedged painfully between the two. They opened the doors and Jerko, flanked by the pair of black suits and dark glasses, limped pathetically towards Orlando. As if on signal, they all stopped a few metres from him and waited. Jerko was cradling his broken right hand with his left one, pain cracking across his forehead. The two *secretarios* compulsively, and each in turn, bent down to dust their shoes with a few dainty swipes of their handkerchiefs, one eye trained on Jerko at all times.

"What have you got for me?" Orlando asked calmly.

Jerko kept his head down and muttered something unintelligible. The two secretarios nudged closer, sandwiching him brutally between their black shoulders. If he had been pounded like a slab of cheap meat last night, he would be paté before much longer.

Orlando ignored his condition. "You will pay dearly for this. Do you take me for a fool, or dare to put me in the same class as one of your small-time crooks?" Orlando knew Jerko had already spent or gambled the money from their deal. If there was anything to spare, by now it was rightfully in the pockets of the black suits on either side of him. "What have you got for me?" His voice was calm and even. The Jerko problem would be easily overcome.

"Look, Señor," he screwed up his face in an attempt to muster pity, "I have my truck, but it's all I have. Please, anything but my truck. I need my truck."

"I want something of value. I don't want that piece of junk. Keep your truck but tell me what else you have, and if you have nothing else, then if you value your life, you'll find something for me."

The two *secretarios* had Jerko compressed so tightly that his shoulders were crushing his own chin and he struggled to open his mouth. He choked and tobacco-stained saliva drooled onto his chest.

"Be creative. Get something of value. I don't care how. I don't care what, as long as it is the most valuable thing in your camp."

"You're asking me to steal from my own people?" He croaked. Incredulous, he stared at Orlando through his bloodshot eyes.

"Do what you have to do if you value your life. My *secretarios* will be at your disposal from now until tomorrow at this same time. They'll bring you and your treasure to me and I'll decide your fate then. I'm warning you, don't test me again."

Unaware that the Santa Sara pilgrimage was to be that same evening, Orlando retreated to his patio, doing his utmost to avoid his mother's continuous diatribe about Jorge's dangerous situation in Santiago. He sat back to count the stars and his money and to pine about María Jacobé.

Meanwhile, the *secretarios*, under instructions to keep Jerko in sight at all times, witnessed the spectacular Santa Sara procession. It began with a flurry of last minute adjustments as Boldo barked commands at young men. His wife contradicted him, converting his order into chaos, which reigned as they waved their hands and snapped at one another until one of them gave up. Eventually the mayhem miraculously turned into an orderly procession and the crowd of gypsies set out from within their sheltered fold at the foot of the mountains.

The entire population of the caravan fell in behind a young couple who had been chosen to carry the black Virgin of the gypsies as they wound through the streets towards the sea, hundreds of candle eyes blinking into the dark. A handsome young woman who followed directly behind the icon-bearing couple sang a pure, lamenting song the likes of which the *secretarios* had never heard. After some lengthy discussion, the argumentative tone of which drew frowns from passers-by, they agreed it had to be a form of *flamenco*. "So pure." Commented one to the other, who nodded in agreement, too moved to speak. It brought tears to their eyes and there was more than one instance when they lifted a corner of their dark glasses to dab their eyes with the same handkerchiefs they used to dust their shoes.

After the traditional Santa Sara rituals and celebrations at the shore where families danced and socialised around bonfires, they fell into the procession to follow the Virgin as she was returned to camp.

The secretarios watched with intense interest as Jerko, custodian of the valued icon, wrapped a generous length of cotton fabric around her and then locked her safely into a heavy wooden crate rather than placing her back inside the chapel. Rumours that the travel ban would be lifted any day had grown very strong lately, and Boldo wanted to be ready to abandon camp at a moment's notice (before the General changed his mind, he said). Boldo had instructed Jerko to prepare Santa Sara for travel. God bless the General.

CHAPTER 15

Manuel Luis Gonzalez

Tocopilla, May, 1974

Manuel Luis Gonzalez-Ruiz relished his habitual solitary walks along the beach. As soon as he jumped off the train at the end of a ten-day shift at the mine in the desert *altiplano*, he headed straight for the north shore.

As he inhaled each breath of salty night air, he thanked Mother Earth for her goodness. He felt sure that the desert heat alone was going to kill him if the mine gases didn't get him first. Although he romanticised about working out at sea, perhaps as a member of a small crew on a fishing boat, his sensitive stomach could not tolerate the constant motion, even on the most calm of days, and he would hang over the side of the boat and vomit until his feet were planted on solid ground once again. As he saw it, in order to one day earn enough money to escape Tocopilla and to live out his dream on Easter Island, his only real choice was to work in the mines. Since the day he was lucky enough to be arbitrarily waved into the underground darkness by a shift boss, he worked diligently and quietly, never giving anyone reason to dislike him or call him lazy. He was not the same as the other men, never feeling the need to participate in their good-natured bravado. Rather he tolerated their witty jibes about his slight frame by simply grinning in response or ignoring them altogether. Truth be told, he rather enjoyed his reputation as 'the walking x-ray' and 'the short garden hose' because it gave him a distinct identity based on truth. He persevered in the mine pits in spite of his slight build and sensitive lungs because he could see an end to it. He wouldn't die young working there. He would be gone long before.

He imagined walking out of the pit on his last day on the job. He would walk straight to the pay office to pick up his final envelope. He wouldn't tell anyone he was leaving. Once he reached the outside of the gates, he would strip out of his coveralls, shedding them like green gabardine snake skin and abandon them to the desert floor along with all the bad memories, dust and gases. And he wouldn't look back. He would run, he would fly, feet barely touching the ground, all the way across the arid flats and down the mountains to the sea. Free as a bird.

Once on Easter Island he would set up a small beach bar that would become famous for having the most festive music on the island and it would attract locals and foreigners alike. He and his happy bar would be featured in pictures just like the ones he had seen in his collection of tourist brochures. He imagined himself the host, the centre of activity, people dancing and gossiping all round him as he served them drinks with a smile and laughed at their jokes. He got butterflies in his stomach just thinking about it, his heart took flight and lifted him to unrealistic heights and he levitated entirely unburdened, smiles of soon-to-become-familiar customers joining him in the crisp evening air.

Every time he completed a shift he was closer to realising his dream. That cool evening in May he calculated that he would have to work exactly one more year before he could leave the mainland forever. He tried to contain his excitement as the train slowed enough for him to jump off and roll down the gravelly hill below the railway tracks at the east side – the railway edge – of Tocopilla. He dusted himself off and tonight because he felt the happy air was pregnant with his plans, he allowed his boots to carry him directly to the sea without stopping at his house to stash his pay envelope, leave his duffle bag or greet the cat.

He was still smiling to himself when, ten minutes later, over the crest of the four big rocks that formed the shape of a reclining dog at the north shore he discovered the almost lifeless body of a young woman floating on her back in the tide pool. His smile disappeared and Easter Island was momentarily wiped off the map. The young woman lay in this shallow watery coffin, arms straight out from her shoulders, eyes closed, and her sandals, having escaped her feet, kicked at the rocky shore in an attempt to alert the earth, to awaken it and bring it to her rescue. Without hesitating, he waded in, grabbed her arms and pulled her backwards to the rocks. With some difficulty he dragged and lifted her onto the closest flat surface and began to pump on her chest as he had seen desperate men do a few times to children on this very shore.

He was not expert. He turned her onto her side and thudded her back with the palms of his hands several times, then rolled her over again and pumped on her chest. He felt a terrible panic and began to tremble, his efforts becoming weaker as a result. But he persisted. After what seemed an eternity, the woman coughed and spit out water. She opened her eyes for a brief moment, moaned and closed them again, her arms and legs tensing and jerking before she fell limp once more. But she was breathing lightly, like a delicate, injured bird.

That was when Manuel Luis Gonzalez suddenly became the strongest man in the world. He bent at his knees, gathered the young woman into his arms and carried her along the quiet streets all the way to his house without stopping once. When he finally dropped her onto his bed, she was still unconscious. He locked her inside and ran back to the beach for his duffle bag and retrieved her sandals that were still floating in the tide pool. When he returned she was asleep in the same position as when he had left.

He knew by her clothing that she was a gypsy girl. He gently untied her wet blouse and skirt and wriggled them off of her limp body, a difficult task given how the wet fabrics stuck to her skin and the fact that she could not cooperate. He turned his eyes away and squeezed them half shut so as to blur the details of intimate body parts and he kept them squinted as he hung her garments on the clothesline in his patio. He dressed her in one of his shirts and a pair of long underwear which, up to this day, had been good only as protection against the cruel dampness of the mine.

It was an entire ten hours before she woke up, during which time he put the kettle on stand-by. He alternated between dozing, head in his arms on the kitchen table, and standing at the side of the bed observing her, wondering if tea was the answer for when she woke up. During this time the negative consequences of rescuing her single-handedly and stowing her away in his bedroom began to present themselves.

He reproached himself for being a good Samaritan. A decision had to be made before he was due to return to the mines in just over two days. He did not want to keep this woman. He had no interest in her or her story. He did not understand why his instinct led him to rescue her, why it had overruled all logic. Moreover, it was the kind of instinct that led to trouble and that he didn't think he possessed. He should have simply run to the police station and reported her lying there, or better yet, just walked away.

Now it was too late. Someone would be looking for her and he would have to spend hours upon hours at the local police station making statements and offering explanations which they probably would not be inclined to believe. They may even lock him up as they investigated and there would be the possibility that his case would be forgotten and he would never be released at all. He would miss his shift at the mines, something he had never done since he started working there ten years ago. His bosses would replace him immediately and his plans for his bar on Easter Island would be delayed indefinitely, if not ruined forever. An even worse thought occurred to him; that they would charge him with kidnapping and he would be jailed for years. He would never survive such a horrific prospect.

The consequences of his heroic actions weighed very heavily indeed until a very simple idea struck him. He would just keep her locked in his house for a couple of days, feeding her sandwiches and tea, allowing her to gain back her strength until it was time to catch the train back to the mine. He would instruct her to leave the house very discreetly after dark once he was gone and she would hide his key under a rock. Then they would both return to their lives as though nothing had happened. In his mind's eye he saw the row of Easter Island monoliths staring wisely across at him, confirming the correctness of his decision.

CHAPTER 16

Orlando Ortega

Tocopilla, May, 1974

The day the General lifted the travel ban and the gypsy caravan was finally allowed to abandon Tocopilla, the *secretarios*, complying with orders from Orlando, headed north along the same coastal road with Jerko sandwiched between them so tightly that he was choking on his gold neck chains. Inside the cab of Jerko's truck that swerved sharply between the rocks to stay out of sight from the highway, they swayed shoulder to shoulder like a Latin musical trio dancing a salsa from the waist up, and the Santa Sara icon slid around unattended in the back, out of time with the beat. Orlando's red Bel Air convertible was already parked at the flats and he sat in the driver's side, door open, calmly kicking at the dirt.

The *secretarios* blessed themselves as Jerko nervously unravelled the layers of light cotton fabric that floated around the precious Santa Sara icon like a protective cloud. He was sweating profusely and his whole body shook. He gagged on vomit more than once, and wiped his mouth with his sleeve, mixing saliva with the salty tears that had begun to roll down past his nose and into his lips. His complexion was yellow and he swayed on wobbly knees that threatened to betray him at any moment.

Finally, Santa Sara was completely exposed. She stood there, vulnerable, as the long swath of cotton briefly levitated above her head, hesitating as though trying to decide which direction to take before allowing the wind to carry it in extended, graceful waves toward the *secretarios*. It washed up onto their chests and settled around their shoulders where it clung, threatening to preserve them like two helpless mummies in mayonnaise-stained black suits.

On a blue planet, one among millions of such celestial orbs, just off the west coast of a continent that stretched to the south pole, hidden among the rocky hills of a long, narrow country's north end, the absolute silence was interrupted only by the crashing of distant surf against the shore.

Mother Earth turned her face lazily away from the sun, and the moon prepared to illuminate the sky. A light wind whistled through caves and lizards skittered in and out between rocks. Three vultures silently and deliberately descended lower and lower, sketching black halos that spiralled from high in the blue heavens. The ore train rumbled, unaffected, on its way down and around the nearby mountain. Seagulls cawed. A fox ventured briefly out of its lair, sniffed the air and retreated. Several wispy clouds formed around the highest mountain peaks and prepared to settle there. Four men stood silently, two of them half swaddled in white cotton, all of them with mouths hanging open, arms dangling limply at their sides as they stared into the sad brown porcelain face of the silent Virgin of the gypsies.

There she stood on top of her crate, temporary queen of a neglected side road kingdom in the Atacama desert, nothing more than payment for a few bags of copper wire, some of which was still in its rubber casing. The gravity of the situation was too much for Jerko and he suddenly yelped as though he had been whipped and collapsed to his knees in front of her, sobbing. The Virgin's downcast eyes were blind to his repentance. With the other men and the looming vultures as unsympathetic witnesses, the hot, thirsty sand mercilessly drank his tears.

A religious icon was the last thing Orlando would have expected to accept in exchange for Jerko's life. He glanced at the *secretarios* who tried to appear noncommittal, although he sensed from their shaking shoulders that they were deeply moved by, and even in awe of, the treasure. He ignored Jerko who now lay prostrate blubbering into the sand, and he circled the Virgin, examining her in silence for several minutes.

Santa Sara was no more than 50 cm high. She was a replica of something much more grand, but the quality of materials and finishing was superb. Her gold crown stood out above all, and golden threads adorned hems and formed intricate motifs on the back of her cloak. The various hand-dyed fabrics (satin, linen, brocade) were finely woven and everything meticulously assembled with rare craftsmanship. Her brown porcelain face with its thin nose, politely down-turned eyes and soft Virgin lips that looked as though they were whispering a secret, suddenly reminded Orlando of María Jacobé. His eyes remained fixed on her mouth for several seconds, trying to decipher what she was saying to him. Her dainty brown hands were holding a rosary made of small pearls. Perhaps her fingers would signal something from Mariá Jacobé. The icon generated both a joy that sprang from hope and an overwhelming yearning. He scanned in detail the brocade edges of the white undergarment and the red lining under the blue veil before dropping his eyes to the Virgin's sandalled brown feet against which rested brightly-painted, carved wooden flowers and red beaded roses, assigning her a certain eternally solid, ever-present quality. Perhaps she would serve a purpose one day.

Without a word, Orlando motioned for his *secretarios* to set Jerko free. Jerko, still crying, sputtered a stream of untranslatable phrases in *Romané* to the Virgin, as he scraped backwards on his knees, head down, ashamed to look around for fear of heavenly or secretarial reprisals. Somehow he reached the door of his truck and crawled in. The gears ground repeatedly before the truck finally understood and disappeared from sight. Jerko's laments echoed down the desert highway. A gypsy Judas in flight.

The *secretarios* extracted themselves from the length of cotton that had wrapped itself around them, helped Orlando re-crate the icon and lift her into the back seat of his car where she would be transported to town. Her crate was crammed in between the two black-suited guardians in dark glasses from whom the odd sob escaped followed by the intermittent clearing of a throat.

Orlando's immediate intentions to somehow meet again with María Jacobé were crushed that evening by his mother's now urgent and constant demands to help Jorge escape certain death at the hands of the military. They were hunting him down along with other members of his syndicate in Santiago. Orlando had to go and do something, and he had to go now. He must get Jorge out of Chile. She would kill herself if he didn't save Jorge. This General and his *junta* were going to kill her one way or the other, she was certain of it. As much as Orlando had tried to push it aside, it had suddenly apparently developed into a seriously dangerous situation.

Orlando had no sympathy for Jorge and his syndicate nor, for that matter, for any such syndicates. And he felt only the tiniest hint of family obligation. It was to escape his mother's incessant nagging and perhaps because of a touch of guilt for missing his father's funeral, that he decided to leave immediately for Santiago where he would take care of business before finally returning to find Mariá Jacobé and some measure of peace.

With many of his old contacts now in Santiago, he knew he would be able to arrange something, and besides, maybe there would be new business opportunities. To travel more discreetly, he decided to leave his car at home and journey by bus and plane. He arranged for his *secretarios* to stay at his mother's house in his absence in order to guard his car, unveil it from time to time and dust it, and since they would be there, also keep an eye on his mother.

CHAPTER 17

Clorinda

Tocopilla, 2001

The first time she spoke to Señor Ortega was only a month before he died. They encountered one another at Santa Elvira's alcove at the cemetery. It was one Sunday afternoon just after she had tended to her father's grave and shared one of their customary silent visits. Now, in his death as in life, caring for her father was a wordless, robotic operation. Nonetheless, she took her time to wipe down the black cross and to sweep the loose dirt from the top of his resting place. She dusted off the old coca-cola bottle with its single red plastic rose, and balanced it at the base of the cross beside the miniature model air plane. Eyes lowered, she offered the ground a familiar, reverential nod and, then planting a kiss on her fingers, she transferred it with a pat onto her father's cross.

On her way out, she paused in front of Santa Elvira's alcove and decided to sit for awhile. An overly-saturated watercolour-on-cardboard portrait of Santa Elvira hung by a nylon thread on the back wall. Clorinda looked at Santa Elvira's face. It showed no signs of stress for carrying the burden of so many petitions. She surely must be a saint, even though the Catholic Church had no plans to make it official. They no doubt received thousands of requests for canonisation from similar *pueblos* around the world.

Clorinda glanced around at the little paper notes and pleas scribbled on the walls. "Dear Santa Elvira... please help my father to get a job. If you do, I promise to burn a candle in your honour every Sunday... please make my mother's cancer disappear... please help my brother stop drinking... please help me pass my final exam. If you do, I will walk on my knees to you... please give us money for a new bed." And then there were notes of gratitude. "Thank you, Santa Elvira, for granting my petition... thank you for bringing my Dad back home... thank you for my new shoes... thank you for keeping my daughter safe..." She decided to light a candle herself and she whispered her only desire, "Dear Santa Elvira, please let Señor Ortega be my friend."

She glanced shyly up into Santa Elvira's eyes and then, humbled by her own spoken request, she immediately hunched forward, losing herself in the flickering candle flame and didn't notice the shadow that fell across the side wall.

She was startled by the sound of the man's voice behind her. "Hello neighbour." She lost her balance, falling over into the wall. She looked up to see Señor Ortega grinning down at her. Clorinda blinked hard. Santa Elvira worked incredibly fast. She instantly turned back to accuse the cardboard saint with her eyes, then crossed herself to close the session and made an additional silent plea, this time for her heart to stop racing.

Señor Ortega's hands were folded loosely in front of his waist like someone at church or at a funeral. His hair was neatly combed, his eyes smiling, and she could smell his cologne. He wore a soft woollen grey vest. She didn't know how to respond. He was within arm's reach.

She should have asked Santa Elvira instead for the blue taffeta she had in mind for a new Sunday dress. She knew what to do with that. But here stood Señor Ortega, her Clark Gable, the man of her dreams, whom she had been dying to touch, wearing a grey alpaca vest that she immediately wanted desperately to taste. The combination of the two desires was overwhelming. She imagined her tongue on the soft wool and her face against his cheek.

He waited politely for her reply as she scrambled to her feet, hands behind her back, too disconcerted to raise her eyes to meet his. She noticed his shiny leather shoes with the neatly knotted short laces.

"*Buenos Días*, Señor Ortega."

"You know my name." The smile was still on his lips.

"Yes, of course. We are neighbours." She said to the ground. She was self-conscious about the earnest looks she shot his way every night from across the road and the secret glimpses she stole from his roof.

There was a long silence. Neither of them moved or shifted their gaze – he looking at her face and she staring at a spot on the ground in front of his right shoe.

"Do you always petition Santa Elvira?"

"No." She dared offer more, "This is my first time, actually." Her face flushed darker as she recalled the nature of her request.

"I used to come here as a boy, you know. This is the first time I've visited Santa Elvira in about 50 years. I don't know what prompted me to visit her today. I thought that maybe she would have been removed from here or maybe the alcove had burned in a fire. But here she is, safe and sound. Maybe she wanted you and I to meet."

Clorinda looked up to meet his eyes for the first time, incredulous. "Maybe." She managed a soft reply.

Out of the corner of her eye, she watched a vulture fly over the cemetery wall and directly into the sun until it disappeared, as though the sun had beckoned it to the heavens with a motion of its golden finger. She remembered her dream of flying across the blue sky into forever, hand in hand with Clark Gable. Maybe it was a sign.

"Well, normally I light a candle to a Virgin of my own. I don't need to petition Santa Elvira." She slapped her hand over her mouth as soon as the words escaped. Why was she telling him this? Besides, as she said it, it occurred to her that maybe she had been wrong to ignore Santa Elvira all these years. Maybe she had been praying to the wrong Virgin just for the sake of convenience.

"Where is this Virgin of yours?"

"In my patio."

"In your patio? What kind of Virgin belongs there?"

"Well, in this case, Santa Sara, the black Virgin of the gypsies."

Although she had not the slightest clue why a Virgin belonged in her back patio, let alone the Santa Sara, Clorinda was pleased with Señor Ortega's obvious interest. Perhaps, he, too, was an authority on Virgins.

CHAPTER 18

María Jacobé

Tocopilla, May, 1974

When María Jacobé awoke, she was in a strange little bed in a cold concrete room, and a pair of worried eyes set on either side of a man's long, sharp nose, were squinting down at her. His thin lips were chapped and they were pursed, shut tight, like the rest of his face that hung motionless half a metre above her own. The man's skin was leathery and it reminded her of a lizard. She opened her eyes wider and blinked hard to focus on this diabolical apparition. Perhaps she was in hell.

Startled, the devil stumbled backwards, his lack of balance not at all lizard-like, and he saved himself when he hit the wall. Several long whiskers, mostly black but some grey, grew out of his chin and a couple of shorter ones had sprouted over his lips but his brown cheeks were hairless. Thin strands from a black, unkempt mop of hair fell over his forehead. His physical disarray, slight build and hunched posture made him a few centimetres shorter than he already was and gave him the appearance of an old man (not a devil at all) which, upon closer study, she could see was deceiving. He was probably less than thirty years old. He stood there nervously wiping the palms of his hands up and down on the hips of his trousers. He opened his mouth to say something, but then swallowed instead and silently disappeared back out of the door. He returned a few minutes later with a mug of steaming tea. "Drink this." Was all he said. And he shuffled awkwardly out of the room again.

She raised herself up onto the pillow and looked around. The only light source was from a window that opened into the interior of the house. There was no glass in it. It was framed with a pair of unpainted wooden shutters on rusty hinges, one of which was loose. The left shutter supported itself crookedly on the corner of the other as though begging for forgiveness. She wondered what the shutter was guilty of.

The grey concrete walls of the room were bare except for a water-marked black and white family photo framed in a warped thin band of black tin. Five sombre faces were looking into the camera. Just like the man, they all had sunken, serious eyes.

There was a wobbly, wooden bedside table with a worn leather-bound bible in one corner. He had set her cup of tea beside the bible. She wondered if the holy book had been deliberately placed there for her benefit or if it was a fixture. The dust on top of it confirmed that it had probably not been moved for half a lifetime. The room's thick wooden floorboards were rough and unpainted. She detected a slight kerosene odour. A grey cat with torn ears sat in the opposite corner licking his paws and when she reached for the tea he stopped to stare at her, twitching his ragged ears, paws frozen in mid-air, yellow eyes around black vertical slits, challenging her to make the wrong move.

The man had sweetened the tea and in spite of her discomfort and confusion and reluctance to accept anything from this stranger, it tasted good. She swallowed and instinctively lay one hand on her bosom, patting her chest as the warm liquid made its way down. Her clothes! She lifted the woollen blankets and peered underneath. She was dressed in a man's heavy shirt and the bottoms of men's long underwear. Her own garments were nowhere to be seen. She gasped and yanked the blankets up around her neck and huddled back into the pillow, hugging the mug to her chest with both hands. What had this man done to her?

She noticed a bare light bulb dangling from the black wire at the centre of the ceiling. A spider was spinning sticky threads from the beam to the bulb suspended below. The spider twisted round with the greatest of ease, like a multi-appendaged circus artist. Mariá Jacobé thought about the poor insects that would be her victims, how they would pull and struggle to be free, all in vain as the spider looked down from her predatory roost, having spun her trap and now having nothing more to do than wait. Mariá Jacobé was like an insect caught up in a strange man's clothes in this grey concrete trap of a house. How had she come to be here?

She listened for conversation but the only sounds were of the man moving things in the kitchen. They must be alone. What did he want with her? Why had he brought her here? And where was this house? She had never slept under a solid roof before and she didn't like it. She felt claustrophobic and began to tremble, tea splashing out over the top of the mug. When she reached over to place it quietly on the table in order to slide out of bed and make her escape, it slipped from her fingers and crashed to the floor. Glass shattered and the cat skidded out of the room, tail like a stiff wire brush signalling an urgent goodbye. She sat frozen staring at the bedroom door, holding her breath.

The man re-entered the room and glanced only briefly at her before moving directly to the floor by the table. He bent down and calmly collected the broken pieces of china. María Jacobé squirmed her way back into the far corner of the bed and shielded herself with the rough woollen blankets, watching his every move.

She could see his scalp through the mess of thin hair on the top of his head. There was a long scar over his left ear. He patiently picked up one piece of the mug after another and placed them into his other hand. His fingers were fine and thin like his face. She dared to think they might be kind hands and she watched him, allowing herself to relax a bit.

He stood up. "It's okay. I'll get you another." He said without looking at her, and he left.

María Jacobé released a long breath and loosened the grip on the blankets.

The man came back later and told her he was leaving in two days and that on the evening of that second day, when it was dark, after she had regained her strength, she must sneak away, leaving his key under a rock. She nodded without a word, keeping her eyes lowered.

He trusted her, he said, not to cheat him. After all, had he not been kind and respectful? She was expected to reciprocate. He reminded her that he had nothing of value in his house and that she should leave untouched anything that he did have. Outside of that, he didn't talk to her and other than wandering into the bedroom to give her tea and cheese sandwiches, he had no contact with her. She kept her eye on the spider who she was sure was observing her from the middle of the ceiling. At last the man left, curtly reminding her that he expected to find the key under the rock and her gone when he returned. She didn't know when that would be.

CHAPTER 19

María Jacobé

Tocopilla, May, 1974

The darkness was deafening. María Jacobé pulled the blankets over her head to block out the profound despair that rained down on her. Tiny black drops pierced her consciousness, wet thorns poking at her memory, jabbing her thoughts, reminding her of her worsening predicament and distracting her from seeing any light that may or may not be present in the obscure air of this suffocating little concrete house.

The man had left that morning, as he told her he would. He made it clear that he also expected her to depart that night after dark. No need to repeat his instructions again. He assured her there was more than enough bread and tea for a couple of days and pointed out that he had also bought cheese and olives to help build her strength. Other than to remind her that this was a very precarious situation for both of them and that she would find her clothes hanging in the patio, he didn't say anything more.

The burden of her situation now weighed even more heavily than it had two days earlier and she found herself unable to move from the bed during the entire day. She was not hungry. She wanted to vomit but the bitterness rose as far as her throat and retreated.

She finally dozed off and woke up again hours into the night. Unable to face her present reality, she fell asleep again, and this uneven rhythm of waking and sleeping continued until morning. An eternity passed before sunlight filtered through the crooked wooden shutters and she pulled herself up to shuffle slowly to the bathroom outside at the end of the patio. Her skirts brushed her head as she walked past them on the clothesline. Maybe she should get dressed and have some tea, but she knew that she couldn't even promise herself that much. The man wanted her gone and she wanted to be gone. Beyond that, she knew nothing.

She managed to make the tea. It was good but she had no appetite and no will to get dressed after all. She wandered, teacup in hand, around the barren house. Aside from the furniture she had seen in the bedroom, the kitchen contained an old folding table and two fragile wooden-rung chairs, a small gas stove beside a short counter with curtains strung across two cupboards and no fridge.

The sitting room contained only an armoire and a worn cane rocking chair with a faded flower seat pad. An unframed, slightly warped full colour reproduction of Jesus with one hand raised, light shining like an exploding star from his heart, hung on the otherwise bare wall over the armoire. Directly below Jesus in the centre of the armoire was an old plastic green radio with black plastic knobs. She opened one of the armoire doors and discovered piles of tourism brochures, several of them about Easter Island. Uninterested, she closed it and shuffled back to bed where she slept the rest of the day and the entire night, without the mental energy to consider, much less obey the man's instructions. She wondered when he would return and what she would do about it should he find her still here, but she was too exhausted to speculate.

After another night where she slept in fits and starts, she wandered out of bed to the sitting room, still dressed in the heavy shirt and long underwear pants. She switched on the old radio. The dial was tuned to Radio Blanco Encalada, arguably the most popular of Tocopilla's three radio stations and the volume was set to a low murmur. She leaned back in the rocking chair and allowed the beautiful, love-sick voice of Englebert Humperdink to penetrate her consciousness. She could only imagine the words he sang, but the concept was universal and tears rolled down her cheeks as she thought of Señor Ortega.

Theme music announcing the hourly news pounced on Englebert's song as it drifted to its sorrowful end. The first news item was of two local political prisoners who had been shot last night when attempting to escape. It was the second such incident in a week. The families could claim the bodies at the Tocopilla military office of legal medical services. The second item was about a search for a missing gypsy girl that had been called off this morning, after three days. It said she had likely drowned after participating in an annual celebration but they had been unable to find her body. Because there had been recent shark sightings near the shore, the military concluded she had been a victim of a shark attack. As an aside, the announcer reported that the General had finally lifted the ban on gypsy travel and that the gypsy caravan had this very morning packed up camp and abandoned Tocopilla after being told repeatedly that extending the search for the girl would be useless. The third news item was obscured by the dark blur that lowered itself over María Jacobé.

She went numb as the news sunk in. She couldn't feel her legs, which were folded over the edge of the seat, toes dangling like ten useless lumps. But she stretched them to the floor and pushed with enough force to start rocking the chair. It gained momentum and banged into the wall behind her, building in intensity until the hammering pain threatened to explode in her head. Finally, she planted her feet flatly on the floor to stop the rocking, dropped her head down between her knees and remained frozen, hair falling across the kerosene-soaked wood floor. She was alone now. Her family had gone and left her behind, believing her to be dead or abducted, perhaps eaten by sharks, maybe taken by the military, possibly kidnapped by a stranger. They would never be certain. She knew they wouldn't believe for a minute that she had drowned and she also knew that the investigation would have been nothing more than a charade. The gypsies knew the authorities would never spend precious resources look-ing for one of their 'runaways.' Like any other gypsy caravan, her father's was not equipped to challenge the authority or artillery of the Chilean military. They were defeated before they could begin. She felt a deep stab of burning pain for her mother and a heavy sorrow for her father. The combination of their loss and the prolonged, stagnant period in one spot would have been too much for them to bear and they would see no other choice but to move on with their people. If only she had died. She would not have had to know this. She was overtaken by a profound yearning to provide them the comfort they deserved. If she had died, they would have at least found her body, they would have known her fate. She had condemned them all, herself included, to life in a purgatory worse than hell.

She pictured the solemn scene at the camp as they prepared to move out. Normally there would be great excitement for what lay ahead, but this time everyone would be avoiding eye contact, moving about without speaking as they collected their belongings. Stoves and dishes clanking into the backs of vans, mattresses and carpets being rolled up, the final disassembling of the tents, children and dogs being rounded up at the last minute. This time it would all been done with heavy hearts. Her father, wearily holding one corner of a large yellow handkerchief out of his van window, the other corner wet with his tears, would signal the vehicles to follow and the caravan would head north towards the Peruvian border, dust rising from behind the wheels that had been stationary for far too long. The tires would run over their own excitement, killing the anticipation of hitting the wide open desert roads. Happiness would be obliterated by the profound sorrow of leaving someone behind. The gypsy camp allotment would be silent now, its cold fire pits smouldered to nothing, vultures circling down to pick through the carcasses among the garbage that littered its useless edges.

Low voices and music from the radio forced themselves back into her consciousness as she resumed rocking, begging for the monotony to provide some kind of comfort. Eventually it brought her complete numbness, the strength from her limbs draining through her fingers and toes and she sagged in the chair, without so much as even blinking. Meanwhile Tom Jones raged on from the top of the armoire as Jesus' eyes looked out from above his open heart.

Afternoon dusk wiped across the windows and she could no longer see the joints on the oiled floor boards under her feet. For several hours, as the radio advertised life beyond, she became little more than a weak composition of molecules within the limited sombre atmosphere of this poor little concrete trap of a house. If only she could evaporate into the emptiness to which she had submitted herself several nights ago. She shivered. Her feet brushed the floor and she started the chair rocking again, her hollow body leaning on the bare wooden rungs, swaying back and forth, back and forth, neither against, nor with her will.

She suddenly felt a great resentment towards the awful man whose house she was in. What right did he have to save her from the fate she had designed for herself? She searched for and eventually found enough energy to slowly move her hands down to her swollen belly, wishing she could remove what was growing there but knowing she had no such courage. She had no valour at all any more, not even enough to escape this house and lie down on the beach again. Physically and mentally battered by her own powerlessness she slept in the wooden chair as the radio stuttered night things into the dark. She stayed there for maybe another day and another night. She didn't know and she didn't care.

In the morning, the sun's slender rays fingered their way silently in through the crevices of the front door and nudged her awake. The sun could offer warmth and light to the house but beyond that even he, the most powerful force in the solar system was useless. María Jacobé responded, squinting around the room that unexpectedly appeared slightly more cheerful this morning in spite of its drab, neglected state. The radio was talking about the conveniently low cost of freshly baked bread and a special offer on a selection of salami and cheese. It was the dawn of a new day and in spite of the physical and mental weariness that had held her hostage during the past days, María Jacobé responded to the suggestion of fulfilling basic physical needs.

She plodded through the patio to the bathroom and splashed water over her face. It was freezing. She jumped back from the shock of it and instinctively spat out a rude gypsy slang. The sound of her own voice and the automatic curse was suddenly funny. She repeated it, first in a low voice and then in a repetitious little sing-song as she pulled her skirts from the line and changed from the man's shirt and pants into her own familiar clothing. Cats had begun to clatter across the tin roofs in search of food, reminding her again that she should eat. She thought of the baby she was carrying and wondered what would become of it whether she ate or not.

She made a mug of hot tea and a sandwich of stale bread and cheese and, with food in hand, she wandered back to the sitting room. Above the drone of the radio she could hear the occasional car passing by and someone yelling a greeting a short distance away. The low tone of a ship's horn sounded from down at the docks and she wondered where this man's house was located.

Carefully parting the heavy cotton curtains that were strung across the single window beside the front door, and keeping her face hidden, she peered out. The curtains smelled of kerosene and she jerked back momentarily, covering her teacup with one hand.

It was a quiet street and she could see all the way up the road towards the mountains. The early mist still clung to the high, steep brown slopes. A few vultures glided on a draft of wind, seagulls were beginning to call to one another. She heard a rooster crow several houses away. She didn't recognise the neighbourhood. The houses looked sad. They were all single storey, side-by-side houses with low roofs and scant windows, and she felt that they were sinking – or being pushed – straight down into the ground. Perhaps the weight of the dictatorship, she thought. Either that, or they had all been in the same place for too long. The iron security bars over windows reminded her of circus animal cages but without the wheels. These ones were sentenced to stagnate for all eternity on the same plot of ground.

Her presence in this foreign neighbourhood – standing in the stranger's house, looking out of his window at this unfamiliar street –

was surreal. In this dream-state, she slowly scanned the houses beginning at the top of the road all the way down, their sad corrugated tin roofs perched atop unpainted concrete façades. Every now and then a house painted bright green or cobalt blue broke the drab chain, reminding her with a pang of the colourful gypsy tents. She continued her survey, only slightly curious. She stopped suddenly when she saw the car across the street.

As though struck by lightning, her whole body jolted with such force that she was thrown backwards onto the floorboards. She skinned her elbows and bruised her shoulder, then relaxed onto her back, looking straight up at the ceiling, her pulse pounding in her ears. After a few minutes, compelled to confirm what she thought she saw, she hauled herself up and tiptoed, trembling, to the window once more. Parked across the street was Señor Ortega's 1957 Bel Air convertible. It was covered with a tarp but it was the same tarp her father had sold him. There was no mistaking the automobile; it had been the pride of her father's collection.

She remained transfixed, nose touching the curtains, her breath drawing the fabric in and pushing it out of her open mouth. Like a mummy come back to life, her eyes burning holes through the cloth, she focused on the automobile several metres away. She blinked, shook her head, pinched herself and tried to clear her head.

The puzzle pieces that were the hodgepodge circumstances of her life had just been thrown into the air and landed in even greater disarray. Now, because she was still alive and Señor Ortega was just across the street, perhaps she could arrange the pieces into a new reality. She could see some of them clearly, but the big picture was shattered into a thousand pieces and reconstruction was not immediately possible.

Señor Ortega had, after all, not made contact with her for more than two months. She felt her way back across the room and lowered herself into the chair, rocking it very slowly. She stared at the shattered bits of china mug on the floor. They were like the broken pieces of her life.

Before mid-morning, she had decided that she must contact Señor

Ortega. But how? She was supposed to be dead. What if a Chileno saw her and reported her to the authorities and they bothered to hunt down her family and return her to them? The shame of her circumstances would be unbearable within her own community. Or perhaps Chilean authorities would jail her for lack of moral standards. What did they do with young, homeless, pregnant, unmarried gypsy girls? No, the answer was not to place herself at risk, where she would once again find herself powerless in someone else's hands. Look where that had gotten her recently. She glanced around at the sad little sitting room. Venturing outside was out of the question. She must try to signal Señor Ortega from inside.

She continued to watch the house across the street. It was very quiet except for an older lady who left and then returned within ten minutes with what must be a bag of fresh bread. María Jacobé remembered momentarily that she was hungry but keeping vigil took precedence over a hollow stomach and she remained at her post, careful not to step on the pieces of broken mug.

Two moustached men in black suits and dark sunglasses emerged from the house, each pulled up a chair in front of the door, whisked white handkerchiefs across their shoes, sat down with a mug of tea and a sandwich, and looked at the car. She waited for Señor Ortega to walk out and sit with them, but he didn't appear. She kept watch on the house for days, but he was nowhere to be seen. She became anxious and irritable and extremely impatient. If only he would come home, then she would know what to do, this impotence would dissolve and everything would be set right. She kept watching.

CHAPTER 20

Manuel Luis Gonzalez

Tocopilla, June, 1974

When Manuel Luis Gonzalez returned home after his shift with another ten days' pay to stash into his Easter Island Instant Nescafe savings tin, the last thing he expected was to be greeted by the ghostly figure of the young gypsy girl staring at him from behind the curtains as he bent down to retrieve his key from under the rock.

If his dream had been in danger of fading ten days ago, then tonight it was at serious risk of disintegrating entirely.

"Why are you still here? Why did you not leave as agreed?" He was incredulous, his voice, a half-whisper, half-croak.

When he was at work, he had been able to partially convince himself that the rescue of the gypsy girl had been nothing but a bad dream. Now the nightmare came screaming back to him in the form of this barefoot female creature in his kitchen. She was going to ruin his life. He knew it. His heart thumped wildly and he began to hyperventilate. He sunk to his knees, head in his hands. He would find a way past this.

Even though she didn't actually say so, he knew that she could accuse him of kidnapping and possibly even – the word sent chills up his spine – rape. What defence would he have? Certainly jail must be worse than working in the mines.

"What do you want?"

"I just need to stay here a little while longer."

"Why?"

"My family is gone. They left last week. I have nowhere to go."

"But that's not my problem. I can't help you anymore. I have my own plans, my own future."

Suddenly she turned angry. "Who told you to bring me here? Did I ask for your help? You ruined *my* plans."

There it was... her first accusation. He knew what she was capable of. He knew he was the one held hostage and, even worse, in his own home. But he couldn't think of a way around it, at least not yet. He pounded past her to the patio demanding that she leave him alone, cursing her under his breath along with all members of the female race. Although he didn't hate them, God bless the resting soul of his dear departed mother, he was never inclined towards women, their manipulative ways, how they twisted logic to suit themselves. He never had a girlfriend, never wanted one. Boys had always been more attractive.

He sunk deep into misery as he washed and changed his clothes, scrubbing his face so hard that it hurt. If she hadn't been here tonight, he would already be walking along the beach, looking out over the Pacific towards Easter Island, towards his dream that was only a year and a six-hour flight away.

He returned to the kitchen to find her unconscious, crumpled up like a rag doll on the floor. This time his first instinct was to run away, leave her alone, escape to freedom and let her die there. Why hadn't he done that two weeks ago? But what if she dies in his house? Then what? Does he bury her in the patio and pretend that life goes on as always? Yes... that's a possibility. But what if someone finds her, even after he's gone? They'll know he was the one who killed her, they'll hunt him down at his bar on Easter Island, people will pelt him with tomatoes and eggs and probably even rocks and call him a murderer. They'll confiscate his bar and an unworthy local will take over and name the bar after himself, pretending to feel terrible about Manuel's bad fortune but secretly gloating over his own good luck.

He was trapped by his own thoughtless impulsive damned act of kindness of a couple of weeks ago. He half lifted her, half dragged her back to the bedroom. She was lighter and more bony than when he carried her all the way home and he realised she had been locked in the house with barely any food. She must be starving. If he didn't feed her, then on top of everything else, he would be accused of having mistreated her before raping, killing her and burying her bony body in his patio.

He had no choice. He ran out and returned with bread and a small amount of mortadella, cheese and more tea. She would recuperate and he would convince her to leave. He gritted his teeth at the thought, but realised he might have to give up some of his savings to purchase her a bus ticket out of Tocopilla. Yes, perhaps he could buy his life back for the cost of a bus fare. There was a glimmer of hope.

CHAPTER 21

María Jacobé

Tocopilla, June, 1974

Without telling the man, María Jacobé had decided she must stay in his house until Señor Ortega returned. But she did not expect to have to wait until after her baby was born, and even then, to be kept waiting. Señor Ortega had simply disappeared. And now, so had his car.

She was devastated by his absence. There was a gnawing hunger in her soul that threatened to consume her spirit. Before long she had eaten herself up, having tried in vain to satisfy her insatiable craving for Señor Ortega.

It was not only the awful yearning to see him, but it was the pain of being forgotten by him that ate away at her. He hadn't tried to contact her since the day they spent together in the *altiplano*. Perhaps she had been fooled by him that day, but how was it possible that a man could feign such genuine tenderness? She was young but she was not naive. No, she felt certain that he loved her.

Perhaps he had been the victim of an accident or had been detained by the military. Or perhaps it was simply the case that he was a very solitary man who found it impossible to share his life with another living soul and he had to escape. The thought of such emotional cowardice endeared him to her even more; it was something she could help him overcome.

She alternated between cursing him bitterly one day and pleading with Santa Sara to bring him back to her the next. She cried herself to sleep at night and then finally decided that he must have been arrested and 'disappeared' by the military. Given the alternatives, it was the only explanation she could live with. As she built a small altar beside the dusty bible on the bedside table and lit a candle, she asked Santa Sara to put a curse on General Pinochet and she prayed to protect her poor beloved's soul. Manuel Luis never asked her about the altar and if he did, she never would have told him. She let him believe it was some sort of superstitious gypsy ritual.

She fantasised that perhaps her misery would cause her to die in spite of Manuel Luis' stupid heroism. One day her broken heart would simply fail, she would shrivel up and be found lying on the floor, a dried, empty corpse. She remembered the desiccated baby condor she had seen once at the shaman's market. It was hanging upside down on a thin cord beside several others of various sizes. The dried carcasses had probably hung there for ages, unsold, pitiful souvenirs of uselessness, not even worthy of a curse. Surely they might have at least served as fertiliser, but instead they were kept in limbo on a string.

María Jacobé's limbo would last a lifetime. Circumstances twisted themselves into knots, and her life was nothing at all what it had set out to be. The fact that she was alive and not in hell was, for her, the first sign that her life was confused with that of someone else. She did not trace back over the days or weeks or even months to discover at which point exactly this exchange of lives might have occurred. But God must have taken his eyes off her for just long enough to switch her fate with that of another young gypsy girl who was also the best singer and dancer of her caravan. But María Jacobé had already forgotten how to sing and dance.

The day that Manuel Luis realised Mariá Jacobé was pregnant, the skies darkened and he was apparently seized by a great internal storm that pummelled him against the walls of his own house and shot him with a million invisible missiles. He tossed himself madly from room to room. He ran out into the patio shaking his fist up at the sky, he raged around and around the place, ran into the bathroom and knocked his head against the one and only mirror in the house until it shattered, turned circles in the sitting room until she thought he would wear a groove into the floor, pounded his fists against the wall in his bedroom until they bled, and finally tore open the armoire cupboard and tossed dozens of brochures into the air, letting them shower down, pelting him on their way to the floor. He grabbed some and ripped them into shreds. At last exhausted and defeated, he folded onto his knees and remained there on the floor in front of the armoire for more than an hour, head slumped onto his chest. She couldn't see if he was crying and he made no sound.

At last he moved. He calmly gathered the papers with his bloodied hands, piled them back into the armoire and gently clicked the doors shut. He looked up sadly as though searching for a rainbow after a storm. He had not uttered a word during his whole rampage; the only sounds that escaped him were those of an injured, incarcerated puppy in immense pain.

When he finally picked himself up and walked straight over to where Mariá Jacobé stood nailed to the floor in shock, she pulled back, frightened that his violence would erupt again. But he slowly leaned down and he pressed his ear to her belly. He never touched her with his hands. He didn't rub her shoulder and ask her how she felt. He didn't offer her a tender kiss on the cheek. His ear lightly touching her belly was the only physical contact María Jacobé would ever experience with Manuel Luis.

CHAPTER 22

Clorinda

Tocopilla, 2001

Clorinda looked down at her hands. They were nearly 28 years old. At least that's what her birth certificate said. 'Female, born December 30, 1974, Tocopilla'. She came into existence at the end of the year, missing by one day the traditional exorcising of bad spirits. Every year at the stroke of midnight on December 31st, all size and shape of papier maché effigies were torched on the streets and surrounding hills. *Tocopillanos* watched as the negative energy from the *barrios* was ignited and burned furiously for no more than a minute – aided by paint thinner and the will of delighted onlookers – before curling away into the night sky, their papier maché ashes falling to the ground around sooty, bent wire frames. The summer sea breeze picked up the black energy and carried it east, up over the mountain barrier where it was dispersed across the wide open desert to do its will. Perhaps it was this accumulation of hundreds of years' of outcast spirits that made life on the *altiplano* more arduous than elsewhere.

The building and burning of the effigies had evolved from an Inca tradition. Now, referred to simply as '*monos*', each barrio scrounged for materials throughout the year, beginning to apply serious effort by October. The Illustrious Municipality of Tocopilla offered several cash prizes for the most impressive *monos*. Competitive *barrios* collected old cement bags, newspapers and wire. They begged for paint from neighbours who might have something left over from a home improvement. They made deals with municipal workers, and electric plant bosses. They exchanged odd jobs for supplies. And then they started. The planning and separate elements of the *monos* were begun in secret in the designers' back patios and a week before New Years, the oversized wire frames were hauled out over rooftops to street corners. Makeshift scaffolding was installed and the *mono* artists went to work in earnest. Eager neighbours became servants. Children ran for water, coca-cola, fish sandwiches, more flour for the paste, more newspaper for the details, and at night, some chicken and rice and wine. Onlookers gawked as evil comic book monsters took shape. They whistled and clapped in awe of the 10-metre high *fútbol* hero look-alikes and the huge rearing 15-metre high unicorn with rider. They watched as Cyclops emerged on the hill casting a shadow over several houses below, and as Neptune wielded his trident above the bakery near the beach.

For Clorinda, the building of the *monos* was incentive to leave the solitude of her little house and wander the *barrios* of Tocopilla. She did so in style. True to her calendar wardrobe regimen, she selected and combined only the finest fabric ensembles to wear on these outings, some years even creating an entire week's wardrobe in anticipation of these special seven days. She loved this time of year because the excitement of the competition drew even more people than normal out onto the hot summer streets which were already teaming with music and laughter. Ancient *microbúses* whose engines barely had enough power to make it to the far end of town, but whose drivers triumphantly completed one round after the next, were jammed with animated, dancing kids with ghetto blasters on their way to the beach. Housewives congregated on corners to plan fiestas and neighbourhood musicians warmed up, testing speakers and electric keyboards outside their front doors.

In order to see the *monos* in progress and observe them taking shape during their final week, Clorinda planned a different route for each evening. So before New Year's Eve she had selected her favourite, and an hour before midnight, she drank a cup of tea and ate her New Year's cheese and salami sandwich before wandering to the corner where her *mono* of choice stood heroically waiting to be set ablaze. She mentally extracted any evil energy that might have invaded her person over the year and telepathically sent it to the *mono*. Then she watched it go up in flames, envisioning her cleansed soul floating and dancing around her body in a pure white muslin religious vestment with traditional lace skirts.

Every year as the *mono* disintegrated – its martyred frame bending, its charred pieces of paper offering themselves up in the smoke-filled air, she was reminded of Joan of Arc. Clorinda too, was pursuing a quest that was directed by her own inner voice and that of Señor Ortega. But the only part of herself that would go up in flames would be the odd garment that she reluctantly donated to the cause of the *barrio mono*. No matter – her life's work would be a great achievement, perhaps not as great as that of Joan of Arc, and certainly less bloody, but inspired by, and an homage to the Clark Gable look-alike god in her life.

New Year's Eve was Clorinda's annual renewal of faith and moment of contemplation, fitting, she felt, for the commencement of a new year. Meditation about life in general, and specifically her life, lasted about as long as it took for the *mono* to burn because life in Tocopilla was not complicated. Her Spanish heritage had apparently, over generations, been overlooked, mixed with other blood, and mostly abandoned in exchange for a life here. Whether or not their condition as a people had improved was still open to question. But she accepted it for what it was. She stood now on the same ground where defeated Inca warriors had fallen and wondered about the significance. She supposed that after more than five centuries, the forced and bloody mixture of cultures was still a work in progress – as was her tapestry. Her struggle to see it through to completion was an end in itself. Clorinda enjoyed making grandiose comparisons in these infrequent moments of reflection, wisely realising that everything was relative, but nevertheless, she felt grounded in her own role as creator.

Soon New Year's Eve would circle around again on the face of this blue globe, bringing inspiration for new monos and hope for the muse she so desperately sought.

In the faded light of the evening as Clorinda sat in front of her loom, stroking its threads, listening for the music that would emerge from her touch, she could see that her hands were mostly red and raw from scrubbing clothes in cold water. These were not the hands of a daughter of a Spanish aristocrat. Her fingernails were broken and it was impossible to remove the dark deposits that had been under them for as long as she could remember. She had been shocked upon seeing the hands of an elegant lady in a downtown shop a few months ago. The lady was a friend of Señor Ortega. She was pointing at some candy in a jar on the counter. Her hands were soft and white with long fingers that were tipped with shiny pink polished nails. Clorinda had stared intently at the lady's hands, moving in so closely to examine the paint on the nails that the lady suddenly withdrew them and clasped them together under her paisley bosom, declaring into the air "How insolent!" Clorinda dared not look up at the lady's face nor did she attempt to excuse herself. Scurrying backwards, she tripped on the uneven wooden floor and ended up on her bottom, legs in the air, her face as red as her own hands. She scrambled out the door and she avoided that shop like the plague ever since.

At the time of the 'hand' incident, Clorinda had been observing Señor Ortega for several weeks. She was dismayed, certain that he would never be drawn to a person with hands such as her own. She had never previously considered the impression given by someone's hands. She pictured Señor Ortega holding his pen and his whiskey glass. Yes, his fingernails were manicured and his skin appeared to be soft, especially for a man. He cared about the appearance of hands. In comparison, the skin of her father's hands was cracked, and he had callouses on his palms, his fingers were rough, the creases of his knuckles stained black. Even Norma's and Angélica's hands were rough in comparison to Señor Ortega's. For the first time in her life, she felt inadequate, maybe even obscene. It was different than feeling conspicuous because of being odd and out-of-step with other people. That, she had become accustomed to. But the man she was enamoured with and the lady she had seen by his side both had hands like something out of a painting. She was excluded from such a picture. She felt diminished. Something evil and jagged streaked through her body, the muscles of her arms and neck tightened and she clenched her rough and ready fists, imagining them coming down hard on the lady's pink fingernails, and punching her knuckles into her matching pink lips. Jealousy was not a pretty feeling.

She crouched like a cat on Señor Ortega's roof that night, driven to discover Señor Ortega's interest in this pink-fingered lady. She could see the lady in his sitting room. She was leaning back into a chair, her legs casually crossed beneath a blue pinstriped linen skirt that appeared to Clorinda to have been deliberately hiked up along her thighs. The lady wore a constant half-smile. Her voice was soft and she gurgled when she laughed. Señor Ortega seemed to be amused by her. They each held a glass of whiskey in their perfect hands, and Clorinda saw Señor Ortega refill them more than once. Soft music drifted out of the radio, furnishing continuity to cordial conversation that was sprinkled with short but polite, moments of silence. Clorinda bit on her tight fists, involuntarily tasting her grubby knuckles. Tears stung her eyes and blurred the scene below. She was absolutely devastated by what was unfolding in Señor Ortega's sitting room. Pink fingernails on white hands were caressing Señor Ortega's grey alpaca vest as he stood beside her chair. She stretched one of her legs and began to gently rub his calf with her foot, his fine woollen trouser leg responding by rising and falling under the discreet motion. Señor Ortega mentioned the name 'Jorge' and the rubbing stopped.

The lady dropped her head onto her chest and mumbled something in a low voice. Señor Ortega repeated 'Jorge' and continued, "Elisia, I saved his life. And yours too, under the circumstances."

The lady looked up. "Yes, but what you did was illegal. And you know it. If I reveal it to the authorities, you could end up in trouble, and at the very least, you'll be the centre of news stories, and probably even gossip reporters. You are aware that Jorge himself was on the news not so long ago."

Señor Ortega sighed and rolled his eyes. Clorinda shrunk back. "Yes," he said, "I'm aware, and I understand the coverage was minimal."

"Nonetheless..." The lady had no grounds to insist and reluctantly let it go.

"Listen, Elisia." Señor Ortega set down his glass of whiskey and seated himself across the room at the edge of the sofa, apparently about to make a point. "Jorge was no hero. No one is interested in what Jorge did, or in what I did to help him. He was my brother. Nothing more. No deep political ties. Maybe if we still lived in a dictatorship it would be a different story. But we have a democracy now, something that you and your friends don't seem to be able to grasp. The fight is over. Besides, look at you," he casually motioned in her direction. "You don't look like you're suffering, like you're fighting an ideological war. You look perfectly comfortable with things as they are."

"Well, I'm not, Orlando. I'm not. And I am suffering. I sacrificed my life in Chile for Jorge and then I gave up a life I had become accustomed to in Canada when we were forced to return to Chile. I could have so much more." She was whining now. Clorinda smiled in the dark.

"Money. You're after money. Why should I help you?"

"Because I'm family, Orlando. I'm the only family you have left. I need your help now. If you give me something to buy a small house, that's all I need. You know that if I wanted to be miserable, as Jorge's widow, I could claim my share of this house." She looked around the room, unable to disguise her distaste.

Señor Ortega rose from his chair without a word. He went to his desk in the little room at the back of the house. Clorinda didn't trust Pink Fingernails, so she stayed put to keep her eye on her. The lady just sat there running her dainty, self-important fingers through her hair. Clorinda saw the sly satisfaction settle across her face.

"Stand up." Señor Ortega bristled back into the sitting room and he almost barked at the lady. Clorinda gritted her teeth in a hard smile.

Señor Ortega grabbed the lady's hand and placed a piece of paper in it. "This is a cheque made out to you, Elisia. It's more than you deserve and the last you'll ever receive from me. I have a record of it and my bank will have a record of it after you cash it. This is your share of the inheritance. You will get nothing more from me, and I don't ever want to hear from you again." He held out a large sheet of paper in his other hand, placed it on the table and instructed her, "Sign this document of acceptance. And don't think that I don't have the means to notarise it without your presence. I'll do so in the morning."

Pink Fingernails tried to be elegant in her acceptance of the deal, but no matter what it was, she had no choice. She signed and smiled coquettishly at Señor Ortega. "Are you sure you don't want me to keep you company tonight?"

Señor Ortega tightened his lips, took the lady by the elbow and led her out the door. Clorinda flattened herself, belly flopping onto the metal roof, hand over her mouth, eyes wide, and watched as they walked to the corner where Señor Ortega hailed a taxi, helped the lady in, and calmly closed the door without a word. He then turned away from the car and walked towards his house without so much as glancing back.

Clorinda raised her eyes to the dark blue sky and thanked the millions of stars that settled like a celestial lace mantel over Tocopilla.

Now in the solitude of her patio, under the generous heavens, Clorinda's broken fingernails were, themselves, proof that they had not been an impediment to her friendship with Señor Ortega. Rather, they were proof that their friendship went far beyond such superficialities. She glanced over at Santa Sara to see if she agreed. But Santa Sara was preoccupied, as she had been for months now, oblivious in an odd, uncharacteristic manner.

As a private Virgin in her own patio, Santa Sara should be absolutely dedicated to granting Clorinda's petitions. All she had asked her for over these past several months was to help inspire her in the creation of her life's work. Nothing else. It shouldn't be an impossible task. Yet Santa Sara had demonstrated either a great indifference or an extreme lack of power in the grand scheme of universal influence. Because of Clorinda's long-standing relationship with the Virgin, she felt obliged to feign her belief in Santa Sara's effectiveness, continuing to light candles at her feet, pray to her morning and night, but, in truth, she had more faith in her relationship with Señor Ortega. Perhaps she should be relying solely on him. She studied her hands, turning them palm up to demonstrate their emptiness. "You see, Señor Ortega, my hands are still capable. But I need you to put something into them for me..." And as an afterthought, "and not a piece of paper." She was amused by her own joke.

"Señor Ortega, as you know, I have the threads of what in my opinion, is your finest grey alpaca vest but I've run them through my fingers a thousand times without feeling their proper destiny." She was serious now, pleading into the dark, "I need your wisdom to help me find the way to pay you the tribute you deserve. Is it so much to ask?"

Clorinda concentrated on her begging palms. Several tears fell into them and dispersed like small rivers in the stained creases. The tears that had built up without her being aware took her by surprise and brought forth yet more tears. They blinded her and when she raised her face to the night, the stars blurred and sketched Señor Ortega' smiling face across the low desert sky. She reached up to stroke his cheek and felt his lips tenderly caress her rough hands.

"Have faith." She heard him say as the fibres of his alpaca vest emitted a holy light from their low position in the Marks & Spencers bag.

CHAPTER 23

Orlando Ortega

Santiago, June, 1974

Santiago was not exactly what Orlando expected. They had constructed some modern buildings, not the least notable of which was 'Diego Portales', the towering brainchild and pride of ex-President Allende, its offices and convention centre completed with extra effort and cooperation of the workers almost on time for the United Nations Conference on Trade and Development. Ironically it was now occupied by Pinochet, his *junta* and other government officials who needed a headquarters after they bombed the hell out of the presidential palace last September. Uniformed and plain-clothed military presence in the city made the air so thick that it was hard to breathe. Pedestrians moved furtively from place to place, no one wishing to call themselves to the attention to one of the many *'milicos'* armed with machine guns, who were strategically stationed on downtown street corners. Pinochet had tied the city in a straight jacket and placed it inside a heavy crate whose lid was locked down securely every night. He was bringing order to the country.

One underground metro line transported passengers back and forth from the city centre to the military school at the east side of town. Entering into the station downtown and emerging fifteen minutes later at the eastern-most stop was like going from one civilisation to another. The wide open streets of the eastern sector, with its lack of visible military presence, its lush tree-lined boulevards, manicured hedges, colourful blossoms that filled the air with pleasant scents, trimmed bamboo dividers and ivy-covered wrought iron fences were in sharp contrast to the craziness of downtown with its noise and traffic, sidewalks that smelled of stale urine, grey walls, corrugated metal window coverings with graffiti scrawled across all surfaces, and the homeless, mangy dogs and ambulatory street sellers who buzzed in and out of busy passageways like flies.

Jorge was hiding in an anonymous corner of a community called San Miguel in the south end of the city, a hodgepodge of mostly adjoining single-story, tin-roofed bungalows fronted by pad-locked metal gates and high cement walls with shard glass from broken green wine bottles embedded at the top. Cryptic graffiti of small-time delinquents was sprayed across decomposing plaster walls, competing with the sometimes artistic efforts of the political underground. The streets here were less verdant and smelled of poverty. The ground floors of poorly-maintained apartment blocks were populated with hardware stores, half-empty produce shops and small barren grocery stores with locked, gated entrances through which clients were forced to point at what they wanted before passing coins through the grill. Long, dark, narrow passageways wound their way back between the buildings to valuable stashes of black market products, which included everything from Russian-made guns to used doors, broken stain-glass windows, and foreign pornography magazines. The walls everywhere cried out with secrets they couldn't describe.

Following the directions Jorge had communicated to his mother, Orlando hired a black and yellow taxi whose door was hanging by a wire. He held it shut with both hands as it wound its way through the *microbúses*, one-ton trucks, khaki green army vehicles, and streams of other black and yellow taxis. Leaving behind the downtown financial sector with its famous cafes and business lunch menus for a southern destination was yet another shift in culture. The buildings became lower, more of them looked deserted or they had simply closed their metal shutters during prolonged *siestas*, their signs stating there was no bread, the roads became more narrow, and life on the street was more sporadic, less hurried. People called out of third-storey windows at passers-by, and others knocked and yelled through windows on the main floor asking to be let in. Finally the taxi driver stopped in front of a nondescript grey apartment building whose only identifying characteristic was a burnt-out green neon sign the shape of a big cross hanging by a couple of wires over the corner entrance to a pharmacy. The taxi driver pointed to a spray-painted address on one side of a padlocked metal door to indicate they had reached their destination and he impatiently ordered Orlando to pay up so he could get out of this godforsaken part of town. Orlando stepped to the curb, latching the loose car door as best he could and the taxi driver accelerated, his unhinged parts rattling and dragging themselves down the narrow street until he disappeared from sight.

A thin, unshaven man opened a metal flap cut out of the centre of the door demanding Orlando identify himself before guiding him upstairs to a cramped attic space. Jorge was seated in a worn, brown corduroy armchair under a window. He was posed like the two-bit king of a dying breed. A bleached blonde woman lounged across the back of his chair. She was rubbing Jorge's ear lobe between her thumb and middle finger and chewing gum incessantly. This was one of the many lairs of the barely-begun and already-defeated Chilean resistance. Orlando understood that there had been many valiant men and women who stood on principle, but he had a hard time believing Jorge was one of them. Many of its leaders had already sought refuge in foreign countries, leaving fewer and fewer 'warriors' to fight for the cause. Jorge saw no choice now other than to do the same. His movements were extremely limited because more and more meeting places had been compromised as *compadres* were arrested and tortured into revealing information. Jorge's name was on 'the list' and it was only a matter of time before he too would be arrested and dealt with according to the military methods of the day. He rationalised that he would be more effective supporting the struggle from outside of the country, informing foreign citizens about the truth behind the dictatorship and suggesting how they could put pressure on the Pinochet regime (boycotts being top of his list) to relieve the Chilean masses of the human rights abuses and help lift them out of poverty and repression. But Orlando could smell his fear.

Jorge was thinner than Orlando remembered. His hair had lost its shine, a bald patch radiated from the crown of his head (the only thing regal about him) and his complexion was sallow. Fear had invaded his organs and he couldn't eat. His eyes no longer fully reflected the light. Either that, or a dark curtain just beyond his cornea selfishly absorbed it all so that nothing bounced back. There was a dankness around him – in his clothes, in his furniture, in the walls, in his girlfriend. He stunk. He needed a bath and a shave.

Jorge said he had connections in western Canada. His contacts had already helped make preliminary arrangements for political asylum. He just needed to get safely to the Canadian Embassy, find enough money for airfare plus something extra – he cleared his throat and looked meaningfully at Orlando calling him *hermano*. If Orlando could not or would not help, then his mother would place the cause of his arrest, torture and death squarely on Orlando's shoulders, like it or not. He cocked his head and raised an eyebrow as though such a thing was unreasonable, but what can you do? The dank, bleached blonde companion, whose name turned out to be Elisia said she had already made arrangements for her escape but she refused to leave without Jorge. The contacts in Canada were her relatives.

Privately, Elisia let Orlando know that she would be willing to do him favours in return for, well... in return for very little, she said. Perhaps some new clothes. And in front of Jorge she admitted that since she had been lucky enough to set eyes on Orlando (she didn't know he had such a handsome brother), when it came right down to it, she might have a hard time choosing between the two. Orlando found her unsupportable but he took advantage of her coquetry once or twice to distract Jorge from one of his typically prolonged communist rhetoric speeches, preaching to the inconvertible. Jorge was not exactly Castro.

Elisia, so confident of her own charm, couldn't have been more wrong. The only effect she had was to make Orlando miss María Jacobé.

He wished he had asked María Jacobé for a keepsake, something tangible to hold, to smell, to bring her close to him. Her face remained clear in his memory but possessing something that belonged to her would have brought a small measure of comfort. He didn't know how he had survived so long without seeing her again. On the bus journey from Tocopilla to Antofagasta he saw her face like a mirage across the desert and in the plane, looking out into the clear blue, he imagined her voice, her smile, the gestures she made with her hands when she talked, how she cocked her head on a slight angle when she looked at him. He would deal with Jorge's problem as expediently as possible and then return to face Boldo. He would ask Boldo for María Jacobé's hand in marriage even though he knew it would be complicated because, being a mere *Chileno*, he was not a worthy man. But he also knew there was a good chance he could win Boldo over with his money, that he could buy off any previous plans for María Jacobé's future.

Orlando realised that his contacts in Santiago were not going to be amenable to helping a communist bastard escape the grasp of the military, so he didn't ask for advice. But the lunches he arranged with them bore fruit. Literally. They informed him of land speculation, of prospective vineyards, thriving orchards, salmon farms, everything of top quality for export, of planned luxury hotel developments and they put him in touch with the military and their appointed government officials with whom he could do business, promising that their recommendations would open all the right doors. They also invited him to dinner at more than one embassy on Avenue America Vespucio, winking and nudging like schoolboys when they referred to the private parties that often followed at a location just down the street, where high class prostitutes did business only with the elite in the luxury of back yard pools and ornate beds. They could introduce him to all kinds of adventures if he was going to stay awhile. Santiago was alive, they assured him. It had it all and they knew where to find it.

Orlando assumed that few of them knew where to find San Miguel, and even fewer had ever driven into its little streets. San Miguel had it all too, but in smaller, darker, flimsier, less hygienic versions, and at much lower prices. It was rife with undisguised crime and corruption where people paid with their own lives and those of their families because someone else decided that San Miguel inhabitants (and those of similar communities) were of little value. They survived with less sophistication and discretion and greater pain and sorrow. He refused to allow his thoughts to wander into and question the clash of class and culture that was part of the Chilean psyche. His principles were simple, sound and practical. They included what was good for himself and nothing more.

Fortunately, at the first dinner he attended on Avenue America Vespucio, he was offered the complimentary services of an Argentinean diplomat's car and driver for a day. The assistant to the ambassador said that if Orlando accepted his proposal he would be doing them both a great favour. There was only one catch. Was he in the market for a 1970 Mercedes Benz? He nudged Orlando's elbow with his own and explained that diplomatic perks allowed for tax-free sale of cars and therefore he could let it go for an excellent price. In fact, he had another car on order because authorities turned a blind eye to diplomatic deals and he would profit handsomely working outside of the regulations. Orlando saw it as the perfect opportunity to transport Jorge and Elisia to the Canadian Embassy without arousing undue suspicion. He raised his eyebrows in feigned interest and accepted the offer.

The next day he took a taxi to Jorge's apartment to advise Jorge and Elicia of his plan. They would dress formally and arrange for their own transport to the Club de Unión restaurant in the downtown financial district. Jorge would have to be clean-shaven and dress in the suit Orlando had purchased for him that morning. Elisia would wear the new dress he had reluctantly chosen for her, something that would not connect her to this part of town. Ignoring her comments about what she would be willing to do in return for the garment, he emphasized the fact that she must not wear jewellery or chew gum and would be advised to dye her hair to something closer to its natural colour. Jorge protested Orlando's choice of meeting place. Before the dictatorship the Club de Unión was frequented by left-wing intellectuals and artists but it had recently been overtaken by right-wing snobs and military officers. Orlando assured him that the reasons he protested were the very reasons that made it the perfect meeting place. Who would expect a well-dressed communist to walk comfortably down the streets of the financial district and into that particular restaurant? And besides, the low-ranking military on the corners would not risk so much as a request for proof of ID, let alone make an arrest at that location for fear of insulting an associate of a VIP, or a VIP himself. Besides, he needed a suitable place in which to pick them up in the Mercedes without arousing the driver's suspicion.

So it was that he delivered them safely to the doors of the Canadian Embassy in a midnight blue 1970 Mercedes Benz owned by Argentina's president, Juan Perón, who unknowingly performed this act of kindness for a renegade Chilean shortly before his own death.

Jorge would later brag about how he and Elisia had had the great fortune and foresight to have arranged a chauffeured limousine and then, through the Canadians, two seats on a flight leaving for Vancouver that very evening. He always added that Orlando couldn't have planned the whole thing better himself.

CHAPTER 24

Orlando Ortega

Tocopilla, June, 1974

Orlando was back in Tocopilla within three weeks. Dusk was settling in under the lazy gaze of the moon and children were play- ing *fútbol* in the streets. A cool, salty breeze drifted across rooftops and dipped into patios, small scraps of paper and bits of garbage sketch- ing lines through the night as the wind moved in to swoop it up and scatter it hundreds of kilometres away, across the floor of the *altiplano*. Some shops were still open and a few shopkeepers, leaning idly against their door frames watched as Orlando stepped off the bus and into a taxi. His heart was pounding as he instructed the driver to take him to the street at the eastern-most edge of town, to the gypsy field. As the bus neared Tocopilla, he decided without a doubt that he would go di- rectly to Boldo's tent and talk to him about his daughter's future, fully prepared to be more than generous in his business dealings with him, perhaps even return the Santa Sara icon if he could find a way to do it without implicating himself in its disappearance.

"Here we are." The taxi pulled up across from a dark, deserted field. The caravan was gone.

Orlando reeled around, grabbing his head with both hands. This was a nightmare. Angry, he got back into the taxi and slammed the door. The driver mentioned off-hand that if he was hoping to do business with the gypsies, he'd likely find them somewhere between here and Peru because their travel ban had been lifted a couple of weeks ago. Orlando cursed Jorge and his mother under his breath as the driver hummed something *flamenco*.

The solitary trip up into the *altiplano* the next morning only added repentance to anger. He berated himself for going to Santiago, and for hesitating rather than immediately talking to Boldo about Mariá Jacobé the day after he knew he was in love with her, for not knowing about the pending lift on the gypsy travel ban, for trusting that Jerko would eventually lead him into the camp, for the fact that the damned gypsies were nomads. Lastly, but no least, he cursed the General for his bad timing. The sun burned into the immense emptiness, mirages undulating across the desert that unfolded into eternity beyond the horizon. They were reminders of the intangible essence of his own dream of a girl who at this moment, was in a gypsy caravan that rambled in and out of sight along one of the desert highways. Last time he was here, it was with María Jacobé and now he was travelling over the very road alone and she was somewhere several hundred kilometres away from him in God knows which direction, bouncing along on the seat of her father's vehicle.

Upon arrival in Tocopilla the night before and discovering the empty gypsy field, he ordered the taxi driver to take him to his house and, stopping only long enough to assure his mother that Jorge was safely away in Canada, and that he would send news from there, he pressed some peso notes into her hand and told her he had to travel immediately on other urgent business. He ordered his *secretarios* to remove the tarp from the red Bel Air convertible and he drove off, leaving them all standing in the dust outside the front door, mouths hanging open. This all took him less than 15 minutes.

He headed up onto the highway towards María Elena and just out of sight of Tocopilla he pulled into a side road and stopped before it narrowed to nothing more than a donkey trail. In the moonlight he could see the deserted *pirquinero* mine shaft about 200 metres further up onto the hill.

He kicked aside the boards at the opening and climbed down the shaky ladder to the first ledge, out of view from the shaft entrance. He illuminated it with a couple of matches, proving that the crate was still stashed snugly against the wall where he had hidden it before leaving for Santiago. He rocked it gently to confirm that the Santa Sara icon was secure inside. Placing it here had been a feat for a contortionist but he had finally accomplished it by tying a rope around the crate and lowering it one rung at a time. He had lost his footing and nearly fell into the abyss as he scrambled to find the ledge. Crouching low and shaking like a leaf, he cursed the icon, blaming her for the scare. He pushed the crate as close to the wall as possible before climbing back up. He rushed, feeling the panic beginning to rise from memories of hanging upside down on a rope in the dark.

If worse came to worst, the Santa Sara icon would be key to his negotiations with Boldo. Having confirmed she was still safely hidden where he left her, he slid on his heels back down the hill to his car and slept there until the morning light signalled the end of the General's curfew.

Orlando travelled along the main interior highway that would take him directly north, mistakenly believing the gypsies would head up to Arica, just half-hour south of the Peruvian border. At the main police checkpoint halfway between Tocopilla and Iquique, he asked as casually as possible about a gypsy caravan that would have passed through about two weeks ago. When he was told that no caravans had passed since the dictatorship began, he accepted the information with outward nonchalance and continued north pretending he was on an overnight business trip. He returned back through the same checkpoint the next day, cursing the loss of time. If Boldo hadn't gone directly north, the only other place he would have the opportunity to earn some quick cash would be in the mining town of Chuquicamata or the nearby city of Calama. It was not until the next day that Orlando came upon the gypsy camp at the outskirts of Chuquicamata. His spirits lifted. His heart raced and he felt the blood rush into his cheeks. Cool. He had to play it cool.

Orlando pulled to the side of the road to observe the movement within the camp. He breathed deeply, willing his heart to slow to a normal rate. Tent flaps were being closed in anticipation of the regular afternoon sand storm and activity was minimal as people prepared to settle down for a *siesta*. A few stragglers were still outside but even the dogs had already fallen asleep, curled up under the trucks. As it was not yet *siesta* hour Orlando decided to make his approach. He stepped lightly on the accelerator and drove slowly along the side road until he reached the camp entrance where he hesitated momentarily before rolling quietly in towards Boldo's tent. He allowed the car to sit idling for a few minutes, the sound of a lion purring in the back of its throat, before cutting the engine. The camp was silent. It was the desert calm before the storm. Orlando remained seated behind the wheel. Finally two boys alerted Boldo to his presence and Boldo exited his tent, shoulders hunched, the usual smile that signalled he was open for business absent from his face.

He looked terrible. Orlando almost didn't recognise him. The old gypsy's hair was totally grey and he looked gaunt as he shuffled towards the car. Orlando could only suspect that he had experienced serious trouble with the military and there had been a tragic outcome. This was not his concern, but it was disappointing because it was always much easier to negotiate with someone in good humour.

"What brings you here, *Chileno*?" Boldo wasted no energy on polite greetings. His voice was low, lacking energy.

"I need to talk to you Boldo. About something... well, someone... very dear to both of us."

Boldo frowned and motioned, without much enthusiasm, for Orlando to get out of the car and to sit opposite him on one of the two crates outside of his tent. The wind suddenly picked up, hurling sand at them, first intermittently but within seconds, unleashing a constant barrage. Boldo motioned at the curious onlookers to retreat into their tents and leave the two men alone. They were forced to yell into the wind that roared around them.

"Make this quick, *Chileno*. We'll be pelted to death out here." But he did not indicate that they should go inside out of the storm. Boldo was holding a black glass bead rosary, his fingers running across it as though he was born with it in his hands, playing it as expertly as he would a guitar.

"Boldo," Orlando leaned forward, "Boldo, I want to ask you, with all of the respect you command and deserve... I am here to ask that you grant me a great honour."

Orlando had never seen such an apathetic response to a request that was framed with such premeditated care. Boldo sat still and looked at Orlando through eyes that were as lifeless as the glass beads of his rosary, waiting. He appeared not to have the desire to participate in this discussion and he continued to finger the beads, more concentrated on them than on what Orlando could offer.

Forcing himself to ignore details outside of the scope of his mission, Orlando pushed forward. "Boldo, I can't explain to you how I know this, or how it even came about, but I am in love with your daughter, María Jacobé, and would like to ask you, from the bottom of my heart, and with utmost respect, for her hand in marriage."

Boldo stared straight across into Orlando's eyes for several seconds without appearing to see him. The muscles around his eyes tightened, his lids twitching. He sucked in his cheeks and his lips puckered, then relaxed. His chin began to quiver, he swallowed hard a couple of times. Suddenly his eyes filled with tears that spilled over and rolled, unchecked, down his cheeks. He said nothing. The rosary slipped through his fingers and fell into the dust at his feet, but he did not move to retrieve it.

"Boldo. I'm sorry. I really am. I didn't mean to offend you to such a degree. I mean no harm. Honestly, I have fallen in love with María Jacobé and I have decided there is nothing to be done about it, other than to ask you for her hand. I know it is unorthodox. But you know I would take better care of her than any other treasure in the world because that is what she is to me... she... well, I can't tell you how much she means to me..."

Boldo was sinking under his incoming tide of tears.

Boldo's wife, obviously eavesdropping from inside the tent, came out, took Boldo by his shoulders and, without looking at Orlando, she walked Boldo inside like a small child under the guidance of a stern nurse. Boldo stepped on his rosary and ground the beads into the sand. Orlando sat, dumbfounded, on the crate. No one came to offer him an explanation, nor did they eject him from their camp. This time he would refuse to leave without María Jacobé. Where was she? He sat for an hour in the wind storm, pulling his collar up around his ears and protecting his face behind his elbows as the sky turned an ugly brown and the sand continued to pelt the skin off his hands. Finally it subsided, sand crystals settling quietly in place, as though innocent of their participation in the recent violence, and people began to emerge from their tents, eyeing Orlando from a distance. Boldo's wife at last raised their tent flap and stepped out, walking slowly towards Orlando. She sat down opposite him on Boldo's crate and studied him with her sharp eyes for several minutes, jaw locked in stubborn concentration. He could feel her eyes drilling two perfect holes into his forehead. He kept his own lowered partly out of respect, but mostly because she intimidated him. He did not attempt to speak to her.

After what seemed an eternity, head still lowered, Orlando dared to raise his eyes to watch from under his brows as, without warning, Boldo's wife rose to her feet. She turned and with the stature of a tall queen, strode away gracefully, as though walking on water and disappeared into her tent. Orlando could only conclude that the reason for her silent presence had been to put a curse on him. But he didn't believe in gypsy curses and he stubbornly remained seated on the crate. Finally Jackza, Mariá Jacobé's sister approached him. She sat down and leaned so far forward that Orlando thought she would land in his lap. She raised her face up to his and he looked down at her, the two of them frozen for a few seconds, eyes locked, noses almost touching.

Jackza half-whispered, mouthing the words very roundly as if she was teaching someone how to speak. "María Jacobé is no longer with us."

"What?" Orlando couldn't make a sound but his lips shaped the word.

Jackza repeated what she had said in exactly the same way. The two of them remained as they were, she looking up at him and he down at her, both stone-faced. The fact didn't register.

"Where is María Jacobé?" He hissed so forcefully that Jackza jerked back, almost falling off the crate.

Jackza took her time to readjust her seating and leaning forward exactly as before, she boldly grasped Orlando's chin with her long, bony fingers and squeezed it so hard he thought his lower jaw would be crushed. "María Jacobé is no longer with us." She said in the same low whisper. But this time, tears welled up and streamed down her dusty cheeks. She dug her fingernails into Orlando's jaw.

He wrenched free of her and stood up. The entire desert picked itself up and began to orbit around him, her words encircling him, hunting him down. They hit their target. His soft brain registered the words, "María Jacobé is no longer with us."

He grabbed Jackza by the shoulders. "Where is she?" He hissed through his teeth again. Why was she making such a ridiculous statement? Now Boldo would have his family hide Mariá Jacobé behind such silly lies?

"She is no longer with us. I told you!"

"Where is she? I won't leave until you tell me where she is. I'll destroy this entire caravan unless you tell me what is going on." He looked around like a wild man, threatening the stoney faces that had congregated, the pairs of eyes, wide and leering at him.

Jackza couldn't shrug him off, so she stood there and screamed into his face. "María Jacobé is 'disappeared,' okay Chileno? She has been 'disappeared' by the military. She's gone from us. They took her. Do you understand? They took her! We don't know where. We don't know if she is alive or dead. Maybe they dropped her into the sea! Maybe they did unspeakable things to her. Maybe she was eaten by sharks. We don't know.

Okay, Chileno? Okay? Satisfied? Now go! Go this minute!" She reached up and yanked several hairs from the front of his head, spat on them, threw them to the dirt and ground them under her toe. "I curse you and curse your mother and curse your unborn children for disturbing us. Leave us!"

Orlando dropped his hands. Somehow his legs carried him to the car, his hands opened the door, and he sat down. Somehow his fingers found the ignition and he inserted the key and somehow the motor started. Somehow his feet applied the right amount of pressure to the clutch and the accelerator pedal and the car moved forward. Somehow he found himself late that night shivering with cold and disbelief under the stars as he lay on the empty white luxury of his leather bench seat, head in hands, in the 'Valley of the Moon,' only kilometres from Boldo's camp, cursing the universe.

This eerily beautiful, desolate place with its dried ridges and prickly inhumane landscape that had etched its scars into the surface of Mother Earth would offer no consolation. On the contrary, its exaggerated emptiness mocked him, echoing through the misshapen blackness that had been carved out by the wind. The shadows that punched violently into the soft stone cracked sneers at him from all directions – You fool – they told him, you left town with such confidence in your ability to turn things in your favour anytime and any place. You forget that your money reign over fate and circumstance. You thought you could return here and offer the icon as ransom for a girl, their icon. – Discordant, accusing voices rose from unholy mouths across the faces of the desert *altiplano*. – You have surely been cursed.

He was a pathetic figure in a fine linen suit lying inside a luxury vehicle that was itself a mere red dot parked on a ridge on the world's driest landscape. He covered his ears and tried to find comfort as he rolled into a fetal position on the soft leather seat of the car he had bought from the gypsy. Orlando cowered from the dark voices. He did not try to respond. He had been beaten with one severe blow and he would never recover. He slithered towards the handle on the passenger door and pushed down on it, forcing the door open just in time for his vomit to splash onto the red rocks below. He had to leave this place.

He decided to return to Tocopilla in the middle of the night, risking being pulled over and drilled by the military for breaking curfew. Maybe he would be better off rotting in prison, or better yet knocked onto the ground with a rifle butt and left there, his broken bones unable to obey his commands to carry him to safety and he would eventually meet his death in the extreme heat and cold of the *altiplano*. He imagined himself lying abandoned on the desert floor, kicked and left aside by a military officer. He visualised the officer jump into his Bel Air convertible, start the engine, and drive off, wind on his face, music blaring from the speakers, smiling into the desert road ahead. Orlando decided to challenge fate. Come what may. It didn't matter now.

He jumped on the accelerator and sped off down the highway, daring the powers that be to stop him. That night a military patrol consisting of recruits too young to shave, was parked behind the rocks just before the sharp curve at the top of the first major slope through the mountain pass. They were exhausted and disillusioned after a day's trek through the hills in a futile exercise to chase nonexistent escapees. What did they care about the red Bel Air that shot past them down the highway? It was probably the son of a general. Who else would own such a car? The commanding officer waved off the idea of a pursuit with the broad swipe of his arm, pulled his hat over his face and went back to sleep, much to the relief of his subordinates.

Orlando arrived safely in Tocopilla just before sunrise. The town was still asleep. He shut off the engine and let the car glide down the hill. He rolled to a stop in front of his mother's front door, went straight to his room and carelessly stuffed clothes into a suitcase. He was beyond agitation and in his muddled state, he wasn't sure what he was taking and what he was leaving. But his mother would not question or care. She would abandon his room as he had abandoned her.

He grabbed his briefcase (at least his documents were always in order), opened the desk drawer and grabbed handfuls of other papers, not even sure what they were, locked the drawer and pocketed the key. He set everything at the front door and turned towards his mother's room. She was sitting upright, terrified by the intrusion and she dropped her shoulders, visibly relieved when she saw it was him.

"Mamá, I have to leave town. But don't worry. I'll still take care of you. Here..." He snatched at her hand and stuffed several notes into it, wrapping his fingers around hers and holding it for several seconds. He could feel her shaking. Or was it him?

She looked up questioning him with her eyes. He knew she was more worried about herself than him but he assured her anyway. "It's all right. It's nothing serious. It's just business. You know how things can be sometimes." Of course she didn't know how things could be, she had no idea how things could be. And he added, because he knew what really concerned her. "No, Jorge is fine, Mother. You'll see. He's safe in Canada now. He'll contact you soon. And I'll send you money every month. You don't have to worry. I'll take care of you."

He kissed her on the forehead and left before she said a word.

The road to Santiago was going to be long and full of patrols, beginning two blocks from his mother's house, but he was desperate to begin the journey. He took the car out of gear and let it roll down the street a block at a time before parking at an auto repair yard and waiting for the curfew to be over.

As a safeguard on the highways between Tocopilla and the Capital, he kept at hand the letters of reference he had received from his newly-made military friends in the Santiago. He hadn't expected the dinners he had attended there to pay off quite so quickly nor in this manner. He surprised himself with his own survival instinct and clear logic, given that only hours earlier he had been prepared to let the sun dry him just as surely as it would dry the vomit he left behind, until he was nothing but a burned carcass. Now he was moving forward as though he knew what he was doing. But he had no plan. He was on auto-pilot heading for the unknown, the quest for Mariá Jacobé driving him forward.

CHAPTER 25

Clorinda

Tocopilla, 2001

Clorinda rushed through the mundane washing, attempting to recall from somewhere in the back of her mind, why stain removal on pinafores was so important. She went through the motions before hanging the baker's aprons on the clothesline in her patio, calling on the sun to bleach the worn fabric, hoping he cared enough to remove the stains in the process. Her real interest, her vocation, was stretched across the loom that leaned against the side wall of her patio. Santa Sara watched over the loom from her altar in the corner, but Clorinda doubted her cooperation. She was all too aware that, to date, the Virgin had failed to provide inspiration, no matter how many candles Clorinda lit at her feet, or how many aprons and coveralls she washed and mended in her honour.

With the last of the baker's large pinafores hung to dry, Clorinda allowed herself to focus once more on her life's work – specifically at the point of union between Señor Ortega's grey patch of warp and her own small red area. She missed Señor Ortega. Lately, her conversations with him had been hollow. Or rather, his responses to her complaints about a lack of inspiration had been dull, as though he was losing interest. She was under pressure to move things along in order to gain his eternal appreciation. She must fulfil her promise to him and to herself – demonstrating her absolute devotion to him – by completing her life's work.

Among other things, her weaving would represent her love, sympathy and compassion for his life. More than an homage, it would be a final statement of truth according to Clorinda. Who better to do this than someone who had observed him closely during his last year of existence, and who had the distinction of being his best friend during his last four weeks on the planet? Señor Ortega's life was entwined with those of countless others. They, too, would have to be represented in her life's work, but the focus would be on the most outstanding section at the bottom left of the frame where she joined her threads with those of Señor Ortega.

She sighed heavily and reached down into her Marks & Spencer bag to extract the square of crushed green velvet and stroke her face with it before pulling out a soft grey ball of Señor Ortega's former vest. She created a shed in the warp within the selected area using a smooth wooden rod she made herself and slid a short shuttle across an area of Señor Ortega's grey life. She packed the first strand into place and then carefully wove the wool back in the opposite direction. Packing and weaving and packing again – it would have been a tedious process if she didn't love the sensation so much. She delighted in not only the physical pleasure but the significance of the work itself. She was designing Señor Ortega's space in the world which was a deliberately irregular patch whose edges were defined by wherever she chose to stop and double back. She noted the variety of rich tones and shades within the grey alpaca wool. These represented important nuances of Señor Ortega's personality, which he had discreetly and successfully blended into the conformist grey so as not to stand out or offend, but which, as he had revealed to her during their friendship, were really quite brilliant.

She admired Señor Ortega's ability to conform, to adapt so well to the norms and expectations of other people. She assumed that his basic nature was one of conformity and that he nurtured it, training his reactions and his tastes not only to be acceptable but ultimately pleasing to others. This, he explained to her, is partly how he earned his money. Did not she, Clorinda, fall into the patterns set out for her by peers and mentors?

Well, yes, some – she admitted – especially her father. Her father had been a hard worker. He never missed a shift up at the mine, and as difficult as the work may have been for him (complicated by the pollution in his lungs), he did not give up.

"I am not a quitter." She said to the warp as she shaped Señor Ortega's grey patch in front of her eyes. She gave the end of the grey thread a tug to emphasise her point.

"But," she declared to the air around her, directing her remark to Señor Ortega, while making a conscious effort to include Santa Sara icon making eye contact with the Virgin, "I have always gone my own way."

Clorinda didn't like to admit that her individual traits were not entirely of her own design. That she had no friends was true, but it was not initially of her own choosing. As a young girl, she had been excited to go to school to meet friends, participate in games, and share secrets. That was before a few of the girls down the street began to ask her questions about her mother that she couldn't answer. They cruelly insisted on extracting the painful memory of the morning her mother had simply disappeared. Clorinda had no answers for them and stubbornly avoided potential contact with all heartless inquisitors.

In her first year at school, however, she clumsily succeeded in making a special friend called Fernanda. Fernanda was a chubby girl whose mother always sent her to school with mayonnaise sandwich snacks. At first Clorinda was more attracted to the sandwiches than she was to Fernanda. Every morning Fernanda nestled into the far corner of the playground on a discarded concrete curb that the caretakers could see no reason to remove and Clorinda could hear her slowly extracting the sandwich from the bag and undoing the newspaper wrapping to expose its contents. Then she took a huge bite and chewed for several seconds, eyes darting around the playground on the lookout for would-be predators. Clorinda was one of them. She circled her like a crooked vulture but she was so cautious that by the time she reached her prey, the last of the sandwich was nothing more than a big bulge in Fernanda's cheek and the wind picked up the crumpled sheet of newspaper from her lap, dispensing crumbs to the pigeons.

One day Fernanda was unusually vigilant as she made her way to her curb. Like a secret service agent, her eyes darted in all directions while she cautiously extracted something from her bag. It was not her usual mayonnaise sandwich. It appeared to be a generous portion of chocolate cake. Under such potentially delicious circumstances, Clorinda had no time to be coy. No time to do her circling vulture routine. She moved in immediately for the kill, sidling so close to Fernanda on the concrete curb that Fernanda was forced to scoot over and she nearly fell off. Clorinda graciously put her hand under the newspaper napkin and saved the cake from falling to the ground. Their eyes met and they silently evaluated each other. Had they been cats, the hair on their necks would have been standing on end, ears back, alert to any eventuality. After only a few seconds, all Clorinda saw was a harmless but delicious slice of chocolate cake. She was not conscious of the spittle at the corners of her lips but she licked them anyway. Fernanda pulled the cake tighter to her body and studied Clorinda in silence.

Eventually, for reasons unknown, she carefully tore away a corner of the chocolate cake and passed the precious chunk to Clorinda. "It's left over from last night." She said. "It was my birthday yesterday."

Clorinda stuffed the chocolate into her mouth and was compelled to sit in silence for a few seconds, eyes closed, letting the chocolate cake feed her senses. "Happy birthday," she said. And after she stopped licking the insides of her cheeks. "It was delicious. Thank you." She was polite and very appreciative.

She didn't hang around for more after her single bite because she was suddenly ashamed of her brazen attack on the fat girl. She left her alone to enjoy the remainder, turning her back to avoid further temptation.

The next morning she wrapped a small chunk of goat cheese in a bit of newspaper and offered it to Fernanda. Fernanda understood and they became friends. Their friendship consisted of 20 minutes of silence every recess, during which they snuggled together on the concrete curb in the far corner of the playground and shared food (mostly it was food from Fernanda's house, whose mother seemed to understand that she was now preparing a snack for two).

Unfortunately, the friendship with Fernanda was cut short because her father was offered a good job in Rancagua, hundreds of miles south and, like Clorinda's mother, Fernanda simply disappeared. After that Clorinda preferred not to attend school because of the reputation she and Fernanda had created as exclusive members of the lonely sandwich club, but more importantly because she seemed to be the cause of people simply disappearing. She missed Fernanda desperately.

Had it not been for the neighbour, Señora Beatrice, she never would have gone to school at all.

After the disappearance of Clorinda's mother, her father paid Señora Beatrice, who lived next door with her brood of six children, a few pesos per month to keep an eye on Clorinda at intervals during the day. Señora Beatrice wandered over in the evenings to ensure Clorinda had eaten the plate of food she had prepared, wished her a good night and promised to see her in the morning. Which she did. She dropped in briefly before eight o'clock to ensure Clorinda was dressed in her school smock and then literally swept her out the door with the broom like garbage into the wind. And in doing so, every morning she reminded her that she didn't want nasty surprises such as Clorinda's unexpected presence at home in the middle of the day. So Clorinda suffered through torturous hours in the schoolgirl world of exclusive giddy groups with private whispers and meaningful glances. She was not good at interpreting the signals and became bored trying. Finally she was saved, when, in her fourth year she discovered the art of truancy.

There was not much of an art to it, really; it just required desperation and a bold spirit. She sneaked out alone over the schoolyard wall when the school guard left his post to buy a cigarette at the nearby kiosk. She then advanced down the streets, flattening into doorways and dodging cars, until she reached her destination hideaway between the rocks at the north end of the beach. The reason for her truancy was not because she was particularly drawn to this place; it was simply because she must not be at school.

Sometimes, she was overtaken by a wave of misplaced nostalgia for something she could only imagine and she wandered into the deserted Bolivian mine ruins whose history had sunk into the black beach sand. She pictured the terrified Bolivian workers fleeing for their lives the day Chilean ships pounded the beaches with their English-made weapons to conquer this shore. The Illustrious Municipality of Tocopilla said they kept the mine ruins as a monument to the Chilean victory. But the truth was probably that they couldn't afford to knock it down. In any case, it was an eyesore. It was stinking and rusted and black. Nevertheless, the rot precipitated a certain grotesque allure. Whenever she entered the ruins, she felt a kinship with the displaced workers who had suddenly been converted to foreigners in what, only yesterday, was their country. They, too, had become black sheep, some trying to disguise themselves in order to conform to rules that made no sense. She saw herself as one of them, a stranger in her own land. When she absolutely had to be in school she tried to make herself invisible by playing mute, sinking low into her chair, never voluntarily speaking up in class, hanging out in deserted areas of the playground, trying to merge with the concrete walls.

In spite of this, when she was very young, curiosity drove her to small twittering crowds. She couldn't resist knowing what the other girls were up to, and she followed groups of them into the washrooms, hung out in toilet stalls and eavesdropped. Sometimes, when a girl was distracted, she inched close enough to extract an uncommonly attractive scarf or even a sweater, from her backpack and steal it home to sleep with it. Even if her classmates suspected her of stealing, which many of them did, no one ever found their precious bits of clothing again. She squirrelled them into a plastic bag which she hid under the far corner of her bed. She kept them separate from her mother's articles of clothing, demonstrating an early skill for categorising precious fabrics. This was the true beginning of her fabric collection.

She did manage to achieve good grades in school, though. This, she assured Señor Ortega, was because she had inherited the 'non-quitter' gene from her father. Once embarked on a project, no matter how distasteful, she saw it through to the end. However, her attraction to yarn and fabrics was distracting and she did call negative attention to herself the first time she tried to lick her teacher's sweater. She was sent to the principal's office but was unable to explain. This incident consolidated her reputation as a nonconformist, some would say 'weirdo.' Since no one associated with a weirdo, Clorinda spent years alone, observing, two eyes looking out from the concrete wall or looking up from a desk, or spying from around a corner. She just watched.

Clorinda remembered how she used to watch Señor Ortega from across the street. To take advantage of the cool evening air she made a habit of sitting in her chair outside the front door as the sun set. This was not only a Tocopilla custom, but probably a universal concept for warm climates. She enjoyed this time of day, especially after Señor Ortega moved in across the street. He, too, began to fall into the habit. In fact, he kept a chair and small table by the door, day and night. In the evenings, he sat there sipping whiskey from a crystal glass. He watched her watch him. Occasionally they both scanned the sea view, but inevitably they returned to focus on one another, in unabashed study.

Clorinda wore one of two light woollen sweaters in the cool of the evenings and often automatically lifted her arm to lick the sleeves because both sweaters had distinctive lovely flavours of pure blends. She licked as Señor Ortega sipped. Late one night, maybe even in the early morning hours, when the streets were quiet and she and Señor Ortega were the only ones left sitting outside their front doors, his phone rang. It was common knowledge that his was the only house on the street with a telephone but this was the first time she heard it ring. Señor Ortega was not the kind of man who would allow neighbours to receive phone calls at his number. Once Jimmy had asked if he could use the number for emergencies, but Señor Ortega was indignant and waved him off, suggesting that no living soul would dream of relying on Jimmy in case of an emergency.

Señor Ortega calmly rose to his feet and entered the house to answer the phone on the fourth ring. Clorinda shot across the street like a bullet and was curled around his front door, peering inside. The phone was on his desk in the little room at the back of the house. She scurried up the neighbour's wall and stepped lightly along her usual route across the roof over to his den. She managed to hear only, "Yes, yes, goodbye." Señor Ortega could speak English. She was impressed. He was truly a man of the world. Her face flushed in the dark as she realised that she loved him even more for his worldliness. There was no end to his wonder. He hung up the phone, unlocked a desk drawer, drew out a folder and flipped through several loose documents. He noted something on one of them before placing them back inside the drawer and pocketing the key. When he returned to his front door, he sat for a few more minutes, sipping on the last few drops of whiskey as he looked up at the stars. She waited until he prepared to go to bed and she tiptoed off the roof, crossed the street and lay for at least an hour looking up at the ceiling above her bed, wondering about her eternal love for Señor Ortega.

Clorinda spent several afternoons weaving the base of Señor Ortega's patch. She adjusted and readjusted the defining edges as she worked one thread at a time, either pulling it back out of the weave or extending it even further across the warp until the area took on a shape she was comfortable with.

After subsequent days of doing nothing more than studying the grey patch, she felt it was right. She selected some deep yellow thread from an ordinary bag, a mundane blend of cotton and polyester. She began to crochet with her fingers, slowly at first and then rapidly and expertly pulling the yellow strands through tight little loops, joining one small oval into another until she had several little golden flower petals. With a fine chocolate brown cotton thread, she formed a smaller and even more tight circle that consisted of dozens of knots and she stitched this dark circle to the centre of the yellow petals. She examined it and decided to attach a few heavily textured green threads to hang out from behind the yellow petals. The finished daisy was about three centimetres in diameter. She sewed it to the joint between her and Señor Ortega and she stood back and applauded. She clapped as though she stood in a crowded theatre full of music lovers, awarding the orchestra a standing ovation for an exquisite symphony performance. The entire incomplete weaving suddenly blossomed with new meaning. She thought her heart would burst with joy. The single daisy was their communion.

CHAPTER 26

Manuel Luis Gonzalez

Tocopilla, December, 1974

His hope was shredded, never to be repaired but always to be remembered and often mourned, in small disorganised heaps of brochures and torn yellowed pages that remained on the shelf in his armoire, even after his death.

Manuel Luis changed his habits. He never, ever went to walk on the beach. He stopped stashing the majority of the contents of his pay envelope in his Instant Nescafe cans at the back of his kitchen cupboard. He painted over the wall in the hallway where he had marked Xs to count down his days to freedom. He never ever pulled out the travel brochures to pour over them under the dim lamp as he listened to the radio in the evenings.

The only habit he found impossible to change was his response to the feelings that seized him every time he had to return to a shift at the mines. His stomach churned and his nostrils contracted at the prospect of the interminable hours of darkness, heat and gases. But he overcame this temporary physical illness in the same way he had done for years, as he had been taught by natives of the *altiplano*. He took a small handful of coca leaves, stuffed them into his cheeks and chewed. He kept a coca plant in his garden even though the plants had long been outlawed in Chile and, ignoring the fact that she had no confidants, he forced María Jacobé to swear on her mother's life that she would never tell a soul. The bush was a hardy specimen that was able to survive this climate with minimal care and despite what the Americans said, as far as he was concerned, the plant did nothing but help miners cope with cruel working conditions. He always packed extra leaves in his pouch which he offered every Friday afternoon to *Tío* the god of ore. He was not religious, but the practice never hurt, and just on the off-chance that he was wrong about *Tío*, he didn't want to give the god a reason to be angry with him.

When it was nearing the time for María Jacobé to give birth, Manuel Luis went shopping. He tugged free all the bills that were stashed in his Instant Nescafe cans and bought a new bed for María Jacobé and the baby, a new rocking chair that he placed on the opposite side of the room to his old one, a sofa, and a fridge.

Lastly he budgeted enough of his savings to pay for the services of a midwife and whatever she recommended for baby supplies. He decided to call upon the services of Señora Lucinda because she had always shown great kindness towards him. Whenever she met him on the street, she invited him for tea. But he always declined. He learned later, through local gossip, that a few years ago Señora Lucinda's son had exiled himself from Tocopilla after the police paraded him in the central plaza along with a dozen other homosexuals. The police routinely rounded them up from 'Bar 13-13' on Esmeralda Street and marched them at gun point, forcing them to high-step in a line, their right hand on the shoulder of the *maricón* in front. Locals stopped and pointed and poked fun at them. "Your mother burned the rice, did she?" "Were you born walking backwards?" For most of the town's homosexuals this was nothing new and they took it good naturedly, winking and swaying seductively in response. Some of them flirted with the police officers, promising they would all enjoy the night together in jail. "Don't bring us cigarettes. We have cigars."

But Señora Lucinda's son was humiliated and vowed never to allow it to happen to him again. He ran away, cutting himself off completely from her and her godforsaken town. She missed him desperately and saw a resemblance in Manuel Luis. She was, therefore, delighted to provide her professional midwifery services even though she was very surprised to learn that Manuel Luis was an expectant father.

There were two types of midwives in town – the type who gossiped and revealed all kinds of intimate details – this type was generally very kind and sympathetic; and the type who was stern and steely, performing only the job at hand without emotion, and never speaking a word about their work to anyone. Contrary to the soft side she had shown him, he knew Señora Lucinda was the latter. Manuel Luis was aware that contracting any type of midwife meant the neighbourhood would get wind of Manuel Luis' new condition of father-to-be and would unleash speculation about his 'wife.' But he knew that he could count on Señora Lucinda for a measure of discretion. In any case, it had to be done, and María Jacobé was agreeable to everything now. She had stopped alternating between being a witch and an angel and had settled into something in between, which he could only assume must be who she really was.

Only days before the baby was born, as Manuel Luis was returning to the mines on the train, he realised that it had been weeks since he had thought about his bar on Easter Island. He and María Jacobé had relaxed into a cordial relationship. Although the house was devoid of conversation, she seemed to respect him, and she managed the house well, always ready with hot soup and fresh bread when he walked in the door after his shifts. Their relationship was cooperative, although mostly silent. He never understood why she dressed in mourning, especially when she was about to give birth. Perhaps the baby's father died, but it was not his place to ask, and even if he dared, he was sure he would not have the satisfaction of an answer. María Jacobé had also cut her long hair so that it fell just below her shoulders and she threw away her bright, layered skirts. She didn't look like a gypsy anymore. He found himself looking forward to his return to the little house, not only because its new furniture made it feel less like a cave but also because it was populated with more than just an unsociable cat. His old refuge was transformed into a pleasant place to be. He sensed it would blossom into a virtual garden of happiness the day the baby was born.

He was deep in the mine when he felt the baby's arrival. The heat and pressure in the shaft suddenly became so unbearable that he thought he would suffocate. He paused as the mountain shifted and he held his breath waiting for more tremors to rumble past them, up to the surface, perhaps building to a full earthquake. None came. The other miners didn't seem to notice; they were still swinging picks in uninterrupted rhythm. When he resumed, lunging heavily forward to make contact with the rock, the entire shaft contracted, undulating from where it disappeared into the darkness at one end, all the way towards the light he couldn't see at the surface. He thought he would be crushed. He looked around. Still no one else seemed to notice the intense pressure. He saw a man cough out a laugh in response to someone else's joke but the man's voice was muffled. He was standing with them, almost shoulder to shoulder but they were in another dimension.

Manuel Luis blinked, wiped the sweat from his brow with his wrist and got back to work. Replicas of the first tremor and the slithering constriction of the shaft along its path persisted throughout the day. He had no choice but to persevere no matter how dizzy and nauseated he felt. Finally, when their shift was over and he emerged with his fellow miners into the evening sky, their counterparts who were just entering for the next shift, were abuzz about the discovery of a large uranium deposit.

The company had not been exploring for it. It was an accidental discovery made only last week they said, and they needed more tests but the ore was apparently so near the surface that their only effort would be to pick it up with their bare hands. Several men folded their arms in front of their chests and rocked them in a cradling motion, "easy as robbing a baby from a cradle." Toothless grins spread across each sulphur coloured complexion at the prospect of an easier grind.

That night, lying on his bunk at camp, Manuel Luis fell asleep with a smile on his lips that had nothing whatsoever to do with uranium and everything to do with a baby.

As the train braked just enough to allow workers to jump off onto the slopes at the eastern edge of Tocopilla, Manuel Luis threw himself down with such force that he didn't stop rolling until he tumbled into the wall of someone's back patio. The impact of his body dented the rusty corrugated metal and he had to use both hands to extract his boot from the hole he made in their wall. Someone cursed at him from the other side. He ignored them, picked himself up, threw the duffle bag over his shoulder and ran home to see the baby.

CHAPTER 27

María Jacobé

Tocopilla, December, 1974

The overwhelming agony of childbirth extended itself from sunrise to sunset during which María Jacobé repeatedly cursed her body for its brutal betrayal. The midwife's experienced hands did nothing to calm her pain.

It was only after she held the warm, wet body of a tiny little girl to her breast that she forgave her own body its cruelty and deception.

Manuel Luis returned home the next night and other than to throw an appreciative glance in María Jacobé's direction, he ignored her. He walked straight to the cradle and with his calloused hands he carefully nudged, pushed and pulled at the swaddled bundle until he managed to lift her into his arms.

"It's a girl," was all María Jacobé said.

"Yes." He responded without looking away from the pinched little face.

He gazed down at the little creature with wonder and adoration and then carried her out to the rocking chair where he settled down, baby cradled in his arms, until she startled him with whimpers that escalated to screams of hunger and he rushed to return her to María Jacobé.

"I will register her birth tomorrow morning." Manuel Luis stated matter-of-factly. "I already thought of a name. It will be Clorinda María, after my grandmother – a proper Spanish name."

María Jacobé understood that she was to have no opinion or decision in the matter. Did he have something against gypsy names? Yes, just as most *Chilenos*, he probably did.

"Clorinda María Gonzalez-..." he stopped, wondering what he should say is the baby's mother's last name, and looked questioningly at María Jacobé. It was the first time he really looked her full in the face since they met. "I don't know your last name. What is your last name?"

"Jankolevich. I am María Jacobé Jankolevich." She informed him. She added as an afterthought, "The eldest daughter of Boldo, King of the gypsies."

Manuel Luis ignored that. " Jankolevich, Jankolevich..." He repeated it several times under his breath as he walked out of the bedroom to settle back into the rocking chair. "Clorinda María Gonzalez-... He couldn't bring himself to add the gypsy last name. More importantly, he could not remind the authorities of Mariá Jacobé's last name because it might alert an astute policeman to the missing young gypsy of several months ago. "I will call her 'Clorinda María Gonzalez-Rosas'. Yes, I like 'Rosas.'"

So it was that another inaccuracy was entered into the Chilean civil registry of births. This one denied Clorinda official recognition of her gypsy lineage.

CHAPTER 28

Clorinda

Tocopilla, 2001

Clorinda sat down on the wooden stool at her treadle sewing machine that had a tarnished golden Singer logo embossed on its worn black enamel body, and positioned the sleeve of the brown gabardine work jacket under the needle, pulling the threads out of the way as she powered the machine with the rhythm of her foot. It was the mundane work she did for survival. Her mind wandered easily and often from the task at hand.

She was contemplating her death. Rather than a sad fact, it was a logical next step. Except for the all-important tapestry she had just undertaken, she had no further desire to continue with her life. She wasn't miserable, did not feel victimised by her unusual childhood, nor was she trapped in a never-ending struggle. She felt simply that once her life's work was complete, she could slip away to the next plane, which she fully expected would be a colourful and limitless textile mirage hovering above the desert, which was also inhabited by Señor Ortega.

One morning when she woke up, there it was… the clear and certain knowledge that she was ready to die. This epiphany presented itself two days after Señor Ortega's death, and she was neither surprised nor frightened by it. It emerged from the pillow of her unconscious where it had been stuffed (perhaps since forever), patiently waiting for her to notice.

She had taken one single concrete step towards the planning of her death but it happened well before she recognised it as a certainty, so it couldn't really be considered part of an official plan.

At Señor Ortega's suggestion, she bought a niche in the cemetery wall right beside his. A week before he died, perhaps on a premonition, he led her to the cemetery to show her his chosen resting place, apparently purchased when he had returned to Tocopilla the year before. Upon leaving the cemetery he pressed several large-denomination peso notes into her palm, telling her to consider where she would be buried.

The next day (she remembered it was a Monday because she was wearing a bleached jeans-skirt and one of her favourite patchwork blouses) she walked her sideways-walk around the corner and up the road to the cemetery to look around. Señor Ortega had chosen a niche in a rather middle-class patio, more than she would have expected for herself. Her father was buried several patios away, in a lower class section, not in a niche, but under the hard dry ground marked by a simple wrought iron cross. There was no space for her there. So she paid for the vacant niche beside that of Señor Ortega, registered it in her name, stashed the registration document in the old folder along with the house ownership papers and forgot about it.

Up until she died, Clorinda would have to continue generating sufficient income for food, electricity, gas and water through a minimum of washing and mending for clients. She would be free to devote the rest of her time to her project, the anticipation of which triggered a warm comfortable sensation that she likened to spun cotton.

Clorinda's needs were minimal. Her only somewhat extravagant desire was to have a few extra pesos to buy chocolate, which, in her very limited experience as a chocolate-eater, filled her with joy and energy that lifted her to a new creative level. Eating chocolate was another reason she missed Señor Ortega.

She finished mending the gabardine jacket and put it aside. Her father used to wear heavy, dark green gabardine coveralls over his patched woollen pants with wide suspenders that he snapped into place over a long-sleeved jersey. During the last few years of his life, his skin took on the same hue as the sulphur at the mines. He used to dress for work in robotic movements, his lifeless eyes always focusing on a soiled splotch on the back patio floor as he pulled on his coveralls. He would pause, staring at this spot, coveralls at his hips, then force them up to his elbows, pause again and carry on until he shrugged them over his shoulders, eyes constantly fixed on the splotch as if pleading for it to release him from bondage. Throughout this dressing ritual, he chewed on a big bulge of a substance that he shifted from one cheek to another.

Clorinda wondered if he harboured a secret desire to travel because he kept a collection of old, yellowed travel brochures in his armoire. She wasn't sure why he kept them because he never looked at them. Once when she was cleaning, she asked if she should throw them away and he answered with a fierce glare. He never talked about it of course, and she could only guess. Her father was a man without options. He kept his mouth shut, his eyes lowered and carried on. He rarely looked Clorinda directly in her eyes and she learned at a very young age to reciprocate. She avoided eye contact with most people.

Clorinda still remembered the night her father's eyes were the most alive she'd ever seen them. The little house became charged with a triumphant energy as soon as he walked in the door, breathing heavily under the weight of a wooden crate that was strapped to his back with a length of knotted white cotton. It was late at night. Clorinda knew she was supposed to be asleep but she was woken by a sudden commotion in the patio. She scrambled out of bed, flattened herself against the wall and inched closer to the activity, stopping to watch from just inside the doorway. She was inspired by her father's exuberant mood and she became his supporter, silently cheering him on in anticipation of what would unfold. But her father's uncharacteristic excitement was cut short, the light in his eyes snuffed out by something her mother told him. Her father had been almost joyous as he uncrated Santa Sara and displayed her under the moonlight on the patio floor. But her mother was horrified. Little Clorinda looked back and forth at her parents during their brief but potent exchange of words. The discussion ended abruptly with her mother snatching her into her arms, shielding her from the little statue, scolding her for being out of bed and striding directly down the hallway as she shouted an order for her father to remove the icon from the house. Her mother forced her to try to sleep, rocking her in her arms, making the sign of the cross over both of them several times and mumbling words in a foreign language. Clorinda couldn't sleep, her wide eyes shining into the dark as she listened for sounds from her father. When her mother finally fell asleep Clorinda wriggled out of her arms, tiptoed to the back patio and watched from the doorway.

She stood in the shadows observing her father as he wearily wrapped the icon in the long bolt of cotton, the same bolt he had used as a strap. She kept her secret vigil as he placed the icon back inside the crate, closed the lid, and stood looking at it for a long time, head low, lost in thought, not moving a muscle. He left the crate in the centre of the patio and he retreated to the kitchen where he sat with a cup of tea, his fingers shaking as he curled them around the mug, looking like he needed to made a decision. Finally, he returned to the far corner of the patio where several boxes, some rusty old tools and discarded metal frames had accumulated over the years. In a slow, determined effort he rearranged the mess to make room for the crate. He placed it in the deepest recess of the corner and piled the unwanted items on top and around it and walked away.

Since her mother's disappearance, Clorinda's young life had been an independent one, cohabiting the same house as her father, always running parallel, careful never to disturb him or upset the household balance. He didn't pay attention to her activities, or at least he didn't comment, and she didn't know if he was aware of her growing desire to touch and taste fabric, which peaked when she was 14. She thought of it as her fabric pubescence, her flowering. Surely it would be something he wouldn't understand and would never tolerate. In order to buy supplies and learn to sew, she would need resources but every peso of her father's salary was already predestined. So at 15 years old, having never had an interest in academic study she officially quit school to help old Doña Rosita with her clients' washing and mending.

Doña Rosita was a dried prune of a woman (Clorinda estimated that she was nearly 80 years old) who lived in the house on the corner. The house had peeling pink trim around the windows and the front door. Clorinda assumed she had it painted this colour to match her name, an easy identifier for her customers. "Just knock on the door with the pink trim. That's my house, *la casa rosada*, she told them, even if they had been there 100 times before. Doña Rosita had operated her clothes washing and mending business for as long as Clorinda could remember.

Her first memory of Doña Rosita was from when she was five years old and Doña Rosita shooed her away from her front gate with a wet tea towel. "Don't hang around here, girl. You'll scare away my customers with those owl eyes of yours on your pinched, old woman face. What's wrong with you, child?" She didn't expect an answer. Like a cat, Clorinda persisted. She returned the next day, and the next, hanging out at the gate for hours at a time, sucking on one of her mother's flowered scarves, watching as people entered and exited the house with piles of clothing.

She visited Doña Rosita's front gate knowing she could escape the eye of Señora Beatrice during the afternoon soap operas, whose dedication to watching kids waned at that time of day, especially for ones that didn't belong to her. Doña Rosita ignored Clorinda for several days, but Clorinda knew there must have been some adult conversation between her and Señora Beatrice (Señora Beatrice was perhaps anxious to spread the word about how poor little Clorinda's mother had run off like the wind – gone in a puff of smoke – disappeared in the blink of an eye – here no more – that simple), because Doña Rosita's attitude towards Clorinda suddenly softened. One day she even invited her inside to sit on a wobbly plastic chair in the patio as she scrubbed coveralls in cold soapy water and staggered under their weight to hang them on the patio clothesline.

Doña Rosita smelled of cheap jasmine perfume and her faded leathery cheeks were heavily brushed with lopsided circles of coral powder that smeared when she flicked flies from her face and scratched them with wet hands. She was a thin woman but her hips had spread out and she tilted side to side when she walked, reminding Clorinda of an upside-down pendulum. Her knees were nowhere near touching each other under her skirt. She wore the same button-down faded flower dress every day, as though it was a professional uniform. Perhaps she had several dresses the same, but Clorinda doubted it because they were all permanently soiled in exactly the same places. Her wrinkled skin was too big for her body now, and it hung, even flopped. Clorinda was fascinated with the sharp collar bones and joints that protruded. It was like a lesson in anatomy, but without the muscles.

Clorinda quietly sidled up to her at the old Singer sewing machine and observed as Doña Rosita's wrinkled old fingers pushed the heavy fabric under the thick needle. She liked the way it punctured the weave in such straight lines, leaving its thread trail behind. She watched as Doña Rosita bit the thread ends and spit them onto the floor and she dreamed that one day she would be so skilled.

Doña Rosita was relieved when, at 15, Clorinda announced that she had quit school and wanted to work for her. She refused to admit that her increasingly arthritic joints would not survive the cold water for much longer, and she was aware that her posture wasn't what it used to be. When she stood up, she was bent forward a full 60 degrees from the waist, and this very often called her attention to her unpainted floor boards. She convinced herself that no one else noticed either her deformed posture or the fact that her floor was in need of paint.

Clorinda accepted the honorary sum that Doña Rosita paid her whenever she remembered. Most of the time it was Doña Rosita who now sat on the plastic chair in the patio while Clorinda washed and hung up coveralls. And it was Doña Rosita who pulled up a chair beside the sewing machine to watch Clorinda's capable fingers pass the industrial weight gabardine under the needle. Sometimes she just sunk into a chair on the patio and fell asleep like a lizard on a rock in the sun.

Señora Beatrice agreed not to tell her father that Clorinda quit school but her silence cost Clorinda half of her earnings. She was careful to keep the same hours as when she had attended school in order not to create a problem with her father. As it was, he either didn't notice or he didn't care.

Doña Rosita became her mentor. It was a sad day when the old lady finally passed away but Clorinda always understood that her advanced age meant it would happen sooner rather than later. Clorinda went to her wake. No one spoke to her. She didn't hear anyone tell stories about Doña Rosita. Mourners came and went. They allowed Clorinda to sit on a wooden chair at the head end of the coffin. She stayed one entire day, politely but silently accepting a cheese sandwich and a glass of coca-cola when it was passed to her. She stood up occasionally to peer into the casket at a perfectly still Doña Rosita who was going to her grave in her flowered uniform. Clorinda communicated telepathically with the body, admitting her sadness but also reminding Doña Rosita of her long and no doubt very fulfilling life. She should be content and she should truly rest in peace now, especially since Clorinda had things well in hand.

Doña Rosita's cheeks were heavily caked with powder, big chalky circles on either side of her sagging skin, and her eyelids were swiped with glittery blue eye shadow. It must have been for the special occasion. Clorinda couldn't ever remember her wearing eye shadow when she was alive. Nor did she pencil her brows quite as ferociously. The makeup artist had very likely been the undertaker, Arturo's wife. Clorinda noticed that Arturo's wife's own makeup style was very similar to that of the defunct Doña Rosita.

Doña Rosita had thoughtfully willed her sewing machine, wash tub and scrub board to Clorinda and recommended her to her customers, promising them that Clorinda would charge them even less than the rate

she had charged them over the past 20 years. She said it was a true bar-
gain, considering that she taught the girl everything she knows.

When Doña Rosita died, Clorinda moved the washing and sewing machine to her house and carried on. That was only months before
Clorinda reached her 17th birthday, which was a solitary celebration that
she marked by stealing a small bit of chocolate when the sweets shop clerk
was distracted, sidling happily down to her favourite rock on the north
beach and losing herself in a very brief but intense chocolate ecstasy.

CHAPTER 29

Manuel Luis Gonzalez

Tocopilla, 1978

When he tripped and fell into the deserted mine shaft only months after Clorinda's third birthday, the only thing Manuel Luis could think of was how they would survive without him. Walking alone on these hills at dusk was a serious risk. But one day when he was squished between two old miners during a train ride home he overheard, between their spits and coughs, how there were often untapped minerals left in the small mines which, for reasons of illness or death or insanity, a *pirquinero* would simply shut down and walk away. Manuel Luis couldn't resist the temptation to investigate at least once.

That night, as Manuel Luis lay bruised on a ledge near the surface of a newly found shaft, he cursed his feet for having more will than his head had brains. The shaft was around the other side of the hill, just a short climb from the path that ran off the main road towards María Elena.

It was the thirteenth time he had gone on one of these night-time treasure prowls. It had become an addiction, when, after his first trip into the hills, he found a small amount of silver. He began to dream about the fortune that was just waiting to be picked up here and there in the hills – shafts all ready to walk into, timbres straining to hold on until he had come and gone – and he was drawn to the black holes in the hills again and again. He had entered 11 other shafts on the same small hill, each time coming home with a few ounces of silver. He tried to persuade himself that it was enough, that he should stop before his luck ran out, but on his thirteenth trip, the best he could do when his feet insisted on carrying him up the side of the hill against his better judgement was to force himself to find a shaft on a different slope. He circled around, clinging to the side of the mountain, trying to talk sense to himself, to see the misguided logic of what he was doing. It was dangerous, but his feet refused to listen to the conversation and they stubbornly plodded him up the rocky hillside.

Besides the hazard of the mountain itself, there was also the danger of being caught working someone else's stake, even if it was declared 'dead' at the time. He was acutely aware of the crime he was committing and that's why he always set out just as the sun was setting. He would blend into the shadows on the brown hills and if he must swing a lantern, his plan was to round the other side of the hill to avoid calling himself to the attention of anyone in town.

Sometimes an inspector would have passed by and marked unsafe shafts with wide plastic tape and a paper caution sign tacked to a board whose letters were burned away by the sun, its warning erased by yesterday's heat or maybe bleached through years of exposure. Mostly however, the deserted shafts – be they decades, or only a few months old – remained untouched even by inspectors, who preferred to sit in vehicles at the base of a hill drinking presweetened Instant Nescafe or Coca-Cola and gossiping rather than climbing up the naked slopes. All in a day's work, nothing done, as usual. But no one was the wiser if they occasionally made an effort to hang one sign here and there.

Multitudes of desolate orifices scarred the steep slopes like the gaping mouths of so many baby birds waiting for someone to feed them. Over the years these quiet holes had swallowed countless human victims, treasure-seekers like himself, digesting them and leaving their remains to small furry creatures who lived in their depths.

Because of his late start, he was forced to take a lantern, which meant that he had to choose a slope that was not visible from town. He adjusted the flame and pushed up the hill, searching for an entrance among the shadows. As he rounded a pile of large boulders, he lost his footing on some loose gravel and he slid down on his back into the entrance of a steep hole that was covered with only a thin sheet of plywood. The plywood gave way.

He tumbled into the darkness, coming to rest on a ledge inside the shaft a couple of metres from the main access. He sensed that it plunged infinitely deeper. He scrambled to flatten against the wall, terrified when he couldn't hear the rocks that he had chipped off the shelf, hit bottom. This one must go to the centre of the earth. Mortified, he held his breath, clutching his chest, his heart hammering against his ribs. He sat crouched in the blackness listening to bats a little further beyond and the scratching of nearby insects as they scrambled up the walls. Hands still shaking, he lifted the lantern, which by a stroke of luck he had managed to hang on to, and after several attempts, he re-ignited it. It illuminated only a couple of metres around himself, a dusty golden-black haze, leaving the rest of the cave a dark mystery. He couldn't tell if they were insects or shivers that prickled up and down his spine.

In the dim light he could make out a wooden crate that was shoved against the wall on the ledge that he had huddled back into. He couldn't be certain, but the crate did not look like it had been there for very long. The wood appeared to be only years, rather than centuries old. He sat for several minutes squinting through the scant light of the lantern. His curiosity aroused, and his heart slowing down to a more normal pace, he dared to move forward. Still crouching and with lantern in hand, he manoeuvred himself over to the crate. He heard rocks loosen and tumble, the hungry darkness far below feeding on the sound. His senses were on high alert. When he finally inched his shoulders into the side of the crate he cautiously raised the lantern to examine it for markings. There was nothing. It could be full of explosives or otherwise booby-trapped to prevent men like himself stealing what was inside.

He hesitated. Manuel Luis Gonzalez was not a gambling man and now that he found himself on a narrow ledge inside a dark mine shaft beside a box of something unknown, he decided not to take more risks. More than for his own well-being, he was anxious about that of Clorinda and María Jacobé – in that order.

Ever since Clorinda had taken her first steps she had become his shadow, her short shape laughing along the walls beside him. A gleeful child's sound, the memory of which had often pulled him out of his own hopelessness, and the darkness of interminable corporate mining cavities.

She was always there to greet him when he walked in the door, her innocent smile and brilliant, happy expression, often too bright for him to meet with his own exhausted eyes, afraid to disappoint her somehow. He rarely heard her cry. She liked to study him quietly from her chair, her big eyes intent on his every move and when he looked back at her, she broke into an engaging smile. In spite of himself, it was impossible to resist her innocent charm but he was unable to express his joy.

He had become very protective of the baby – his baby – and when he was home, even María Jacobé had to stand back as he coddled her and carried her outside to look up at the stars. Clorinda had captured his heart in the way only an innocent child can, producing a love that he could never have imagined. How such a small creature could take hold of him so profoundly was a mystery he would never solve. Outwardly he was still the quiet, solemn man he had always been, but inside he glowed with a new warmth and vitality.

Perhaps it was this that drove him to become more adventuresome in his attempts to procure money. His salary was too low to feed three mouths. He wanted something more than basic subsistence for the girl. Perhaps she had awoken a new spirit in him, given him a new ambition, replacing his dream of owning a bar on Easter Island. The bar now seemed trite in comparison and although it was not apparent to anyone else, he saw himself a changed man, a family man, albeit out of step.

Having fallen so violently into the shaft Manuel Luis knew he was lucky to be alive. He was afraid there would be no easy way out of this place. He was prepared to scrape and crawl his way up the wall. It might take several hours or several days to escape such a hole. He hoped they would not search for him and that he would not have to be rescued. A rescue would raise questions about his purpose here, and perhaps he would be accused of thievery of whatever was in this box. With these and numerous unpleasant scenarios haunting him through the darkness, already preparing to stave off ridicule or even death, he couldn't believe his luck when he raised the lantern to examine the cave walls.

Through the dirty golden light he thought he saw a ladder. Still crouching, he rocked forward and stretched out his trembling fingers, unfolded his uncertain legs and felt his way up the roughly hewn means of escape. He puffed out a laugh that bounced back at him off the walls. The laugh became a roar of delight, which shot like a rocket up into the starry sky when he set foot on the surface. Safely back on the gravelly slope, he looked down only once into the darkness where he knew the wooden crate would sit forever unless he returned.

During his next 10-day shift at the mine, with each swing of his pick into the rock and with each tired breath before he closed his eyes on the narrow cot each night he thought about the crate. What if it wasn't a booby trap, but a treasure? He ruled out pirate treasure because the crate was too new and too far from the sea, but it occurred to him that it might contain antique jewellery or ornaments from an escaping Bolivian general who had fled during the War of the Pacific. The timing was reasonable – only 120 years ago. Or perhaps something more recent like a smuggler with art from a church. He recalled the news report of how some gold-plated icons had been looted from a church in Iquique when he was just a boy. The thieves had been caught but even under severe interrogation had never revealed what happened to their booty and it was assumed it had been smuggled out of Chile. He dreamed of a collector's gold and silver coins, but considered the crate too big for such a prize. Perhaps it contained guns and ammunition, a thought that made his blood run cold. He ruled out gold or silver ore because a miner would have sold it immediately. Perhaps it was valuable art from Europe. There were plenty of stories of wealthy Nazi war criminals who had passed through and even stayed in Chile, and it was well-known that they did not travel lightly. There were abundant rumours about the single German man who built the huge Spanish-style villa on the rocky shore just off the main street in Tocopilla. He stayed to himself, rarely leaving his fortress. The house faced out to sea and rumour had it that he was constantly on watch for Nazi hunters. They said he had even constructed elaborate escape tunnels. Maybe this was his treasure. Maybe he had forgotten it or could not find sufficiently discreet means to rescue it and therefore had given up hope of displaying it in his comfortable home that probably housed other such fine works.

Lying awake on his bunk during the seventh night of his shift, he convinced himself that whatever was in the crate, it was not a booby trap, but a treasure. He decided to return one last time, promising himself that afterwards, he would never again venture into the shafts. If he was right, he would also never have to return to work in a mine. The temptation was too great to resist. He could feel the adrenalin pumping through his veins and he determined that he would indeed achieve the superhero status he saw in Clorinda's little girl eyes.

By the time he returned to Tocopilla, he was absolutely and totally obsessed by the crate and its contents. He didn't notice that the mussel soup María Jacobé had prepared was the best she had ever made. He did notice that Clorinda had grown more in the short ten days since he had seen her, and that her eyes still followed him everywhere. He sat with her until dusk, playing with her toes and wrapping his fingers around her own small hands, enjoying the feel of her soft young skin, a pleasant distraction until he could set out for the hills. As soon as María Jacobé gathered Clorinda into her arms to prepare her for bed, Manuel Luis left on his excursion.

This time he trod carefully around the rocks and felt for the ladder leading into the mine entrance. He took a deep breath, gripped the lantern and, trembling, he slowly lowered himself one rung at a time until he reached the flat ledge. He carried with him only a screwdriver. It was enough to pry open the lid. He brushed away some of the dirt before sliding it off and gently placing it against the wall. The lantern revealed one large shape wrapped in soft layers of light cloth. Always conscious of the narrow ledge, Manuel Luis set the lantern down and carefully tilted the crate. He located the end of the cloth and began to unwrap whatever was inside. There were at least a dozen metres of cloth and he thought it would never end, but he continued unravelling, getting closer and more anxious.

When at last he saw a golden crown, he gasped, his voice a high note that echoed too loudly in the cave. His eyes darted around into the darkness. He must calm down. Too much excitement was dangerous. He stopped to breath for several minutes before resuming. A golden crown. What else? His eyes were two black saucers. He couldn't contain his excitement and he murmured nonsense sounds and mantras to help ground himself in reality, to prevent his thoughts taking him to an imagined paradise because with one careless movement, he could lose his balance and plunge to the depths.

Gazing down on her from above, Manuel Luis blinked hard several times, and pounded his temple with the heel of his hand as he recognised the black Virgin of the gypsies, Santa Sara in all her sad, lonely glory. He was afraid to touch her. He let the box thump back squarely on the ground, roughly gathered the shroud and threw it back on top of what was inside, and stood, eyes staring into the cruel light that played tricks on him, hands raised above his shoulders as though the Virgin had just drawn a gun and was holding it to his chest.

He tried to comprehend the presence of this omnipotent figure in an obscure, deserted shaft and he struggled to breathe as the air around him suddenly became very oppressive. Who could have imprisoned the Virgin in such a sadistic and unusual manner? Surely a gypsy would not risk performing such a malicious deed for fear of the curse it would bring upon him and his family. Therefore, it must have been stolen and hidden from the gypsies, perhaps as revenge. But, thought Manuel Luis, what ignorant man would not understand the power and consequences of a gypsy curse?

Running it through his mind, Manuel Luis knew that during the moments he stood pondering the dark destiny someone had designed for the black Virgin, he had suddenly been injected with superhuman strength and a creative force, probably a gift from the Virgin herself. Working with nothing more than intuition, he replaced the lid and tipped the box back at an angle, leaning it against the rock wall. He began wrapping the metres-long white cloth around and underneath the crate and knotted it at the top to make a secure handle. He then hoisted the crate up the ladder towards the entrance, one precarious step at a time, aware that the Virgin knocked around loosely, unprotected, inside her wooden space. Slowly ascending the rungs, he maintained his balance and kept a firm grip on the cloth handle. The crate rose with him towards the open air. When he reached the surface, the moon was watching, her white face tilted sideways, her half-smile illuminating the path back to town. He slung the crate onto his back and, using the white cloth as shoulder straps, he made his way back home.

CHAPTER 30

María Jacobé

Tocopilla, 1978

It was well past midnight when Manuel Luis returned home from wherever he had been going these many evenings after work. This time he arrived staggering and short of breath under the weight of a wooden crate he had obtained through mysterious circumstances. He waved her off when María Jacobé attempted to help him remove it from his back. He made his way directly to the patio and bent his knees very slowly as he lowered the wooden box to the ground and slipped out of the make-shift strap.

The cotton fabric strap looked oddly familiar.

Without saying a word, Manuel Luis opened the lid, tilted the crate on an angle and reached in very carefully to extract the Virgin from her wooden prison.

If Mariá Jacobé had been at all prone to fainting spells, she would have passed out then and there. She fell back on her heels. Stunned, unable to believe her eyes, she gazed at Santa Sara who now stood on the patio floor looking back at her, pitiful and wretchedly out of place.

"She can't be here, Manuel Luis! She can't be here. You have to at least allow her to stand on something. Don't leave her on the floor like this." María Jacobé shrieked and pointed both index fingers at the Virgin, arms shaking, extended with such force that she nearly dislocated her shoulders. She was indignant. The shock of encountering the Virgin in their patio was compounded by the fact that she had been placed directly on the ground, just like any other common object.

María Jacobé leaned onto the patio wall because her knees failed her. She braced herself against the rough concrete as Manuel Luis obediently overturned the crate and lifted the Santa Sara to stand on top of it. He stood back and beamed. But not for long.

It was not necessary to examine the icon further. There was no question that it belonged to her father's caravan. How long ago was it that she had last danced in her honour. She had lit candles and prayed at her feet. The memory made her want to vomit, spew out the pain of the years that she no longer owned, that had slipped back behind the present day like cowardly ghosts behind a screen.

The Virgin's presence here caused her great confusion. She studied Manuel Luis' face for answers, but his jaw was locked tight. He was angered by her negative reaction, and now he would never talk. She could not imagine him stealing the icon. Surely he would understand the grave consequences of such an act. Had he rescued it from somewhere? Another one of his famous rescues? How could it be that it was not safely with the caravan? It was one of the most precious and well-protected items they owned. The caravan would never move on without it.

Santa Sara looked straight across at María Jacobé unprepared to reveal anything.

"This is a gift for you." Offered Manuel Luis again with a nervous half-smile. He could feel his face crack with the effort. He was not accustomed to smiling.

"This is not something that you give to one person. You are not authorised to give such a gift and I cannot accept it. This is not something you give and take, Manuel Luis. This belongs to the gypsies, to my father's caravan."

"Well, the gypsies are not here. They left it behind. What am I to do with it then?" She could see his disappointment. Although he didn't understand the ethical code of the gypsies and the depth of their reverence for Santa Sara, he understood her importance and her value "You are a gypsy. It belongs to you. Who better to take care of it, to pray to it?"

"No, Manuel Luis. This belongs to my father and his people. If we keep the Santa Sara, we will be cursed. She will not answer our prayers under these circumstances."

"But I rescued her..." He stopped himself.

María Jacobé refused to hear more and she turned on her heel, shouting back at him over her shoulder. "Take her back where you found her, Manuel Luis, for everyone's sake. Please."

"Please." She repeated under her breath.

María Jacobé could not sleep knowing the stolen Santa Sara was in her house. She scraped Clorinda's little bed towards her own and when that wasn't enough, she lifted the child into the protection of her arms. She thought she felt an earth tremor, and cowered with the child under the blankets. But it was only some minor shifting, perhaps just a warning. If Santa Sara decided to take revenge for being stolen under whatever circumstances by even the most well-meaning of men, no one, including this innocent girl would be safe.

Manuel Luis had performed another of his unwelcome rescues-gone-wrong, inspired by something she could not imagine and would certainly never understand.

CHAPTER 31

Manuel Luis Gonzalez

Tocopilla, 1978

Manuel Luis was not a man to sit in a bar with friends on his days off from the mine because Manuel Luis didn't have any friends. He was solitary by nature. That's why his old dream of owning a bar in Easter Island was so attractive. He would have been the invisible protagonist, the necessary fixture behind the counter who filled orders with an ever-pleasant smile. He would never really be the centre of activity but he would be the king pin. Should he ever be absent from the picture, the drinks would stop flowing, the bar would be dry, he would be sorely missed.

Walking past *El Gato Negro*, the corner bar, he caught a glimpse of the bar tender throwing his head back, laughing and pointing a finger at a customer who was laughing so hard he was unable to finish his story. Several other men, elbows on top of the counter, were caught up in the joke, shoulders shaking, a couple of them hammering the counter with the palm of their hands. The raucous laughter spilled out of the door, and it was irresistible.

For the first time in his life, Manuel Luis was overcome with a desire to join the men, to be one of the crowd, maybe even the one to make them laugh. He could sardonically recount the story of his treasure and how María Jacobé had thrown it back in his face, ordered him to get rid of it. Aware of the need to wash away the bitter taste on his tongue, and without a second thought Manuel Luis allowed himself to step inside. He pulled up a stool at the near end of the bar, smiling, something so unnatural for the muscles on his face that when he saw his reflection in the mirror behind the bar he thought it was the joker, the man at the bottom of the deck. When the bartender finally stopped laughing long enough to notice him, Manuel ordered a beer. By then the joke was over and the raucousness had died down to a loud male murmur.

Manuel Luis was slowly sipping his beer when a thin gypsy who looked worse for wear, wandered in and sat down on the empty stool beside Manuel Luis and ordered a whiskey. They must have both had 'loner' written across their foreheads because no one paid them any mind. After his second glass of whiskey, the gypsy struck up a conversation with Manuel Luis.

He was in town with the travelling vegetable and fruit market he said, something he had been doing for several years since striking out on his own, away from the caravan.

"My name is Jerko." He held out his hand.

Manuel Luis accepted it and introduced himself.

"Do you work around here?" Jerko asked.

"Yes. Well, that is, I work up in the mines."

"A hard life." Said the gypsy. "I wouldn't want to chain myself to it."

Manuel Luis nodded. He knew enough about gypsies, he thought. This one seemed pleasant enough but it was always best to play it safe and keep one's distance. Look what happened the last time he performed a kindness for a gypsy. He was heartily wounded by her rejection of his gift and he could not rid himself of the bitterness and disappointment of it in spite of swigging back nearly a pint of beer. He had defiantly stashed the icon with his tools in the patio. It would be better off there than in the cave and one day he would decide what to do with it.

Jerko ordered another whiskey. After his fourth glass he began to look for sympathy and his bleary eyes brimmed with self-pity.

"You know, *Chileno*," he droned, "I was once a very important man in our caravan, but I lost something. Something very important. And I knew I would never be able to tolerate the looks on peoples' faces when they discovered my failing. Before I could be ostracised, I left. It broke my heart but they would have kicked me out anyway. I ran off, you know, I just ran off. I had to live on my own, missing my family. It's been more than four years now, but I cannot return. Well... maybe if I could find a way to redeem myself. But that is one chance in a million. I am doomed to live alone, travelling forever from one town to another selling fruit. That is my lot in life now, one that weighs on me very heavily."

Manuel Luis had his own sorrows to drown and, although the drunken gypsy was leaning into his shoulder, Manuel Luis didn't interject with so much as a sympathetic mumble. He sipped his beer until there were only a bit of foam in the bottom of the glass, stood up with nothing more than a nod in Jerko's direction, and left Jerko in mid-sentence trying to catch his balance. Jerko continued to complain, now very drunkenly. He didn't seem to notice that Manuel Luis was gone, perhaps never really noticed he was there in the first place.

Manuel Luis went home to bed and forgot about the pitiful gypsy.

The next morning, María Jacobé asked Manuel Luis if he would watch Clorinda for an hour because she was going to buy produce at the travelling market.

He never saw her again.

CHAPTER 32

Clorinda

Tocopilla, 2001

There are some things you don't tell even your best friend. Not because you don't trust your best friend, or not because you don't have one, but because these things are too painful to recall, never mind that an unexpected onslaught of unspent grief would destroy you. Clorinda was vaguely conscious that in her mind there existed a void, more like a vacuum in which gentle waves would pull her into the sea and its incoming tide would have the power to overtake her. This void was perilous in its very existence, let alone its potential as a personality assassin. She knew it was related to the disappearance of her mother and she avoided it.

Therefore, although Clorinda occasionally allowed herself to recall the few memories she had of her mother, she refused to dwell on questions about her disappearance, and what had suddenly prompted her mother to leave her life with Clorinda and her father. She learned from her father how to protect the stubborn silence not only between the two of them but also in the corners of her mind.

Her father had never explained the sudden and mysterious disappearance of her mother. One morning her mother was simply not there. She had been replaced by Señora Beatrice whose black eyes sunken into a sombre face between her thick mop of grey-streaked hair and her seriously striped apron at Clorinda's bedroom door. She was there to help her dress and prepare breakfast she said. After that, Señora Beatrice was present for half an hour or so every morning, poking her head in again at mid-day and finally reappearing each evening to supervise the cleaning of the kitchen and to send Clorinda to bed.

For the first few months, Clorinda expected to see her mother walk into her bedroom, but after being repeatedly greeted with bitter disappointment in the form of Señora Beatrice, the expectation was downgraded to hope and, eventually even the hope shrivelled up and died. She became heartsick and couldn't eat. Señora Beatrice prepared a cheese sandwich each morning and sat Clorinda at the kitchen table in front of it, then rushed next door to attend to her own household. When she returned at mid-day, Clorinda was still sitting, shoulders drooped forward, arms limp at her sides, staring at nothing, dried tear stains on her cheeks, the sandwich untouched except for by houseflies.

During these first few months, Clorinda asked Señora Beatrice about her mother, and Señora Beatrice just shook her head, and clucked her tongue, saying, "She ran off, Clorinda. Your mother ran off." She never attempted to soften the fact or concoct a story that would transform her mother into a heroine or an angel or even a martyr. Clorinda knew by her father's constant dark moods that such kind fabrications would never come from his mouth so she was left with this void, this deep mystery about her mother's whereabouts.

She instinctively created a place where she could meet her mother, and although she knew it was make-believe, it provided some comfort, which was more than she received from the adults in her life. Señora Beatrice had said her mother had run off, so Clorinda imagined her mother running alone across the desert in her thongs and skirt. Where else was there? In her mind's eye, Clorinda followed her across the high plains. She closed her eyes to observe in detail how her mother's diaphanous layered skirts floated across the distance, shimmering like mirages over the burning sand. Her mother always turned around to look at her, smiling, reaching back to catch Clorinda by the hand and they travelled together at the speed of the wind.

Señora Beatrice informed Clorinda's father that Clorinda was capable of sitting quietly for ages on the floor of the patio or in the rocking chair in the sitting room, apparently doing nothing. Manuel Luis didn't comment and for months Clorinda was left undisturbed as she and her mother got caught up in the breeze over the arid desert landscape of her mind.

Beginning the week after her disappearance, Clorinda gathered her mother's scarves, cotton blouses and night clothes into a pillow case and slept on them so that when she closed her eyes she was comforted by her mother's smell. Eventually the air in their house swallowed the last of her scent, but the pillow case was still a lottery full of memories. Every night she closed her eyes, reached in and let her fingers decide which memory she would be comforted by.

She then lay a piece of her mother's clothing directly under her face, pulling a corner of the fabric into her mouth and niggled on it.

She couldn't remember any other children being slapped across the mouth as they ran their tongue up their mother's long-sleeved cotton blouse or sucked in small bunches of her one-and-only silk scarf that was tied loosely around her neck. These reprimands became powerful, romantic memories which she delighted in subjecting herself to again and again as they precipitated her nightly maternal reunion. Try as she might, she had no memory of her mother ever singing to her. She could not recall and did not know any lullabies.

After Clorinda started to sing to fill the hollowness of her house when her father died, questions about her mother threatened to surface and Clorinda had to beat them down. It was because Norma and Angélica said that her songs were gypsy songs, that they had the distinct sound, and although they were not experts on the subject, there could be no doubt. This, they insisted on leaning into her ear and whispering, was because Clorinda's mother was part-gypsy. Why else would someone just up and leave their home? She was restless, they said, typical of gypsies, they said. And besides, they could tell by her complexion, her habits, her light but still unmistakable accent. Because of this, Clorinda was unsure whether a vague memory of her mother speaking another language was true or something she had invented based on Norma's nasty stories.

The question only became more complex by the presence of the black Virgin of the gypsies in her patio. But she knew for a fact that the icon belonged to her father, and in his own silent way, he made no secret of the fact that he hated the gypsies. His ownership of the icon, then, was all the more puzzling. He waved his hand dismissively whenever anyone mentioned gypsies and he abruptly turned his back and walked away from any such conversation. Luckily for him, gypsies seemed to have erased Tocopilla off their maps. It had been years since the municipal gypsy camp had been occupied. This greatly diminished Clorinda's sources of information and eliminated any possibility of first-hand investigation. She eventually ignored the rumours and became decidedly hard-headed in her denial of any gypsy connection whatsoever. Her music was her own music and her songs her own songs.

Initially she sang without a hint of self-consciousness. Her lyrical expression was a natural response to the silence in her own house. But one evening she became aware of a growing crowd outside her front window and she heard someone yell out, 'Olé', joined by more voices in a steady chorus of '*Olés.*' Curious, she padded to the front of her house and was confronted by a dozen sets of eyes peering in through the glassless frame in her wall. There was applause and some were calling her name. The crowd itself then became its own attraction, drawing more and more curious people to her front window. Shocked and embarrassed, she shooed the people away with broad sweeps of both arms. She was utterly clueless about what had just occurred and retreated to her back patio to watch the stars appear one by one, and to ignore the murmuring voices on the street.

However, she couldn't not sing, and in the days and weeks that followed, neighbours remarked that she had the voice of an angel. Passersby stopped to listen to the melodies that floated out of her window. Norma and Angélica stole garments more frequently as a reason to loiter at Clorinda's window. Mostly it sounded like gypsy music but no one could be sure because although some words sounded like *Romané*, no one could identify the tune or indeed verify the lyrics.

Angélica, being a neighbour and the closest thing to a friend that Clorinda had, became the self-appointed Clorinda expert. At every opportunity, Angélica stationed herself outside the house to inform passersby of Clorinda's natural talent. Always careful to mention that she must not be disturbed, Angélica prohibited any attempts to approach the little house, assigning to herself the authority of a stern museum guard, accepting soiled, ripped coveralls and stained baker's aprons as she saw fit. Before long, Angélica had converted Clorinda to an unwitting celebrity, and visitors to Tocopilla were guided past her house in the same way they were directed to the Bolivian mine ruins or the local man-made beach. Clorinda, with her eccentric calendar of loud, home-made attire, her odd manner of walking, and her sweet singing voice became one of the town's unofficial but essential tourist attractions. Visitors from the desert or from the south would pause in front of her house in the same way visitors passed by lion cages at the zoo, waiting and hoping that she would break into song or better yet, exit the shadows of her lair and make an appearance. For this reason, Clorinda became semi-cloistered, coming out mostly at sundown to sit on her chair outside the front door and gaze across the town as it drew itself in at the end of the day. Later she had the added pleasure of gazing over at Señor Ortega.

CHAPTER 33

María Jacobé

Chile, 1978 – 1982

After a week on the road Mariá Jacobé still didn't know if she had been kidnapped or rescued. They were headed south in an old Ford pickup truck in need of a new muffler, in pursuit of Boldo's caravan. She glanced sideways at Jerko. He hadn't changed much over the last few years except to be even more gaunt and smell as though he bathed in stale whiskey.

She remembered how their eyes had locked that morning at the market. Jerko saw her first. She was choosing some cactus pears, a special treat for Clorinda, who, during her three years of life, had not yet tasted them. María Jacobé was leaning very closely into the fruit, selecting it by smell to avoid touching or squeezing it so she would not be clucked at and shooed away like a dog by the fruit vendor. When she looked up after her close inspection, about to make her request, she found herself staring straight up into the green blood-shot eyes of Jerko.

They stood looking at one another in disbelief. He whispered in *Romané*, "Are you a ghost? On top of everything else, have they sent you to haunt me ?"

It had been four years since someone had spoken to her in her native tongue. She was moved to tears at the sound of it, this intimate language of family that went missing the night Manuel rescued her. She stared back, Jerko's face blurring behind her sudden tears. Tocopilla died around them for several moments – the sound of its cars, the dogs barking, children crying, sea gulls cawing, vendors advertising their wares in their repetitive, staccato style – all became silent. She too, became mute out of shock, fear and confusion.

Jerko reached over and grabbed her wrist with his bony fingers to pull her closer. His eyes grew round and their bloodshot whites filled with more red. He was terrifying. "You." He hissed. "You have caused them much more pain than I." His face contorted with a kind of demented hatred. He squeezed her wrist so hard she thought her bones were going to break but she didn't pull away.

He said more loudly, still in *Romané*, "You... wherever you have been... you have been alive... all of this time. They have mourned you from the moment of your disappearance and you did nothing to console them. You ripped their hearts out. And it is I, I who have paid, I who was rejected, thrown to the dogs like an old bone to slowly chew up and spit out."

Mariá Jacobé did not understand why he mumbled about being cast away. The sounds of Tocopilla penetrated her consciousness once more and she looked around. There were no other gypsy sellers and this was not a gypsy market. She did not know why Jerko was here alone. She felt his grip tighten on her wrist. He yanked at her like she was a disobedient dog, pulling her around the piles of fruit to the back of the stand. She tripped along helplessly behind him, almost falling onto the packed dirt.

He looked up at the sky and smiled a twisted smile and then with a sudden ugly glare, "You're coming with me. You are my redemption."

He opened the driver door of his rusty pickup truck and pushed her roughly along the seat before bouncing into place behind the wheel. He leaned over to her, his nose almost touching hers, the rancid smell of his breath adding disgust to her fright. "Don't even try to leave. That door," he nodded towards the passenger side, "doesn't open, so you will have to climb over me to get out, and that will only happen over my dead body. And I can tell you with a great deal of confidence that there will be no dead bodies in my truck."

He stepped heavily on the gas and they spun out from the curb behind the fruit market, abandoning his produce to rot. His reward, he muttered to her through the side of his mouth, would be worth much more than a few kilos of overripe fruit. She steeled herself for the ride, wondering where they were going and for how long. What about Clorinda and Manuel Luis? She trembled uncontrollably, and without asking for permission from Jerko, she rolled down the window and vomited, the sour remains of breakfast blowing onto the side of the truck. She hung her head out the window for as many kilometres as it took for there to be nothing left to throw up. Her throat was dry. Her head was spinning. The sun was harsh and the wind hissed obscenities in her ears. Either it was the wind or Jerko. She couldn't tell the difference. They had both appeared out of nowhere and whisked her away, along with the sorrows that a kinder wind would have gathered to sow over the desert. See what you can reap from here, this unlikely, infertile habitat.

Exactly one week after the disastrous morning at the fruit stand, she could see the bright dots that were Boldo's tents staked on the desert plain at the eastern outskirts of Ovalle. They had zigzagged through every possible town from the coast across the *altiplano* to Chile's eastern border. Initially travelling much too far north, Jerko finally turned the truck around and headed south again on information from an old man who was selling ice cream along the side of the desert highway in the middle of nowhere.

They'd slept crumpled on the bench seat in the cab of the truck the first two nights. Or, at least Jerko slept but she lay staring up at the lonely roof of the old Ford, looking for a sign etched into the rusty metal. Jerko had said they were still too close to Tocopilla and how did he know that she wouldn't run away? And he added as a 'by the way,' she must know that Tocopilla was a cursed town. The gypsies refused to return to it since her disappearance and the loss of other precious cargo about which he did not elaborate. She pictured Santa Sara in her patio and could not imagine how Manuel Luis had come upon her. Surely Santa Sara's curse was behind this twisted turn of events. María Jacobé was paying the price already.

Finally on the third night Jerko allowed María Jacobé to stretch out in the back of the pickup, but he slept beside her and with some thick twine he tied her wrist to a hook – as a precaution, he said. She shivered throughout the night under the cold desert sky with only a fruit tarp and two old woollen blankets for cover.

María Jacobé didn't know if she was coming or going. Obviously Jerko intended to return her to her parents in exchange for his old place in the caravan. Why he had to win it back was still a mystery and she didn't understand the things he constantly mumbled under his breath. But by now, she was certain it had something to do with the icon in her patio.

Over the past four years, she had dreamed of holding both her parents in her arms and never letting them go, feeling the security of Boldo's thick whiskered cheek against her own and his strong arms almost crushing her back in his embrace. She could smell the oranges on her mother's breath as she hugged her tight, their tears mixing in each other's hair and ears. She could feel her mother's hands pat her shoulders, and feel their way up her neck to her cheeks, the light pressure of her thumbs at the corners of her mouth. Jerko had brought her to the threshold of her dream, and she would soon step across and see her family.

But the brightness of the dream was obscured by her longing for Clorinda. Each night she pictured herself draping Clorinda in her favourite flower print scarf, Clorinda's sparkling eyes studying the fabric details. "Just for a few minutes..." she would tell her. "This is not for little girls." She felt Clorinda's small fingers wrapped inside her own as they walked down the dirt roads in the neighbourhood. Clorinda would dart behind her legs, grabbing at her skirts to spy on other children whose own undisguised curiosity was expressed at the ends of their pointed fingers. She forbade Clorinda to play with other little children and this only served to fan rumours about what the mother must be hiding about the girl. She thought about Clorinda's odd habit of licking her clothes, how she could sit for hours stroking her alpaca sweater and how she picked at Manuel Luis' only woollen vest until it began to unravel. Such a strange, but lovely child. There was no doubt that Clorinda was blessed with a special gift but it was too soon yet to know exactly what. Her aching for Clorinda had burrowed into her soul where, like an unwanted intruder, it insisted on curling up to live with all of its baggage. It was so profound, she couldn't cry. And it was so secret she couldn't talk.

She hadn't spoken a word to Jerko since he had thrown her into his truck. He didn't seem to notice because he was in a constant, crazed state, always talking to himself, smiling and often laughing aloud like a mad man.

It was fortunate they came upon her father's camp when they did because Jerko's truck was inhaling its final drops of gas. He had filled the tank at least a dozen times, but paid only once. The other times he threw the truck into gear and sped away from the gas pump, leering into the rear view mirror as the poor gas attendants ran themselves into exhaustion in his dust. The old Ford finally sputtered into Boldo's camp, Jerko behind the wheel like a victorious white knight, champion of the world. María Jacobé leaned far back into the seat, watching familiar members of the caravan emerge one by one from their tents. They followed the truck as it rolled in on its remaining fumes to halt exactly in the middle of the camp. Boldo and her mother were the last ones to arrive and they walked directly to the truck as the crowd parted like the red sea.

Jerko flung open the door and jumped out, laughing like the madman he was. He yanked María Jacobé's arm, pulling her roughly to her feet just outside of the truck and held her by her shoulders like a prized treasure he won in a formidable but extremely successful battle.

Boldo and her mother stood absolutely still as they stared at María Jacobé and the colour drained from their faces. It was Jackza who first jumped to María Jacobé. Screaming and crying, she pounced on her, knocking her to the ground and she covered her face and neck with kisses. María Jacobé lay incredulous, elbows digging into the ground, trying to sort out the reality of the week's bizarre events, to comprehend how she came to be lying on her back in the sand, under an hysterical sister who she hadn't seen for years, dozens of feet surrounding them, a circle of teary eyes staring down from above.

She knew it was in vain, but she searched between the legs in the crowd for Clorinda's eyes to be staring down at her too.

She felt Boldo pull Jackza off of her and draw them both to their feet. Tears streaked down his puffy face and he rolled her into a long, bear hug. Her mother threw her arms around both of them and rocked them all side to side as she moaned and intermittently looked up to the sky to give thanks. Then the entire caravan population surrounded them, first crushing in on them, and then withdrawing. Hands joined in the air, they formed a wide circle. The colourful crowd slowly and repeatedly contracted and expanded around the family, inhaling and exhaling in long, wide breaths that fanned out into the desert. Their happiness rippled with the wind across the dusty high plains.

That night, they roasted a pig on a spit, music razed the midnight sky, dancers went wild, and drinks were mixed with tears and laughter as fires burned well past dawn. María Jacobé sat between her parents, her lips upturned into an unfeeling half-smile, as she looked on silently through the film that had dropped over her eyes. She couldn't remember how to dance and this didn't surprise her.

She wanted to be alight with the joy and happiness that her parents shared, but inside there was a hollow void where Clorinda's voice called her name over and over, each fresh little girl lament audible before the echoes from the previous cry died away. She ached to answer but she couldn't speak. In only a week she had become a zombie, her senses had numbed behind the fragile crystal screen she had deliberately constructed to preserve her baby's voice, to touch her little girl hands, tousle her fine little girl hair, and gaze into the brilliant, innocent little girl eyes.

This world of loud, lively music and dancing could not touch what was behind the crystal shield. Mariá Jacobé recognised another face that the wind had etched into her crystal barrier. It was Señor Ortega's. He was trapped in the glass, watching both worlds. She needed to protect him too, to prevent his thin clear prison touching either world, one in which he had never belonged, the other from which he was lost. If she allowed him to escape the crystal, her barrier would disintegrate and her worlds would collide. In the worst case scenario – which was the only possibility – she saw him turn to dust that would be whisked far and wide across the desert, turning him to nothing, as though he had never existed.

As her parents jostled her between them in time with the rhythm, she felt that she was being compressed, her life draining from her into the thirsty ground beneath. She would end up nothing more than a dry skeleton on the floor of the desert, to eventually be eaten by the sun, her bones picked dry by dozens of dancing, hungry vultures.

She never escaped this delicate state of mind and several years later, as she was strolling with her mother and four other gypsy women at the foot of Santa Lucia park in the centre of Santiago she passed a man who exactly resembled Señor Ortega. Her mother was holding her hand as they meandered along the sidewalk, the fingers of her other hand rolling across rosary beads behind the folds of her skirt.

María Jacobé knew her mother prayed constantly for her to recover from her lonely journey – "wherever it has taken you, 'my little gem', it doesn't matter." She prayed "Please return her to us," on each bead of the rosary, all day long. She considered cutting out her own tongue if it would help María Jacobé to find hers. She even suggested it to Boldo, but he said he didn't want to have two silent women in his tent, no matter how rigorously he used to complain in years gone by.

The tall, well-dressed man had a ruggedly handsome face, a touch of grey hair and a slight limp. She could smell his musky perfume in the air after he passed. She drew in a sharp breath and held it, suddenly freezing in mid-step. Only her eyes moved. They followed the man as he rushed to descend the steps of the metro station. She watched as his head bobbed lower and lower and he finally disappeared.

Somehow Señor Ortega had escaped her thin crystal prison and he was sucked into the ground by the Santiago crowd. Now his dust would be transported to the north where he belonged. Señor Ortega's crystal barrier had disintegrated and there was nothing to keep her worlds separate. Suddenly Clorinda's voice invaded the city streets. María Jacobé bolted around sharply as the little girl called out for her, becoming more insistent, more shrill and too loud to block out. María Jacobé's mother was shaking her by her shoulders, her words disappearing as they tumbled, useless letters of a mute alphabet, one over the other in the confused air between them. Her mother's eyes frantically tried to follow her as Mariá Jabobé stood on the spot and visibly withdrew from the world in front of the helpless gypsy women. María Jacobé slipped through the doors of insanity and into the safety of a private darkness where she was caught up in the wind that chased unknown realities in an eternal search for Señor Ortega's dust and for their baby daughter.

CHAPTER 34

Orlando Ortega

Santiago, 1974-1982

After months in Santiago during which he pressured his friends and military acquaintances to help him investigate a missing young gypsy girl who was 'disappeared' by the military in or around Tocopilla, Orlando found it impossible to accept that no one – from the regional General down to the lowest ranking soldiers stationed in the north — had heard a single story about a missing girl other than the same story that had been announced once, and only once, on local radio after several days' search, and in one small insertion on the back page of *La Prensa de Tocopilla*.

He disguised his true interest in her by saying that she had stolen some silver from the back seat of his car when he had turned his back and that, no matter what the value of the loot, this crime must not go unpunished. This was credible in the minds of the upper circles of the right wing and military in which he now found himself, where individuals from lower social class were painted almost exclusively with the broad brush of 'thieves and undesirables.' The popular opinion was that if the girl had been 'disappeared' – careful to point out of course, that the military did not participate in such disappearances which were nothing more than urban myths – the girl had probably paid for her crime and Orlando should let it go.

Orlando noted that in Santiago more than in the small towns in the north, Chileans from all classes were conscious of the social strata into which they were born and likely to die, their destiny in their final resting place matching that of their birth– either a marble tomb in the family mausoleum which was designed by a noted architect, located in the upper class sector of the cemetery or a lonely, rented concrete niche alongside thousands of others in the walls or the barren ground of the poorest cemetery patios. There wasn't much in between.

Resentment towards the wealthy was agitated by the military rule that favoured them. The cruel treatment extended by the upper classes towards the poor, with their false superiority based on accident of birth more than anything else (itself sometimes a bold deception) was unforgivable. But the poor classes continued, in one way or another, to live up to the less than favourable standards that the rich had set for them. They belligerently struggled to survive with some scrap of dignity, but in the eyes of the rich, this only demonstrated the proven, nonconformist lack of education and breeding. Neither class understood the struggles of the other, nor could they see through them to any common human ground.

If the walls of the city could talk, they would cry in outrage at what they had seen, many would have crumbled (and some did) under the weight of it all. Far too much for one city to endure. The walls protested that they were nothing more than innocent bystanders, brick structures designed and built in good faith. But they moaned that they were not impervious and over several decades, hatred and resentment was absorbed into their mortar and seeped into the very substance of their brick so that even they, the once-neutral city walls could not be trusted to impart fair judgement.

The walls themselves began to fight with one another. A few of the more sympathetic older buildings in the financial district who remembered their neutrality and refused to take sides, crumbled under the pressure of their peers, bits of cornices falling down to kill unfortunate municipal workers on the street below. The poor, stricken building would then sink into helpless decay, its elevators would stop working, bannisters would weaken, windows would refuse to open and doors would stubbornly refuse to close. Surrounding buildings would look on smugly, a chorus of the creed of the status quo ringing out from their windows.

Despite all outward appearances, some good will managed to reside in the chinks of some walls in even the wealthy downtown streets. The Catholic Church was not the owner of such buildings. In those circles, their concern was more about wealth and influence than righteousness. In reality, the morals preached by the Church were more readily absorbed through a spirit of good will and ignorance and into the spartan chapels of lowly suburban and rural parishes.

It seemed that even Mother Nature was under military command. Some of the city's buildings whispered stories through about the inhumane way in which they were forced to imprison left-wing political sympathisers, but the events they witnessed were ordered to be swept up by the wind, carried to the garbage dumps and dropped. These testimonials, unwanted by the establishment, were also known to be scattered over deserted grounds at the city outskirts to be buried along with other terrible memories. But the seeds of the memories germinated underneath newly-formed shantytowns and the stories, like the makeshift shelters, sprouted into fresh crops of social resentment.

The walls were much older than the dictatorship. Earlier they had witnessed the exchange of hundreds of political favours for personal power. They saw ideologies thrown onto the back shelves of corner closets where they were forgotten and covered in dust. They saw publicly righteous men privately horde brown paper bags full of money. They saw illiterate individuals awarded posts that required higher education in exchange for temporary party loyalties. They witnessed uninformed decisions out of concert with the ruling parties but in keeping with personal ambitions, causing havoc and opening the way to civil unrest.

For centuries, the walls of congress were privy to the methods used by elected officials to allow foreign and local companies to reap profit at the expense of the people. In fact, some walls became cynical, amused by the growing skill with which elected representatives manipulated their

public, convincing the *pueblo* that not the government, but the corporations were at fault for stealing the country's resources. At the same time,
the government sympathised with the corporations' complaints about
workers who asked for too much. The cynical walls applauded and gave
the shrewd government members a standing ovation for their unmatched
skill as prevaricators. Representatives congratulated each other for their
artful fuelling of resentment between the companies and the workers
while they innocently washed their hands of any responsibility.

Orlando had managed with his wealth and friends in high places to present himself as a man of stature. Others dared not question for
fear of offending him. This cultivated deference was what provided him
with his tight circle of security. He was careful to appease his acquaintances (Orlando never had any real friends) so that they never had reason
to investigate his background. It was very unlikely that someone from
Santiago would be sufficiently motivated to travel to Tocopilla to discover
who he really was. He was a master chameleon conformist. Only the walls
within his lavish 3-bedroom apartment in the privileged neighbourhood
of Vitacura knew of his private negotiations and less than lawful manoeu-
vres, but buildings in this part of town had a certain reputation of being
complicit in white collar crime.

Orlando's investigations into Mariá Jacobé's disappearance led
nowhere. If they knew anything, the walls jealously guarded the information he desperately sought. Sometimes he found himself wandering along
the streets opposite the national archives at the base of the Santa Lucia
park because he knew the gypsies frequented its sidewalks to offer palm
readings and gypsy blessings. Over the past few years he had become accustomed to this bitter-sweet exercise in spite of the fact that he knew it
would fail to bring him comfort. After each episode he would return to
his apartment and pour a few extra glasses of whiskey to help him sleep.

One day he was sitting on a bench in the park examining the faces
of passersby, hoping as always, but knowing deep down that he would
never see Mariá Jacobé's face among them. He looked down at his watch.

He'd been there for hours and it was the third time this week. The sun was setting and he had wasted yet another entire afternoon. He thought back over countless similar days and suddenly something inside of himself switched off and permitted the obvious question. Maybe it was time to let go. But it would mean he'd have to admit defeat, admit she was really gone. He'd have to mourn María Jacobé and he couldn't imagine his life without the hope of seeing her again. He suddenly realised that this hope had disguised itself as his reason for living. It woke him up every morning – Rise and shine. You've got things to do, money to make, perhaps a new lead to follow or even a surprise encounter. But at the end of each day, it laughed in his face because he had come up empty.

Today, for the first time, he saw that this hope was nothing more than a traitor that was slowly killing him, beating him to death one evening at a time. In fact, it was torture in disguise, and in a twisted way, he had become trapped as its sadistic participant. This afternoon he realised with a certainty that dropped without warning from the blue sky that it was time to move on. For the first time since driving away from Boldo's deserted camp in Tocopilla those years ago, he resolved to stop searching. Suddenly it became the right decision, and for the moment at least, he steeled himself for it, convinced he would be capable. With fresh determination, he stood up to leave, promising himself this would be the last time he would come to this park. Resisting a strong urge to scan the group of gypsy women who brushed past him to enter the park, he quickly crossed the street and was picked up by the crowd that pushed its way down the stairs to the metro station.

CHAPTER 35

Clorinda

Tocopilla, 2001

"Señor Ortega," Clorinda exhaled his name in a prolonged sigh. She was sitting across from him at his niche, which looked particularly dull and bleak today. Even the skies were not as blue as usual. Morning haze lingered over the mountain peaks and foamy grey waves rolled in from a dark sea over the dismal, uninviting beach. It was almost time for *siesta* on a mild Tuesday afternoon. She had gladly exchanged a restless hour laying on her bed looking up at the stained wooden ceiling for an early visit with Señor Ortega. Clorinda had wisely donned a heavier than usual long-sleeved sweater that hung past the hips of a what she now considered a boring blue knit circle skirt.

She did not feel particularly inspired by anything today and, although she tried not to transmit an unnecessarily depressed state of mind to Señor Ortega, she was afraid he had already detected it. She reached up to brush some dust from the sill of his niche, checking to ensure the pen she had hidden behind his name board was still there. She replaced the dried carnation with the new one she had lifted from a nearby grave. Just one – she said to the soul in that grave – just one, it won't be missed. Bless you for your contribution.

"How is my tapestry progressing, you wonder?" She posed to the niche the same question that she herself had been pondering since early this morning. The day had started badly, already destined for gloom. It was nothing she could put her finger on, perhaps just the constant worry over the lack of progress of her life's work.

As was her habit, she had walked directly to her loom after she got out of bed, pausing to look at the yellow daisy communion between her and Señor Ortega, reaching over to lightly touch the grey patch that was himself and to wish him a good morning with a quick lick of her tongue. Normally that gave a spark to her day, but today Señor Ortega still appeared to be asleep. Disappointed, she stepped over to Santa Sara, picking up a cloth to absently brush some dust from her head and shoulders. Santa Sara smiled down appreciatively.

That morning as Clorinda sat at her table in the patio sipping tea and nibbling on day-old bread and black olives, she addressed herself to the most important section of her otherwise blank tapestry. "Señor Ortega, you appear more grey than usual today." She glanced up at the dull sky and then back at his grey threads. They quivered slightly under the light breeze that swooped down into the patio. It was well beyond time to employ some of the bright fibres from her plastic bags that waited patiently to be put to use. Several months had passed since she had guaranteed them a future on the front lines of her life's work. She had picked and coaxed them from their current situation in an English knit jersey, separating the colours from one another, undoing their alliances and in return for their cooperation she had promised they would be part of an important scene in her tapestry. Unfortunately, she was still unable to envision that scene.

She reached over for the bag containing the balls of English polyester-cotton blend and dragged it towards her chair and, as an afterthought, she pulled over another bag, this one branded with the nationally-recognised red 'Ripley' logo. None of the fibre in either of these bags was anything special but she was fond of the colours – one was strong red and orange and the other was deep forest green and heavy navy blue. She stored them in separate bags not because they were categorised as one type being more refined than the other, but simply because she had recycled the different colours at different times.

This morning she felt the impatient balls could be placated for her tardiness if she experimented with them a bit, and who knows – maybe the playfulness would be inspirational. So she emptied both bags onto the table, unravelled some of the balls, enjoying the feel of the strands between her fingers as she twisted one with another, and moved them around like pieces on a game board.

"Don't pout, Señor Ortega, we are experimenting here." She winked at the grey patch that was frowning at her from a few paces away. "I am aware that these samples contain a high percentage of man-made fibre, but there is no need to show your elitist side. After all, there is a place for every type and quality in my work. Although I understand the difference, I do not judge based on class." She wagged her index finger at Señor Ortega's grey patch. "I expect you to be as tolerant and patient of these less-refined materials as I am. We are partners in this now and it's important that we have an understanding. Why do I have the feeling you woke up on the wrong side of the bed this morning?"

Now as she looked up from her seat in front of his cemetery niche she sensed his mood was still solemn and she berated the mid-afternoon sun for its half-hearted effort to brighten the sky over Tocopilla. She turned her face to Señor Ortega's concrete façade. "We need a change. Maybe I should invite you for a walk. We've never done that before. I can show you my favourite places." Her heart fluttered as she pictured Señor Ortega smiling down at her as they strolled along the streets of Tocopilla. He would shorten his long strides to accommodate her smaller steps. His distinctive, slight limp and her crab-like sideways style – two different aspects of a shared soul leaving their footprints over the same ground.

Clorinda explained in a half-whisper as she set off. "I haven't visited the Virgin on the hill for years because I have my own Virgin and I also reacquainted myself with Santa Elvira at the cemetery... but it will be nice to pay a visit to the grotto on the hill. You never know where you'll find inspiration." She smiled hopefully and felt Señor Ortega warming her side. She leaned towards him, which exaggerated her off-kilter style of walking.

She climbed around the hill, and up the stoney path that hadn't changed much over the years. She stumbled awkwardly up towards the grotto, slipping on the loose gravel, occasionally leaning into the ground with her fingertips for balance. It was a steep path and further from the edge of town than she remembered. She stopped to catch her breath and looked down over the tops of buildings towards the sea.

The landscape was littered with rows of rusty roofs between grey asphalt roads and oil-stained cement back patios, garments dotting the clotheslines, dogs asleep in the middle of everywhere, cats stretched out along fences, vultures circling above it all. The cemetery, which covered several blocks of land in the midst of residential streets, was a miniature city of its own, with walls and brightly painted, dense structures that were more alive – with their decorative awnings, striped umbrellas, *fútbol* team flags – than the rest of the town. Señor Ortega's official home was there now.

"We can see your niche from here, Señor Ortega." Clorinda pointed it out, one eye closed, lining it up with the index finger at the end of her outstretched arm, like the sight of a telescope. She shifted her telescopic finger to the left, and squinted down on what would be her tapestry hanging on the loom in her patio, her life's work with Señor Ortega's grey patch, as yet physically unassuming, but actually overpowering in the sheer knowledge of its presence.

"There is a story about two lovers who came to visit this Virgin. They were young and their families forbid them to be together but they knew they could not live without one another. Do you know this story, Señor Ortega?" She didn't wait for a response. "So they made a pact. They agreed to meet here, beside this grotto, they embraced one another and then threw themselves, still wrapped in each other's arms, down the hill. They rolled, hanging on to each other, from here all the way to the sea, and they were found dead, battered by the fall, on the beach still embracing."

Clorinda herself, had always felt somewhat distant from this story, unable to relate to the passionate determination of the lovers to defy their families in such a way... in a sense the young lovers' revenge. She stood looking at where she imagined the lovers' bodies would have been found, from here just broken dots on the black sand.

"What do you think of such a story, Señor Ortega?" She sensed a cold breath on her neck and shivered. "Let's leave." As she stepped and slid down the gravelly path she had the sensation that she was intruding, erasing footprints that were meant to be there for eternity, dangerous steps that forbidden lovers from two different cultures had taken years ago. Señor Ortega was agonising, uncertain, reluctant to follow her down the path. She coaxed him. He had no choice but to go where she led him, his mood increasingly dark.

She set her sights on the beach now, a place on the north side of town. The first time she had walked along this end of the beach was when she was about 12 years old. She escaped her class on a whim in order to run to the garbage dump beyond town in the hope of finding a woollen or perhaps a silk scarf that someone undervalued and had grown tired of.

She cut down past the rocks on the beach in order to keep hidden, just in case Señora Beatrice or any of the neighbours happened to be on the main road. Here she discovered a tide pool that was encircled by huge rounded boulders like inert sea lions warming themselves in the sun. Light glinted off the shallow waters that had settled between them, creating a peaceful, magical atmosphere above a fairy tale pond. Unable to resist, she climbed around the rocks and slid into one of their smooth indented shelves, leaned forward with her elbows on her knees, chin in hands, and she watched as the sea gently washed in and retreated. She sat for hours, forgetting entirely about the possibility of the potential wool or a silk scarf at the garbage dump.

The tide rose slowly and as she watched, mesmerised, a mermaid/angel creature magically took form in the centre of the pool. The mermaid lay flat on her back, layers of ethereal satin and lace undulating around her body, her mermaid tail hidden by beautiful sea-blue patterns on cotton circle-skirts. Flowered gossamer angel wings sketched themselves back and forth across the surface, and long dark mermaid hair floated in and out around them. The water in the pool rose with the tide and the mermaid silently disappeared into the deepening blue.

Before Señor Ortega returned to live in Tocopilla, and especially after her father died, Clorinda often took refuge in the tranquility of this tide pool. She got lost in the timelessness and other-worldliness of it. At first she tried to will the mermaid to reappear, squinting her eyes to conjure the image. But over the years, she learned that it was beyond her control, that the mermaid appeared sometimes and other times not, but either way, when she finally stood up to take leave of the place, she felt a heavy sadness mixed with uncertain joy. She never analysed the feeling other than to admit it was irresistible. It was the memory of this mysterious, contradictory emotion that attracted her time and again to the location.

Today Clorinda sensed the same magic as she sat on the smooth boulder at the edge of the tide pool. Señor Ortega sat silently beside her and she could feel his deep inhalations as they watched the mermaid rise to the surface, water rippling around her arms that were covered in an embroidered long-sleeved cotton blouse, her young rapturous face looking up towards Señor Ortega. They were like two spirits captured in a wave beyond time. Clorinda studied them both. He seemed to have forgotten about her in the presence of the mermaid.

Clorinda turned to reprimand Señor Ortega for excluding her. After all, the mermaid was her discovery. And Señor Ortega was her closest friend.

That either spirit should threaten to come between them was unacceptable. She vowed to keep him away from her tide pool in the future. She would, instead, force him to focus his attention on her life's work. After all, once her work was completed, he would be rewarded with her company beyond this lifetime.

CHAPTER 36

Orlando Ortega

Santiago, 1983

Making money in collaboration with government officials was so easy that he often sat alone in his apartment at the end of the day, whiskey glass in hand, threw back his head, and laughed out loud. After nearly nine years in Santiago, he no longer had to make an effort. They were calling him for favours. Government coffers that were filled with 'reserved funds' meant that public disclosure of how money was spent was not required by law. The majority was for military use, but they also spent on voyages, parties, gifts for wives and prostitutes, overseas properties, luxury vehicles, on their children's private foreign education, on their wives' plastic surgery.

In rare cases where spending was required to be more discreet but appetites couldn't be curbed, other methods of obtaining government department money had to be utilised. Orlando benefited most from such instances as a player in the triangulation of funds. He very simply supplied the government with an invoice for nonexistent services, accepted the cheque in payment for nothing, and split the cash with the official who had arranged it all. Since there were no audits or compulsory public disclosure of records, corruption was rampant and Orlando saw no reason not to profit from it.

Because he spoke English, he was invited to participate in negotiations for the purchase of military supplies, first for small-ticket items like

land vehicles. Later he began to lobby on behalf of the salesman of heli-
copters and small war planes. Foreign companies expected to pay money
under the table to help win their bids and Orlando profited handsomely.

His life became one, long cocktail party in which he drank on the
terraces of backyard pools in the evenings, and on weekends he drove his
Bel Air through the central valleys and along beach-side highways and
found his way to quaint hideaway restaurants. He went deep-sea fishing
on friends' yachts and learned how to sail his own sleek boat. He played
at being the owner of three vineyards and a couple of orchards, and even
invested in a salmon farm in the south.

He avoided businesses that were outwardly violent, because he had
discovered the genteel, more civilised white-collar techniques of turning
a profit, and he learned that even a man from humble origins such as his
could deceive the most highly respected personalities of the time. There
was no need to mix with less educated, more brutish businessmen, and
if he inadvertently crossed their paths, he quickly turned a blind eye and
moved away. He never rocked the boat and never exposed his personal
prejudices. The key was the all-important first impression, maintaining
a cool head, confidence and style. He often recalled the sales pitch Boldo
had made just before he bought the Bel Air and wondered if Boldo was as
wise as his own advice. Orlando maintained the car's impeccable condition in order to keep up with his reputation as 'the man with the mint red
Bel Air convertible.'

By now, the majority of his wealth was safe in Swiss banks and off-
shore investments, including accounts he had opened under his mother's
name, she being too naïve to understand what she had signed and he, of
course, possessing full power of attorney and absolute control.

Orlando met Colonel Rodrigo Müller-Von Koffman one warm
summer evening at a modest cocktail party thrown by another medium-
ranking official, who was a friend of a friend. It was good business to keep
widening his circle, and he had a nose for accepting only the most useful
of invitations. Experienced in the game, Orlando firmly believed in the

old adage of 'it's not what you know, but who you know,' the basic law of the Chilean jungle which held true in regards to anything from obtaining a top political post to getting the freshest cut of meat at the corner butcher shop. That particular evening, his nose set him on a winding path that would eventually lead him to a destination where he never in his wildest dreams would have thought to find himself.

Orlando's interest was piqued more by Rodrigo's name than by his mid-grade military rank. Probably Rodrigo's German last name, given the prestige associated with immigrant families from Germany, was the sole reason he had been invited to the party. Rodrigo, a fair-skinned man who also happened to be from the north (the town of Mejillones, about 2 hours south of Tocopilla), interested Orlando not just because he would have expected him to be a dark-skinned '*moreno*' like most northerners, but because he was a slippery sort of character who, had he not been so obviously comfortable in these surroundings, would have been suspect. There was something about him that made the hair on the back of Orlando's neck stand on end.

At the time, Rodrigo was staying at a posh downtown hotel, having produced a letter from a general stationed in Antofagasta, guaranteeing him the full attention and support of local authorities while on an undisclosed military mission. Rodrigo had arrived, he said, with two other officers who were, from what Orlando was able to deduce from Rodrigo's discreet inferences, agents of DINA, Pinochet's secret intelligence agency. DINA was something Orlando preferred to stay clear of, having seen their less-than-subtle tactics employed not only in service of their country but for personal gratification. He did not want his reputation soiled by even the slightest hint that he may have a connection to the group. Therefore, he decided to gracefully depart the company of Colonel Rodrigo and managed to avoid him for the rest of the evening.

The next time he encountered Rodrigo was a year later. Upon initiating a plan to submit several invoices for another of his lucrative never-to-be-completed studies that he had negotiated with an associate inside the department of public works, Orlando's assistant reported a troubling new series of stamp duty taxes required to set up the new company through which to run the invoices. Finally annoyed with this abusive and nonsensical process that proved to be a roadblock to future contracts, Orlando stormed into the Civil and Corporate Registry office to deal with the matter himself. He insisted on seeing the man in charge and after several false starts and brief phone calls, was led by a stone-faced secretary who clicked along with an air of frigid self-importance out of the building, down the street to another government building, and finally upstairs to a spacious office which overlooked the Plaza de la Constitución. "This way, Señor." She theatrically waved Orlando into the main office foyer with a mock bow and wry smile.

The office was decorated with furniture made from the finest Chilean hardwood, a modern, elegant sofa and two matching chairs with an end table over an expensive Persian rug, a fully stocked bar, a Chilean flag and coat of arms and the standard-issue framed photograph of General Pinochet with his presidential sash across formal military grey. A man was sitting in a high-back swivel chair, his back to the door, observing the plaza below through his expansive 12th storey window.

"Enchanting view." He said without turning around.

"Quite."

"Help yourself to a drink. Whiskey is it?"

"Thank you." Orlando walked to the bar. This was not quite the scenario he had expected, but he would cooperate in his customary coolness and play a game of wait-and-see.

Glass in hand he settled down into one of the armchairs and waited in silence. When the man behind the desk finally swivelled around Orlando found himself facing Colonel Rodrigo Müller-Von Koffman, grinning from ear to ear. "I'm delighted to see you again."

Orlando leaned forward and gently placed his glass on the table as he tried to absorb the situation without revealing his surprise and sudden discomfort.

"What happened to your uniform?"

"I don't wear it anymore. My military duties have been replaced by a more important civilian role. I don't question the powers that be."

Orlando suspected this was a cover for a newly-assigned position within DINA but he couldn't understand how it would be connected to this office. He reached for his glass again and took a sip. "What have you got to do with the excessive stamp duty?"

"Oh, that." Rodrigo executed a brief royal wave of his hand through the air. "Well, don't worry. I fixed that little problem while you were walking over here." He explained it without explaining it. "Tell your assistant he need only mention your name next time. I have put you on my special list."

"Much appreciated. You're very kind."

"No problem at all, my friend. It's my pleasure."

Orlando did not like the reference of 'friend,' but he held his tongue and waited for whatever would come next, fully expecting Rodrigo to launch into some unwelcome gossip about people in high places. But Rodrigo was apparently a man of greater discretion than Orlando gave him credit for. Rodrigo rose and walked around the desk to shake Orlando's hand in a polite gesture which suggested the meeting was over. Orlando was content to have underestimated him in this instance, but he could feel his skin crawl.

"I'm having a small dinner party tomorrow night. Please come. My secretary," he gestured towards the outer office, "will give you the details." Orlando's acceptance of the invitation was taken for granted.

The party wasn't as small as Rodrigo would have had him believe. When Orlando pulled into the gated villa on Málaga Street, he recognised several vehicles belonging to other of his business associates, both in the private sector and in the military. Tasteful Latin jazz filtered into the air outside and upon entering, it faded behind the deep monotone fog of male voices mingled with women's polite laughs and high-pitched girlish twitters. The scene was a mixture of muted colours with mostly black

suits and military green. Had it not been for the khaki green, they could
have been on the grounds of any Hollywood mansion owned by one of
the movie stars of the time.

Orlando accepted a glass of whiskey from a waiter and mingled
with the crowd, greeting acquaintances as he made his way towards the
pool at back of the house. It was there that he saw Rodrigo in an animated conversation with the men he recognised as DINA operatives. They
all glanced in his direction and averted their eyes before casually parting company. Glasses in hand, fixed smiles under heavy moustaches, the
DINA men nodded politely at the ladies and brushed Orlando's shoulders
as they walked by, one on either side of him, like two dogs sniffing raw
meat. Rodrigo had turned with a broad smile, beckoning Orlando to follow him across the patio.

"So glad you could make it. What do you think of the place?" He
swept his arm in a wide circle with the power of a symphony conductor
about to signal a thunderous finale. There was a glint in his eyes, something sharp, like the tip of a knife. Orlando faced him, a million short
hairs fiercely prickling the back of his neck.

"Let me tell you a most interesting story..." Rodrigo briefly touched
Orlando's arm, indicating they should walk away from the crowd and
towards the privacy of the manicured hedges. Their conversation was
mitigated by the gurgling fountain whose water spilled over into the garden and trickled between the rocks. As Orlando listened, whiskey glass in
mid-air, he could feel his life wash away and sink into the sand where the
fountain drained into Rodrigo's back garden and beyond.

CHAPTER 37

Orlando Ortega

British Columbia, Canada, 1983

Señor Orlando del Transito Ortega de Riveras' escape from Chile
was silent and without incident. The flight attendants in the first class
section of the plane, true to their promise, ensured that his trip was pleasant – uniformed Canadian airline employees satisfying requirements of
comprehensive rules that he would later recognise as characteristically
Canadian in precision, efficiency and courtesy.

He breezed through customs at the Vancouver international termi-
nal, exited the building to stand on the sidewalk and looked up into the
sky. There was a cold wind and he pulled his sweater to his chin as he tried
to find his bearings.

The sky and the waters of the Pacific Ocean would be his only connection to Chile but he couldn't see the ocean. To say he felt lost was an
understatement. He was going to travel inland to a northern interior mining village called Wells located in the Rocky Mountain foothills of British
Columbia. He thought of 'Wells Fargo.'

Jorge had highly recommended the town of Wells to Orlando, making several obscure references to its benefits as a small community in a
gold mining region. It had apparently been abandoned by bigger corporations because of low profitability but was perfect for small operators
who knew their business, especially if the market price peaked, as was
predicted. Other than that, Orlando knew nothing.

Orlando's ride north was on what he could only describe as a third-world bus, a relatively small and mundane grey machine with the illustration of a starving dog racing across its metal exterior. Its quiet blue and grey interior was conducive to muscle cramps that uncomplaining passengers accepted in silence because they did not expect any more from their buses. The bus crew consisted of only a driver, not even a steward to offer tea and sandwiches and no first-class option. He looked around at the other passengers who were a mixture of elderly pensioners, hippies past their prime and native Indians.

He was a foreigner in the midst of what could easily be described as a group of local aliens, all cramped into this racing dog machine that didn't race at all, but panted and crawled its way north, first past expansive farms with modern equipment and storage facilities, then along canyon roads that were wide in comparison to the ones he was accustomed to. The countryside was impressive with its densely forested hills and snow-covered coniferous trees. At first he was amazed by the never-ending forests but long before the end of the trip he grew tired of seeing nothing but identical tree trunks and the eternal telephone wires strung between poles on either side of the road.

The highways of this wealthy northern civilisation teamed with logging trucks with red flags waving off the ends, auto carriers lugging up hills towards new owners, produce trailers, many of them probably hauling Chilean fruit, and cattle trucks with their wide-eyed, soon-to-be-slaughtered cargo. Zooming past the bus were more pickup trucks than he had seen in his entire life. They were driven by men wearing baseball caps, usually unaccompanied. He suddenly felt lonely and longed for the familiar silent nakedness of the Andean roads and the barren copper-coloured mountain peaks that reached up into the clear blue Chilean sky. He pictured the fishermen's wooden houses sprinkling their poverty along the rugged Pacific shore, small colourful boats bouncing on the waves that washed between the rocks. He tasted homesickness for the first time, and cursed this sadness that threatened to poison the start of his new life.

It was less than a month ago that he was standing beside the fountain in Rodrigo's elegant Santiago garden. Orlando recalled the thick lump of panic in his throat and the throbbing in his temples as Rodrigo coolly recounted how he had scraped together certain important details of Orlando's life and explained how, should one of them in particular be brought to the attention of the General, it could cause him a serious amount of grief. Rodrigo bent down to gather some dry leaves and held them in the palm of his hand. He crushed them with his fingers and let them fall into the stream that bubbled its way through the rock garden. They were carried off on the surface of the lightly gurgling, laughing water.

Orlando gazed out the window at the monotony of power poles and tree trunks and remembered the series of events that resulted in his current reality.

Orlando's first response to Rodrigo's threats was not to run, but to launch a counterattack. He had been ambushed but would not remain on the defensive. Two could play this game. He wasted no time initiating his own investigation into Rodrigo's background. Fortunately, Rodrigo's earlier mention of his northern origins gave Orlando a place to start and he called his *secretarios* into action.

The *secretarios* boarded the first bus heading south from Tocopilla to Mejillones. Orlando pictured the bus squeaking to a brief halt in the dirt off the highway in Michilla, the secretarios' dark glasses reflecting images of miners who descended the bus with their backpacks and waited to pile onto a truck that would take them up to the mine. Some things would probably never change.

The secretarios would get off on the main street in Mejillones, and wander into the central plaza to chat with the toothless old men who sat there for a good part of each day regurgitating the week's gossip. The plaza was typical of all small northern towns. Its wooden benches with broken backs and sloped seats distributed in no specific pattern throughout, stone walkways in disrepair lined the perimeter and crisscrossed the plaza alongside dusty would-be flower beds, the occasional palm tree offering a bit of shade. A few dogs curled up to sleep in the dry fountain, no one would remember the last time it was filled with water.

The buildings surrounding the plaza were mostly two-storey wooden ones that had seen better days. Worn paint, once beautiful lattices still supporting a few naked vines that refused to die, stained lace curtains hanging limply out of dusty windows, a small chalkboard leaning against the windowsill of a cafe with its misspelled words advertising the menu of the day.

The important buildings were around the corner and along the waterfront, including the museum that was once a small Bolivian fortress. Undoubtedly the most well-kept building in town, its painted white walls, red trimmed tower and roof stood out as the local architectural marvel. Rows of residential buildings fanned out from the centre of town, the majority with unremarkable wooden sides and tall double-door entrances flanked by grilled windows.

The *secretarios* hit the jackpot when they ran into old José-José the chief gossip of the plaza, most respected because of his accurate, long-term memory. Sharp as a razor, they were told. Beyond that, no one understood how José-José could have become the hub of news and information because he had a terrible and often debilitating stutter. In fact, his nick-name used to be José-José-José in reference to the number of times he spit it out before finally making the leap to pronounce his last name. His nickname was eventually shortened to José-José for the sake of expediency.

In any case, José-José could be relied on to tell a story from beginning to end, even if it took him from noon until midnight. He considered himself, and perhaps rightly so, an indispensable local figure whose public cried out for him. It was either his stoic public service or the sheer challenge of finishing sentences that provoked him to stand in front of his bench each day to entertain his seated audience. He jerked his nose towards the sky as he stalled on one word after the other and his public nodded their heads in unison like a flock of woodpeckers on a perch. If anyone dared to intervene, finishing a sentence for him, he would shoot them an annoyed glance and, as a form of unusual punishment, would retreat to the beginning of the phrase where he repeated the whole thing again with exaggerated intonations. Therefore, experienced listeners did not dare to interrupt. Not if they wanted the entire story in a reasonable amount of time – which the *secretarios* did.

Interpreting José-José's stories not only required patience, but a keen ear because the stutter was compounded by his toothless pronunciation. Nevertheless, he had no competition as the best source of information in town. What he lacked in public speaking skills, he made up for with elastic ears and a brain that was a sponge for details. The *secretarios* persevered and José-José did not disappoint. It took four full days to extract the juicy information about Rodrigo, during which they sat on the bench looking up at José-José through their dark glasses, frequently removing them to wipe off the constant rain of spit and often massaging the backs of their necks to alleviate the strain of so much nodding.

On the fifth day, they tripped over each other in a race to rent a booth at the local telephone company to report their findings to Orlando.

First and foremost, Rodrigo Müller-Von Koffman completed his compulsory 2-year military service more than 15 years ago as a private. He had not served recently in any capacity, especially as an officer.

José-José had it on good authority that Rodrigo was nothing more than a lazy *mamón* (big mama's boy), and that he was known around town as a small-time con artist. His father was a tailor, now a fragile old man, who was forced to continue working long past the days, months and years that he should have retired because he had no pension and his son was useless.

As the *secretarios* jostled for position in the cramped phone booth – each one in turn grabbing the receiver to interject, knocking each other's glasses off and generally tussling like two overgrown schoolboys in shiny black suits – they summed up José-José's four-day account in 15 minutes. After that, Orlando picked up the investigation through contacts in Santiago in order to paint the full picture.

Rodrigo's last name was indeed Müller-Von Koffman; he had been honest about that. His parents were first-generation from Germany, and the rumour was that his father's brother (who brought the family to Chile) was an officer in Hitler's army. Although no one could be certain, the basis for this assumption was that he jealously guarded two valuable paintings that he had brought with him from Europe. The paintings disappeared right after his death, his own brother (Rodrigo's father) selling them for almost nothing to an art dealer from Santiago before the old man's tomb had even been sealed.

Rodrigo's father was not a good businessman, and what had once been an elegant tailor shop in the centre of town, was soon figuratively and literally hanging by a thread. He was forced to sell the property and buy a smaller house, which served as the family residence as well a location for what was left of his tailoring business.

Less than a decade into the dictatorship, Rodrigo saw an opportunity to play out what resulted in the most successful con of his life. One night at the corner bar, he made the acquaintance of a young military clerk named Carmelo who worked in the local sergeant's office. Rodrigo was about to abandon the conversation when an offhand comment drew him back in. After several mugs of beer, Carmelo chuckled about how it was possible to do anything if one was a military officer, bona fide, or not. Rodrigo's eared visibly pricked up, his face stretching into an engaging smile as he encouraged Carmelo to continue.

As Carmelo confirmed a very interesting possibility indeed, Rodrigo's smile became so elongated that the corners of his lips extended beyond the sides of his head, like an out-of-control rubber band. He learned about the *junta* had a headache trying to deal with impersonation of military officers. There had been a number of instances in which resourceful men had illegally obtained documentation and military uniforms in order to demand (and be awarded) free food, travel, and lodging. Carmelo told him that it happened more often and more easily than most people realised and a memo had been circulated to alert all military offices. However, in Carmelo's opinion the problem would be mostly ignored simply because of numerous other concerns that took precedence. His commanding officer, for instance, considered the memo nothing more than a busy-body piece of work that added to his workload.

This unlikely bit of information, divulged for no other reason than to make conversation in a shoddy corner bar in Mejillones changed the course of both Rodrigo's and consequently, Orlando's life.

As it turned out, Rodrigo's father had recently been commissioned to mend military uniforms and so he was in possession of a full range of standard military-issue fabric, lapel tags and insignias. Rodrigo would have no problem looking like an officer; the only thing missing was documentation. So he went to work on Carmelo.

After a few weeks of employing his own cunning charm, Rodrigo converted Carmelo into a most devoted admirer. He knew how homesick Carmelo was for his family in a small town at the southern tip of the country and played to his desire for a father-figure. Rodrigo could see the admiration in Carmelo's eyes and when he was certain he had brought him far enough along, he decided to play his hand. He took the high road.

"I need your help, my good friend. I am about to embark on a mission that will serve our little town, that will help bring us out of poverty, enable our port, empower our fishermen, and generally improve life as much as possible during these difficult times."

Carmelo was attentive and unquestioning. Even though his hometown was thousands of miles away, he could relate their situation to that of the port town of Mejillones. His eyes watered with the memory of the green, tree-lined coast and his mother and sisters in their heavy woollen sweaters waving goodbye to him from the porch the day he left in service of his country. If he could do anything at all to alleviate their plight, he would, but given that he was more than 2,000 miles north, the best he could do was contribute for the good of the locals here, in the name of his mother and sisters. Besides, Señor Rodrigo was a generous, intelligent man currently without means and he would be honoured to lend a hand.

"Carmelo, I have an important contact in Santiago but neither he nor I have the finances to carry out my plan. I need to ask for immediate help from somewhere much more powerful, from the only institution that cares about our country. Unfortunately they have much broader responsibilities at the moment and are not aware of, and therefore are not able to concern themselves with the specific troubles of our town. I would ask them myself, but you know how slowly the military can work sometimes..."

Carmelo nodded and waited, his eyes glassing over, failing to comprehend where Rodrigo was leading him with this, but eager just the same, to understand the logic of someone so intelligent and well-intentioned.

"Yes, well, Carmelo," he continued carefully, in his just-right, smooth, instructive tone, "In many ways the military is the most efficient institution in Chile, but if they don't understand the gravity of a situation, the problem will be passed around on a sheet of paper from one desk to another, perhaps even fall into someone's garbage bin by mistake and it will get lost, therefore missing an opportunity to save our community. A case in point is the memo about officer impersonation you, yourself, told me about some time ago."

"So, I was thinking that perhaps... just perhaps..." He conjured his most thoughtful and somewhat pained expression, "if I sacrificed myself by doing something that we both know is ever so slightly illegal but at the same time the right thing to do, the necessary action can be taken for the good of Mejillones. But I have to go to Santiago to deal with the men at the top."

Carmelo raised his eyebrows but was unable to form a question in response. This was a little bit complicated.

"What I'm asking Carmelo, my loyal friend, is for you to help me to do the right thing."

Carmelo nodded again, eyes still slightly glassy. Try as he might, he could not clear the fog that hovered around his brain.

"I need to do just what you had told me about the first night we met. Remember? We talked about men disguised as 'militaries' in order to obtain food and travel."

The clouds in Carmelo's brain dissipated slightly. He nodded affirmatively and Rodrigo nodded with him.

"Yes, I need to become a 'military' in order to get to Santiago and help my contact take action to rebuild the commerce for this area."

Rodrigo's altruistic plan was bound for success if Carmelo would agree to take the responsibility (and therefore the credit) for one very tiny but extremely important duty. And of course, it would be something he could proudly relate to his family back home.

"Yes, yes I can help."

Even if Carmelo questioned the legality, he had no problem seeing beyond to its truly righteous core. The next day when his sergeant was on duty at the port, he agreed to take dictation from Rodrigo, and he typed, in standard military jargon and format, on official letterhead, instructions that bore the forged signature and personal stamp of the General in Antofagasta.

This was to be the official letter of introduction and passage which bestowed on Rodrigo the rank of Colonel and ordered that he, as bearer of this letter, be awarded the full attention and service deserving of his illustrious status, by all military, governmental and private institutions and companies.

Letter in hand, Rodrigo returned to his father's house and ordered a full set of military uniforms, fit for a decorated colonel of the highest standing, to be paid for by the military *junta*.

Then he set off from Antofagasta for Santiago on a first class seat of a Ladeco Airlines flight, paid for by the military *junta* and installed himself in a sixth floor suite of the Hotel Carrera, also of course, paid for by the military *junta*.

It was from the lobby of this hotel that he made his initial contacts. He was flawless in his role as Colonel on a hush-hush mission and received all the benefits deserving of such an outwardly accomplished and cultured man. Bellboys bowed low, the desk clerks were charmed and vied for his attention, even the cleaning lady left an extra flower and chocolate on his pillow each day. Being quick on his feet he skilfully sidestepped questions and improvised through one situation after another. The fact that his mission was secret was a great advantage. His practice as a small-time con man paid off remarkably well in this new arena and he wondered why he hadn't thought of it earlier. He looked up to the sky and mouthed "Thank you, Carmelo," and that was all the thanks the young recruit ever received. Carmelo was a patient young man and never questioned the outcome of Rodrigo's mission, let alone the lack of communication until he let slip his complaints, over a few beers with one of the harmless gossip friends of José-José a few weeks later. After that, rumours and conjecture floated between the old buzzards in the plaza, where they chewed it over, never mentioning it to anyone else until the *secretarios* went asking.

Things went so well for Rodrigo that before a full month had passed, he was invited into the same circles as Orlando and learned how to turn a quick invoice for a false study. From there he learned from whom he could acquire information on recently expropriated properties and which foreigner paid the best bribes for which services. He met his two DINA associates at a cocktail party and together they designed a small but powerful information gathering network after which they all set up secret foreign bank accounts.

With his DINA associates, and the plethora of information, he then moved easily into the dark but lucrative business of extortion and blackmail. He decided it was time to 'retire' from the military after their first successful big-time blackmail scheme showed unlimited promise. In fact, it was this blackmail victim – none other than a top Minister – who helped position him in the department of corporate registration, through which he eventually arranged to meet Orlando.

General Pinochet had selected Rodrigo's DINA associates to investigate the Minister, an extremely delicate assignment to be carried out with utmost discretion. Pinochet was reluctant to investigate one of his own, but he was under heavy pressure to increase international trade revenue and he knew that someone from inside was interfering with the country's all-important fruit exports. By chance, a DINA operative in Peru heard the name of the Chilean Minister mentioned rather furtively by a Peruvian fruit exporter. From there, Rodrigo's associates were assigned to follow his trail.

Chile's situation was this: feeling helpless and angry, Chilean exiles had helped convince international syndicates, through protest and public education of activists in their new homelands, that the Pinochet regime had to be punished, and that the most effective action was to boycott Chilean products. As a result, organised dock workers at ports of entry to these many countries refused to unload Chilean fruit and it rotted in the containers at the docks. The Chilean export businesses lost money and couldn't afford to pay workers, had no money to transport food within the country itself, and the national and regional economies took a tremendous hit.

Babies in Chilean families from the south to the north were lost to starvation at alarming rates. The government withheld the increasing child mortality figures from the public in order to avoid dealing with these unwanted complications. It had become a very delicate issue.

Therefore, when General Pinochet discovered that an individual had orchestrated a scheme to profit from the situation, he was furious. His fury turned to rage when he suspected it might have been one of his own trusted Ministers who was among those undermining his economy for personal gain.

Because it was common knowledge that fruit was left to rot in foreign ports due to the boycott, the scheme consisted of filling containers destined for North America and Europe with already over-ripe fruit and vegetables, topped with a thin layer of good quality produce. The good fruit that was originally destined for these ports was directed instead to Peru or Bolivia or Argentina. From there it was shipped to its final destinations, falsely labelled as Peruvian or Bolivian or Argentinian produce.

The unsuspecting dock workers unloaded it and bins in stores everywhere were stocked with Chilean fruit, the profit for which went into various private pockets along the way.

Ironically the unsuspecting Chilean exiles who had claimed victory with their boycotts were among those buying and enjoying this Chilean fruit while babies of friends and family at home in Chile died of starvation and as Pinochet and his family and friends remained unscathed.

Sure enough, the investigation literally bore fruit when the trail eventually led the two DINA agents to the Minister in question. Even as professionals they couldn't suppress their excitement about this rich prospect. Instead of reporting their findings to General Pinochet, they reported them to Rodrigo. The three of them plotted to hide the truth from Pinochet, declaring the Minister's innocence, and in the process bringing Pinochet a great measure of relief. He would gladly look down another path, thank you very much.

Meanwhile, Rodrigo arranged a meeting with the Minister and explained rather coolly over a dry martini, that he held the Minister's fate in his hands. The rest was easy. They agreed on a large, regular 'discretion fee' in addition to Rodrigo being awarded the cushy post as head of the corporate registry department through which passed valuable information on new companies and their owners.

Rodrigo concentrated most of his efforts on his new extortion business, gleaming tidbits here and there about businessmen and officials in high places through the department. Most of them were wealthy enough to pay what Rodrigo considered modest amounts of regular 'discretion fees'. It was quite by accident, however, that Rodrigo discovered something he could hold over Orlando's head. He had heard that Orlando was as wealthy, or more so, than most of his usual 'clients,' so it was with great pleasure that he listened to a most interesting story about Orlando's dissident brother (the unlikely source being an Argentinean chauffeur).

As he looked beyond a million tree trunks along the side of the road from the window of this bus that was lumbering through western Canada,

Orlando recalled the night, now just over a month ago, that brought him here. As he and Rodrigo cordially sipped their whiskey beside the gurgling pool in the fairy-tale setting in the garden beyond the pool, Rodrigo was playing his blackmail hand. He revealed what he knew about Orlando helping to smuggle his 'wanted' communist bastard of a brother into the Canadian Embassy in none other than a Mercedes Benz owned by the government of Argentina. Rodrigo congratulated Orlando on the audacity of the operation.

They both knew the grave crime Orlando had committed, especially in light of the national security situation of only a few years ago. Therefore Orlando was 'invited' to join Rodrigo's list of clients, requiring that he pay a hefty sum each month. If Orlando dared to challenge this accusation, Rodrigo would arrange with his DINA associates to release the information to none other than General Pinochet himself, with whom they enjoyed a direct relationship, and Orlando's promising future would be abruptly ended when he was positioned in front of the firing squad.

Orlando's planned counter-attack, in spite of the information uncovered by his northern *secretarios*, would not succeed. He realised that even if he managed to squash Rodrigo like the bug he was, the larger problem of the DINA partners remained. And, considering their power and resources, that would be insurmountable.

The bus lurched to a halt and he found himself disembarking along with the other passengers, at a coffee shop inside a grand log structure on the edge of a snow-covered highway at an unlikely place called '100 Mile House.' One hundred miles from where? – he wondered.

CHAPTER 38

Orlando Ortega

Wells, British Columbia, Canada, 1983-1996

One doesn't live in a country for 13 years without becoming accustomed to places with names like 'Spuzzum' 'Robber's Roost,' 'Moosejaw,' 'Devil's Canyon,' or even 'Wells.' But you are always surprised when you walk down a street in one of these places and you collide with the drifting aroma of fried beef, cumin, onions and garlic and for a fraction of a second you are transported back to the 100-year-old *empanada* emporium on a bustling corner of downtown Santiago. Then for the next two days, all you can think of is standing shoulder-to-shoulder in a Spanish speaking crowd eating a steaming hot *empanada* and drinking Instant Nescafe from a small plastic cup.

Likewise you are knocked off balance by an unexpected wave of sentimentality when, through a second-hand store window, your eye catches a cheap print of a lonely rail car in the middle of a vast desert, and in the background a snow-capped volcano. And suddenly you feel out of place in these other majestic, forested mountains.

Or one morning you find that you can't contain your excitement at the familiar appearance of fresh baking powder biscuits because they are reminiscent of Chilean-style flat bread. And then you are disappointed because they are not.

Orlando had sent his roots into the earth in the small town of Wells, British Columbia and waited for them to take hold. But it was like trying to transplant an organ into a donor with mismatched blood type. Either the place considered him an unwelcome foreign invader or his roots couldn't find enough sustenance in the unfamiliar soil. Whatever it was never became clear. What had recently become obvious however, was that he missed Chile and decided, after all these years, that he was going to go home. He would return a changed man.

Jorge had gone back to Chile almost immediately after Pinochet declared amnesty in 1988. Brave warrior returning to the scene of the battle after it was declared won and over. Although they never contacted each other directly, Orlando's mother had told him that Jorge was back, that he had visited Tocopilla with his wife Elisia and that they were moving south. There were gaps and inconsistencies in the stories about what really happened to Jorge in Canada, but because of his penchant for working towards the greater good and his fluent Spanish he was apparently recruited by the RCMP to work as an undercover narcotics agent. He was 'uncovered' by the dealers and had to flee once again for his life. He returned to Chile and decided to dedicate himself to the cause of the *Mapuche* natives in their battles over land rights in southern Chile, and he settled in Temuco.

Their mother passed away more than five years ago. The official cause of death stated simply 'old age' but Orlando read 'loneliness, abandoned by her sons' in between the lines. At the time, Orlando decided that returning for her funeral was inconvenient, that it was much more simple to wire Jorge money for funeral expenses. He told himself it would be best if he stayed away, spending money on her funeral rather than wasting it on an overseas trip to fight with Jorge in person. But now he admitted that he had been wrong, that he had allowed the antagonism between him and Jorge to be more important than his love of, and loyalty towards his mother (as much as, he had to admit, it was not reciprocated).

Jorge later mailed him photographs of the funeral and the flowers at his mother's niche, saying simply "Wish you were here," and it drove Orlando to a two-week-long drinking binge. He sat in the popular 'Jack O' Clubs' Hotel pub and cried in his beer, blubbering things in Spanish to the young, clueless lumberjacks. A few compassionate drunks shook their heads at each other and patted him on the back. Orlando bought rounds for the house, one after the other, and his sympathetic *amigos* grew in number until his immediate cash ran out. He returned alone to his rented room at the back of the Wells Hotel and when he woke up two days later, he reflected some more on his immediate and not-so-immediate life, something he had become expert in during his years in Canada.

Six months ago Jorge's wife Elisia contacted him to say that Jorge had died after he agonised in hospital for two days, struggling to survive a bullet that had passed through a lung. There had been an armed standoff between some radical *Mapuches* and police at a forestry site. Jorge, not the front-line warrior he always imagined himself, was fatally wounded. His name and photo were flashed twice and for only an instant each time on national TV news reports, and then he was forgotten. All his life he strived for personal fame, seeking recognition as the next Che Guevara. Orlando suspected that Jorge looked down from wherever he was now, shaking his fists and cursing the news editors for not expounding on his history, for failing him, lamenting that his sacrifices had been in vain and that he had been passed over, unappreciated.

Elisia didn't sound heart-broken as she conveyed the bad news about her husband, but Orlando knew it was because she was primed on tranquillizers. He avoided returning for Jorge's funeral, citing the distance as too great, just as he'd done when his mother was buried. The truth was that during his whole life, he'd never felt close to Jorge and the idea of feigning a sorrow that didn't exist and accepting sympathies from people he'd rather forget made him nauseous. Another reason for not returning was that he wanted to avoid Elisia because she would latch onto him like a bloodsucker. So he sent an overly elaborate flower arrangement accompanied by a formal message of bereavement that he hoped expressed the profound sorrow of a loving brother.

Perhaps the relatively recent deaths of his only family members caused him to contemplate his own situation. He had family neither here, nor there, but he felt a thread pulling him back towards Chile. He was being recalled – perhaps for repair – he thought. He was a flawed product who had to return and make things right. It was a time of reckoning. Besides, he was not well.

His decision to return to Chile was not a rejection of Canada; he was content with what this country offered him and he was fully aware that he had not tasted from its vast array of cultural flavours, from its prairie towns and cosmopolitan centres to its Atlantic villages and northern tundra. But he wondered whether he had settled into this peculiar half-forgotten little village for a reason. Perhaps Jorge's curse had been Orlando's blessing. Orlando suspected that Jorge had recommended this forsaken little mining town which was now just a shadow of its former self, in a mean-spirited attempt to frustrate Orlando, to jest, make a mockery of his gold-mining businesses, a payback for him for not joining the South American revolution. But Jorge's plan backfired.

Although he wasn't aware of it when he first arrived, Wells became a hibernation heaven at a time when he needed it most. He hadn't stopped to take stock of where he was or where he would go since the day he ran out of the mine with the rock full of gold in his crotch. Come what may, he had dedicated his life to the pursuit of money. Maybe he had been happy. Maybe not. When he found himself snowed into this little town inhabited mostly by harmless peace-seekers and several misfits who had retreated from society, he forgot that he was himself an alien, and he tossed aside any bitterness he had about leaving Chile to lay back and go with the flow. And no one here was flowing anywhere. So he stayed and learned to appreciate the simple things in life.

The town of Wells was isolated in a beautiful forested setting about 1,200 metres above sea level in the big, silent, cold, heart of the Cariboo Mountains. Its long winters extended into June. He could never have imagined a place with so much snow. But the town was prepared for, or at least accustomed to, it. The houses were designed with steep tin roofs so the snow could slide off before they caved in. Nevertheless Orlando often saw boys with shovels on the roofs, pushing chunks of snow that slid off in thick white crusts. The snow fell into piles at the base of the walls, breaking off long icicles from the eaves troughs on its way down, the sharp, pointed icicles jutting out of the white mounds like so many knives warning you to stay away. The snow piled up and blocked windows, providing extra insulation between the bitterly cold exterior and the cosy interior hideaways.

Orlando often woke up to a white blanket that had fallen silently over the town during the night. He felt he was in a magical wonderland where the landscape of the previous day was wiped out and converted into millions of brilliant crystals glinting into the sunlight, offering a fresh start. The first sound in the morning was the rhythm of someone scraping the sidewalk with a shovel and tossing snow aside as they cleared the way from their front door to the street.

Children who were bundled up in thick one-piece ski suits, mittens tucked into their sleeves, little faces wrapped with woollen scarves, trudged to school in knee-deep snow leaving snowmen and snow angels in their paths. In the afternoons he saw pink-faced children on wooden toboggans racing out of control down steep slopes, small icicles forming on the tips of their hair. He was reminded of the kids in northern Chile sliding down sand dunes on pieces of cardboard, the heat of the sand and the friction burning through the cardboard and sizzling into their bottoms. Amazing how children from extreme climates found entertainment in exactly the same way.

Wells' location in this high valley was a skiers' paradise and years ago someone had cleared the slope of a mountain looking towards town and built a rope tow and a long wooden ski jump (now worse for wear). From their kitchen windows residents could watch skiers zigzag down the slopes and fly off the end of the ramp. Perimeters of nearby lakes (of which there were plenty) were cleared and converted to skating rinks. The local curling rink down on the flats was a hub of social activity, especially during 24-hour bonspiels and the two hotel pubs filled up each night warming the bellies of loggers and a few old gold prospectors with more beer and whiskey than they could handle. Pickup trucks loaded with snow mobiles could be seen parked along the side of the road as they paused in town to buy last-minute provisions before heading into the snow-covered wilderness beyond.

Orlando was fascinated by this life in winter. He bought a hardcover notebook with 100 sheets of lined paper and began to write descriptions of his first impressions. Should the wonder and novelty of the place ever wear off, threatening to make life here appear normal, he could read his journals and remember how bizarre it really was. This notebook was the first of Orlando's dozens of journals.

When the snow finally melted in June, the town and the hills around it blossomed. Cold, clear water began to trickle down over rocks and around the base of tree trunks, playing hide and seek under spongy moss that thrived among the thick undergrowth. Dogwood flowers and wild roses bloomed. Wild strawberry plants unfolded their leaves. Buds opened up on the trees, sap ran down the bark and all manner of bugs and insects came to life. Birds returned and built nests in a flurry of activity. Moose foraged in the swamp on the flats at the eastern edges of the town. Mother bears and their cubs could be seen at a distance. Beaver and otters swam in the creeks beside the highway.

The breeze that drifted through the valley absorbed all the smells of an abundant, fresh new life. Orlando was dizzy with the mountain scent of spring. Of everything he knew he would miss when he left this valley, it would be the pure forest air. Something as simple as breathing was cause to give thanks to the universe. In Wells he learned to appreciate nature.

In summer the town was alive with local festivals and artists' workshops, the area's natural beauty a source of inspiration and wild ideas. Tourists passed through Wells on their way to Barkerville, now a government-sponsored ghost town whose reason for being was to celebrate its short-lived boom as an old-west gold rush town of the 1860s. Its narrow streets now gone quiet, had once bustled with all class of people, from Chinese immigrant workers, international businessmen, to prospectors and prostitutes from everywhere, all profiting from the gold in the hills. Residents loved to brag about how Barkerville was once larger than San Francisco and how a fire that started in a brothel brought the town to its knees.

Nowadays, because Wells was also the entrance to a pristine national park with a chain of protected mountain lakes, the area attracted hikers and outdoorsmen. Like snowmobilers in the winter, the summer adventurers crowded into the few small cafes to take advantage of the last-stop at the edge of civilisation before heading into the forested mountains and lakes beyond.

Between the time he decided to abandon the town and when he actually departed for Chile, Orlando spent most of his days strolling through its streets and wandering up into the surrounding hills so he could look down onto the innocent, stoic wooden structures with a growing nostalgia.

After 13 years, Orlando had 87 hardcover volumes of hand-written accounts that began as observations and descriptions of experiences in this little town. The world had opened up to him more in this half-deserted, snow-covered, pathetic-looking, wooden little *pueblo* than through any of the places he had lived in Chile, from desert town to capital city. In large part it was because the place afforded him time for reflection. As the years passed and he became accustomed to his new surroundings, his written description of the northern idiosyncrasies digressed into comparisons of life as he knew it at opposite ends of the world and then took a leap into documenting his personal philosophies, expounding on everything from the meaning of life to the relevance of field mice.

His life here was not the business venture he had initially anticipated and he woke up one day after a few years and realised that he couldn't remember when he had last dreamed up money-making schemes, calculated the potential of a mining stake or considered return on potential capital investments. He had evolved from a human calculator to someone not altogether identifiable, but with whom he felt somewhat satisfied. His penchant for making money was expropriated by his newly found love for writing prose.

When Orlando moved to Wells in the winter of 1983, the town was well-past its prime, the two gold mines having closed nearly two decades beforehand, taking more than three-quarters of the population with it and leaving small company houses empty. Only the shadows and ghosts of former residents remained. Of the less than 300 people that now inhabited the town, most were loggers and provincial transportation employees. Scant others stayed to provide basic services, which included a school, a few cafes, a motel, two hotels with pubs, a curling rink, a Royal Canadian Mounted Police office, a general store and a gas station. Some prospectors and a few fur trappers lived in cabins somewhere in the surrounding mountains, visiting the general store infrequently.

Residents who would not define themselves as loggers or truck drivers or mining prospectors, at one point or other all converted into one or all of these things when they needed the cash, but in general they were artists with a nonconformist view of life.

When Orlando first arrived in town, he stepped out of the 'Wells-Barkerville Stagecoach' – an 8-seat transport van that made trips once a day to and from the next populated centre of Quesnel and inhaled a long breath of fresh air. If the Stagecoach had no passengers, it simply fulfilled its mission of delivering mail and newspapers to Wells residents. He felt he had been transported back to a mythical time of innocence and something – he wasn't sure what – reminded him of small towns in Bolivia. He half expected to see a Bolivian street vendor sitting in the back seat of the van with her arms wrapped around her stack of home-made alpaca sweaters.

From the front of the post office where the Stagecoach dropped its passengers, Orlando wandered across the street, suitcases in hand, to the Wells Hotel, its pristine sign with old western-style lettering inviting him inside. A little bell jingled when he opened the door, he walked to reception, requested a quiet room at the back with a private bath and he lived there for the next 13 years.

Orlando soon became acquainted with everyone in town, although he made friends with very few. Jim, the owner-driver of the Wells-Barkerville Stagecoach was the closest to what he could call a friend. Jim had nicknamed him 'Orly.' They spent hundreds of hours over the years chatting during Orlando's frequent trips back and forth to Quesnel where he had arranged his banking affairs. Jim, an outgoing man who had grown up in Wells, was a wealth of historical information, most of which left Orlando scratching his head and later scratching across the pages of his journals.

Jim informed him that back in the days when the mines were operating, each of the two mines produced a gold brick at irregular intervals. Jim was entrusted with the transport of said bricks as far as Quesnel. The night before a brick was ready, he would be advised to pick it up in the morning from the steps of the Good Eats Cafe, a small restaurant on the corner of Main Street. The brick was placed on the wooden steps to the entrance and people stepped over it on their way in to eat breakfast, not blinking an eye. Jim picked it up and threw it into the back of the van along with other cargo and drove off. He remarked that if this had been 100 years ago, he could have expected masked thieves to ambush him about 30 minutes away, in a short canyon called Robber's Roost. But, Jim said, society had matured. Orlando rolled his eyes.

The arrival of Jim's Stagecoach every afternoon was also reason for communal gathering. Residents stood outside the post office and waited for Jim to unload bags of mail and for Roger, the postmaster to sort it. The post office doors remained locked until the job was done. Orlando watched the lady with blue plastic curlers in her hair drop one cigarette after another and grind it into the dirt at her feet. He had never seen her without a cigarette in her mouth or without the curlers and wondered if she ever removed them. A few burly young men stood around chatting with each other, all constantly scratching their beards. Orlando eyed an ancient bent-over man with a cane who in turn eyed an extremely wrinkled old lady with thinning hair and a case of advanced Parkinson's disease. Two little boys played at sword fighting with willows as dogs jumped and bit at them. The crowd around the post office didn't change much from day to day. It was as if the regulars were expecting something that never arrived but for which they never lost hope. Once a month a sizeable group of new faces crowded in front of the General Delivery counter, anxious for their unemployment insurance cheques.

Orlando spent his fair share of hours at one or other of the hotel pubs, rubbing elbows with the locals, listening more than talking. Very infrequently, after chugging back several beers, a curious young logger asked too many questions, but other than that no one seemed to care where Orlando came from or why. He knew there were rumours about him, but they were harmless and people seemed to enjoy the speculation. Some said he had escaped from prison in Chile... "You know, another one of those South American countries that is run by a dictator." Others said he was more likely one of their military officials who had stolen from the dictator and was on the run. Don't you notice that he always seems to have money and hasn't worked a day since he arrived here? The most amusing story claimed he was an ex-CIA agent whose life was in danger and that they had given him a new identity and had to hide him away in this out-of-the-way town. Was not Wells the perfect location for something like this? The answer was always a resounding "Yes." Orlando had always benefited from rumours and wasn't about to intervene now.

In all the years he lived there, Orlando never had a romantic relationship. The first reason was that there were so few eligible women in town, and the second was that he enjoyed his self-imposed solitude into which he could lose himself and from which he could emerge on a whim without explanation.

For instance, when he visited Bertha in her hotel kitchen, she never questioned why he had retreated to his room for days on end, or why he had stayed in Quesnel for nights in a row, or why he was suddenly more amicable than normal. Bertha, with her rosy cheeks and hands as scraped up and rough as the vegetables she peeled, her red hair blazing over her green eyes as she yodelled bits of songs, allowed him to sit on a stool as she scraped and peeled and chopped and stirred. She was happy, she said and had faith that her husband would one day come through on his promise to have her 'farting through silk.' Her lively optimism reigned supreme. Even in her kitchen, Bertha dressed like a Mexican party. Her bold floral dresses with heavy ruffles around the bottom that swished when she shifted her weight, her long dangling earrings and bracelets that constantly jingled, were expressions of her celebration of life.

Sometimes Orlando accepted invitations to fund raising events for the war veterans at the Royal Canadian Legion, which consisted of drinking beer and buying raffle tickets for prizes such as a quarter of a moose, its meat wrapped and frozen, or three bottles of Canadian Club whiskey. He was introduced to Lucy, one of the regulars at the legion who wrote letters to the Queen of England twice a year and always received a polite reply. No one knew the subject of her letters, but she saved them all, often showing off her stack of envelopes with a stamp of the Royal Mail, each containing a valuable letter, surely from the hand of the Queen herself, she would say.

Orlando was not such a recluse that he didn't become familiar with other local characters. He was introduced to 'Diamond Lil', an older heavy-set woman who never actually wore diamonds. He met 'Shaky Kate', the old lady with advanced Parkinson's disease. And he often passed 'Forty-Below' on the street, a bent-over ancient Chinese man who was 100 years old if he was a day. His nickname was a reference to his complaint about having to survive in minus-forty-degree temperatures. Forty-Below's photo appeared one day in the local paper, above an announcement that he was going back to China to die.

Orlando had the luxury of observing their lives from the outside, never having to get involved in anyone's problems. For him, Wells was a paradise. Therefore it could not have been the cause of his weak heart.

After one too many episodes of severe shortness of breath and a fainting spell where he fell off the stool in Bertha's kitchen, he finally agreed to let Jim drive him to a doctor in Quesnel. The tests were conclusive. He suffered from something the doctor called cardiomyopathy which could be caused by a variety of factors, all of which Orlando discarded. He had had for some time now, the sensation of an invisible thread that had wrapped itself around his chest. It pulled at him, insisting, sometimes yanking him with such force that he fell forward and he struggled to maintain his balance. It was shortly after these episodes began that his senses played tricks on him, converting local smells, sights and sounds to poignant memories of Chile.

The thread dug into his chest, slicing his heart in two. One half was filled with the peace of this less-than-ordinary town with its mixture of odd inhabitants, and the other half was a scrambled milieu of Chilean culture, including everything from its food, to its wealth, poverty and corruption, to its barren northern landscapes and rugged coastline. He longed for the desert and fell victim to nostalgia for things such as his red Bel Air convertible. He reviewed his journals for answers. Clearly he was straddling two continents and it was wearing him down. But it was probably what was not written in his journals that was the cause of his broken heart. Even as he skirted around the edges of such a conclusion, he felt the thread tighten around his chest and he backed away from memories of Mariá Jacobé, and he forced something else to come forward. That was when he conjured up one of the few happy images from his childhood.

He pictured himself holding onto Jorge's hand when they were little more than toddlers. He had dragged a crying Jorge out to stand in the middle of the dusty street outside their house. "Wait for the wind to come and carry your sorrows out to the desert." He told Jorge. "Just wait for the wind." They stood there, two innocent, expectant little boys, hand in hand and waited until a small gust of wind from the sea swirled in around them and they turned to watch as it carried Jorge's sorrows up over the mountains. Maybe now, Orlando thought, it was he who was waiting for the wind.

Orlando arranged his return trip and it was with both a heavy heart and an excited anticipation that he packed his few clothes in the same bags that had arrived with him 13 years ago, plus one extra for his notebooks, and for the last time, and without saying goodbye to anyone other than Bertha and Jim, he set off on the Wells-Barkerville Stagecoach.

Three days later, he was flying over the barren brown gradient peaks and valleys of the Andes.

CHAPTER 39

Orlando Ortega

Santiago, 1996 – 2000

Santiago was Santiago and although Orlando was not the same man who had escaped it in 1983 it was all too easy to assume he could fall back into his old routines. What he didn't realise was that the ground had shifted just enough to tilt him off-balance and he ended up running alongside new bureaucratic vehicles like a dog chasing after the wheels of power. The four years since his return to Santiago from Canada passed in fits and starts because of it.

During the new democracy that officially began in 1990, General Pinochet and his military ministers had been replaced by civilians, even though Pinochet had arranged his own post as senator for life. There were many new (and some not so new) faces in the government halls these days. Pinochet had recently returned from London where he was detained while the Spanish judge tried unsuccessfully to extradite him on charges of war crimes. When he returned home he was eventually stripped of his status as lifetime senator, and opened up to prosecution.

The old fight was still going on. Orlando was at once bored and fascinated by it. As always, however, he remained outwardly neutral, seeking only to take advantage of the situation.

Rodrigo had picked over and sold Orlando's properties, all ownership documents lost or modified without question. Orlando contacted old associates and although, in true Chilean style, they never said No, to his requests for help, infinite delays and lack of initiative said it for them. He would have to pay dearly for having dropped out of the circle. He never found out what became of Rodrigo but assumed that a man with so many enemies would have one day encountered an unpleasant end. Perhaps Rodrigo had exiled himself out of Chile as well and was now running scams in an unsuspecting country that innocently welcomed him. Orlando decided not to investigate further. Maybe it was because of a weak heart, maybe a weak will, or maybe just finally, a fully-faded interest.

Out of habit and lack of new direction more than desire, Orlando had spent the last few years trying in vain to wriggle his way back in through some crack of armour in the old guard. The national 'reserved expenses' budget was increasingly less as the government tried to comply – at least for the sake of appearances, if not honestly – with international requests for greater transparency. This meant there was less money for bureaucrats to play with as freely as they had in the past.

There were, however, still gaping holes in federal laws, or at least a blind eye was turned to them. In addition, some laws passed by Pinochet's regime were still in force, affording the current democratic government a more than reasonable amount of power in such modern times to manipulate departmental budgets. Therefore, it was still corruption-made-easy but most of the players were different and Orlando had not found a key contact with enough will or influence to enable him to resume his old practices. He also admitted to himself that he had lost a certain ambition and perhaps lacked his old vigour and tenacity.

In any case, he turned more and more often to his journals, picking up where he'd left off in Canada. He wrote in earnest, documenting people and places from his heyday in Santiago – meticulously detailed accounts of past and mostly illegal negotiations. He included names and accurately cited dates and sums from his old records. The journals contained enough information about important people to mount at least two dozen potentially explosive corruption investigations, not to mention human rights abuses. Perhaps he did this out of spite. He did not do it with false hope in a cosmic justice, and certainly without hope for justice to be meted out by men, especially his own countrymen.

He was driven, perhaps obsessed to write for reasons he had yet to define. The journals were a private occupation through which he attained an unreasonable level of inexplicable satisfaction and were never meant for eyes other than his own. Therefore, he was extremely cautious in the matter of their security. Should anyone at whom he pointed his pen, discover his records, he would be in danger. Sharks would emerge from dark waters to encircle him. He would be stripped raw, no friends to turn to for protection.

In Chile, justice historically moved in blocks. Loyalty was the name of the game. The appearance of righteous unity was paramount. If a crate contained one bad apple, rather than risk its exposure and maintain an uncontaminated box, it was covered up by the good apples, causing the entire crate to rot with it. These crates of rotten fruit (which were positioned across the political spectrum) ran the government from one term to the next.

This brand of block justice was not limited to one or other political party; it appeared to be part of the Chilean genetic composition. Sometimes Orlando wondered whether the official posture that was inscribed in the national coat of arms, which boldly stated 'By reason or by force,' should have been 'By blind loyalty we shall maintain power.' He had become a sad cynic.

Orlando's bad heart was getting worse. While in Canada he received ongoing treatment for cardiomyopathy and a doctor in Chile recently warned him of likely heart failure and recommended an operation, Orlando resisted. His heart condition did not fill him with fear, and he rarely complied with advice regarding diet and exercise.

On more than one occasion over a short span of time, he experienced severe pains and found himself gasping for air and decided that rather than return to the doctor, he would move to Tocopilla.

The old red Bel Air was still in his possession. He could not imagine how it escaped Rodrigo's mad grab but by some stroke of luck or sloppy oversight (or perhaps even, with the help of a rogue man who had his own score to settle with Rodrigo) the prized car had been covered in a garage for nearly two decades. The mere sight of it was an injection of pure youth. He was jubilant as he stepped on the accelerator and sped north towards Tocopilla.

When he arrived, he was filled with nostalgia for what he had rejected as a younger man. However, there was no doubt that he would have done everything exactly as he did then. No regrets.

The town had changed for the worst almost immediately after the outset of the dictatorship. The combination of the closure of most saltpetre mines in the *altiplano* and the concerted efforts of Pinochet to punish the town because it was a notorious nest of socialists, had converted it into a depressingly colourless place with only past memories as fuel – and they were now dwindling.

There was a time when the downtown streets were shoulder-to-shoulder with people bustling to and fro – noisy Bolivian street sellers, women guiding their children who tripped along with freshly scrubbed strawberry faces in school uniforms, American and English mining engineers bumper to bumper in company trucks, freighters from all over the world anchored at a safe distance from the harbour waiting their turn at the dock, small, colourful fishing boats bobbing in waters at the shore, brazen prostitutes hanging over the rails on the boardwalk, hopeful workers from the south disembarking from one intercity bus after another, ore trains clanking up and down, practically brazing the crowded houses on the edges of town.

Now several downtown store fronts were boarded up and graffiti was scrawled across the yawning, empty spaces. The street that used to be lined with shoemaker shops was all but deserted. Only one shop remained open, its faded sign which was a cut-out drawing of a hand pointed down to the single shoemaker who leaned idly against the door frame. It used to be that these shops couldn't keep up with demand. The shoemakers, clenching a dozen small nails between their front teeth, barely had time to look up from their labours to respond to requests. They were skilled at speaking through their teeth without dropping a single one of the small tacks and clients nodded, somehow interpreting the words that were forced out between the teeth and nails. Now the single remaining shoemaker was toothless, his hands idle.

The wealth of the town was reflected by the state of the *fútbol* stadium. Just as pesos left town one by one in the pockets of desperate, disappointed workers or fleeing political asylum-seekers, the green blades of grass fell dead one by one into their mass grave of sand. Now the caretaker sprinkled water sparingly over the raked gravel to keep the dust down. Even so, the ball disappeared in brown clouds as sweaty players made awkward, bouncing passes.

Boulevards once bloomed with flowers and tropical bushes; now municipal grounds keepers swept dirt from broken sidewalks and picked up litter from the narrow wastelands. Freshly painted houses of all colours with healthy patches of green grass, flowering hibiscus, birds of paradise and orange trees had once brightened each side of the unpaved residential streets; now the thirsty grey-walled houses with graffiti and their rusty corrugated metal patches blended into the grey asphalt of the roads, heavy rocks on each corner of tin roofs to prevent the wind stealing the metal sheets from over their heads.

High fences with locked gates opened to walls which were topped with shards of glass or ragged wires, whose locked doors were still not enough to reassure homeowners that the few possessions they had would be safe. Everything was as precious as the ore and as fleeting as the sand.

Residents made the most of life under conditions against which they halfheartedly protested but mostly resigned to as something ordained by God. '*Si Dios lo quiere...*' the phrase that fell habitually from everyone's lips. 'God willing...' nothing more to be done, so let's laugh and enjoy our life for what it is.

Orlando paused to note the music that spilled out from square holes that were windows in vacant-looking grey cement walls. White lace curtains danced to a tropical rhythm as the passing winds tugged them outside, and waved them like flags of truce to passersby. The little houses filled were with children born of unwed teenaged mothers who lived with their parents. The young laughter and happy childish screeches echoed off back patio walls and filled the neighbourhoods with life. What the town lacked in colour was more than compensated with sound.

Orlando decided to stop for a beer at The Three Lions Pub on the main street before going up to his mother's house. He noticed the plaster from one of the lion's tails at the entrance was chipped away, exposing a hollow metal frame. He sat down at the bar and the only other client there, a large bleached-blonde lady wearing painted-on blue jeans sidled up to him.

"Nice car." She commented and nodded to where Orlando had parked it in plain sight in front of the door.

"Thank you."

She was chewing gum and looking at him rather intensely. "What do you know about Tocopilla?"

"Enough, I guess."

"Well, I can show you more than you have ever dreamed existed here." She winked.

"I'm sure." He half-smiled and lifted the smudged glass containing frothy beer to his lips.

"For instance, we have a nice little beach, and a monument to our victory of The War of the Pacific."

Orlando nodded, "Yes, I remember."

"Well something you probably don't know about is our colourful little mouse of a girl whose reputation is well-known maybe even as far away as María Elena. She sings, you know. Very good too. She is called Clorinda María Gonzalez-Rosas and she lives up on Calle Poniente, only a block from the cemetery. You know where that is?"

"Yes, actually, I do."

"Right, well she lives there. Three houses down from the top corner.

I'm a very good friend of hers. Maybe I can meet you there sometime and introduce you... my prince" She winked and touched her hair, half-dozen bracelets clanking down from her wrist, her other hand reaching for his knee.

He didn't finish his beer.

Up on Calle Poniente Orlando sat for a few minutes in his convertible, motor running and music streaming from the radio as he adjusted the rear-view mirror so he could see the young woman across the street. That must be her, the famous local singer named Clorinda. It was the right house. Everyone here watched everyone else. He had forgotten how it was in small towns.

He studied his mother's house and for the second time in his life, regretted not being here for her funeral. Other than more layers of dust, the façade hadn't changed in several decades. Surprisingly, looking at it didn't tug at his heart or trigger a parade of images from his childhood. It was just an old but familiar, abandoned, undisturbed house.

He shut off the engine, music falling silent, the street dropping into forlorn greyness without it, and he walked towards the front door.

When he finally succeeded in unlocking it he smelled loneliness spiked with the wretched scent of purposelessness. He held his handkerchief in front of his nose and proceeded through the entrance way. Nothing here had been needed by anyone for a long time. He wondered if his mother felt like she was just another one of the useless, abandoned items. How had she coped all the time he and Jorge were away? Perhaps she was thick-skinned like himself. He realised that he didn't really know much about her. He had never paid attention. He continued to wander around, touching almost nothing, just looking, half-searching for a clue as to why he had paid so little attention to his mother. He would never know how she felt and nothing here was going to tell him.

He wandered through the entire house, including the patio and returned to the small room at the back to collect some papers he remembered leaving in the desk drawer. Probably nothing relevant by now but he would read them at the hotel. There was certainly nothing else worth bothering with. He would arrange to have the house cleaned and painted before moving in. He noticed the tips of the shoes that belonged to the girl named Clorinda protruding from under his front door. He smiled to himself, closed the door and locked her inside.

CHAPTER 40

Clorinda

Tocopilla, 2001

Standing alone in the still of the house, listening to the sound of Clark Gable's red convertible roll away down the road, Clorinda prickled with his lingering presence. More than lingering, it was saturating. Clorinda let her fingers play across his desk. She could feel his tall Latino charm ooze out of the wood, taste it in her skin and smell it in the air. She let it penetrate before exploring the rest of his environment.

The ease with which she helped herself to a cup of tea in this stranger's house was, by all standards, including her own, surprising. Discovering gas still remaining in the small tank after an unknown number of years was even more unexpected. Browsing leisurely around the house, teacup in hand was bold. But it all added up to destiny.

She sat down at the table and let her eyes wander around the kitchen. It was not remarkable, and although it had been years since someone lived in it, it was perfectly functional. She imagined the woman called Doña Miranda washing the dishes and preparing the food and performing her household duties just as any other woman in town did, using the same methods as her mother before her. The same spices (cumin, paprika, with garlic and basil) flavoured the soup, the same fish and meat was being served with the same simple lettuce and onion salad. Clorinda was curious if her own methods would be comparable since her mother never taught her to cook. She learned by tasting what Señora Beatrice brought over from next door and then by trying to follow the indications her father gave her when he stood at the stove no more than two or three times per month. By the time she was 12, Clorinda did all of the cooking and, having invented her own recipes, had no sure method of comparison. She didn't know if her food preparation was typically correct, and if so, if she cooked a satisfactory meal or an outstanding one. She and her father both ate for practical purposes – to fill their stomachs – not to have a gourmet experience. For an exquisite taste experience, God had invented chocolate. But it wasn't important anyway since her fascination with fabrics far outweighed any fleeting inclinations towards food recipes – traditional or exotic.

Clorinda's investigation of Doña Miranda's house – or was it Clark Gable's house – naturally fell in line with her personal priorities. She spent very little time in the kitchen, a little more time sipping tea at his desk in the small back room (lightly placing her own fingers over the fingerprints he left on the dusty surface, shivering at his almost-touch, and sniffing the air for the remains of his scent), a minimal amount of concern in the sitting room and patio, and the majority of her time in each of the three small bedrooms, rummaging through closets and drawers, checking the bed linens and blankets.

That the house and everything in it was musty was to be expected. How many years of neglect had it suffered? The amazing thing is that no one had touched anything. Either Clark Gable's family was extremely lucky, or the house itself had a mysterious protective aura. That it had not been ransacked or claimed by squatters was extremely unusual. On a shelf in the master bedroom she noticed a photo of Doña Miranda and two men in shiny black suits and dark glasses standing beside Clark Gable's red Bel Air. There was also a large photo in an ornate frame of another young man with a beard and a bleached blonde woman, who it could only be assumed, was his wife, hanging at the head of Doña Miranda's bed, the location usually reserved for people's Jesus pictures. A half-hidden braided palm leaf hung from beneath the frame, a decorative maternal blessing for her son, via the priest on Palm Sunday. There was a faded antique photo of a young Doña Miranda and her husband on their wedding day, laying flat on the bedside table (maybe toppled over during an earth tremor). It was so heavily coated in dust that Clorinda almost didn't notice it. She blew on it to uncover any resemblance between the husband and Clark Gable. It was impossible to see the detail. She didn't see any photos of Clark, himself. Maybe that is what he took from the desk drawer.

Family pictorial history aside, she pranced excitedly back and forth the bedrooms. She found an intriguing collection of clothing in a locked cedar chest at the foot of Doña Miranda's bed, which she pried open with a kitchen knife. Clorinda gushed with excitement, exclaiming to the air.

The quantity of new cloth far outnumbered anything she would have received at one time from Angélica or would have been able to collect from the dump or from behind the used clothing store. As well as a fabric treasure, it was also a wealth of family information. Her fingers tingled as she took her time fondling the private items, but she firmly denied the temptation to steal anything.

It was obvious what belonged to Doña Miranda of course. There were a few possibilities within her collection, the most outstanding of which was her yellowed satin wedding dress that was wrapped in layers of tissue inside a brown paper bag. It had far outlived both partners. Clorinda knew which unremarkable shirts and scarves and trousers belonged to Doña Miranda's deceased husband and which she had guarded for the other son. None of Clark Gable's apparel was in the trunk. After nuzzling and tasting a few of the most precious items, including the wedding dress and a pale blue chiffon blouse, she closed the chest and adjusted the small crocheted afghan so it concealed the slightly damaged lock.

As though she owned the house, she wandered, unhurried, into the room that must have been Clark's. In contrast to the rest of the house with its light, pressed board shelving and chairs with hollow metal legs, Clark's room was furnished with heavy solid wood items. His bed had a tall, slightly curved headboard beside which was one night table with three drawers. It was empty. His wardrobe was an oversized floor-to-ceiling imported oak cabinet with carved double doors. Clothes hung inside – three sports coats, two formal suits, a few pairs of trousers, some light blue pinstriped and white long-sleeved shirts (whose shoulders were now hopelessly yellowed) and on the top shelf was one grey felt fedora and one tan one. The top drawers down the side were empty but the lower ones contained three neatly folded summer woollen vests, two fine alpaca sweaters, two men's silk scarves which made Clorinda swoon, and some argyll socks. She stayed to play in Clark's room.

The sheer pleasure of the touch and exotic flavour of the man! The luxury of sliding a shirt that belonged to Clark Gable over her shoulders and burying her face in its front – the ecstasy of the personality-soaked, fine alpaca fibres of his sweaters. She stripped out of her shift and pulled on his pinstriped shirt, taking her time, breathing heavily, as she fastened each small button. She donned the trousers and double-breasted jacket of the navy blue Italian wool suit and stood, hoisting the trousers with one hand, then the other, as she rubbed the fine textiles against her body and licked the sleeves. She exchanged the wool suit coat for the summer Italian linen, pulling the collar up under her ears, her thumb under the lapel, posing like a gangster. She put on his tan Bailey fedora, tilting her head on various angles in front of the bathroom mirror.

She pranced barefoot around each room of his house, out into the patio, almost climbing the walls in delight. She consumed him, his essence seeping into her blood through her pores. She slowly disrobed in a clumsy striptease out of suits that were too big, and tried on his sweaters, inhaling their fibres to preserve them in her memory. She felt she was stealing away his soul. Clark Gable would be hers. Finally, she carefully laid out the sweaters and scarves on the bed and still half-naked, gently rolled over them from one side of the mattress to the other, stopping face-down to breathe in and taste her movie star hero.

She imagined him walking down city streets, perhaps those of Santiago, perhaps Buenos Aires, perhaps even New York or Paris, wearing these clothes, these very clothes that she now draped over herself.

She pictured him, a figure of impeccable style, outstanding as he roamed crowded streets, stopping at busy sidewalk bars to sip drinks, perhaps smoking a cigar, everyone turning their heads. And she imagined him confidently leaning into the plush white bench seat of his convertible, hair blowing wildly, shirt ripped open by the wind, as he sped down country roads.

Now in nothing more than underpants and a silk scarf, one end gliding over her chest and the other tossed across her shoulder, she prepared another cup of tea and settled into a kitchen chair to drink it. How was it possible that she had been oblivious all these years to this amazing collection of clothing that had been stored away in this little house? How could she not have smelled it? Spitting the tea to the floor, she raised the short fringes of the scarf to her mouth, and staring vacantly ahead she niggled on the fringes before sucking in the scarf itself, and soaking a large corner section with her saliva. She would leave something of herself behind as a token of her appreciation for today's delightful visit – some of her hair, her saliva, her breath. She felt she owed him more than this but she would pay him back in other ways one day.

Finally she returned to Clark's bedroom to neatly fold and hang the clothing, to restore order. She danced around the room once more before preparing to leave the house via the patio and over the roof. She hesitated at the doorway of the small den at the end of the hall. Clark had retrieved some papers from the desk. Perhaps, although she had no real interest in documents, but simply because she found herself inside the house, she should investigate. The top desk drawer was empty. She tugged on the drawer below, fully expecting it to be empty too. But it slid open so easily that when she thought about it later, she realised it had been an invitation.

The dying rays of the afternoon sun pointed through the window to the item in the drawer, in the same way that the north star shone on the baby Jesus to guide the three wise men to his manger. Clorinda must have been chosen to find the chalice veil. Just like the baby Jesus, oblivious to its own power and destiny, it lay there as nothing more than a humble swatch of fabric inside a loosely folded yellowed tissue. Clorinda leaned forward to examine the holy cloth, carefully pressing her finger-tips around the edges. It was clearly a misplaced item from a liturgical set. How had a priest been so careless with something so splendid and significant? Clorinda identified it as an antique – hundreds of years old – probably from the time of the Spanish. This off-white raw silk veil was embroidered with red roses and detailed green leaves outlined with gold threads. The square cloth was finished in fine gold-trimmed appliquéed edges. She could still smell the incense. She recognised it from one of the books about religion in South America that the librarian had insisted she browse through. This was exactly the type of work a Carmelite nun would have created. According to the book, the nearest convent of this type was in Potosi, Bolivia. Clorinda imagined an old nun with a constant devot-ed smile on her lips sitting in the light of a cloistered garden, face bent lovingly towards the small veil that she decorated with her meticulous stitches, and with each jab of the needle into the fabric, a prayer. Perhaps a Spanish aristocrat had donated the fine silk to the convent as part of a dowry for one of his daughters and the nun set about converting it to this thing of rare beauty.

No meaning to be ungrateful for this grand discovery, but unable to resist, she searched the remaining drawers for similar treasures. But it was alone. All the more precious.

She carefully laid it out on top of the desk and watched as a golden aura grew around it. Clearly the chalice veil was delighted to have been found. Clorinda had been chosen to rescue it, just as she had rescued Santa Sara from her undignified situation under her father's rusted, greasy old tools and dirty wooden crates in the corner of the patio.

Clorinda wondered what Santa Sara's opinion of the chalice veil would be. Would the Virgin saint be jealous of what was destined to be Clorinda's second treasure? It was akin to introducing a second child, or perhaps a second wife into the household. Clorinda recalled how she had recovered Santa Sara from beneath her father's patio trash only a few days after he was buried. Initially, her rescue was out of simple pity for the figure, but more importantly, it was because she felt that an elegantly adorned, beautiful statue did not deserve to be cloistered in such horrid conditions. Although Clorinda had never seen a gypsy caravan or visited a chapel in which the Virgin presided over her chosen public, she had seen photographs and read articles in the library. Even before her father died, at Clorinda's timid request, the librarian dug up several magazine articles and found reference to Santa Sara icons in Chile. Clorinda's heart fluttered when she encountered an image of a Virgin that resembled the one crated inside her patio, and the librarian obligingly hunted down the library's single book containing popular myths about Santa Sara. Then Clorinda understood the historical significance and did not underes-timate the personal value of such a figure. After that, she noticed how popular Santa Sara really was. She saw her face on small ornaments in store windows, printed on wallet-sized cards that hung at the corner ki-osk and on a pendant around the neck of the lady who worked at the bakery. Fate had brought Santa Sara to her patio. But it was clear that not even a martyr should suffer so. Truth be told, the rescue of the Virgin after her father's death was not only for the sake of the Virgin herself, but also because Clorinda longed for intimate friendship, even the sort derived from the inanimate icon's cracked porcelain face and painted eyes.

She performed a ritual the evening of Santa Sara's resurrection. After she released the icon from her years of incarceration, she turned the wooden prison upside down, covering it with a heavy linen mantel and converted it to an altar. She positioned the Virgin in the centre and scattered rose petals at her feet. With her lips close to Santa Sara's veil, she serenaded her with a soft, melancholic melody, lamenting her long, undeserved imprisonment. As she meticulously dusted the brocade gar-ments, and carefully washed her porcelain hands, face and feet, restoring the icon to its former self, she shifted the tone of her song to one of joyous celebration. She placed six candles on the altar and lit them in Santa Sara's honour. Then she sat with her for hours and talked about her father, begging forgiveness for his ignorance, reasoning with Santa Sara that as a lost soul he was deserving of her intercessions.

Thereafter she noticed how the Virgin beamed at her from time to time and how her head was always lowered in gracious appreciation. Clorinda only asked that there never be confusion as to who rescued her, and that she should please keep it in mind whenever Clorinda petitioned her for favours.

The chalice veil would not be the companion that Santa Sara was, but it would be a sacred item that she would cherish for its beauty. She studied the cloth back and front, before returning it to the folds between the tissue paper and she slid it into her pocket with great care. She left the house through the back door, scaled the patio wall, tiptoed across the roof and lowered herself down the neighbour's wall, all the while, her right hand protecting her pocket.

Although the chalice veil was also a religious masterpiece, it did not belong alongside Santa Sara. Clorinda emptied a large, flat tea can with a hinged lid and lined it with padded cotton before arranging the small veil, rose pattern facing out, one appliquéed corner folded back on itself. She carefully closed the lid and placed the tea box on her bedside table. Each night before she crawled between her sheets, she opened the lid, leaning in to breathe the golden incense and bless the nun who had created it. She also blessed Clark Gable and his mother for making available such a precious work of art. Surely it had been their gift to her.

Clorinda acknowledged that although united in their common beauty, spiritual value, and inspiration, her three most prized possessions were private from one another. Señor Ortega's grey patch didn't know the story behind the black Virgin, the Virgin was ignorant of the chalice veil and to the chalice veil, both were irrelevant. Clorinda appealed to each of them in turn for inspiration for her life's work.

Although he wasn't exclusive, Señor Ortega in his grey patch was, without question, her greatest connection and most important spiritual guide. He was both the subject and object of her life, he was her alpha and omega. She studied the grey patch that was Señor Ortega and leaned forward to touch her cheek to his threads. As usual, he was warm and responsive, always there for her. She consulted the grey patch daily, and her life's work became a joint project with her at the helm. She navigated between the patio and the cemetery niche, and looked up at the stars for guidance, counting on the sun and moon to help her maintain a daily balance for her existence between realities.

CHAPTER 41

Orlando Ortega

Tocopilla, 2001

Orlando's pleasures in life had been reduced to three single, habitual activities that he spread across the waking hours of each day. Every morning he made entries in his journal after sleeping on the previous day's events and contemplating their relevance. Every afternoon he drove his Bel Air convertible along the wide-open desert roads for the sheer pleasure and freedom of racing with the wind. He rarely if ever, encountered anything new on these excursions. He always stopped to buy an ice cream bar from the desert highway ice cream seller who never uttered hello, thank-you, or goodbye. All he said was "100 pesos." The mere existence of a man in the middle of the barren plain selling something cold was uplifting. It was like finding life at the end of a scorched, forgotten street to nowhere. The mute ice cream man covered the same desolate three-kilometre stretch of the Pan American highway every day and there was no sign of his ice cream storage or personal accommodation. Orlando considered him something of a northern miracle.

Finally, each evening Orlando sat outside the front door of his house, cup of tea in hand, to gaze across the town and over the sea. Enjoying how the evening sea breeze caressed his face and his bare arms, he surveyed the streets that descended row on row to the beach. They were illuminated (except for during sudden, frequent power cuts as the electric plant sacrificed local convenience in order to send extra volts up to the mines) and he could see activity at the dock. Usually there were just one or two ships in the harbour. Boys with *fútbols* wandered by and people returned from corner stores, most of them acknowledging him but never initiating conversation.

The girl Clorinda, sat across the street every evening without fail and stared at him in silence. She never raised her hand to wave, never even nodded in his direction. She just observed him as a vulture might keep vigil over a dying dog. He had become accustomed to her odd presence which, more and more, felt like it was closing in around his doorstep.

After several months he felt a bond forming between the two of them. He looked back into her constant gaze. She was unselfconscious, like a baby turning around and staring unblinking, over her mother's shoulder. He had the impulse to wink at her, and one evening he did wink and added a discreet nod of the head but he received no response. Just the same steady stare. He laughed to himself, shook his head and wandered back inside the front door. All evening, each time he recalled the incident, he laughed out loud and could be heard laughing to himself until he turned off the lights. Even as he lay in bed, looking up at the ceiling, arms folded under his head, the bed shook as he laughed and finally fell asleep.

He left on his daily Bel Air excursions a little later each day because he found himself loitering in front of his house, curious to see what Clorinda was wearing that day or perhaps to hear her sing a few bars, or even an entire song. When he eventually did start the car engine and motor off towards the highlands, the desert landscape was littered with images of Clorinda, her odd way of walking, her habit of her pressing a swatch of fabric to her cheek, even seemingly scrubbing her face with it, and sometimes sticking out her tongue to lick it like she might lick a popsicle. He was delighted by these random 'Clorinda moments' that inexplicably materialised through the afternoon haze. He added them to his list of recent pleasures, bringing the total number of joyous pastimes up to four – more than any man of his age and health could ask for.

For the first time in his life Orlando del Transito Ortega de Riveras considered himself a happy man. Although it perhaps didn't factor logically into the question of happiness, he debated whether or not this pleasant state of mind also meant that he was a good man. Was it because his conscience was clear? – his slate was clean? – all the water had now flowed peacefully under various bridges? If he was a good man, it was not out of anything he'd done, but rather it was due to the passage of time, as though time was all he needed to be forgiven his earlier transgressions. For the most part, he was satisfied with this notion but was sometimes nagged by the idea that there was something in his life that he was terribly guilty of leaving unattended.

One day as he bolted across the desert in his red Bel Air convertible, he was musing about Clorinda's unique wardrobe and he suddenly realised that she marked the days of the week with her outfits. Angélica had tried to tell him something about Clorinda's wardrobe the first day he returned to Tocopilla, and he dismissed it without consideration. Now he found it highly amusing. It had taken him a few months to recognise this idiosyncrasy but as he drove off that day, which was a Wednesday, he noted that she was wearing a jewel-neckline shift which she accented with a yellow daisy tucked behind her right ear.

He looked forward to seeing her on Thursday especially to observe her attire – a caftan with a wide, sweeping purple leaf pattern. – Yes! – he slapped his knee and chuckled. She was staring back at him with her usual silent unflinching gaze. He stopped laughing, stood up and bowed to her, a low, sweeping motion, as though he had removed a hat. And he credited her for her personal genius with mock applause.

She tilted her head and furrowed her brow only slightly, hesitated and raised her hand in greeting. She smiled.

This was the beginning of their slow, silent salsa. They stepped in and out of it in the relaxed rhythm of smiles and polite nods, always at the same distance, never approaching each other from their respective sides of the street. It was a steady, conscious dance that continued for months.

One evening just before dusk, the routine sounds of the street fell silent under a song that rose from within the walls of Clorinda's house. Passersby stopped, cocking their heads to one side. A colour like bliss tinged each person's cheeks, transforming them all into seemingly innocent angels. This enchanted multitude had congregated just as Orlando went outside to relax. Careful not to distract them, he advanced and blended into the crowd. It was a rare pleasure.

He had never – even in private high society recitals of Santiago – heard a voice with such naiveté, clarity, strength and emotion. Her song, the words of which were not clear – nor even logical within the common sense of lyrics – conveyed fleeting concepts that struck him. The melody seemed to weave its way through layers of history, revealing centuries-old wandering souls that mingled with static ones, and it was finally reflected here on the faces of stragglers on a street outside her house in Tocopilla. She interpreted the sound of a humanity that had spread its wings around the world to merge beyond the layers of time. She was a vessel that had absorbed the magic stories of the continent, which on selected quiet nights found their release in the sound of her voice that spiralled out of invisible flutes and played through nonexistent harps, at once jubilant and melancholic.

She was a miracle. She was a butterfly on a soft breeze. Above all, she was hauntingly familiar.

Orlando decided it was long past time to make her acquaintance. It was less a cognitive decision than an intuitive command. Thus he arranged a chance meeting with her the following Sunday morning.

CHAPTER 42

Clorinda

Tocopilla, 2001

Although there was no clear evidence of progress, dividing her time between washing and mending and her life's work turned out to be much easier than Clorinda had predicted. With Angélica's more and more frequent and overbearing presence outside her front door, clients began to avoid taking their uniforms to Clorinda, preferring instead to deal with someone without 'a rotweiller.' Therefore Clorinda was able to complete her work-for-pay projects before siesta nearly each day, leaving the cooler, late afternoon hours for her weaving.

She decided that her life's work was far too grand for a basic tapestry so she expanded it to include anything related to threads that intertwined or intersected and fabric that could be attached with any kind of yarn or otherwise woven into the warp. She included 'sculpting' with fabric, a simple example of which was her crocheted daisy which, up to this point, was still the only thing she had added to the tapestry surface.

Day after day, she sat looking at her strung loom without adding to it. She sang songs and imagined thousands of colourful patches springing up like the desert in bloom across the warp, with endless added varieties of textures and three-dimensional shapes reaching up to pay homage to the sun. She rummaged through her yarn and fabric bags, unravelled balls of wool across the length of the patio floor to admire them, lingered over various threads for untold periods of time, tore some off for the pleasure of their taste, licked fabric remnants for the luxury of it (mostly the silk ones) and finally replaced everything, having done nothing more than play and dream of all the possibilities. Exhausted, she would kiss her and Señor Ortega's communal daisy and go to bed, but not before noticing that the moon always shone directly on their flower, giving it special power. It was the last thing she saw at the end of each day.

One night, shortly after he was buried, instead of going to bed, she crept out her front door and walked her slinky, crooked walk down the street, around the corner and up the hill to the cemetery, scaled the wall beside the locked gates and didn't stop until she reached Señor Ortega's niche. She sat down on the wooden visitor bench, stared up at him and cried in silence until dawn. Her hands, folded on her lap, were damp with salty tears. The sun was so moved by her pain and devotion that he asked the moon to remain a little longer to offer some kind – any kind – of maternal celestial solace. The moon stayed on, shining her knowing half-smile, drying the tears on Clorinda's cheeks and stroking her hair before disappearing into the waking sky. Exhausted, Clorinda climbed back out over the cemetery wall, slowly walked home and fell into bed, ignoring the baker's assistant who was pounding on her door with an arm full of aprons.

That day without knowing what moved her to do so, she extracted one of the three glass-bead roses from the foot of her Santa Sara statue and attached it exactly in the middle of Señor Ortega's grey patch. It felt like the right thing to do. The tiny bits of shimmering glass reminded her of when Señor Ortega sometimes smiled down at her for reasons she didn't understand.

She couldn't help but picture him lying in his dark chamber, legs outstretched, no shoes (the sock on his left foot sinking into a space where his two smallest toes had been 'disappeared'), hands folded across his chest, eyes closed. It hurt to think of Señor Ortega lying motionless in a box, not even attempting to escape. He should be shooting across the desert sand in his red arrow.

They took their first and only trip up to the *altiplano* two weeks before he died. He said she really should see what lay beyond the Andes, this awesome *cordillera* that encroached on Tocopilla, and threatened to nudge it, one house at a time, into the Pacific. He said that he applauded the little town for stubbornly standing its ground against the towering rock. She didn't know what he meant until they were driving through the pass. The scale of the mountains was awesome. She had taken them for granted all of her life but now that she was passing through them she realised they deserved a greater respect. They ascended so quickly that her ears popped almost immediately after losing sight of the town. The winding road took them up past dozens of small, rough holes that had been blasted into the steep rock on either side. Señor Ortega explained that these belonged to the *pirquineros*, who eked out a living taking a small share of the mountain god's ore to eventually sell on the world market, all the while constantly armed with the hope that they would discover the mother lode.

Once up on the flats, they passed one of the many abandoned mining settlements where now only a caretaker remained, a dusty cactus leaning into his cement wall, nothing else in sight. The caretaker stood motionless against the arid backdrop, vast blue sky dwarfing him and his little buildings in the middle of nowhere as he stood, thumbs hooked into wide, red suspenders (the only colour for kilometres), mouth hanging open, squinting into the sun, watching them fly by.

There were small train maintenance yards with pieces of iron and wheels on axles strewn about at the end of narrow paths that hung off the main road. Only one worker was needed there these days. Not enough ore trains passed any more. Now the only one that ran on these tracks was the world's last remaining saltpetre train, and it whistled its lonely claim to fame only a few times each day.

She listened to the eerie sound of wind through the power lines that ran parallel to the highway along most of the distance. For her, this sound was the most scary thing about the *altiplano*.

Within 45 minutes they had arrived at the town of María Elena, a half-deserted town owned by the saltpetre company whose processing plant was across the highway. Señor Ortega drove directly to the plaza and parked on the street near a row of black and yellow taxis whose drivers leaned against a dusty palm tree and cooed over the Bel Air. He paid one of them to watch it and led the way to a small restaurant for lunch. Everyone stopped eating, spoons in mid-air to stare at them as they walked in the door. They eyed the young woman in her bizarre outfit who had a strange sideways style of walking, and her tall, elegant male companion. Why was this man in María Elena with this odd crea-ture? Where did they come from? No one spoke. After several seconds they resumed sipping their soup, spoons clanking against the sides of their chipped china bowls with the worn pink floral patterns but they continued to steal sideways glances at the couple.

Señor Ortega motioned for Clorinda to sit at the small wooden table in the corner and he ordered 'the menu of the day' for both of them be-cause it was the only thing available. They ate their consommé in silence, aware that every pair of ears in the place was stretched towards their cor-ner. The waitress sighed as she cleared the soup bowls and plunked down a plate of rice and greasy roasted chicken in their place. In the midst of the otherwise silent room an old man whispered to a companion that he knew who the stranger was. He is "the evil son-of-a-bitch from Tocopilla who ran off to Santiago with the bags of money he made from cheating *pirquineros*. He is a thief."

Clorinda glanced across at Señor Ortega who didn't blink an eye. They finished their meal, he paid and they walked out without uttering a word. All the way home Señor Ortega was immersed in a dark silence. He parked the car outside his house, offered a half-smile and tipped a nonex-istent hat to Clorinda as they parted ways.

Clorinda wondered if one so kind could be a thief. Perhaps it depends on what one steals. She stole chocolate more than once but didn't consider herself a bad person. And Angélica and Norma stole clothes on a regular basis, but they were good people too. Was Señor Ortega really a thief? And if so, did he steal something big enough to make him an evil man?

Picturing Señor Ortega in his niche, Clorinda tried to move on to more pleasant memories, but her mind returned to things that were stolen. She thought of Señor Ortega where he would always and forever lie flat out, immobile. She remembered the conversation they had days after their trip up to the *altiplano*, his conscience prickling and prodding at him to discuss something with her. He wanted to talk about things that he stole, mostly money, perhaps to justify stealing or to put it behind him. She told him about how she, too, had stolen something – chocolate – but she didn't mention the chalice veil or all the clothes she stole from schoolmates when she was young. She had not been completely honest with Señor Ortega. She wondered whether or not he noticed the missing veil from his desk drawer. He had never said anything. She couldn't tell. Now her conscience pricked at her. She remembered something else that she lied about, something quite big, something quite important, that she had never admitted to him.

The remarkable first day when they met at the Santa Elvira alcove in the cemetery, when he appeared like an impeccably dressed saint, just after she had asked Santa Elvira to make him her friend, when she chatted nervously about petitioning saints and bragged about having her own Virgin in her patio, and not just any Virgin, but Santa Sara, the black Virgin, when he asked her how it came to be there – she lied.

"I found her stashed in the furthest corner behind wooden slabs and concrete building blocks." Clorinda had told him. "She belonged to my father, God bless his soul." She said it with such confidence that she almost believed it herself at that moment. She had always wanted to believe that it had been awarded to her father in special recognition for something, that he was, somewhere in his soul, a righteous man who had earned such a prize. But the events of the night of Santa Sara's arrival – her mother's indignation and rejection of the icon, admonishing her father for offering a gift of something that was not his to give – would forever deny her wish for her father to be a hero, and for the icon to have truly belonged to him.

Señor Ortega remained silent and she was afraid he'd tell her politely that it was time to go and wish her a good day and then she'd never have this opportunity again.

She didn't want to lose the momentum of this encounter. It was a true miracle that she was not absolutely speechless. Surely their meeting had been predestined. This idea filled her with confidence.

She dared offer, "Would you like to see her?"

"That would be very kind of you, Señorita Clorinda."

She remembered how they walked in silence back to the house, Clorinda carefully keeping a polite distance and suddenly self-conscious of her sideways walking style. She couldn't change it now though and risk an untested walk beside someone who himself walked with such long, confident strides. What if she fell down? She was relieved when they reached her front door.

Señor Ortega was obviously very impressed with the black Virgin. So touched was he by her beauty that the colour drained from his face and he raised his right hand to clutch his chest. Clorinda lifted her chin and puffed out her bosom in silent pride.

Santa Sara granted this audience with Señor Ortega from her position on the makeshift altar in the back corner of the patio where she had been since Clorinda placed her there after her father's death. Clorinda interpreted the Virgin's trademark half-smile to mean that she was content to be here in the patio. She certainly appeared happy enough.

Fine cracks like blind fingers felt their way in and out of the details on her brown porcelain face. In spite of her years she was still beautiful.

The Virgin's almond-shaped downcast eyes were in holy synchrony with the perfectly arched brows, fine nose and proper, not too voluptuous lips – all portraying purity. Once-shiny locks of dark hair disappeared properly under the blue head veil that was bordered in gold lace. Her head was topped with an ornate gold crown. The veil hung beyond her hips, the red underside defining the folds in a perfect rhythm along its edges. The main garment was white, trimmed with gold brocade at the neck and lower hem. The Virgin's hands were clasped in prayer and a tiny rosary of pearl beads hung from her fingers. The brown porcelain fingers were all intact, with only hairline cracks the same as on her face. Brown sandalled feet tipped out from under the embroidered outer garment that covered a white linen skirt. Brightly painted carved wooden flowers were glued around the base as though reverent worshippers had laid them at her feet.

Señor Ortega stood in front of the statue for a long time without remarking at all. Clorinda suddenly became uncomfortable and turned to lead him towards the door.

He said, "I understand the Santa Sara belongs to the gypsies."

"Yes," Clorinda was relieved he had come back to life. "Yes..." she repeated. "I guess she does."

"Do you know how this Virgin come into the possession of your father?"

"Well, no. I really don't know that for certain. My father never told me anything. He always had her stored away to keep her safe, I think. I don't know how Santa Sara came to be here." She couldn't tell him that the Virgin never saw the light of day when her father was alive, how he had lumbered into the house with it strapped to his back like a thief in the night and offered it as a gift to her mother, which she rejected. Or how her mother said the icon had to be returned or they would all be cursed, and how it didn't belong here. The lie was told, and it was too late.

He pondered before responding, "I am like a gypsy myself I guess. I have travelled a lot in my life. Here in your patio, I find a static Santa Sara. She should be travelling with gypsies but she's not. I should be travelling out of habit, but I am not. Maybe it's a sign."

CHAPTER 43

Orlando Ortega

Tocopilla, 2001

Orlando's heart almost failed him as he stood in front of the black Virgin in Clorinda's patio. Time stopped. For one eternal second he saw the faces of María Jacobé, Boldo, and Jerko. They took turns accusing him, waving their index fingers under his nose. He blinked and concentrated on the delicate feet of the statue, willing the faces to vanish.

How many years ago had he sentenced their precious Virgin to an eternity in an abandoned mine above the hills of Tocopilla? How long was she was forced to exist in dank obscurity before she somehow made her escape? Equally, how many poor souls had given their lives to that same wretched shaft in exchange for the promise of either salvation or riches?

In the case of the Virgin, it was salvation. He was astounded at her good fortune. Perhaps she really was a blessed entity. He had left her swaddled in a length of white cotton inside a wooden crate on the ledge of a narrow cavern somewhere in the Andes. And yet here she was staring past him into the girl's back patio.

The years had treated her well. She looked the same as the one and only time that he laid eyes on her. But the sight of her now brought him back to the most important turning point in his life, something he had forever-after endeavoured to wipe out of his consciousness.

María Jacobé was like a black hole in his mind whose darkness was surrounded by danger signs, warning him not to go near at the risk of falling into something out of which he would have neither the desire nor the strength to dig himself out. He obeyed the signs, but at this moment, he found his toes very near the edge of the abyss, its soft shale edges threatening to give way as his missing toes tingled.

He almost dared himself to remain there, toes dug in, arms outstretched, like a super hero ready to fly. Instead he asked Clorinda about the origin of the icon knowing full well that if she even mentioned the name 'María Jacobé' that he would plunge into a darkness that his mind had prepared for him decades earlier.

She spoke instead of her father. He was saved.

"Do you like chocolate?" He asked.

CHAPTER 44

Orlando Ortega

Tocopilla, 2001

Clorinda didn't talk much. She expressed herself through her limited but creative wardrobe, a repertoire that was determined by the days of the week – or perhaps the other way round. Her daily routines relieved her of the uncertain prospects of navigating through unexpected situations. They provided her with predictable and therefore, controllable social interaction.

Her songs, on the other hand, were totally without reservation and unlimited in their variety and spontaneity. She sang unselfconsciously but perhaps that was because she always sang in the privacy of her home. Her songs were far and beyond anything that remotely invited conversation. They were a monologue from which no dialogue could possibly ensue. Thus Clorinda got a message out to the world, which was open to individual interpretation, but somehow tied to the cosmos.

It must be said that no one in Tocopilla truly understood what her songs were about in a cerebral way. Her music, when it reached someone else's ears, penetrated their souls and carried them off to a place in the cosmic unconsciousness, where everyone quite simply comprehended everything. Some of the young people were of the opinion that listening to Clorinda's songs was better than smoking pot. Thus there was a lot of slow nodding of heads among listeners as they made eye contact with one another outside of Clorinda's front window. Orlando likened it to a hippie love-in.

One afternoon as they sat outside Orlando's front door sharing some chocolate Hershey kisses, Clorinda was moved to talk more than usual. She confessed that she did have one ambition in life.

"What would that be?"

She licked her fingers, sticking each one of them far into her mouth and making loud sucking sounds as she pulled them back out. "I'll be right back."

She ran across to her house and returned with three plastic shopping bags. One of them was a bag branded 'Marks & Spencer'. Where on this earth did she find such a bag?

"Oh, I get them here and there."

"Well, when did you get that one?" Orlando pointed to the Marks & Spencer bag.

"The last time..." was her only explanation, and he had to be satisfied.

"Look, look. Look at this." Her eyes were shining and she had spittle at the corners of her mouth. He was intrigued that she unconsciously salivated with excitement.

She pulled out a ball of deep pink yarn. "Look. It's raw silk." She plucked at the ball untucking the end and then she raised it to her mouth, touched it lightly on her tongue as though tasting the first and only ripe cherry of the season, and she closed her lips around it and sucked.

Orlando watched without blinking. Clorinda's face suddenly reddened and she yanked the precious silk from between her lips and carefully re-wrapped the ball. "I've never shown anyone my collection before. You are the only one."

Orlando felt privileged and more than a little curious. She pulled out three balls of fine ocean blue cotton. He noticed that the balls were made of threads joined with knots. She must have picked something apart and he pictured her concentrating on the task, eyes focused, trying to steady her excited fingers.

Clorinda pulled out one ball of yarn after another, handling them all with the love and care of a mother holding a newborn baby. He noticed her stifle the impulse to put some of the yarns in her mouth again, and he looked away, granting her the dignity of controlling this habit in his presence.

"I want to make something," she confessed, "and I have been very carefully selecting and saving these yarns for a few years now. You can't..." and she looked up at him very seriously from under her furrowed brows, "...you can't just use any old yarn for a special project like mine."

"May I ask what it is you have in mind, Señorita Clorinda?"

"That's the problem. That's the really big problem." She glanced up and then lowered her gaze to fight back tears. This was obviously extremely important to her so Orlando said nothing. He reached across and touched her arm ever so lightly. She jumped back. He retracted his hand and waited.

"Señor Ortega, I have the most powerful desire in the world to tell a story with my wool. But I don't have the means." She suddenly slumped forward until her face was hidden in her lap and her shoulders shook with silent sobs.

Orlando sat there looking at her, hands on his lap, feeling very much like a helpless fool in the face of this young woman's outpouring. He was honoured by her trust in him. And he wondered at something that felt like happiness building inside his chest. At the same time the grief about her own predicament, about which, he had to confess, he had not the slightest idea, was heart-wrenching.

He waited patiently for her shoulders to stop shaking, not because he possessed the wisdom to do so, but because he was at a loss. More than ten minutes passed and the two of them remained inanimate – him looking down at his hands in his lap, and she with her head buried in her skirt. It was a Thursday so her head was buried in her flowered Hawaiian-style caftan.

Finally she turned her face and peeked up at him from under the petals between the folds. He allowed his eyes to meet hers but was uncertain if she wanted him to look at her, so he returned his gaze to his fingers.

"It's okay, Señor Ortega. It'll be okay." She spoke in a low, soothing tone, as though he was the one in need of comfort.

She carefully returned the balls back into each bag, placing them like each one had a numbered or preordained spot. Then she stood up and without another word, walked back across the street with her three bags of wool and disappeared through the front door of her house. What was that nursery rhyme he had heard the children in Wells recite? Something about three bags full...

The following afternoon, after his customary drive along the desert roads, Orlando knocked on Clorinda's door and waited, listening to her footsteps as she shuffled from her back patio.

"Yes? Who is it?"

"It's me, Señor Ortega."

Silence.

"It's okay. I'm okay now."

"May I talk to you, Señorita Clorinda?"

The locks clicked and she opened the door a crack, revealing her nose and one eye.

"I found something that I think you should have. I would like to give it to you."

"Go back to your house, Señor Ortega. I will meet you outside in a minute." Once again her tone was one of consolation, as though she was about to do him a favour, as though it was he who needed to be comforted.

Orlando was sitting outside his front door as she approached him in her crab-like sideways slither. She was wearing heavy cotton trousers with an oversized sky blue t-shirt, one of her casual Friday outfits.

"Can I serve you some tea?" It was the first time they would share tea and sandwiches. He had arranged a small table outside his front door in order that she would understand he was not trying to lure her into the privacy of his lair.

"How kind. Yes, thank you, Señor Ortega. I take 4 spoonfuls of sugar, please."

She sat back and leaned into the wall, waiting to be served, as though it was a common occurrence.

They slurped their tea and ate the cheese sandwiches in silence. Then Orlando stood up to clear the cups and saucers from the table. "Wait here please. I have something for you."

When he returned she appeared to have fallen asleep, slumped back in her chair, her arms hanging limp at her sides, face turned up to the sky. He quietly placed the large wooden frame on the ground in front of her feet, stepped back and waited.

CHAPTER 45

Clorinda

Tocopilla, 2001

The day of their first shared tea outside Señor Ortega's front door, when he said he had something that belonged to her, she was unable to contain her excitement. She couldn't imagine what. Other than the fabric from Angélica and the chocolate Señor Ortega shared with her, she was not experienced in receiving gifts. It was a new concept. She was uncomfortable and tried to relax. Perhaps if she closed her eyes and breathed slowly.

She sensed Señor Ortega's cool shadow crossing her face but she couldn't bring herself to look up at him. A full five minutes passed before she opened her eyes to see him smiling down at her. He indicated with a glance what he had set on the ground before her.

The wooden frame of the hand loom became blurred by the tears through which she saw it. Of course words failed her. Such a gift was beyond her greatest expectations. She was afraid to look up at Señor Ortega who stood, hands folded patiently in front, watching her with his steady smile, and she was afraid to look away from the loom in case by doing so, it would disappear. So she sat for a very long time gazing at it before finally leaning forward to touch the frame. It had a satin varnish finish with authentic, smooth metal posts and perfectly notched wooden corners. Such a loom was apt to accept her most exquisite threads. The thought of them stretched from top to bottom sent tingles up and down her spine.

Finally, she looked up at Señor Ortega, and, not knowing how to express her genuine gratitude, she boldly reached for his hand and kissed it several times, surprising them both.

Señor Ortega sat down and they gazed in silence at the loom until he told her that he thought she should take it home and get to work.

She nodded, picked it up and carried it across the street.

The truth was that she didn't know where to start. She was too overwhelmed to focus. All of the ideas she had had for weaving a masterpiece tumbled through her brain, ending up on the floor in a pile of colour and texture that she could no longer interpret. She made several attempts to string the loom but they all failed. Nothing felt right. She was absolutely discouraged and was surprised to admit that she almost hated Señor Ortega for ruining the concepts that had worked so beautifully in her mind year upon year and now that she was faced with making them a reality, she had to admit failure. She petitioned Santa Sara for help.

She lit a candle at the foot of the icon each morning and waited in vain for a sign. But finally it was Señor Ortega who provided the answer she sought. It was during this time, upon later reflection she could testify that their bond of friendship was woven so tightly that even her own best efforts would never have the power to unravel them. Now, instead of sitting across the street from each other every evening, she went to sit with him in front of his house. They watched the sun set over the ocean and her visits habitually lasted well into the night, until people began to disappear behind the walls of the houses, streets became empty, lights were switched off and the sound of televisions and stereos was silenced one by one.

Early each evening Señor Ortega went into his kitchen and returned with a different type of sweet which always contained chocolate. Sometimes it was an eclair or marzipan or dark, bitter chocolate sprinkles on a lemon square, sometimes candy-coated chocolates and even liqueur-filled chocolates (the taste of which made her she shiver). He placed the treat on the table in front of Clorinda, assuring her with a smile, that it was good for the soul.

She thanked him with a nod, closed her eyes, opened her mouth, stuck out her tongue with a reverence equal to accepting holy communion and pulled it inside, where she held it for as long as possible, keeping her eyes closed in order to fully appreciate the exquisite chocolate sacrament that melted through her senses. Therefore, she spent much of her time sitting there, face slightly upturned, with her eyes closed, moaning from the base of her throat as Señor Ortega sipped whiskey from a glass. Neighbours walked by and nodded, often without being acknowledged in return.

As the evening wore into night she listened to Señor Ortega's accounts of how he used to work in the mines when he was just a boy. Not the same mine as the one her poor father laboured in year after year but, he assured her, with all the same health risks. He explained something about selling gold and copper ore and how the rest of the world ultimately determined how much money a Chilean miner took home to his family, and whether or not he worked at all. Most of the details escaped her but she loved the sound of his voice as it took on a serious, businesslike tone and she sat up straight, in awe.

He spoke about his life in Santiago, his brother who had died not so long ago, and the years he lived in a small town in Canada. He had to get an atlas to point out exactly where he had travelled. Even so, it was impossible to imagine. He even mentioned a man called Rodrigo, but that part was particularly unclear. Sometimes he told her things about Bolivia, how the children of Potosi gathered on Christmas Eve to dance barefoot in the plazas in the hopes of receiving a candy. How, if you gave them candy or even a toy, their parents often took it away to sell it. Such was the poverty and desperation. He wandered from topic to topic, connecting one event to another across the years in what she considered a nonsensical way. But he told her that life was a series of random events and one simply jumped from one to another, like stepping stones across a stream, the water washing away the footprints. She didn't understand the concept of stepping stones because she had never seen a stream. He then explained that perhaps it made more sense to consider that one's life consists of a series of threads of all colours and textures. You select the ones you want and weave them into something that resembles who you are.

Señor Ortega's thread analogy was the inspiration for her life's work which was strung across the frame that now leaned placidly in the shade of her patio wall. It was sadly lacking the connections she knew Señor Ortega referred to although his grey woollen vest patch, the daisy and the glass rose bead that adorned it, still satisfied her. She knew they were perfect, and she wanted to find just the right threads to represent whatever came next. She knew that whatever it was would be a continuation of their relationship and connection with others. But what was it? She was struggling very hard to interpret her life in context with his. The daisy and rose were representative of their cherished bond. But the more she thought about it, the more she was convinced that she understood too little and she did not trust her own interpretation. She crocheted two more daisies with her fingers and added them to her collection.

She remembered that Señor Ortega seemed to be interested in her parents, particularly her mother, but there was little she could tell him. He also asked many questions about gypsies, another subject about which she knew very little. He noted that the gypsies had not been in Tocopilla this year at all, the municipal allotment was strangely vacant month after month. Clorinda paused to realise that she could never remember a year in which the gypsies had visited Tocopilla. Sometimes Angélica and Norma teased Clorinda with stories and descriptions of the fabulous fabrics the gypsies used to sell. "They travel the world," Norma said. "They can get anything from anywhere. You never know what you might find amongst the gypsy bolts." Clorinda could feel saliva building in her mouth and she listened for news of the arrival of a caravan. But it never came. She listened attentively to Norma's stories of gypsy visits and customs. She had no way to know if Norma was telling the truth or exaggerating in order to make an impression, but she remained attentive. She remembered that she had once overheard on a downtown street that Tocopilla had been cursed by the gypsies but more than that she didn't know. She wasn't sure if she believed in gypsy curses but some said that the town was depressed for no apparent reason and therefore the gypsy curse must have taken hold. She said that as far as she could tell the town had always been as it is today. Señor Ortega reminded her that she didn't get out much and perhaps didn't notice and besides, she was young. When was the town cursed? Well, apparently around the time she was born. She told him she remembered wondering if her father's constant sadness was because he too, was a victim of the black spell.

One evening after Señor Ortega gave Clorinda a special chocolate treat, a rich piece of chocolate cake that he called a 'brownie' in English, and after he had sipped dry his second glass of whiskey, he entered his house and returned with a blue folder containing some official documents.

"Señorita Clorinda, I have taken the liberty of drawing up some legal papers in case something should happen to me."

"What kind of thing? What kind of papers?" This was out of the blue. What on earth was he thinking?

"*Bueno*. I am not a young man anymore..."

She interrupted him. "Oh, no Señor, you are wrong. You are a very young man. It's just that you have had a long experience."

"Yes, maybe it's that. But my heart is failing me."

Her face contorted and something like a long squeak escaped her lips, like the distant sound of a vehicle screeching to a halt.

"I have a serious heart condition, Señorita Clorinda." He stated matter of factly.

She felt like he had just hit her in the chest with a hammer – repeatedly. Her own heart suddenly felt weak. How could this be? How could her Clark Gable have a heart condition? And what exactly was a heart condition? She knew it was grave. And how could he make it go away? She was suddenly desperately short of breath. He had to make it go away. She felt hollow. Her knees turned to rubber. Her arms fell limp and she slumped forward onto the table, resting her forehead very near where

Señor Ortega's arms were crossed over top of the blue document folder and she refused to look up.

He slowly stretched his fingers towards her head and she thought she felt him touch her hair. Her skin tingled. Eventually, after what seemed like an eternity, the strength returned to her muscles and she raised her head but her shoulders and arms remained limp.

He shook his head. "I'm sorry, Señorita but we cannot change this thing." He spoke in such a calm voice, "I need to make you aware of these documents because they are very important for your future. After I die..."

She looked up at Señor Ortega, her chin now resting on the table opposite him, her mouth clamped shut and her eyes pleading for him to retract what he had just said, the word 'die' screaming in her head.

Then he forgot about his blue folder and he started to talk about life and death but she couldn't hear it because the pain was too loud, so she excused herself and went home, leaving him there alone with his mysterious folder full of papers.

After that, she avoided Señor Ortega for three precious days. She peered out from behind her curtains and saw him sitting on his chair at his front door, and she longed to hear his voice telling her fantastic things, but she couldn't face him now. She could not find the strength to look into his face and pretend that she was not thinking about him dying. The concept was too painful even from across the street, even when she sat at her Singer sewing machine stitching zippers and mending seams, and especially when she looked at the loom in her patio. She opened the tin lid where the chalice veil lay in its cotton padding, always acquiescent, ready to be of silent service and tried to distract herself with its beauty. She examined the fine embroidery, praising the accomplished old nun for her inspiration and skill. But it was to no avail.

The whole world ached. The air around her throbbed, sadness crawled relentlessly up the beach in waves, one after another. One morning Señor Ortega left a chocolate outside her front door. She bent down and picked it up like someone would pick up an injured bird. She cradled it in her hand, her fingers lightly wrapped around it and she held it to her chest. She walked inside, closed the door behind her and paced in front of her window, chocolate clutched to her Tuesday cotton blouse. She saw Señor Ortega uncover his red Bel Air convertible and get in and drive away. He returned late that evening and she thought he was stooped over as he walked to the house. He left the car uncovered, normally a sacrilege. He disappeared and didn't come back to sit outside. She knew because she kept vigil until two in the morning.

CHAPTER 46

Orlando Ortega

Tocopilla, 2001

Orlando often sat, pen hovering over the pages of his journals as he thought about Clorinda, but he never wrote about her. His days had become much more meaningful because of her nightly visits. Her presence alone was reason for him to ponder. Given the limited opportunity for experience in her physical environment, he initially underestimated the quality of her companionship. But as exhibited through her amazing knowledge and self-taught skills with fabric and yarn, to say nothing of her uncanny talent for recognising its origin and qualities, her intuitive and spiritual wisdom was astounding. On top of that, she delivered song in a voice as pure as a wind that played through leaves in a forest or that glided over the top of grassy meadows. Ironically, she had never seen a forest or been in a meadow.

She was a young woman of very few words but she never failed to strike a chord in Orlando when she asked astute questions. She had the unique ability of pulling ideas seemingly out of the blue and connecting them to events not obviously related. It was a talent bordering on genius. She provided a rich and rare companionship and he looked up to the heavens wondering if he was in debt after all to a power higher than himself for providing him with such an intriguing young neighbour. The pleasure, especially at this juncture of his life, was immeasurable. Even though he did not classify himself as an old man, he knew he was going to die soon. He could feel it. Perhaps only a few weeks left.

Without pressuring her, he wanted to spend more and more of his waking hours in her company. She had accepted, without hesitation, his invitation to drive to María Elena. A pain stabbed and twisted into his chest when, for just a second, he recalled the other young woman he had invited to ride with him to María Elena nearly 30 years ago. Danger signs were flashing in his brain. He dared not allow himself the pleasure or pain of that memory. So he and Clorinda set off on what promised to be an enjoyable excursion. It took only one remark from a stranger in a restaurant to turn it sour.

Orlando wanted to talk to Clorinda about this, to explain, to set the record straight. She was not going to tell anyone, and if she did, it would be of no consequence. He had no reason to hide from anyone now and besides, he would soon be lying on his back in the niche he had purchased for himself last year, nothing more than fodder for gossip.

The next day, instead of going for his usual afternoon drive, he covered his Bel Air with a soft canvass protector, unsure if he would remove it ever again, and he walked with deliberate strides to Clorinda's door. His missing toes ached and he marvelled at how his body could remember what was no longer there.

With an unnecessary amount of caution, he asked her if she would please come across the street to his house, and would she mind stepping inside? Orlando had always been conscious of neighbourhood gossip and did not want to provide people with more reason to talk about Clorinda. Although people appreciated her rare talents, she was also the subject of jokes and some derision on account of her odd manner of walking, her uncommonly mute behaviour and obvious eccentricities to do with eating wool, dressing flamboyantly, and avoiding eye contact.

Clorinda obliged, immediately locking her door and following him across the street. Orlando motioned for her to sit on the sofa and offered her tea, which she politely declined suggesting it was still too early in the afternoon for the bakeries to have filled their bins with fresh buns.

"*Bueno.* Here we are, Señorita Clorinda, you and I."

She leaned forward waiting.

"Yes, well, here we are." He stood up and paced in front of the window. She leaned further forward, to the point of falling off her chair. He kept his back turned as she scrambled back up.

"We are friends. Are we not?"

"Yes."

"Friends trust one another with secrets, with events from their past, with things they have done that they are proud of and not so proud of. " It was a statement, not a question. She waited.

"The other day in the restaurant in Mariá Elena.... what that man said...." he stopped pacing and then resumed. "I guess lots of men believe those things of me. I was a businessman. My purpose was to make money. I was not a charity. Every man takes care of himself. Some of us are better at it than others."

She surprised him when she challenged him with a response, a direct question. He had expected blind support. "Are you saying that being a thief was your business? Were you in the business of thievery?"

"No, I wasn't in the business of thievery, but I tricked many people because I was smart."

"Was it wrong?"

"I don't know."

"Was it wrong?" She repeated.

"No. It was not wrong for me. It was the way people played the game in those days. It's the same way people play the game now. Maybe it's wrong if you are the loser. But if you are the winner, like I was, then it's okay."

"Did you actually steal anything in the way that I have stolen chocolate once or twice? Just by taking it and running?"

"No. I never did anything like that."

"So it was all just clever tricks then?"

"Yes, clever tricks that made a lot of money."

"Do you believe in God, Señor Ortega?"

"No." He turned to look down at her, surprised by the change of subject. "Do you?"

"Well, I guess I do. I mean I pray to God through Santa Sara and the Virgin on the hill, and even Santa Elvira. Sometimes I ask Jesus for things directly."

"Does he listen?"

"Yes, of course he always listens when someone speaks to him."

"But does he care?"

"That is what I don't know." She said, dropping her head a little. She continued, "That is what I don't know. Everyone says that God cares. But I wonder if he really cares, because why would he take someone's mother away, and I wonder why he gave my father all of those travel brochures without giving him the chance to use them? Maybe he was testing, maybe he was teasing, but God has his reasons."

"And is God the one who tells you what is right from wrong?" Orlando ventured.

"Well, do you know right from wrong?"

"Yes."

"Then if you know right from wrong and you don't believe in God, I guess maybe it is not God who tells people. He just reminds them." She responded thoughtfully.

"Did I commit a greater wrong by tricking people so I could make lots of money? Or did you commit a greater wrong by stealing the lady's chocolate and running away?"

Clorinda was objective. "Your wrong was greater than mine because you did it more often and it was a lot more money and probably you tricked a lot of people."

"Because I don't believe in God, I don't have to confess these things and ask for forgiveness, but you know what, Señorita Clorinda? I want to ask your forgiveness."

"And why is that Señor Ortega? You have not hurt me. You have only been good to me."

"Because you are the only person who matters to me, and I think I am the only person who matters to you."

She nodded affirmatively and waited.

"Then it matters to me that you forgive me my wrongs no matter what they might be. It is important to me that you see me as a good person in spite of my shortcomings, for which I am now sorry."

"Then I forgive you Señor Ortega." She rose to her feet, thinking their conversation had come to a satisfactory end. It was the most intense conversation she'd had in her life. She was exhausted now and needed some silence.

However, Orlando was not finished. "Come here. I want to show you something." He led her to the room at the back of the house and unlocked the door. She recognised this room as his sanctuary. Furnished with a heavy wooden desk on top of which was a row with three ballpoint pens, a fountain pen, a lamp and a calendar, tucked under which was a big chair and beside which was an old armoire with locked doors, the room was a haven for his opinions and observations as well as hundreds of his darkest secrets.

He unlocked one of the armoire doors and waved his hand in front of it. "See these notebooks?"

She nodded.

"These are my journals that I started writing nearly two decades ago." He opened the other armoire door to reveal yet more stacks of the same type of book.

Her mouth hung open.

"These books, Señorita Clorinda, contain written accounts not only of my thoughts and experiences, but also details of my business dealings over the years. Do you understand?"

She nodded affirmatively but her eyes were blank.

"There are many important secrets in the pages of these books Señorita Clorinda. They contain the names of many important people who might even be in our government today."

"Oh, that's very impressive." She cooed.

"You could say that, I suppose."

He locked the armoire and the office door after they stepped back outside. "This is what I wanted to confess to you Señorita Clorinda. These are my tricks, my business dealings. Everything is written in my journals for you to see."

"Yes, well, thank-you Señor Ortega. Thank you for asking my forgiveness, and yes, I do forgive you. I forgive whatever you might have done wrong." She clearly did not grasp what he just tried to explain and she shifted her weight from one foot to the other, impatient to leave the room.

Orlando was only slightly disappointed in her lack of comprehension. The important thing was his truthful – if not absolute – confession and her willingness to forgive. She absolved him of all wrongdoing, whether it was something he remembered or not, whether he had inflicted grave injury or not. All that mattered was that the only living person of any consequence had given him blanket absolution. He was born again.

CHAPTER 47

Clorinda

Tocopilla, 2001

Clorinda sat looking at the chocolate Señor Ortega had left at her door. It was now soft and slightly misshapen, having begun to melt over the edge of her bedside table. She bent into it to take a small nibble, followed by another and finally licked the bedside table clean. Miraculously she drew enough strength from one small chocolate to confront Señor Ortega's 'condition.'

She was grateful that it was Wednesday. She selected her brightest Wednesday jewel-neckline shift, the one with bright pink and purple flower clusters in between large green leaves and added a pink carnation which shouted out from behind her right ear. It was the perfect outfit to demonstrate a positive attitude and her willingness to support Señor Ortega. She finally reached the conclusion that this situation must surely be more difficult for him than for her.

Picking up a smooth pebble from the ground, she used it to rap on his front door. It was uncharacteristically unlocked. He didn't hear her so she wandered inside and found Señor Ortega sitting hunched over his desk in the small room near the patio, his back to the door, pen in hand. He was studying his book very closely, no distance between his face and the paper. He didn't hear her walk in so she tapped lightly on the wall just inside the room and approached him without waiting for him to turn around.

"Señor Ortega." She whispered so as not to startle him. She had never simply walked into his study before and was nervous about being so bold. "Señor Ortega." She repeated, whispering more loudly this time.

He didn't answer. She approached the desk worried now that he was angry. "Señor Ortega. I'm sorry I stayed away. I mean, I was..." No response. Why did he refuse to turn around? She was unworthy, of course because she had hurt his feelings. The ache in her chest throbbed with contrition. She touched his arm very lightly. Nothing. Then she reached for his hand. She would apologise gently. She would coax him into listening to her, to understanding the reason for her absence.

But he didn't turn around. Ever.

His hand was cold. Too cold. It sent a jolt shooting through her fingers, up past her neck, striking a place in her brain where she'd only been twice before. She was deafened by the sound of his stillness. Her heart leapt with great force in her chest. Her hair stood on end. She jumped back. "*Dios!*"

She recognised the persistent hush of it, the silence upon silence of it, the hollowness of it, the utter finiteness of it. The only other dead persons she had ever seen were her father and Doña Rosita, but lack of experience was no match for certainty. She knew she couldn't argue with it.

She leaned into him to breathe his musky smell, to taste the collar of his shirt, to feel the coarseness of his unshaven cheek, to put her face against his chest, to sink her nose into his thick hair, to bend her cheek into the soft wrinkles on his neck. She wrapped her fingers over his, caressing his hands, touching his manicured fingernails. She licked the British wool sweater and stroked the light Italian weave trousers. She rubbed his soft leather shoes, and then worked her way back up to his face, finally lightly kissing his eyes that he must have closed at his last breath. Or maybe he fell asleep first. Maybe he tired of writing.

Clorinda went to the kitchen and dragged a chair back to the little room, placing it so that it touched Señor Ortega's chair and she sat down beside him at his desk, knee to knee, hand lightly on his arm, her head touching the desk, looking up at him and gently demanding his attention, as though comforting him at the hour of someone else's death, giving him counsel.

"I hope you did not feel any pain Señor Ortega. I hope I carried all of your pain home with me when I left the other night. I wanted to relieve you of it. You are a good man, Señor, even if you tricked people so that you could make lots of money. You only did whatever you had to do. Maybe you needed a lot of money. Maybe your plans required it and you had no choice."

Clorinda didn't question his drive for material wealth, nor did she resent his accumulation of it. People, especially those you love, are forgiven for what they have had to do in the circumstances that are their lives. She was relieved that she had been there for him, able to free him of his sins before he died.

"You have been my inspiration, Señor Ortega, since before we even met. I will create a great homage to you."

She gently removed the pen from between his fingers and laid it down perpendicular to the top of his notebook. She withdrew the notebook from under his hands and closed it gently, seeing only that the last word he had written was her name. "Clorinda..." The 'C', 'l', and 'o', were strong and the rest of it was scrawled, until the 'a' fell away under the weak pressure of the pen, in what must have been a final, light drag of his hand across the sheet. She tried not to dwell on images of his final moments.

She reached inside his desk drawer for the key to his armoire and unlocked the doors. His numbered notebooks were all stacked in order. She gathered them into her arms, a dozen at a time, and carried them across the street to her house. She found his blue document folder as well as other coloured folders and she put them into the same basket she had seen him use for his papers the day he arrived, the same day as when she had stood at his doorway, spying on him.

Then she went to the same kitchen cupboard where she had also gone that day more than a year ago and was surprised to find tea leaves still in a can. She put the kettle on, made herself a cup of tea and returned to the den to sit down beside Señor Ortega. This was the same room she had sat in that first day she spied on him, after he had locked her into his house. This time, as last time, she had no permission to be here, and was equally alone although this time Señor Ortega was leaning into his desk.

Clorinda sat during that entire afternoon and all through the night with him. She confessed her love for him, her low voice pronouncing word after word, ever so softly but clearly, how he had not only enabled her with his gift of the loom, but also inspired her to create her life's work.

"From the moment I set eyes on you, I knew that whatever you did was very important, so I watched because I didn't want to miss any of it. I wanted to be your friend. You know I even asked Santa Elvira to help me with that? And she answered my prayers, so maybe she told you something too? What did she tell you Señor Ortega? How did she convince you when she had never been able to convince anyone else in Tocopilla? Do you know that you are the only true friend I've had in my whole life? I'm going to miss you... I'm going to miss you like you can't imagine. I wonder if you know the pain of missing someone? How do you advise me to live with the ache of you being gone?"

She leaned into his side near his chest and blessed his heart with her salty tears. She bent close to his ear and hummed soft melodies to him, her voice breaking in and out of whispers. They were private, lamenting songs, songs that belonged only to her – and now to him – they were her invention, of her soul. She didn't see how her music could have come from the gypsies. Even if her mother was a gypsy, she had never heard her sing. She serenaded Señor Ortega, but softly, because it was something private.

"Señor Ortega, I have always wanted to fly with you across the mountains, to go where ever is beyond María Elena. Just like you were Clark Gable and I was... I don't know who, but I would be the one with you. When we drove through the desert in your car.... Well, I've only been in a Tocopilla taxi before and your Bel Air is another class of car, like from another world. Just like you."

She reached up to touch his hair and let her fingers linger there, combing it with short, light strokes.

"Maybe you are flying over the desert right now or maybe you are in heaven already. No, I don't think so. I think you are still here with me. You wanted at least one more conversation before you left. You were going to show me some papers in your blue folder. But also I need to make my confession to you. You cannot go before giving me absolution too. *Por favor*, Señor Ortega."

She could feel him listening.

"They say we are all sinners, Señor Ortega and so I must be a sinner, but on the life of my mother I can only confess to two things that I know of, and that is the stealing of chocolate and fabric items, sins I committed before I knew you. I ask you to forgive me these sins. The other sins must be hidden within my soul, but maybe my soul is so dark that I can't see them. I have searched now and then for things. I have asked the priest several times and he told me to come back to him when I was prepared to be honest about my confession. He reminded me that the only woman ever to be free from sin was our blessed Virgin Mother of Jesus. He seemed angry that I did not confess more. The truth is that I have lived my life alone in this town. I don't bother people and they don't bother me. I haven't had the chance to offend anybody. So maybe if my sins are not in my actions they are in my thoughts. Maybe my selfish ambition to adorn myself in lovely fabrics, submit to the feel and smell and taste of it, is a sinful act. Maybe God is clucking at me or clapping his hands so that I stop and pay attention to such vain transgressions. Now that you are above all of this, you can see clearly and must have the answers. I ask your forgiveness of my past sins, whatever they are and please Señor Ortega, I ask that you also forgive me the sins I will commit in the future because I don't know if I'll have a chance to ask you again. Please release me from them. I'm sure you will, or at least you might show me how not to be a sinner. Of course I release you from the need for that conversation about your papers. I assure you that your papers are safe all with me. I won't disturb your documents or interfere in your private journals. I will take them with me to my grave. You have my word."

She stood up and threw her arms above her head. "Go with the wind, Señor Ortega, because I think your soul must be free. You are a traveller, like a gypsy, you said. So you must be on your way."

Señor Ortega was leaning forward on the desk, no sign that he heard her. "Go." She whipped her arms up from her hips into the air above her head in several wide, ungraceful gestures like she was chasing away pelicans at the beach or shooing cats from her roof.

"Go Señor Ortega. You have already left me. Why hang around? I won't hold you here. I love you too much to tie you to this chair."

Two things happened at once. She burst into tears because she was overwhelmed when she heard her own voice say, "I love you." It was the first time in her life she had been able to say those words. A soft breeze entered the room, brushing against her cheeks and it whispered back to her "*Te amo también*, Clorinda." – "I love you too, Clorinda." Like a small tornado, his words spiralled around her, lifting and empowering her but making her weak at the same time.

She was so broken by the simultaneous pain and joy of Señor Ortega's departure that she fainted, folding silently onto the floor at his feet. She lay there in her crumpled Wednesday jewel neckline shift for an unknown number of hours. Perhaps she had travelled with Señor Ortega through the sky and over the mountains. But she was never sure.

She woke up when Angélica, who was standing between two policemen, repeated her name, the voices first entering her consciousness from far away and then suddenly, rudely, close to her ear.

She rose awkwardly to her feet.

"What happened here?" It was the policeman, his voice expression soft and sympathetic.

"Señor Ortega died, God rest his soul." Clorinda responded matter-of factly.

"Yes, we see that. How? When?"

"What day is it?"

The policemen exchanged glances. "It's Thursday."

Angélica looked at Clorinda's clothes. "Clorinda, you've been here since yesterday. Have you been here since yesterday?" Her expression was serious, and she looked confused.

Clorinda looked down at her pink and purple Wednesday shift. "Yes, yes, it was Wednesday."

"Then this man has been dead for a day already." The policeman announced.

"Well, no... I don't know. I mean he was here when I came to see him in the morning."

"You mean he was already dead when you arrived?"

"Yes, yes he was."

"The judge will be here any minute and then we have to remove him. We can't leave the corpse here any longer. Sanitation laws don't allow it. He is... he was... Señor Orlando del Transito Ortega de Riveras?"

Clorinda cringed at the word 'corpse' and Angélica nodded affirmatively with authority and ownership, as though she too, had been Señor Ortega's friend. Clorinda let it go.

"We must advise his family."

"He has no one. I am the only one he has." Clorinda puffed out her chest and made herself taller. "I am his best friend." She looked at the policemen one by one, her eyes focused on the buttons on their chests and then squarely at Angélica.

"Then you will come with us, complete some documents and take care of all that has to be done for him. You know what has to be done Clorinda."

The policeman turned around and ushered in the man who had been standing in the shadow of the hallway, jittery and anxious as though he was waiting for the starter's gun at the beginning of a race. Clorinda recognised Arturo the undertaker. He was one of two undertakers in Tocopilla. The other was his brother Eduardo.

Clorinda remembered him and Eduardo from when she was a young girl. Even then their physical aspect used to frighten her and she hurried to cross the street when she saw them approaching. Both brothers had thin grey transparent skin that hung over their small frames like a suit that was too big. They had deep-set eyes that never smiled. They were frail and walked hunching forward, as though they would at any moment be called upon to catch a rebound from the ground in front of them. Their, mother, a plump woman who wore bright flower patterned dresses, bless her soul, always combed their thin hair, parting it neatly to one side, but it didn't help.

After their father died, Arturo and Eduardo split the family business because of an irreparable quarrel between the two. Now their competition was literally to the death. Arturo was the youngest but even as adults both brothers looked the same, like albino vultures, their complexions as pale as death itself, their scalps partially covered with fine, sparse grey feathery hairs that hung across their bony brows above a pair of dark, beady eyes. They were probably the two most hated but essential men in Tocopilla.

Arturo, like his brother, cruised about town, often on foot, with a measuring tape draped around his neck, on the off-chance he would need to take measurements for a coffin. If they weren't cruising, they were hanging outside the emergency entrance of the hospital, each leaning on their battered station wagon that doubled as a hearse. They had fought so intensely over their father's original hearse that one of them ended up lighting it on fire. They blamed each other but nothing was resolved in the street or in court. The hearse was burned beyond any hope of repair and still sat in front of their mother's house as a monument. To what, no one was sure.

They both guaranteed the highest quality and best price for their wooden boxes that were custom-built in their back patios by underpaid, sweaty, young men who sang to tinny *tecno-cumbia* that erupted from a portable radio, hips swaying to the beat while making bad jokes about corpses. Both brothers added value to their service by offering free sandwiches and presweetened instant coffee for funeral wakes. Arturo's only advantage over his brother was that his wife made better sandwiches, and that he could be more easily persuaded to supply a few free litres of wine.

And today, he happened to be first on the scene.

No one came to Señor Ortega's wake, which had to be very short (only two hours) because he had already been dead for about two days and under these circumstances there was no time for anything elaborate. No sandwiches or loose cigarettes served on flowered china plates for Señor Ortega's last goodbye.

Because of the rush, Arturo had instructed his sweaty coffin makers to carry one of his biggest boxes directly to Señor Ortega's house. Two of them swaggered along the streets as per Arturo's instructions, empty coffin with tropical music blasting from the portable radio they had thrown inside. They carried it high on their shoulders, sometimes unable to resist throwing in a few spontaneous salsa sidesteps to the beat, which threw the other guy off balance, resulting mostly in harmless insults but in one instance, nearly dropping the coffin to fight it out.

There was no time for preparation, the wake would be a closed coffin affair, no need to shave Señor Ortega or comb his hair or even change his clothes. He would have to be buried in his British wool sweater and Italian trousers. She hoped he would consider it an appropriate outfit for all eternity.

Clorinda sat alone in an almost all-black Thursday outfit (she rushed home to change while the sweaty young men helped Arturo place Señor Ortega in the box). She pulled up a chair right beside his coffin, sat silently, leaning into it for two hours, a puddle of tears at her feet, and then she walked behind the car as Arturo drove Señor Ortega slowly down the street and around the corner to the cemetery.

Arturo had kindly offered, during this most painful time of grief, to relieve Clorinda of any worries concerning the cost of the funeral. Although he would have to make a sacrifice, he would do it in exchange for Señor Ortega's 1957 red Bel Air convertible.

He rubbed his hands in pure delight before he backed the convertible up to the front door and Clorinda helped him manoeuvre the coffin along Arturo's specially designed ramp (which had demanded another hurried trip by the sweaty helpers) and they hoisted it into the trunk of the red Bel Air. Arturo wriggled and adjusted the custom-made box until its weight shifted securely towards the back and bottom of the trunk. Drops of sweat rolled freely, pausing momentarily on the feathery tips of his thin hair before running down the back of his neck. Inside the coffin, Señor Ortega slid down in this undignified posture – feet elevated, practically travelling on his head. Arturo patted the coffin and leaned in to tell Señor Ortega to relax and enjoy the ride. He tied the coffin in place with heavy elastic ropes with hooks, and pulled the trunk lid tightly over the coffin so it wouldn't bounce and disturb the dead on the road to the cemetery, but more importantly to prevent marking the paint of his new car.

When he was satisfied, the three of them took their places – Señor Ortega in the trunk, Arturo behind the wheel (suddenly much taller and more handsome than ever before in his life) and Clorinda walking behind. Arturo thoughtfully inserted a cassette and played a sombre march along the slow road to the cemetery.

As a result of Señor Ortega's funeral, Arturo gained a distinct advantage over his brother. The red Bel Air convertible was the novel trend in Tocopilla funeral offerings. It was applauded as the newest, most fashionable, if somewhat most unconventional hearse in town. Now, instead of chasing business on foot or from behind the wheel of the brown station wagon, clients actually sought him out. His funerals were one of the most spectacular weekly (at least) events. People lined up at the end of one of Arturo's processions even if they weren't acquainted with the newly departed who was jammed head-first into the open trunk, flowers hanging out all sides. Arturo cleverly adopted Coca-cola marketing techniques. He inserted the funeral march cassette and turned it up to maximum volume, announcing the imminent march of any given funeral several minutes beforehand. It was equivalent to the Coca-cola theme song at the build-up to a televised *fútbol* match. It got people's adrenalin running.

Before long, Arturo was a local celebrity. He cruised down main street in his red convertible, sporting oversized sun glasses, four thick golden neck chains and a red (to match the car) plaid felt newsboy cap. His grey skin took on a happy pinkish hue and he gave the local funeral services industry a makeover. Many young boys were heard to announce to their fathers that their dreams of being a *fútbol* star were replaced by ambitions to enter the funeral services business. Consequently, demand for measuring tapes increased as it became fashionable to drape them around one's neck. The knock-on effect also included a small boom for local hat sellers.

CHAPTER 48

Clorinda

Tocopilla, 2001 – 2003

From that week on, Clorinda struck Wednesdays from her calendar. She lit a fire in her barrel in the patio and threw all of her jewel-neckline shifts into the flames (13 in all) and watched until there was nothing left. Because she could not simply replace Wednesday attire, she was forced to wipe the day itself from existence. She noted that when she first set eyes on Señor Ortega, it was also a Wednesday. This presented a short-lived conundrum, but she managed to rationalise her decision, because no matter what, it was essential that the guilty day should pay for its crime. So she went to sleep each Tuesday night before midnight and she slept until Thursday at 0:01am at which time she resumed her week. Her sleeping hours on what used to be Wednesdays were spent dreaming through the desert, looking for Señor Ortega. Sometimes he left traces of himself behind. She could smell his musky perfume. Other times she saw his smile in the clear blue sky and she almost caught up to his footprints before the wind erased them from the golden sand dunes. On rare occasions he joined her as she walked across the mountains just east of Tocopilla, his strong gliding steps helping to steady her as she climbed the rocky slopes. The day that used to be Wednesday became her period of dream quests and she looked forward to the timeless ventures chasing and sometimes almost catching up with Señor Ortega and they cajoled like children through flowered tapestries and blue-green variegated wind-blown gauze.

The day on which she had assumed she would be ready to die had long since passed. This was because her life's work was at a standstill and there was no end in sight. She sat for hours at a time in front of the loom contemplating the work at hand, mindlessly crocheting yellow daisies until her fingers were raw. By now she had dropped hundreds of them, one by one into a plastic bag. The chalice veil, beautiful as it was, turned out to be self-serving, offering none of its creative secrets for free. Even if it had been forthcoming, Clorinda wouldn't have known how to repay it.

She made daily visits with the exception of nonexistent Wednesdays, to the cemetery where she pulled up a wooden stool in front of Señor Ortega's niche and they commiserated over the sluggish progress of her tapestry. Initially he listened patiently but she sensed that he was becoming agitated by the repetitive nature of the conversation. Admittedly it was a monologue of complaints about her lack of muse, but she did make a point of stopping now and then to take a breath, leaning an ear towards his niche and listening for a response from within. He was attentive, considering the circumstances. Gradually she came to the conclusion that advice from Señor Ortega, especially regarding her life's work was, in fact, written in his journals, that he had already answered almost anything she could possibly ask. So she planned to delve into the books.

After this realisation, even before the day she unlocked her father's old armoire where she had replaced the travel brochures with Señor Ortega's notebooks, the tone of her visits to Señor Ortega changed to something less whiney and she noticed a marked improvement in their relationship. Miraculously there was universal harmony for the hour each afternoon that she spent with Señor Ortega at the cemetery. A light breeze caressed the bare skin on her arms, neck and face and during her visits she was spared the stench of the fish plant. She was able instead to take delight in the scent of fresh carnations, one of which she usually felt that she had been given divine permission to move from a neighbouring grave to place on the shelf of Señor Ortega's niche. Of course, she asked his forgiveness for this habitual petty theft.

She relaxed in the peace and quiet of the surroundings in Señor Ortega's cemetery patio. Over time her daily visits were transformed from wrestling with her loneliness and longing for Señor Ortega into what she smugly defined as healthy communions between kindred spirits. She still missed him terribly when she was at home by herself, but sitting in front of his niche brought back to her the companionship they shared before he died. Sometimes she regretted not introducing herself to Señor Ortega after the first day that she set eyes on him, but she forced those ideas away, reminding herself that every minute they eventually did spend together was very rich.

The afternoon she decided to seek her muse from within Señor Ortega's journals, the town had just settled down for siesta. The dogs had stopped barking, and the cats were stretched out on tin roofs soaking in the sunshine that forced itself through a layer of cloud. Housewives were seated comfortably in front of their televisions watching an episode of their favourite soap opera. Waves rolled softly onto the beach. Small groups of vultures circled here and there above the streets and pelicans stood on the railings of the dock looking sleepily out to sea. The ore train had just rattled its way down to the port and was now quiet. Even most taxi drivers were off the roads, now snoring, arms folded on a chair in their patio or laying flat on their backs on a bed with their shoes on. The town would be peaceful for a few hours. It was the perfect atmosphere for Clorinda's new project.

She rearranged her work space, washed the floor and waxed her wooden side table. She organised the piles of mending and repositioned the scant furniture in the room (table, chair, sewing machine, and narrow book case) so it looked more spacious and welcoming. The room was transformed into a sort of working chapel, not necessarily a place of worship, but a space into which she felt comfortable introducing Señor Ortega's journals, which were sacred. This was her father's former bedroom, may he rest in peace. She had never before disturbed its contents other than when she replaced the bed with her sewing table and shelf, but now she needed him to share some of his space. She planned to use his armoire for Señor Ortega's journals so she removed her father's old travel brochures and stacked them into respectable piles on the bookshelf. She couldn't bring herself to throw them away. Even though they were of no use, they must have held great value for her father. She browsed through a few of them, blowing dust from the yellowed covers. She found among them, an old government publication about the rights of Chilean mainlanders on Easter Island and looked for some signs, a mark perhaps or a note in the margin, to indicate her father's purpose with this information. But there was nothing. She turned back to the journals, which would now be safe under lock and key in the armoire.

This done, she retired to her bedroom and lay down on her bed and looked up at the ceiling. All of her earlier energy was drained and she needed to sleep. She noted once again, how peaceful it was at this hour and consciously relaxed. She stared blankly up at the ceiling as she methodically tightened and loosened toes, knees, buttocks, arms, shoulders, neck, and exhaled a long breath.

She was about to close her eyes when her father silently entered the room in his green gabardine coveralls. It was as though he had just returned from his shift at the mines. He still had his packsack over his shoulder and his coveralls were dusty from throwing himself off the train and rolling down the hill. At first he didn't say anything to her.

She lay there, limbs frozen, heart pounding, her voice caught in her throat. Her eyes followed her father as he approached the bed. He was floating soundlessly, not trudging and puffing as he used to.

The characteristic emptiness was gone from his eyes. He looked at her as though he was seeing her for the very first time. "I can't tell you why your mother left." He said. "I still don't know, after all these years of searching. I haven't been able to find her. I will keep looking. I'm sorry Clorinda."

Then he leaned forward and his hand brushed through the air above her shoulder and she felt the coldness of his ghost. "But we all do what we have to do, Clorinda. You are a good girl. Your mother's disappearance wasn't your fault and it wasn't mine. It was a gypsy curse. That much I know." He vanished from the room.

She blinked her eyes into the dim afternoon light, her body tingling, senses alert, not attempting to move, not knowing if she could. She could smell the kerosene that had always stained his coveralls still hanging in the air. She heard the sound of his voice very clearly and she repeated in whispers over and over again what he told her. He had spoken to her past the silent years of his life. Where did he find the words?

She was suddenly absolutely exhausted and she fell asleep before she had the answer. When she woke up she wasn't sure if her father's presence had been a dream. But she felt a peace that she realised she had been missing all her life and she went outside to the patio, raised her arms to the sun and whispered her thanks to him, wherever he was now wandering.

She approached Señor Ortega's journals with confidence and new energy. His handwriting was meticulous and easy to read. Her initial trepidation, evident as her fingers shook at the mere touch of the pages he had set his pen to, was washed away when, as she read, she began to hear his voice and often heard a smile between his words. He was giving her the courage to continue.

Clorinda turned the pages slowly and kept her face very near the surface of each sheet, her head moving back and forth like an old typewriter carriage, mouthing the words under her breath. It was very tiring and the motion made her dizzy. In addition, Señor Ortega's vocabulary was more extensive than hers and she didn't have a dictionary. She did her best to interpret the meanings of unknown words and found that if he used the same one often enough, she was able to assign a concept. She persisted steadily through long afternoons and it became easier as she worked her way, line by line, page by page, through the stacks.

His first journals, begun when he moved to Canada, were of his early perceptions and he qualified it with the awareness that he was living within a slice of the culture in a tiny quadrant of the whole. Therefore his experience of Canada was a very limited one, and he judged it as such. She felt that this was her first important lesson.

After his early remarks about his new life in the new land – the snow and the cold, this foreign society in which information was warmly shared and efficiently dispersed, rules were respected, schedules and deadlines that were met, employees as well as employers assumed responsibility, the level of honest compliance and general lack of suspicion was a national characteristic – he began to digress.

After that, Señor Ortega used his journals to reflect on his own life and his encounters with others. He commented on naïve individuals and corrupt systems, on good, hard-working men and on sleazy characters looking for an easy way out – or in, as it were.

In one journal he wrote a great deal about his brother Jorge, much more than what he told her on their evenings together outside his front door. This journal seemed to be an attempt to analyse his relationship with Jorge but he was unable to reach a satisfactory conclusion. He rarely mentioned his mother except in reference to her health and finally in a relatively short entry after she died. Clorinda judged that by the lack of entries regarding such an all-important subject as his own mother, it could only mean that it was too painful for him to write about. From there she deduced that he probably omitted other equally or perhaps, even more deeply important, people or events in his life.

She read through dozens of notebooks about his business dealings in Chile and her attention piqued each time she recognised the names of elected officials and important businessmen. These same names sometimes ran in big letters across newspapers that hung by clothespins to nylon cords outside the corner kiosks of her neighbourhood.

In between reading Señor Ortega's notebooks, Clorinda sat down in front of her loom and studied the warp that she had strung months ago, squinting her eyes, still waiting for inspiration to wash across it, like ghost images painting themselves onto her woollen canvas. She often unravelled balls of yarn to look at them in the sunlight and then rushed to re-wrap them so they wouldn't fade. But sometimes she forgot herself and before she knew it, she was standing in the midst of a maze of coloured threads that were strewn from one end of her patio wall to another at various angles and heights. Depending on her mood, she either stepped playfully in and out or she scowled and furiously followed a thread to its end, re-wrapping it into a tight, hurried ball and cursing her own silly behaviour under her breath.

Her collection of crocheted daisies grew dramatically. She ran out of the same yellow cotton and began to make them out of white and then orange and even blue. She filled more plastic bags with daisies.

Santa Sara watched her without sympathy from her altar in the far corner of the patio. In spite of the Virgin's ineffectiveness to date, Clorinda continued to light candles, asking for the inspiration that simply failed to materialise. Considering her slow progress, Clorinda's promise that she would die when her tapestry was complete meant she would live to be 200 years old. She became very discouraged.

Finally she opened the last of Señor Ortega's numbered notebooks and read the final entry, the one in which her name was scrawled, firmly and then nothing more than a thin line that disappeared into the air above the page, his last thought before fading away from her. The writing on this page made no sense to her. It was simply an unbroken list of names of people, both men and women. The list which was not really a list at all, but a single paragraph, beginning at the top left of the page and continuing down, line after line, left to right, names separated by commas, first names randomly interspersed with last names, as though all of the names were either unified, each having been given an equal amount of importance, or all names, both first and last, were meant to be disconnected.

CHAPTER 49

Clorinda

Tocopilla, 2003

Clorinda was tormented by her stagnant tapestry and her search in vain for a direction. Contrary to what she had expected and hoped for, it was not among the names and events so scrupulously detailed in Señor Ortega's journals. She repeatedly returned to his hard-cover notebooks looking for something she must have missed. It had all been of sufficient importance for Señor Ortega to write about it and, he warned, too important for anyone else to read. Why, then, did he risk writing it down? What sort of fatalistic satisfaction did it bring? Was he tormented by the events of his own life? She sincerely hoped not.

His most perplexing theme, which was mentioned repeatedly through the years of journals, was something he called cosmic justice. He rambled on about inequalities, good and evil, paying for your sins or reaping rewards for good deeds – always something in exchange for something else. He said these were not ideas from the cosmos at all, but something invented by men. Even an orderly universe did not exist, he said, so it was impossible that it could keep track of good and evil deeds or saintly lives, much less an accurate accounting of due reward or punishment. She didn't fully comprehend the concept and initially she thought it was synonymous with 'God' and maybe for Señor Ortega it was. He said he didn't believe in cosmic justice and she knew that he also didn't believe in God. "I believe in you," he had said to Clorinda one day when she asked him. And he smiled. This was the part that confused her the most.

His journals revealed many of his transgressions with a varying amount of detail. Had she known the extent of his youthful deviousness when he had bestowed the power of forgiveness on her, she might have at least demanded some penance before relieving his conscience. She imagined herself ordering Señor Ortega, as a priest might do, to say the rosary or to repeat the Lord's prayer ten times. She tried to picture him creeping silently out of a confessional, head bowed, taking his place alone in a back corner of the church and kneeling down with his beads in hand. It was an absurd notion and she couldn't complete the image in her head. Señor Ortega would not do penance. Her face reddened at her wild imagination.

She had been privileged to see his softer side when he was alive, and she came to understand some of his admitted weaknesses through his writing. Some of the words in his journals were dampened with a certain impotence that even a strong, wilful man like Señor Ortega was apparently unable to overcome. She wondered what he was not saying, what he refused to mention by name, what was so painful that he could not recall. This mysterious weakness of his begged for true balance in judging the man (if there must be judgment). It weighed towards sympathising with him rather than seeing him only for his dark deeds. The question of Señor Ortega was not a black or white one; there were many tones in between. She congratulated herself for her choice of grey wool for Señor Ortega's patch on her tapestry.

Clorinda was certain that although the journals were full of detail and personal reflection, Señor Ortega didn't include in them the things that affected him most profoundly. She noted more than once that he did not ruminate about his mother as he had on Jorge. Perhaps writing about his mother – may she rest in peace – would have tread too heavily on his wounded soul. Clorinda sympathised with the pain of dwelling on lost loved ones, mostly her mother. She couldn't allow herself to speculate about her mother's abrupt and cruel disappearance because it precipitated an agonisingly fruitless exercise in which she would circle around and arrive back at the same question, defeated and haunted by a renewed feeling of loneliness.

Her mother had dropped into a void, the type of which Clorinda did not know existed until she was a young woman living by herself in the immense silence after her father's death. She dipped her toes into the void a few times, testing it like one tests the temperature of the sea before going for a swim. It was dark and warm and mysteriously attractive. She waded into the void a few times. Fortunately she had been spared its emptiness because something always brought her back to the safety of its shallow edges. Usually it was the memory of a gift of fabric from Angélica or her own mental reminder of a cashmere sweater she had seen in the window of one of the American-style second hand shops on main street.

Now, for nearly a year, her saviour had been Señor Ortega and even after he left her alone, she knew he stood guard at the fringes of her void with his arms outstretched. His journals distracted her from its shores. She interpreted this to mean that he was encouraging her not to abandon her purpose.

Although Señor Ortega never mentioned Clorinda in his journals except when he scrawled her name as he breathed his last breath, her full name was typewritten on several official documents filed inside the blue folder that Señor Ortega had wanted to show her the day he gave her the terrible news of his weak heart. One of the documents was called a 'Power of Attorney' and there were others clipped neatly behind it. Some looked like forms, several boxes neatly filled in with typewritten letters and numbers. On other sheets were several paragraphs of formal language that were much too sophisticated for her to interpret but she recognised her name among them. Yet others that were not even in Spanish, but what she knew must be English, mentioned Switzerland and London and New York with names that included the words 'Investment Bank.' Each document was imprinted with various official logos (she noted with amazement that some were even metallic gold and silver) and several pages were embossed or stamped with ink in the shapes of eagles and diamonds. Almost all were signed with a hurried, flowing signature. Señor Ortega's name appeared underneath and on some, a black thumbprint was pressed beside them onto the paper.

She used the tips of her index finger and thumb to cautiously turn the sheets over, one by one, avoiding even the slightest possibility of accidentally smudging the ink or bending the corners. She leaned into them, flaring her nostrils to inhale and identify the ink. With her eyes so close to the surface that she couldn't focus on the letters, she dared to run a finger over the raised type of the logos and stamps. To satisfy her curiosity she selected one bone-coloured linen textured sheet and very slowly extended her tongue until it touched the bottom right corner. She licked along the edge, only for a few centimetres, and resisted sucking the paper into her mouth. She'd never seen nor tasted such beautiful, textured papers in her life.

Señor Ortega's journals and secret papers were beginning to keep her awake at night. Although it was very seldom, if at all, that anyone entered her house, she worried that somehow, someone was going to discover them. She knew there was no basis for this concern because no one knew the journals existed much less expected to find them in her house, but the unreasonable fear manifested itself just the same. It began to weigh so heavily that she couldn't concentrate on her mending and it distracted her from seeking the necessary inspiration to continue with her life's work. Her worry over the safety of the journals gradually took control of her. She compulsively jumped out of her chair to see if the key to the armoire was in the drawer where she left it. And as if that wasn't enough, she became obsessed not only with the safety of the journals, but with the security of the key to the armoire where they were stored. She tied it to a shoe string and hung it around her neck under her clothing.

She found two old padlocks among her father's forgotten tools in a grimy box at the end of the patio and she slipped them into metal harnesses she clumsily screwed across her front door.

She repeatedly unlocked and re-locked both cupboards of the armoire. She would walk out of the room, reach only as far as the doorway before doing an about face, and return to double check that the armoire doors were really locked. The obsession continued to build. It didn't take long before she succumbed to a compulsion to count the number of journals in the stacks to be sure none of the books were missing. It got worse – she then felt compelled to open and review the numbered journals to ensure none of the pages had gone missing and then it escalated to the point where she scoured the pages one by one to ensure the words themselves had not disappeared. She didn't know the source of this fear but it had stubbornly evolved until it consumed her and she was absolutely under its control.

She started at the beginning and read each notebook through to the end. It occurred to her that she was missing something or that as she read through one of the journals, something was being mysteriously stolen from another. She was forced to read the series of notebooks again. Then she re-read single pages, going back over paragraphs and finally repeatedly reviewing single sentences, scanning for missing letters. The intense relentless labour of the revisions was exhausting.

She was indisposed for days upon days. The mending piled up. People began banging on her door, demanding their clothing. Angélica stood outside her window, whining at first, and then ranting. Clorinda lifted her nose out of the journals only to shriek that she wanted to be left in peace. The word on the street was that she had finally tipped over the edge and had gone absolutely crazy. Instead of passing by her house in the hopes of hearing her songs, neighbours now paused, hoping to catch a glimpse of the crazy woman through the window of her lair.

She forgot to eat, once in awhile making a cup of tea, only to be left untouched and grow cold on the shelf far from the desk in order not to spill a single drop on any of the pages. She forgot to light a candle at the foot of Santa Sara and the icon stood mutely admonishing her, her smile transfigured to an expression of righteous disdain.

She lost sight of everything except for the journals, their demand

for her concentration drained her mental faculties and her head was spinning. She didn't know if it was day or night. She forgot to dress accordingly.
She was unable to track her revisions with any confidence. There was to
be no end.

She was reading the first page of journal number 1 for the 121st
time. Like the needle on an old record, she was caught in a groove from
which she would never escape, reading the same lines again and again.
It was Señor Ortega's description about how the snow fell silently over
Canada, day and night, and of the people who trudged through it each
morning, their voices white and muffled – when all at once, she was called
to stop. Her ears perked up and the hair on the back of her neck stood
on end. She slammed journal number one closed, scrambled to kneel in
front of the armoire and ran her fingers along the stacks of books until she
reached the last one. She pulled it out and turned to the last page, to the
last word of the last entry.

It said, "Clori-i-i-n-d-aaaa." She read it again, "Clori-i-i-n-d-aaaa."

She looked around. She could hear Señor Ortega's smile in the air
around her. She could smell his musky perfume. He was inviting her. But
she couldn't go and visit him at his niche, at least not under the current
risky circumstances. He must remember that she had promised to guard
his journals.

The last word of his last entry spoke to her again, "Clori-i-i-n-daaaa."

He was insisting. She would have no choice but to go to him. Her
only option was to take the journals with her.

She ran to her front window and yelled at the first boy that passed by
on the street. He nervously obeyed her request to come closer. She was a
crazy woman that he dare not disobey for fear of weird consequences, ones
he knew he was incapable of imagining. He crept timidly to the window.

"Boy, get me a wheel barrow. I need one in a hurry." She ordered.

The boy ran off and she scurried to the back of her house where she
gently removed Santa Sara from the top of the wooden crate. She searched
and found a replacement altar amongst the pile of rusty, spare bicycle and

refrigerator parts, a metal bed frame, and sundry cardboard boxes that still populated the far corner of the patio. Two cats escaped out from under, jumped up to the roof, and turned around to observe, craning their necks, eyes round and staring.

She dragged the crate to the centre of the patio and in between bustling inside to check on the contents of the armoire, she scrubbed years of dirt and grime from all of the crate's wooden slats. She hauled it down the hall and placed it in the centre of her work room. She unlocked the armoire cupboards, removed the journals and carefully piled them into the wooden crate. As an afterthought, and after hesitating more than once, she also gathered all of Señor Ortega's coloured document folders, including the blue one with her name on many of the papers, and tucked them carefully beside the journals. Then she nailed the crate shut, sat on top of it, elbows on knees, head in hands, and waited until the boy returned with the wheelbarrow.

He helped her load the crate into the wheelbarrow, and together they wheeled it down the road, around the corner and up to the cemetery. It was a solemn procession with the same number of people that had accompanied Señor Ortega to his burial, but this time in a much less elegant hearse. Clorinda leaned into the box, reaching to steady it as the boy wobbled and almost dropped the wheelbarrow more than once.

She instructed him to follow her through the patios until they arrived at Señor Ortega's niche and to leave wheelbarrow there with her. She paid him with the coins she had scraped from the bottom of her empty coffee can. He left shaking his head, and she stretched her arms as far as she could reach around the crate, keeping lookout. Maintaining such vigilance made it impossible to visit with Señor Ortega. She was preoccupied with her cargo. It was much too vulnerable, far too exposed. This was a thousand times worse than being at home with the journals. She must do something else. So she remained draped across the crate in the wheelbarrow, eyes darting suspiciously in all directions, until a solution occurred to her. She called out to the cemetery caretaker as he walked down the path.

"Señorita Clorinda, this is a very unusual request and I don't know if I can help you."

"But Maestro, I am the registered owner of this niche. Go and check the office records for yourself. Besides, I am not burying anyone. I am storing some of my things. "

"How do I know this crate does not contain someone's remains?" He tested her with his superior, sinister accusation.

She was insulted. "Because I say so. That's how!" She placed her hands on her hips. "Smell it if you want."

He declined. "*Sí*, but there is still paperwork that needs to be done. This is extremely uncommon. I can't just seal off niches without proper authorisation."

"I'll take care of it afterwards." She couldn't decide whether to plead or demand. She hadn't eaten in days, had barely slept, and was going crazy reading the same sentences time after time after time. Soon she would believe it was snowing over Tocopilla. She didn't know if it was Friday or Saturday, or heaven forbid, a nonexistent Wednesday. She probably wasn't dressed properly. And she hadn't truly conversed with Señor Ortega in ages. She was totally disconcerted and desperate to bring this to an end.

The caretaker stood silently studying her from head to foot as she blubbered a lot of nonsense, at once pleading and demanding, and after several long moments he acquiesced. He would bend the rules just this once. Perhaps it was her offer to sew two brand new pairs of coveralls in exchange for his work that convinced him. She assured him that she had just the right pieces of blue gabardine and could add some of the heavy striped linen, perhaps even a patch of flowered canvas here and there. She inhaled a satisfied, creative breath. He would be the best-dressed caretaker in all of Chile. She looked up into the sky, thankful that she had finally managed to find a solution and concentrate for even a second on something other than the journals. She glanced over at Señor

Ortega's niche and promised him under her breath that she would be there shortly for a proper visit.

The caretaker assured her that professional cemetery caretakers such as himself had methods to insert much bigger and heavier boxes into niches, so sliding in the crate full of whatever-this-was would not be a difficult task. He turned unceremoniously to the job at hand, attempting to lift it. He grunted and finally angled it until he manoeuvred one corner onto a shoulder and he indicated, veins popping out on his neck, that Clorinda should help him hoist the box higher into the air. When he slipped on the gravel, lost his footing and nearly broke his shoulder, he cursed and shot a dark glance at her.

The box toppled over, several nails popped out from one side and two slats sprung away from the frame. The blue folder fell onto the ground just out of Clorinda's reach. In her attempt to stretch across the ground and trap it under her foot she slipped and did an awkward split, pulling a thigh muscle. She yelped as at that moment the wind swooped down and grabbed the blue folder full of papers, hurling them helter-skelter into the air. She jumped about holding her thigh with one hand and leapt awkwardly to catch the papers with the other. The wind teased her, making the papers perform crazy acrobatics on wild updrafts. A few of them sliced across the air in front of the caretaker and he reached out to grab them. Otherwise he stood by uselessly, seemingly enjoying the spectacle as Clorinda's ridiculous dance continued. Finally she retrieved the papers but had a heavy suspicion that a few had escaped and had been blown into far-off patios within the cemetery, and were now irretrievable. She glanced apologetically at Señor Ortega's niche, tears in her eyes. She prayed she had not let him down.

The caretaker helped her stash the folder and documents, all worse for wear, back inside the crate and used rocks to hammer the slats back in place. She did her best to help by wedging her shoulder in beside the caretaker's and holding the bottom of the crate as he heaved it, at last putting it to rest on the shelf of the niche. The caretaker tried to chase it further back into the cavern with curses, but it would only go so far. He told Clorinda they would have to be satisfied with that position because it left him just enough space to slide the concrete slab across the front. Clorinda was reminded for a second of how someone had rolled a big rock in front of Jesus' tomb. She made a mental note to return in three days to ensure that her tomb was still closed.

The caretaker glanced at Clorinda for a signal to seal the niche with freshly mixed concrete, and she stood vigil for 20 minutes as he unceremoniously slathered the grey mud around the sides and locked the journals away into their vault.

She was almost giddy with relief as she dragged a wooden stool in front of Señor Ortega's niche to pay him a long overdue visit.

"My apologies for my lateness and my state of dress, Señor." She began formally, suddenly conscious of her unkempt appearance. "I beg you to understand my reasons for sitting with you today as I do. I assure you, it's not due to lack of respect." She bowed forward so deeply that she fell off the stool.

Trying to hide her embarrassment, she clambering back up, brushing her skirt and she sat primly, hands folded on her lap with as much dignity as she could reclaim. "As I promised you, Señor Ortega, I have taken your private journals to my grave. They will forever be safe." She almost exploded with pride at her own ingenuity.

She could sense his approving smile and she relaxed, feeling she had returned to a sane world.

"Now things will go back to how they were. You know, some clients are very angry with me. But I'll convince them that everything is all right now...." She turned her face up to focus on the grey wall behind which he lay, surely attentive to her every word.

"I will be free to come and visit you every day again. And, Señor Ortega, I will make progress on my life's work. You'll be very pleased. Of course since I'm doing it for you, how can I not continue? My life's work will not be denied."

She added as an afterthought, "And if you want to review your journals, they are conveniently next door. I also included the official documents in your blue folder and, well, all of your folders with all of your important papers. So nothing has been left to chance. Your history is safe with you and me and the walls." She winked and pointed to the wall in which he and the documents were stored. Her cheeks were flushed with a pink satisfaction.

As she inhaled before her next bit of monologue, she heard Señor Ortega's moan from inside the wall. It was loud and long and forlorn and there was no smile in the sound.

When she returned after three days to check the niche, she walked past the flower sellers and failed to notice that more than one flower bunch was wrapped in a paper cone that was made from lovely textured paper imprinted with golden and silver seals in the shape of diamonds and eagles with her named typed underneath and the words 'Investment Bank' and Señor Ortega's signature at the bottom.

CHAPTER 50

Clorinda

Tocopilla, 2004

Clorinda leaned back in the low wooden chair in front of her loom. Santa Sara was standing on her altar across the patio, two candles burning at her feet. The glass-beaded rose in the centre of Señor Ortega's grey patch glistened in the morning sunlight. It was Sunday, a day which would surely bring inspiration and insight. She sensed a nervous glow from within the bags of yarn and fabric swatches, as they anxiously anticipated her plans for them. Dozens of bright butterflies (unheard of in Tocopilla because of its lack of vegetation) fluttered up from within the multitude of branded plastic fields filled with fabric daisies and disappeared into the blue sky.

She selected a bag of local and synthetic yarns, nothing special to begin with. She was planning to weave the interaction between Señor Ortega and the *fútbol* club of which he had been president and she would intersperse the story with snippets of Bolivian and Chilean gold and silver miners.

She had already decided that the work would not be pictorial as were traditional *arpilleras*, rather it would be impressionistic. This inspiration had struck her like a bump in the night and thrilled her so much that she tickled inside. It gave her permission to capriciously combine threads and create three-dimensional elements by stitching swatches of fabric into soft, abstract and geometric shapes before attaching them to the warp. She felt entirely free to work from her intuition. Shapes emerged from the shadows of her mind and she assigned them personality and energy.

She would begin the warp at the top left corner and jump around her woollen canvas, attaching colour and texture as she proceeded from one patch to another until it finally joined the grey patch that belonged to Señor Ortega, the focus of the piece, the light of her life.

Over the months during which she toiled she wasn't aware of the exact moment at which the grey patch and Señor Ortega became one and the same. She spoke to the grey patch as though she was speaking to him. She asked its advice about her choice of colours, whether or not some shapes were too whimsical, if the texture was too heavy, if the tone was just right.

Her life's work became a joint effort. She deferred to the grey patch at all times, always coming back to it for affirmation and using it as her point of reference. While the patch remained a plain grey shapeless space with nothing adorning it apart from the beaded rose in the centre and the yellow daisy that joined it to the red that represented herself, she eventually filled in everything around it. At the same time, because of her constant close association with the grey patch she began to notice fine, new strands of various distinct tints within the grey threads themselves.

She squinted her eyes and leaned in closely, a tantalising intimacy between herself and the wool, her eyelashes nearly brushing the threads, her tongue feeling the fuzzy hairs of the yarn. She scrutinised every millimetre of the grey patch. Surprisingly this exercise enabled her to extract new information about Señor Ortega and as the strands that made up the threads began to take on a life of their own, she was struck with previously unknown details about Señor Ortega's personality and felt she had come to know him so completely that they had truly become one in spirit. She expressed to the grey patch her silent yearning for her mother which had inexplicably presented itself to her more and more often as her relationship with the patch blossomed. She felt the grey patch's sympathy.

The tapestry was developing into a beautiful three-dimensional mélange, reflecting she thought, the texture of Señor Ortega's life. "Don't you agree, Señor Ortega?" She asked as she stroked his wool. She gave it two quick soft licks. She considered her relationship with the grey patch a democratic one, and was comfortable in her egalitarian, interactive approach. However, she had to admit that Señor Ortega, being the grey patch of her own creation, was under her absolute control. She tried not to take advantage of him. Although she was careful not to put words in his mouth, she was amazed at how many choices they were in complete agreement upon, and how the exact same idea would simultaneously occur to both of them. She consciously avoided heavy-handed tactics that would force him to see things her way, and the relationship worked smoothly, ideas and opinions always perfectly synchronised.

"I have two questions Señor Ortega. The first is, why did you write your journals? And the second is, why did you tell me about them?"

The grey patch responded to her, smiling as always, "To be honest Señorita Clorinda, I started to write the journals in Canada because without the possibility to work in the manner in which I was accustomed, I became bored. I didn't really need the money, I found that once I started writing my journals, I quite enjoyed it, it allowed me to reflect, and I was in a very peaceful place. When I returned to Chile I continued with the journals only because I found myself once again in a position where I couldn't work in my usual manner. It became a lifestyle – the writing, I mean. And the answer to your second question is, I don't know."

"Yes, you know Señor Ortega." She wagged her finger and chided the grey patch. "You know, and you can tell me." She poked at his greyness a few times to coax him into admitting it.

He spoke from his heart. "*Bueno*. To be honest, I am not really sure, but I think all of a sudden you were the most important person in my life and I wanted to show you that I was not a totally bad man. It only made sense that I should ask you to read my journals so you could see for yourself how things were done. Also I needed you to guard the books. I couldn't let them fall into the wrong hands."

"So were you using me? Or did you really want me to understand you?"

The voice paused in his grey space before answering. Clorinda sat up straight, making eye contact with the glass-beaded rose in the middle of Señor Ortega's patch, threatening it to come up with the answer she wanted to hear.

It answered her with a glint, "How much can someone really understand someone else unless they are presented with the same circumstances that offer the same sets of choices? That being said, I felt that you would sympathise with me."

She relaxed. "That's what I was hoping to hear Señor Ortega. I think we two are quite alike, and for that reason we do understand each other as much as this world will ever allow."

"Or..." she looked at the grey patch suspiciously, "Or, did you really hope that I might turn in your journals to someone after you were gone? Then the dirty details would be exposed to the public and you would be safe where you are now once the scandals broke? You didn't really expect me to place myself in the centre of controversy did you? I mean, if I thought you really wanted me to do it, I might have... I'm not sure."

"I honestly don't know, Señorita Clorinda."

She moved on. "And the names, Señor Ortega, the list of names in your last entry... I don't understand why you wrote so many names. I mean..."

"Oh, that." The grey patch interrupted her with a laugh. She loved the sound of his laughter and she chimed in, her own voice echoing off the patio walls.

"Señorita Clorinda, I was dying. I could feel my mind getting soft. I wanted to wake myself up, to test my memory. So I began to make a random list of the names of all the people I ever met in my life. I didn't get very far, but I did manage to list the important ones, I'm sure. It was really just a mind game."

"My name was the last one."

"Yes, I saved the best for last."

Señor Ortega was such a charmer. He always said what she wanted to hear. It warmed her to the bone. She beamed back at the grey patch and bent down to pull a yellow daisy out of her bag as a reward for him. She stitched it in place next to the one she had attached at their red and grey meeting point ages ago, and stood back to admire it, humming. They made a lovely grouping – the daisies and her and Señor Ortega.

She studied her red patch, a small but bright, triangular shape beginning at the base of Señor Ortega's grey. It should really be interwoven more with the grey. Although they had spent very little of their lives together, they had formed a formidable bond – isn't that so, Señor Ortega?

The grey patch was in vigorous agreement.

With a thick needle, she wove some of her red wool into the edges of Señor Ortega's grey, like bloody fingers scratching his grey surface. She stood back, tilting her head to one side and then the other. No, it wasn't enough. The red needed to reach up further inside the grey. They needed a stronger, more imperial bond. She added a bit more, and then a bit more, and yet more, daring to move higher and higher into the grey patch, until Señor Ortega was covered in heavy vertical red scratches. She leaned forward and, flicking her tongue, she tasted the wool, licking several stripes, one after the other until she was satisfied that the flavour was consistent. Yes, she had managed to combine the very different yarns into a perfect savoury combination. It was delicious.

The grey yarn looked back at her from inside its red prison bars where she knew he would always be safe, just as his journals were safe inside her tomb. No harm would ever come to any of them.

The two daisies looked lovely and maybe she would employ more. She pulled her bags of daisies towards herself – which now added up to eight of the large *Mercado Central* branded bags – and she dumped them all out onto the patio floor. There must be thousands upon thousands of them. Ooh, they were beautiful. She crouched onto her knees, delved into the mounds with her fingers, threw the cotton daisies high up into the air and let them rain back down onto her upturned face and outstretched arms. She repeated the movement again and again, gaining momentum and velocity. She looked like a windmill propelled by a strong wind under a steady torrent of daisies. Finally she ran out of breath and collapsed onto the patio floor, head buried in her elbows, a broad smile pushing at her reddened cheeks. She raised her head and looked around. Daisies everywhere, a few had even come to rest on Santa Sara. Clorinda squinted at the icon's face and saw an expression of subtle but pure delight. She rose to her knees and raked the daisies with her fingers, spreading them across the patio floor. They had magically converted her drab concrete floor into the flowering desert, covering no less than three square metres. Thousands of daisy faces were raised up to happily acknowledge the sun and testify to the fine state of the world today.

Still kneeling in the midst of her desert garden, she glanced up at her tapestry. How incredible that it had finally taken on a life of its own. It was so colourful, with patches of flat colour, one blending into another, loose threads crisscrossed, hanging like children's swings here and there over the section she referred to as 'el escenario canadiense'. She had combined plenty of white wool with deep green, thick yarn bunched in vertical shapes in and around strips of celestial blue satin, confident in her interpretation of the Canadian landscape. The blue blended into a slightly deeper tint, that was repeated throughout the entire weaving. This represented the Chilean sky. It was, of course, interrupted by the Andean peaks with their rugged tops of golds, browns, bronzes, oranges and reds. Over these backgrounds, she added scrimps and shards of colour to retell the stories from Señor Ortega's journals.

She incorporated characters, both dead and living, as Señor Ortega had described them. No one was exempt from the truth as she knew it. She personified the man called Rodrigo, for example, with the army green woven into heavy black that lurked in the shadow of powerful chartreuse. She connected shimmering silver threads that insidiously entrapped an entire section she had named '*compradrismo*'. Caught in this shining web were the names which, according to Señor Ortega, must remain unspoken. But she recognised their deeds. She represented many of them with wicked three-dimensional patches. The unidentified players knew each other intimately, all holding some power, one over the other, and she bound them closely, linking them like gnarled fingers of several old hands, all clawing and applauding at the same time. She represented the skyscrapers of downtown Santiago with their woollen cornices and mesh windows behind which lurked shadowy twisted threads. She added daubs of colour for the bright spots in Señor Ortega's life, his early satisfaction when he counted his money, the pure joy as he sped in his red Bel Air convertible across the open desert. She wove shimmering red satin so that it appeared and disappeared in a straight line across an expanse of golden raw silk. She depicted with lush, heavily textured green and brown squares, his quiet time tucked away in a small room in western Canada, and then his soft, yellow joy in the friendship he shared with Clorinda.

Clorinda considered her life's work a piece of art. It represented all of the things that people do for their own reasons, things that she learned about from Señor Ortega who was an expert on living in the wider world. She was still obsessed with her life's work, but not in the same static way that she felt when she was searching for her muse. Now it was because, although she had woven the colour and texture into meaningful and representative shapes and spaces, she intuitively knew that it was not yet finished.

She had not forgotten her plan to lay down and die upon completion of her tapestry but it was not yet ready and one cannot simply leave this earth with their work undone. For that reason her destiny was in the hands of the mysterious creative powers that be, mostly in the form of the grey patch that still peered at her from behind the red bars.

She wondered what would become of her life's work when it was finally complete and she could lay down in peace, arms folded across her chest. No one else knew or cared about it and no one was capable of sharing her satisfaction. In reality, the fate of her tapestry was irrelevant because she created it to fulfil her personal desire, and not for any glory, real or imagined, fleeting or sustained, that might result from it. She commented to the grey patch about the similarity of her work with his journal writing. The journey through her work, and not its destiny, was what mattered. As with one's life – the grey patch responded – it is to be lived with vitality, you must take up the challenge, because even with faith, there is no certainty about the destiny of one's soul.

She did wonder what 'they' (who would be in charge? Angélica, perhaps, or maybe just a municipal worker) would do with her body and her calendar of outfits. Would they unseal her tomb and slide her into the niche where the journals now lay. Probably. Would they entomb her clothes along with her body as was the practice of ancient ancestors? She doubted it. She honestly didn't know and didn't mind not knowing.

Her single remaining desire was to complete her creation, and in doing so, continue to experience the touch and taste of her fabrics, sing her songs, and, every now and then, be sufficiently lucky enough to savour some chocolate.

She resumed her habit of sitting outside her front door each evening to watch the sun set over the ocean and listen as the town settled down to sleep. Every night she spoke to the ghost of Señor Ortega as he sat smiling at her from across the street. They conversed in the cool of the late afternoons when she visited him at his niche. And every day she spoke to the grey patch in the quiet comfort of her patio.

These habits continued well beyond the next few years as she built on her tapestry.

One day, as she sat in her patio following the threads that appeared and disappeared, in and out of her eclectic fabric canvas, she was inspired to attach a few more daisies to it. She stitched one in place, and then another, and another, and another. Each day, she added more daisies. And each day, the number of daisy additions grew. If she added ten one day, then the following day, without planning it as such, she felt moved to add fifteen. And the next day twenty, and so on, until there were no more daisies left in her *Mercado Central* plastic bags.

Before long, her weaving was entirely covered with a single layer of daisies. Then she made more daisies and added another layer, and another, until she lost count of the layers. Her tapestry grew heavier and extruded out into the patio, encroaching into Santa Sarah's space. The Virgin tilted back into the wall, her cold eyes staring disapprovingly as the fabric monster grew out of control. There were yellow, white, orange and blue crocheted cotton daisy petals on every square centimetre of the canvas. The characters with their lives, their plans and their ambitions, good deeds and corruption were safely buried beneath the countless layers of fabric flowers. It would take ages of meticulous excavation to find the truths and the lies underneath, never knowing the difference between one and the other. Even then, she speculated that someone would unravel them and they would undoubtedly be recycled.

The players, with all of their faith in themselves and whatever lay beyond were woven in this jungle that was a lost civilisation. The journal stories had been obliterated by her self-indulgent, abundant, unrealistic flowering desert. As the timbre of Señor Ortega's voice rose to the surface through each daisy petal, the importance and the details of his existence became more and more nebulous to everyone except for her. Clorinda revelled in the life her tapestry had assumed. She could feel Señor Ortega's all-encompassing energy.

She was oblivious when the gypsy caravan returned to Tocopilla after a 32-year absence. The convoy of vans arrived silently, pulled in by the wind that had pushed them away so many years ago.

After the dust settled from behind their wheels three young men extracted a stained blue velvet armchair from the back of the largest silver van. They assisted a thin, old Boldo from the passenger seat of the lead vehicle to sit in this chair. He settled there like the king he was and directed the unpacking and erection of their tents, every so often stopping to scan the panorama that was Tocopilla and the ocean beyond.

He had never fully recovered from Mariá Jacobé's disappearance, re-appearance, and her resulting insanity. He wasn't sure how María Jacobé's pathetic state was connected to the lost Santa Sara but several weeks ago, it occurred to him that they should return to this place and attempt to lift the curse that his wife had made in the name of their missing daughter and the lost Virgin. The coincidental disappearance of the Santa Sara icon and Mariá Jacobé had, over the years, merged in his mind to become one and the same. Perhaps by means of something beyond his understanding, re-visiting this place would help bring an end to Mariá Jacobé's tortured condition. On her deathbed several years ago his wife had made Boldo promise to take care of Mariá Jacobé no matter how much of a burden she would become. For the first time since then, he decided to put his faith in a miracle and he wondered why he hadn't thought of it earlier.

Boldo raised his arms to welcome the bent, bony woman that was María Jacobé. She now had long white hair and eyes that saw inside her-self to another reality. She was pale and listless. Jackza guided her to sit on a large cushion on a blanket at Boldo's feet. Together they watched a ship sail out of the harbour and he surveyed the shores to the north. It meant nothing to Mariá Jacobé but Boldo ached with the memories of her last dance in the circle of fires on the black sandy beach. They sat together in silence and he reached down to hold her hand.

"Wait for it." He told her. "Wait for the wind to come and carry away your sorrows." He ignored the fact that she had no tears as he wiped his own with the back of one hand. And he prayed for the arrival of the familiar desert wind, spiralling, as it inevitably would, a small breath from heaven, out of nowhere, to carry away their pain, alleviate heavy hearts, and disperse it somewhere far and away over the *altiplano*.

For an instance he thought he heard Mariá Jacobé singing, her pure voice offering hope to his aching soul. He glanced down at her, a moment of unrealistic expectation. She sat idly looking out at nothing. Still, the memory of her voice would not let him go. He could hear it from this place overlooking Tocopilla, as clear and vibrant as it had ever been.

In the grey patio at the back of her little house, Clorinda sang as she worked. She was absolutely and entirely content as she attached more crocheted daisies to her tapestry. Señor Ortega's voice was answering her, rising from between the grey threads and up through the fabric flowers that she had covered him with. The wind pulled at one of the yellow daisies on a layer above Señor Ortega's patch, wrestling it free. It flitted playfully around the patio before disappearing over the wall. Her eyes followed it through the sky for a second after it was gone and then she automatically reached into her bag for thread to crochet a replacement.

A yellow crocheted daisy blew up to the gypsy camp and settled as softly as a butterfly on the unfeeling lap of María Jacobé. It touched down only momentarily before being pulled into the centre of a miniature spiralling gust of wind and was whisked up beyond the mountains and into the sands of the *alitplano*, where all of the pain disappears.

Spanish Word Reference

Adiós	goodbye
amigos	friends
arpilleras	decorative embroidered and/or 3-dimensional fabric designs that tell a story
Azúl Unido	fictional name of soccer team, 'Blue United'
altiplano	high plains (in this case, found in northern Chile, carrying on past the borders into Bolivia, Peru and Argentina)
barrios	neighbourhoods
buenos días	good day, good morning
bueno	good (also, "well")
campesinos	farmers
chicha	alcoholic drink made from grapes or corn
Chileno	Chilean
compadre	brother in arms
compradrismo	nepotism
cordillera	the Andes mountain range
Don	dignified title, Sir
Doña	dignified title, Madam
el escenario canadiense	the Canadian scene
el gato negro	the black cat
empanada	meat pie
flamenco	gypsy music and dance coming from Spain
fútbol	soccer
hermano	brother
junta	group, council
la casa rosada	the pink house
Las Tres Marías	a constellation of stars, The Three Marys
Latino(a)	Latin person or Latin thing
mamón	Mama's boy
maricón	slang for homosexual
matagatos	cat killer
microbús	city bus
milico	nickname for military personnel

mono	literally 'monkey,' but also used for imitations, ie., stuffed toys, fantasy creatures
moreno(a)	dark-skinned person
pirquineros	small, independent miners
pisco	Chile's national alcoholic drink, distilled from wine
por favor	please
pueblo	town or 'the people'
Quechua	Indigineous people of northern Chile, Bolivia, Peru
Romané	Romanian gypsy
Salud	health, and used to make a toast, 'to your health'
secretarios	secretaries, in this case, assistants
Señor	Mr
Señora	Mrs
Señorita	Miss
sí	yes
Si Dios lo quiere	God willing
siesta	nap
tango	music and dance style from Argentina
Te amo también	I love you too
techno-cumbia	fast electronic dance music
Tío	uncle, the god Tío is the god of ore
Tocopillanos	people who live in or who are from the town of Tocopilla

Brief Notes on Culture, Geography, History

(Noted only as mentioned in context of this novel)

Cerro Rico (literally 'Rich Mountain') is a mountain in Potosi, Bolivia. Rich in gold and silver, it has been mined for centuries and gained the nickname, 'the mountain that eats people' because of the number or miners who have died there (beginning in the time of the Spanish Conquistadors).

Che Guevara, born in 1928, an Argentinian doctor who became a Marxist revolutionary in struggles throughout South America, is best known for his role in the Cuban revolution. He was executed in Bolivia in 1967 at the hands of the Bolivian military who were assisted by the CIA.

Coca plant is a hardy bush whose leaves are used by Indigenous people for religious purposes and to stave off hunger and altitude sickness. The leaves are chewed and held in the cheeks to absorb their nutrients. Especially miners are known to chew coca. Just as grapes are not wine, nor are coca leaves cocaine. Only after 'processing' do the coca leaves convert to a drug.

The **General** in the context of this story refers to General Augosto Pinochet, the man who was dictator of Chile from 1973 until 1990. He overthrew the coalition government of Salvador Allende and reliquinshed power 2 years after a democratic referendum in 1988 (but not before setting himself up as Senator for Life).

Saint **Padre Hurtado** was a Chilean priest (1901–1952). He was a champion of social causes and founder of "Hogar de Cristo", still Chile's largest national charity. He was canonised in 2005.

Mapuche are the indigineous people who live in southern Chile (from approximately Temuco and south). They were never defeated by the Spanish and have been struggling for centuries to be recognised as owners of their own lands.

Saltpetre was mined and distributed worldwide from huge mines in northern Chile for use as fertilizer until a chemical substitute was found. Today, the only remaining saltpetre mine in the world is just outside of María Elena, Chile, and the company town is now half deserted.

Salt flats are huge stretches of desert salt in the altiplano of Chile and Bolivia. Salt is still mined here.

Salvador Allende was president of Chile from 1970 until 1973 when he died during the Coup d'Etat headed by General Pinochet. Allende was Chile's first Marxist leader, elected in a tight race to become president of the socialist coalition government. He began a process of nationalisation of resources (mining, banking, etc).

Santa Sara, represented as a dark-skinned icon, is also known as the Black Virgin of the gypsies. She is their patron saint. There are several different versions as to her origin and some say she was the daughter of Jesus and Mary Magdalene.

The **seasons** in the southern hemisphere are opposite from in the northern hemisphere, so for instance in Chile, the month of March is the end of summer/ beginning of Autumn.

The god **Tío** is a god who is believed to live in the mountains and is owner of the ore. Miners pay homage to this god in various ways. Most often there is an effigy of him somewhere in a mine and miners make offerings of coca leaves, cigarettes and alcohol in order to appease him and also thank him for the ore they are extracting. Some traditional miners regularly sacrifice llamas as offerings to Tío.

The **War of the Pacific** was a war between Chile, Peru and Bolivia. Chile came out victorious in 1876 and claimed land that once belonged to Bolivia, which includes many rich ore deposits. The original Bolivian territory extended south to Tal Tal (see map) and is now Chilean territory. The Peruvian border remained largely unchanged.

14143416R00182

Made in the USA
Charleston, SC
23 August 2012